MAELSTROM

A.V. Pham

Book cover design: K.M. West Creative

ISBN: 979-8-9888296-0-7 (paperback)
ISBN: 979-8-9888296-1-4 (ebook)

To my friend Victor,
without whom Malcolm Ly would not exist.

To my beloved Andrew,
without whom this novel would not exist.

1

The rain swept sideways through the streets, crashing violently on the concrete. Six o'clock on a summer's evening and the sky was already the color of strap molasses. Most rational people leave the office early on a day like this, fearing the rash of flash floods that follow a sudden bout of heavy rain.

Most rational people. If I were most rational people, I would have moved out of Houston years ago, Mal reasoned, as he pulled the drawstrings of his rain jacket tighter against his face. He clutched a brown paper bag inside the jacket, hoping the slick material would provide some refuge for his rotisserie chicken sandwich. He should've gotten the salad; his meal would've been protected by a plastic container. Scanning the key fob, Mal made his way down the hall, leaving a trail of rainwater and mud in his wake.

Damn, broken again. Stairs it is. The odds of riding the elevator in this building were worse than winning the Texas lottery, but the rent was cheap and it provided a mailing address that wasn't his home.

I should have left Houston when she left, he reasoned as he trudged upstairs, each step heavier than the last. She didn't want to be a part of his life anymore, giving every excuse under the sun for why she needed to "live her life".

Whatever that meant.

Her litany of complaints was endless.

He was never home (partly true, but she made it unbearable to stay home). She was stuck raising their son alone (also only partly true; she was a stay-at-home mom, but she always parked their kid with the grandparents). His job was too dangerous. That part? Well, that part ended up being true, and he should've listened to her.

Not to reconcile. Gods, no! But at least then he would still have his son.

The doors to the fifth floor snapped open, pulling him back from his thoughts. His neighbors walked out to the landing, nodding to him in passing. He wasn't sure what they did for a living, but their office and clothes often reeked of pot and booze.

As long as they can pay rent, I guess.

Anyway, it wasn't his business anymore. He was no longer a cop.

Malcolm Ly, Private Investigator.

Somehow, the fluorescent lighting and dingy yellow paper gave the sign a duplicitous feel. Was he an investigator? He hadn't accepted a job in months. He didn't even know how the phone lines and lights were still on. The now-soggy sandwich dropped onto the broad, paper-littered desk. Mal jerked when his cell phone buzzed. He rummaged through his wet pockets, the vibration helping him track it down, until he finally found it and accepted the call.

"Where the hell are you?" the voice on the other line shrilled.

Shit. It's Friday.

"You forgot, didn't you?"

"No, of course I remember." *Then I forgot.* He knew he should have paid attention to that weird feeling he got standing in that deli line.

"Son of a bitch. Well, I'm almost at your office." Kasey was always a step ahead of him. Oftentimes it was annoying; at the moment he was grateful. He cast a disparaging glance at the soggy pile on his desk. The tattered brown bag did nothing to make the sandwich inside seem appealing or edible.

Ten minutes later, she buzzed him through the broken intercom. "Co- get me, assho-"

"Hello to you too, sunshine. Be right down." A few moments later, he emerged from the fire door and smiled at a small, shivering figure in the foyer. "You look like a wet rat."

"You smell like one," she shot back, handing him the damp pizza box and stomping towards the elevators. The aroma of piping hot cheese and pepperoni made his mouth water.

"Uh… the elevator's broken. We're going to have to take the stairs, princess." He motioned in the opposite direction.

"Damn it. I should make you carry me up for forgetting about today," she whined. Kasey Khuu was the type who considered walking a vigorous activity and once said that she would transfer her consciousness to a robot so she would never have to worry about working out. She was joking. At least, he thought she was.

"I'm not going to carry you like a child!" He laughed. "The most I'll do is carry your beer."

He grabbed the six-pack dangling from her lanky arms.

"And I don't want to hear you bitch about it for five stories, either," he teased.

"Remember that one time in Professor Barnouw's class when the elevators went out, and you carried me to class? I think we should re-enact that," Kasey said breathlessly as they made their ascent.

"First, your foot was broken." Mal rolled his eyes. "Second, that was two stories, and I was doing Bruce a favor."

"Would it help if I broke it again?"

"Don't even joke about that, Kase. Only you would break your foot walking ten feet to class."

Mal and Kasey met in college in their freshmen year. As improbable as it seemed, they shared a love for 19th century literature. By the end of the semester, they were inseparable. The following year further cemented their friendship when Kasey started dating Mal's best friend, Bruce.

"Why do you have a plant in your office?" She turned her nose at the half-wilted fern in the room's corner.

"Chicks dig vegetation," he quipped.

"I'm sure you get a lot of action in this place." Kase rolled her eyes.

If you only knew. He pictured a breathless Gwen bent over his desk, with her pleated Ralph Lauren skirt hiked and the sliver of her thong pulled to the side. He could still hear her soft moans as he pumped vigorously before climaxing on the small of her back. That was last week. Right before she told him she couldn't see him anymore because things were getting serious about what's-his-face, the lawyer. Or was he an accountant? He wondered what "serious" meant when they only moved in together a few months earlier.

"Anyway, you'll never guess what Director Dick announced today at our monthly meeting." Kasey twisted the cap off her beer and tossed it on the floor.

"Enlighten me." Director Dick was how Kasey expressed disdain for Richard McDonald, lab manager of the forensic biology section. As she told it, Dick only remembered which side he was on when there was an audience. She couldn't stand his unscrupulous mustache or that floppy bucket hat he wore to cover his receding hairline. For the first two years, he called her by the wrong name, even though there were only two Asian people in the biology lab, and the other was a man. He spent more time rubbing elbows with politicians than at work, but it was all for the "greater good" of the lab. According to him, the more "presence" he put in, the more funding the section received, funds that eventually went to fatten Dick's wallet. It was the only explanation they could find since the lab was still working with instruments from the Eighties and the supply room still leaked every time it rained heavily.

Which, in Houston, seemed like it was every other day during the fall.

"Dick says the city is awarding us two million dollars this year to go towards new digital media programs and a Hamilton," Kasey declared between chews.

"Remind me, what's a Hamilton again?"

"Big fancy machine that can run high-volume DNA extractions."

"Exciting."

Kase rolled her eyes at his attempt at sarcasm. "Please. He's been promising a Hamilton for the last three years. It's a wonder we get anything done in that lab."

Mal stared, amused, as his best friend took another swig of her beer, wiped her mouth with her sleeve, and grabbed another slice.

"Use a napkin, you filthy animal." He chortled at his own joke, tossing the used napkin in his hand at her. Unfazed, Kasey unrolled the napkin and wiped the grease from the side of her lips.

As they had every Friday for the last four years, they ate dinner together. Kasey did most of the talking, while Mal listened quietly, interjecting with advice, solicited or not. This ritual started as a forced coping mechanism for Mal. After losing his son, things got dark.

Kasey and Bruce wouldn't give up. They came over every few days to throw away the untouched food and make new batches for him. He didn't know how they managed it, but they paid his bills and cleaned his house. They would pull him out of bed, force him to eat, drink, do more than just breathe. And when the taste of cold metal in his mouth wasn't just a thought anymore, Kasey was there to slap the shit out of him. Eventually, those forced family dinners made life tolerable again.

"So, I just landed this case, and it's looking kind of shady. The girls and I are taking bets on whether it's an inside job."

"God, Kase, that's kind of morbid, isn't it?"

"Stop making assumptions! It's a burglary. Nobody was hurt." Kasey defended.

"Go on." Mal cocked his head, slightly intrigued despite himself.

"We got a call on Monday afternoon that this guy's house has been burgled. Fifty million dollars' worth of art, gone! What's weirder is he and his wife were in the house, along with three of his aides." Mal listened intently as Kasey became increasingly animated. She might be a drama queen, but was a great storyteller. She continued with more details.

"Five witnesses, but not a single one heard anything as the mansion was being cleared of precious paintings, sculptures, and statues? The smaller busts could be swiped quickly enough, but how did the thieves clear larger paintings secured on the walls? I don't get it."

"He then comes downstairs, sees his front door open, and grabs a .22 pistol from the bedroom before heading outside. There he sees one trying to flee on his daughter's scooter. He fires and gets a shot off, but the gun jams. The guy disappears around a corner, and it was too late."

"Who steals a scooter when they've absconded with fifty million dollars' worth of loot?" Mal thought it was a good question.

"I knew you would pick up on that." Kasey beamed. "And that, my friend, is why we're taking bets."

Mal groaned. Yes, on the surface, the case reeked of insurance fraud. But Mal couldn't shake the feeling something far more sinister was brewing.

2

Selena sauntered into her plush, modern corner office on Wednesday morning, triumphant, as was her custom.

Though exquisitely decorated, the office was remarkably sparse and impersonal, a reflection of its inhabitant. She was the investigatory edition of a ghost, unknown and seemingly unknowable. Selena Parish strolled into Mutual Financial Protection, a large New York insurance firm, one fine autumn morning, a week after a missing Matisse sent everyone in the building into hysterics. When she talked her way to the C suites, she assured them she could find the painting. In exchange, she wanted the largest office on their floor and a hefty commission for the find. John Bausch, the CEO and the man who would have to answer to the stockholders, had no choice but to agree. It was even money whether he was swayed by her beauty or her audacity.

Two weeks later, Selena returned in a sleek blue Hervé Leger dress and silver heels, carrying a black aluminum cylinder over her shoulder. Murmurs and whispered conversation followed her progress, but she seemed oblivious as her heels click-clacked on the tiles. She strode past Bausch's secretary, ignoring the woman's protests, pushed his office door open, and stopped a careful pace away from his desk. Selena uncapped the tube, carefully unfurled the Matisse, told him to authenticate it, and "not pay the little weasel a dime".

The explanation took longer. It had been stashed in a vault in the Hamptons the whole time. The idiot filed a false claim after he had gotten in over his head with gambling debts and a gold-digging mistress. Unoriginal, perhaps, but men were predictable, and it made her job easier. Soon after, Bausch moved Kerry Gentry, his former top investigator, out of his office and Selena in. The office gave her a breathtaking view, but she appreciated the staggering salary more. No one blamed Bausch, despite Gentry's years of loyalty. She had saved the company nearly eighty-one million dollars. Of course, there were whispers that Selena was involved in the theft, but the internal investigation revealed nothing. Rumors continued to swirl, probably fanned by Gentry and his clique.

"Girl, don't you ever wear pants?" Selena's assistant balanced a cup of coffee atop a fat file folder.

"Gia, sweetie, there are only two things a man notices in a professional woman - subtle cleavage and a short hemline. Wearing pants will only threaten their fragile egos. How would I ever get any information out of them that way?" She batted her eyes, lips pouty and full.

"Mm-hmm. I'm sure that's how my cousin Tina got that black eye, too." Gia joked. Watching her boss walk into work was like having front row seats to New York's Fashion Week every morning. To celebrate her latest victory, the recovery of a near-priceless Rodin, Selena chose a magenta La Robe de Chiara Boni sheath with strappy nude Valentino heels, her signature coif, and a touch of gloss on her heart-shaped lips. Gia pulled at her stuffy knee-length skirt and wished *she* had worn pants to work today.

"Let's go to Pastis tonight for dinner." Selena cooed. It was true, the act of recovering the art gave her more of a rush than the paycheck or the lifestyle it afforded, and she'd ride the high for days if something didn't derail her.

"Not so fast," Gia protested, disappointment reflected on her face. Selena was a tempestuous bitch, but when she was happy, she was generous with her time, money, and attention. Her long-suffering assistant was usually on the receiving end of that generosity. It made up for the bitch who surfaced when Selena was bored or stressed. "You've got a fresh case. I'd say pack for humidity and despair." She placed the giant folder in front of Selena.

"Where are we going?"

"*You* are going to Texas. Wealthy attorney in Houston claims some thieves stole fifty million in art right from under his nose. His wife and three other aides were in the house. It was mid-afternoon, and he shot at one of them. Get this." Gia paused until she was sure Selena was paying attention. "One of the bastards made off with his daughter's scooter."

"Fifty million in art and *a scooter*? Oh, well, that seals the deal." Selena balked at the absurdity of the story. "I'm going to need the—"

"Police report? It's in there. I've also compiled photographs of the missing pieces, the insurance policies, and any other tidbits you might need. Here's the kicker–he just announced his run for Mayor–which he's *funding* on his own." Gia knew what her boss needed, when she needed it, and Selena smiled. Her assistant may be sassy and a poor dresser, but she got the job done. All of this compiled before she had her first cup of coffee.

"So, tell me something. Are you going to call up that fine piece of man while you're in town?"

"What are you talking about?" Selena feigned ignorance.

"Don't play coy with me! The one with the jawline that looks like one of your dead artists chiseled it. The one with the ass!"

"You are so vulgar." Selena put the right air of dismissal in her voice, and Gia rolled her eyes as she walked away.

It's been a while since I saw Malcolm, Selena reflected. She scrolled through her contacts.

I wonder if he still has the same number.

3

"A scooter? Are you fucking kidding me?" the voice bellowed over the line. "I pay you forty grand to pull off this job. I give you a *fucking* step-by-step guide even idiots like you can't screw up, and you stole a fucking *scooter*?"

"Take it easy, boss. It's not like we got caught." Tory tried to sound confident, though sweat trickled down his temple. So maybe they almost botched the job, but almost didn't count. They weren't going to get caught. The boss had given him a good plan, and he'd followed it to the letter. They both wore gloves and masks, he followed instructions for renting the van, made sure it was plain with no distinguishable marks and removed the license plates. He even filed off the VIN number under the dash, not that it mattered. He dumped it in Third Ward, a part of the city so seedy that an unlocked van would be dismantled in hours. The plan was flawless.

If only his cousin, may his name forever be cursed, hadn't stolen the scooter and then tripped over it.

"Well, the cops are sniffing around. You know why? Because it smells rotten! Because no competent *professional* would steal that much priceless art and then take a sixty-dollar scooter." The voice grew more and more agitated.

"We followed your instructions, and we got away clean. No evidence. My cousin just wanted the scooter for his daughter.

He figured no rich dude would miss that cheap piece of shit," Tory reasoned, putting on a brave face.

He was always cleaning up Jamal's messes, and this was no exception. Six weeks ago, Jamal came to him fresh out of prison. Three years in the pen for grand theft auto. He wanted a new start, go legit for his daughters, but work was sparse for a criminal and he fell back in with the same crowd, and Tory decided it was time for a what did they call it? An intervention.

"Hey, cuz, you and me, we're family. We gotta look out for each other." Tory spoke between puffs from their shared blunt. "I got this gig. Real easy, real clean. I'll split it wit 'chu, fifty-fifty. Then you're out. Take the money and set your kids up somewhere nice. I don't want you anywhere near this shit again."

Jamal eagerly agreed, and the planning began. The best thing about working with him was he asked no questions. He never questioned how Tory contacted the Boss, or even who the Boss was. Which was good, because Tory didn't know and didn't want to know.

He received a burner phone in his mailbox one day with "Wait for my call" written neatly across the envelope. He tossed it on the counter and forgot about it for an entire week. When it finally rang, the clichéd Darth Vader voice gave him directions to a particular park bench. That led to a key for a gym locker, which led to a set of typed instructions. It was cheesy and contrived, like something straight out of a bad spy movie. Despite the tacky cat-and-mouse tactics, everything had gone off without a hitch until Jamal screwed up.

"With the money I'm paying you, you could have bought ten scooters! I have half the mind to turn you both in." The voice was panicked, almost desperate now, and Tory sensed weakness. This was his chance to salvage this train wreck, save his own ass. He might even save Jamal's ass, too.

"You don't want to do anything stupid now," Tory warned, trying to keep his voice calm and level. "You turn us in, and I might start talking."

"Talk about what? You don't know shit about me." The voice shrank until it was breathy and small.

"All's I know is you turn us in, and I'm going to have to turn everything I have in to 5-0," Tory tested.

"Y-you were supposed to burn it all!" Tory guessed right. Darth sounded scared now.

Fuckin' amateur.

"Being in prison as many times as I have, I learned if you're going to get your hands dirty for some other cat, you better have some insurance. Y'know, in case things go sideways." He grew a little cockier. "Matter o' fact. I think the stuff we took is way more valuable than what you're payin' us. I think we're looking at a hundred grand for this job, or I flip to 5-0."

Silence. *Did I push too far?*

"Fine," Darth Vader ground out. Tory could hear the clenched teeth. "You'll get your money by the end of the week."

"A hundred grand?"

"A hundred grand." There was a soft click and then only the sound of Tory's racing heart. He blackmailed his way out of this shit hole.

4

Levi Stevenson looked up from his desk and across the hall. Abigail was scribbling intently. A strand of ash blonde hair laid across her face, half covering her impish features. His daughter seemed out of sorts lately and it was worrying him. The old Abigail would never show up to the office in a frizzled updo and wrinkled blouse. Last Monday, she absentmindedly left her purse in the car and almost ran into oncoming traffic going back to retrieve it. At first, he thought it was all the work piling in the office. Ever since the oil spill debacle and subsequent lawsuit, their accounting firm had been fielding clients, from smaller, individual accounts to larger corporations. It was way more work than Levi anticipated, and they had to take on two junior accountants over the recent months. Then, he thought back to a few weeks ago when she confided she had been seeing a man, that it was serious, and that she was in love. Maybe there was trouble in paradise.

"Abigail, would you like to have lunch with your old father today?" He figured a pleasant lunch would cheer her up, or at least take her mind off things.

"Not today, Papa. I don't really have much of an appetite," she replied without looking up. "I have a lot of work to do."

"Abby, you're worrying me," Levi said gently, walking over to her doorway. At over six feet, he was an imposing man. "Tell me what's wrong. Maybe I can help? I know one or two things."

It was a pointless offer. Even as a young girl, she had been stubborn and strong-willed. When she fell off her bike, she brushed his hand away and picked herself up. When she didn't get into her first-choice college, she called Admissions until she secured an interview with the Dean. Levi didn't know what made her so independent, whether it was growing up without a mother, or if he had not offered enough help or attention. Right now, he wanted more than ever for her to open up to him.

"Abby," he clucked, and pulled her chin up. Dark circles surrounded her pale blue eyes, making them look childishly vacant.

"Okay, okay." He could tell she was humoring him, complying so he'd leave her alone, but he'd take it. He shuffled out of the room, concern hooding his eyes.

Abigail watched her father leave, wishing she could tell him the truth. The last few months had been challenging enough. Her married lover was extremely vague about divorcing his wife, stringing her along, holding out hope. At least he had. Now? He flat out told her it would be too damaging to his reputation, his career, to divorce the witch. Abby made some veiled threats of exposing their relationship and all she discovered to his wife and to the world.

Surprising nobody, it didn't end well. He didn't back down, and now she was left wondering what went wrong.

God, when did my life become such a cliché? she thought.

#

They met at some charity gala. Funny, she couldn't remember what event it was, but she distinctly remembered the blue pinstripe suit that caught her eye, the sideswept hair resting above the crest of his forehead, and the way his slightly crooked teeth softened the too-masculine jawline. As a statuesque blonde walked over to him and gently placed her hand on his shoulder, Abby felt her stomach drop in disappointment.

Of course, he was taken. A man like that couldn't be single.

Abby walked over to the buffet table and made herself busy, glancing around furtively for a familiar face. She wished her father wouldn't make her go to these things; they were eternally banal, an endless circle jerk with the same moneyed faces and lousy food.

"Abigail," a silky voice called out. She twirled around, an enormous smile spreading across her face. She recognized that voice anywhere.

"Bethany!" she exclaimed, relieved. "Thank God! I thought I'd have to chat up one of the living dead."

"How are you, dear?" Bethany asked, planting soft kisses on both of Abigail's cheeks. Bethany Tremel was heiress to one of Houston's largest oil conglomerates. Sultry and soft-spoken, people often misjudged her, pegging her as nothing more than a dainty fixture on her father's arm. Most failed to realize that behind those deep-set brown eyes lay a vicious financier and scientist. Aldrich Tremel had been leveraged up to his eyeballs in unfortunate investments and near-sighted purchases. It was his daughter's socioeconomic genius that catapulted his company into the technological age of oil production. Now, a semi-retired Aldrich spent most of his time with his golf buddies, while his daughter oversaw the day-to-day operations.

"I've been to a hundred of these and they're all blurring together. Same people, same food." Abigail complained. "Can't rich people think of anything else to serve besides cold shrimp and lukewarm deli meat?"

Bethany erupted into joyous laughter. Her friend's frankness was a welcome contrast to the veiled nuances and duplicity that were her everyday world.

"Well, I can't help with the catering, but I can keep you company." Bethany grabbed her hand, and they circulated the ballroom. As they stood, captured by a tedious political consultant and trapped into tortuous conversation, Bethany caught her shy friend sneaking glances at a couple.

"Handsome, isn't he?" she whispered, making an excuse and

escaping the talk of the next election.

"I don't know what you're talking about." Abigail flushed, trying, but failing, to sound nonchalant.

"Oh, don't worry dear, half the women in this room wish they were married to Marc Sandoff." Bethany smirked. She took a sip of her champagne, leaving a rich maroon stain on the glass's lip. "Houston's most eligible bachelor until that bitch Lenore snatched him up. It was quite the scandal, you know."

"What scandal?" She knew Bethany was baiting her, but her interest was piqued.

"There's talk Lenore poked a few holes in some *prophylactics*. They had only been dating a few months when, suddenly, he announced their engagement. Their twins were officially 'premature', and six pounds and seventeen inches. Ha. Honestly, I wouldn't put it past that conniving tramp to do something like that."

Abigail stifled a gasp. It wasn't polite to indulge in such trashy gossip, but it certainly livened up the night. She looked up from her wineglass as her friend eagerly waved Marc and Lenore over.

"Marc! Lenore! How are you, dears?" Bethany switched gears from catty to charming in an instant.

"You know what another gala means. More shoulder-rubbing and ass-kissing." Marc boomed. There was a surprising smoothness to his voice, like hot glaze cascading on a freshly baked donut.

"Honestly, Marc, do you need to use that kind of language?" Lenore chastised, before looking Abigail up and down. "And who's your little friend, Bethany?"

"I apologize. How rude of me. Marc and Lenore Sandoff, this is my close friend Abigail Stevenson. She and her father own an accounting firm. They do some consulting for me." The casual mention was priceless, Abby knew. Someone Bethany Tremel went to for advice? "Abigail, meet the most brilliant attorney in Houston. His firm represents Tremel Holdings."

"Nice to meet you." Abigail held out her hand, expecting Marc to take it. She was surprised when Lenore clasped her fingers around Abigail's hand in the manner of royalty forced to interact with commoners, not fully touching them. Abby shifted uncomfortably at Lenore's icy gaze, feeling small and plain standing across from the towering figure in her blue silk Marchesa gown. Strands of blond tresses fell naturally, encasing her sharp chin and elven features. Lenore dropped Abigail's hand in dismissal.

"My pleasure, Abigail. You're Levi's daughter." Marc, in contrast, offered a warm and comforting handshake. She shivered with excitement at the touch. "I'm quite familiar with your father. Is he here tonight?"

"No, unfortunately, my father couldn't make it." Abigail replied meekly, still trying to recover from his touch.

"Well, it's not a complete loss. You're here." She detected a twinkle in his eye as he fired off the compliment. "You're just stunning, aren't you?"

She didn't know how to react. Anyone standing within ten feet of Marc and Lenore could sense the tension between them. Was his comment genuine or made to irritate Lenore?

"Marc! Leave my girl alone. Aren't there enough lovely ladies here for you to tease? You're standing next to one," Bethany said pointedly. Abigail silently thanked her for the rescue. "Anyway, we should get going. I think the Lehmans just walked in."

With that, she whisked Abby on to the next couple, leaving her feeling a little wistful she couldn't bask in Marc's presence a little longer. The rest of the night passed in a blur, and the young accountant's last thought that night was of Marc Sandoff's smile.

An exquisite bouquet of sunflowers was delivered to the accounting firm the following Monday. The note simply read, *Thought sunflowers might be more your style. Dinner, 8pm tonight?*

This was followed by a phone number. Abby gulped. She hoped to see him again, but to admire him from afar, not have dinner. She had no intention of launching into some sordid affair. He was also fairly presumptuous to tell her what flowers she should like. But it didn't irritate her. It excited her more.

All the men she dated were sweet but predictable. They treated her like some precious porcelain doll; they waited for her to make all the decisions in the relationship, afraid to upset the balance of her life. One former boyfriend even confessed, post break-up, that he stayed with her for another year because he was waiting for her to dump him. Marc was different. He took charge; he made the first move. She sucked in her breath and dialed.

The next six months were a whirlwind of fancy restaurants, fancier hotels, and lavish vacations. He spared no expense as he spoiled her with extravagant jewels and brand-new wardrobes. For Abby, it wasn't about the money. It was Marc's emotional maturity. He nurtured every half-dreamed desire and indulged her petulance. He was there to hold her hand through bouts of depression and made desperate love to her when she was lustfully manic.

She became insatiable, obsessive. She would fret every time he left her apartment, knowing he was going home to his wife, wondering if he was going to fuck her just because she was there. The part-time relationship they had no longer satisfied her. She had his love and affection; she wanted his time. She wanted him to come home to her.

A month ago, after an especially steamy mid-day session, she confessed her love.

"I don't want our relationship to be a compilation of stolen moments and clandestine weekends anymore. I love you. You have no affection for Lenore. Please leave her. Be with me," she pleaded.

He casually pushed her arm off his chest and started searching for his briefs. Her eyes brimmed with tears as he buttoned his dress shirt.

He finally spoke, his voice soft, but with a subtle hint of

bitterness. "It's more complicated than you think. Look, I have to go. I have a meeting in twenty minutes. I'll call you."

She had never seen him run out so fast. He didn't call for three days. When they finally spoke, he explained he loved her too, but what they had was all he could give her at the moment. He emphasized she needed to give him time to figure things out.

"You know how much this divorce would cost me. We have kids."

The discussion went on and on. Finally, exhausted, she gave in. She rationalized that having Marc part-time was far better than losing him completely.

Soon, her phone stopped ringing as frequently. He became busy with work. When she started the affair, Bethany had warned her to be careful; that all men were fickle, and they never leave their wives. During her affair, Bethany played the role of supportive friend, giving them alibis and lying for them. Now Bethany was her only place of solace.

They were sitting on the balcony of one of Bethany's high-rises, overlooking the city.

"Sweetie, he has been busy. I don't think he's ignoring you on purpose. We're not his only clients, you know." She clasped a faded cigarette between her fingers.

"I wish I said nothing."

"Fuck that." Bethany clearly had had too many glasses of wine. "You said what you said. No regrets and don't apologize."

Abby wondered if she had become lackluster and transparent in his eyes. Maybe he had already moved on to the next shiny new toy. As if in response to her thought, right on the balcony, he called her to say divorce was simply out of the question. Bethany threw the phone against the wall and she fell apart.

#

Levi draped his brawny arm around his daughter's shoulder as they walked to her favorite ramen joint. He wanted to take her somewhere nicer downtown, but she protested that she didn't feel like going too far. Her demeanor seemed to have lifted a little, so he pushed on about his date with Susan and the failed casserole debacle.

Abby was happy for Levi. He spent her entire childhood alone, trying to minimize the distractions so he could maintain some normalcy and consistency in her life. He recently met a gracious lady at the synagogue, and though she couldn't cook to save her life, Susan truly cared for her father.

"Papa, I'm really glad you met Susan," she began. "She's good for you. You're smiling again."

"I always smile when I'm around you, sweet girl," Levi interrupted.

"I just mean, you know, I don't want you to be alone, in case…" She quickly recovered. "In case I move or get married or something."

"Are you trying to tell me something?" His brows furrowed. Could the secret boyfriend have proposed and all this time his daughter had been distraught at the prospect of leaving him alone?

"No." She smiled. "I'm just saying. You know… *in case*. I can't stay here forever. I have to spread my wings too, you know."

"Well, spread your wings close by. Austin, maybe, or Dallas. If you leave Texas, my heart will break forever."

She rolled her eyes and smiled dolefully. She wanted to confide in him. He would immediately know what to do. She was envious of her father's clear perception of right and wrong, the fine line between them. If she could go back, she would tell her father everything from the beginning so he could stop her from making those mistakes. Now, if he knew everything she had done, it really would break his heart. A teardrop formed at the edge of her already swollen eyes. She gave him a bear hug.

"I love you, Papa," she whispered. His response was drowned out by the screeching sound of a vehicle rounding the corner. The last thing Abigail saw was a celestial glimmer atop the hood of the car before she was thrust violently onto the ground.

Levi also saw the SUV, but from his vantage point, he saw an object peeking through the open window. He threw himself on top of his daughter as the sound of firecrackers rapidly popped off through the air.

5

"Excuse me, Mr. Ly?"

Mal dropped his shoulders and sighed.

Shit, is rent due already?

"I'll have it tomo—" He turned to see a disheveled young woman. She carried a toddler on her hip and a little girl stood beside her, sucking her thumb.

"Yes?" he asked, curiosity getting the better of him.

"I need your help." The sleeping child stirred slightly in protest as she shifted her weight from one foot to the other.

"I'm sorry. I'm not taking cases right now," Mal lied, glancing down at the faded track marks on her free arm. He could sense she was a heap of trouble, and trouble never paid.

"No, please, it's not what you think. Please! Hear me out," she pleaded, her eyes growing wide with desperation. He tried to close the door, but she stuck her foot in the doorjamb.

"I have cash, and I'll pay up front. Whatever you ask, I just need you to listen to me. I'll give you all the money I have and if you don't want to help me, that's fine. You can keep it, but I need you to listen to me!"

Mal dropped his shoulders for the second time. The little girl wiped the drool from her mouth and stared at her mother with curious eyes. Mal recalled his son at that age, gazing at everything with innocence and wonderment. Young children didn't understand much, but they understood emotions. He couldn't turn away a desperate mother, even if she were a junkie. Against what little better judgement he had, he motioned for her to come in and shut the door behind her.

"Sorry, the place isn't much, but I'm not around often." Another lie, since he practically lived there. He hoped she didn't notice the dirty laundry piled by the copier as she walked in. He snatched a chair propped against the back wall and motioned for her to sit. The child immediately jumped on the ratty couch while the toddler nestled against her mother's bosom, stirring slightly before her breathing evened out again.

"How can I help?" He wanted to say "show me the money" but thought he ought to be polite.

"My name is Ericka Thomas, and you've noticed the needle marks on my arms." She extended her right arm, revealing faded scars around the crease. The faint bluish-black discoloration told Mal her vein had completely blown, but not recently.

"I'm showing you because I don't want to hide who I am, or rather, who I was."

"I didn't even notice." Another lie. He was racking up quite the tally today. "Please, tell me what you need."

Then I can get rid of you, he thought.

"I'm not a junkie off the street, Mr. Ly. I went to college; I had a family who loved me." She tucked a strand of hair back into her tightly wrapped bun. "I met my boyfriend and fell in love. I started doing hard drugs, dropped out of college, started hooking to support our habits. Nothing you haven't heard before as a police officer, I'm sure."

She's done her research.

"Then Jamal got picked up on an auto theft charge, not his first, and he went away for a long time. That was my wake-up call. I had to fix myself for my girls."

"That's all really commendable, but what does this have to do with—"

"Let me finish." There was a hint of iron in her voice, and Mal folded his hands, concealing his impatience.

"I found a job doing clerical work for a good man. He kept me clean, housed me and my girls, and paid me a small salary. Not much, but I didn't have to pay rent as long as I stayed clean. For the last two years, we were in a good place. I visited Jamal often and told him that if he didn't straighten up when he got out, I couldn't stay with him."

"When he got out, things were good for a while. Jamal did odd jobs, stayed away from his old crew, and I continued working for Mr. Pram. We saved up enough to move into our own apartment. Then Mr. Pram suddenly died, and his daughter closed his office. I was out of work and Jamal couldn't find anything permanent. He started running with his old crew again, staying out nights, coming home intoxicated. I was afraid he was using, or worse, that he was boosting cars again."

Ericka cleared her throat before continuing, her voice shaky but firm.

"About a month ago, Tory, his cousin, not his real cousin," she clarified. "He pulled him into some kind of job. They were always off talking, keeping secrets. Then one day, he comes home with a packet and told me to hide it. He said he found a job, a big one, that would solve all our problems. He said he would take me and the girls away and we could start over."

Tears were now falling freely from her ashen face. Mal looked around for a tissue, not expecting to find one.

"I told him it sounded too good to be true, but he wouldn't listen. He said jobs were scarce for someone with a record, but that this was our best opportunity to make a life together. The next part, he was real specific. He told me your name, made me write it down. Then he said—" Her voice broke, and it was a moment before she recovered enough to continue. The little girl looked at her mother, wide-eyed and unmoving. "If things broke bad, I should come to you and give you this. He said you were the only cop who ever treated him fairly."

Mal sat stunned as Ericka pulled a brick-like bundle wrapped in a tattered newspaper from her diaper bag, unmoving, as she untied the twine and tore at the wrapper.

"Mr. Ly, this is five thousand dollars, and it's all yours, but you have to help Jamal."

"Things broke bad?" Mal asked softly. His mind raced as he tried to remember Jamal. He never worked Auto Theft. His career had been mainly focused on Homicide and then Organized Crime.

Was Jamal an informant? Impossible, he remembered all his informants.

Ericka nodded.

"How bad?"

"Tory and Jamal were arrested for a double murder. His lawyer, the one the court gave him, said he did a drive-by as part of some gang war, and two pedestrians were caught in the crossfire!" Ericka was now sobbing uncontrollably. The toddler in her arms woke and added her voice to Ericka's misery, and the child on the couch followed her mother's lead.

"Okay, okay. Please stop crying," Mal pleaded. "I'll look into it."

"No sir, you don't understand, not yet. Jamal and Tory are not violent criminals. They run with a rough crowd, but they're thieves, not murderers. They've been running away from gangs their whole lives!" Ericka stuttered between sobs.

"I believe you." Another lie, at least regarding this Tory. Jamal? Mal was willing to give him the benefit of the doubt. For now.

"It gets worse. They were stabbed in central booking. Tory didn't make it and Jamal's in the hospital. He can't go back to jail. He won't make it out again."

6

K ase, I need a favor," Mal wheedled, happy she answered her phone. "I need to see the files on a double murder. A shooting that happened in midtown?"

"That was fast. How did you hear about it?" Kasey replied, pulling down her face mask and stepping away from her bench.

"A client." Mal replied curtly.

He'd spent the afternoon pulling details out of Ericka and considering the answers before calling Kase.

Were the two victims of the shooting simply unlucky bystanders? If what Ericka said was true, it sounded like Jamal and Tory had been set up, but to what end? Besides, could he really take the word of a junkie? That was the five-thousand-dollar question.

He comforted Ericka and assured her he would look into it. Before she left, she gave him Jamal's room number at the county hospital. Mal tried to visit, get answers directly, but was frustrated by a rookie who didn't recognize him and wouldn't give him access. Even his private investigator's badge didn't persuade him. Worse, Mal's protégé, Joe, who became team lead after he left, was out in the field and unreachable at the moment. That he couldn't remember Jamal added to his irritation.

"You have a client?" Kasey asked, incredulous. "Well, you won't get much right now. I'm still working on the evidence, and Gwen hasn't started the autopsies yet."

"What do you have so far?" Mal snapped. This case, despite the hefty chunk of cash that came with it, was irritating him. The sooner he was done with it, the better.

"Mal! That's not how this works! You know that. It was a drive-by. I'm still swabbing for blood. There's probably no contact DNA and I haven't ran any of the samples yet." Kasey snapped back, then lowered her voice. "And even if I did, I still can't tell you anything."

Mal dropped his voice to match. "Why are you swabbing for contact DNA if it was a drive-by?"

"Because the higher ups ordered it to waste my time," Kasey continued in a hushed tone. "Mal, this case jumped the line. It seems someone at HPD wants it closed. Yesterday. Or sooner."

"Who's the lead?"

"Baker."

Mal rolled his eyes.

Well, this sucks. I'll never see that file.

He and Terrance Baker never got along in the short time they worked together. They were partners for a month before the Lieutenant had to tear them apart. Mal would follow leads while Baker stuck to the rule book. The younger detective thought his partner reckless and a menace; Mal found the young buck lazy and unimaginative. Unsurprisingly, Baker made no attempt to hide his pleasure when Mal resigned from the force.

"When are you going to have any information to share?" He probably sounded more irritated at her than he should have, but he was pressing.

"Why don't you go talk to your little girlfriend at the ME's office? Maybe she'll give you something more than just nookie." The soft *click* told him he'd pushed too far.

#

Mal sauntered through the halls of the county morgue. His steps resonated through the dimly lit corridors, giving it an almost supernatural feel. He walked without slowing past

Gwen's office towards autopsy and knocked. A surprised intern held the door slightly ajar; her protective gown and mask were half off.

"Can I help you?" she asked, concerned and scrutinizing his dirty trousers and crew neck t-shirt. Non-morgue personnel weren't usually allowed here.

I probably should have changed before coming to the Medical Examiner's office.

"Can Gwen come out to play?" he asked with a hint of a bite, amused as the girl's face switched from concern to utter confusion.

"Dr. Bixby?" the girl called. She was unsure if she should disturb her boss, but if he was legit, she could get in trouble. "I think someone's here to see you?"

"Who is it?" a voice shouted back. "Tell them I'm busy and to make an appointment."

"But I want to play now," Mal responded loudly, thinking that he was making it his mission to irritate all the women in his life today. A figure emerged from a doorway, quickly taking off her personal protective equipment. Even in scrubs, Gwen was a vision. Her auburn hair hung loosely from a makeshift bun, the olive-colored eyes piercing him with questions.

"Hey, beautiful." His attempt at charm fell flat.

"Mal, what are you doing here? How did you get past the front desk?" she quizzed, leading him out of autopsy and speaking to her assistant. "It's okay, Claire. I've got this. Why don't you go inventory the supply room right now while you wait for me?"

The girl nodded and disappeared.

"Seriously, how did you get past the front desk?" Gwen demanded.

"Nancy," Mal said, simply.

She rolled her eyes. Nancy Carrigan was a smart girl in all aspects except where Mal was concerned. He knew all the buttons to push to get his way. The first time he came to the

ME's office uninvited, he charmed a visitor's badge and free run of the lab out of a newly hired Nancy. Since then, she was under strict orders to escort him everywhere, unless he was with Gwen.

Gwen didn't know how he talked himself out of that restriction, but here he was, standing in the doorway, hair unkempt, clothes disheveled, and handsome as all hell.

"You're not here for personal reasons. You wouldn't be so brazen. What do you need?"

She shifted uncomfortably; arms folded across her chest. Her stance was defensive, guarded, but her heart was ready to burst. When they last spoke, she broke off their affair. She could see a future with Henry and she could no longer see anything with Mal. That was his problem, or maybe it was hers. When they were together, he clouded her judgment and made her lose all inhibitions. But he was unstable, unreliable, and never completely hers.

Then again, she was never completely his, either. When she first met him, she was already engaged to someone else. He exuded a tragic sadness that made him more attractive. She had always been drawn to broken things; it made her an effective doctor and an even better pathologist. It also created chaos in all her relationships.

Gwen started an affair with Mal.

Soon after, she called off her engagement, breaking the heart of a young cardiologist she had been dating since med school. Six months later, he was engaged to his scrub nurse, and Mal had broken her heart.

"Look, I'm not here to annoy you," Mal retreated a little. "Well, I am, but I also need help."

Gwen eyed him suspiciously.

"What do you know so far about the double homicide? The drive-by in midtown?" He clarified, since homicides were regrettably common, even multiple homicides.

"How did you know about it?"

"A client."

"You have a client?" Gwen asked, incredulous. "Since when did you take proper jobs?"

"Since they paid five thousand cash up front, okay? Now, can you please help me out?" Mal grew impatient. He was tired of having to explain himself. Then he softened his tone. "My client is in a lot of trouble. Please, Gwen."

She melted.

"Mal, your bleeding heart is going to get you into trouble. Wait there and don't touch anything." She gestured to her office, then disappeared behind the double doors.

Gwyneth Bixby was the one with the bleeding heart. She was on the board of multiple philanthropic committees, worked at a free health clinic in her spare time, and had been a big sister to a young girl from Third Ward for many years. By Mal's calculations, the girl was probably headed to college now. As the only child of world-renowned surgeons, Gwen grew up in a world of privilege, but it was a solitary life. Her parents were constantly trying to save the world, so Gwen's closest family were her au pairs and tutors.

Then her life took an unexpected turn. Homeschooled most of her youth, she was unprepared for the temptations that college presented. Soon after her arrival at Duke, she became known as the "it" girl around. She had a dealer on speed dial ready to supply her with the best eight ball money could buy. Despite her clear aptitude, she barely made it into medical school. The deciding factor was an unsubtle call her father made to the dean. In med school, she straightened out her life, but not in the direction her parents imagined. They were disappointed when their only child became a county Medical Examiner instead of continuing their legacy.

As a reminder of her life outside of work, Gwen's office was in stark contrast to the sterile corridors of the morgue. Tasteful art covered the soft-hued walls. Photos of family and friends stood on her desk, and plaques and certificates lined the shelves.

"Levi and Abigail Stevenson." Gwen announced, walking in with a large case file under her arm. "Multiple gunshot wounds to the arms and back for him and arms and chest for her." Gwen opened the thick file and shuffled through photographs of both victims.

"She's young. What a shame," he commented.

"She was a sweet girl." Gwen stared at a portrait of Abigail printed from the firm's website. Her blond hair was curled and brushed neatly to one side. The starched collar of a maroon blouse peeked through a well-tailored cashmere cardigan. Her lips curled into a neat smile, as if she had a secret.

"You knew her?" Mal looked up from the preliminary photos.

"Only casually. She and I crossed paths a few times. We ran in the same charity circles. Levi was a firm believer in giving back to the community." Gwen sighed. "From a cursory look, Levi and Abigail were as clean as they get in this town. Nothing in their backgrounds to suggest any vendettas. No secret offshore accounts or funny money trails. It looks like they were collateral damage. Random gang violence."

"No one else got hurt? What about whomever the shooters were aiming for?"

"Witnesses said there were some suspicious guys walking behind them. One African-American, one Caucasian. Low hanging jeans, large black tees. You know the look." Mal nodded. He certainly did. "They were playing their stereo really loud. It drew some attention. They dodged and then ran off after the shooting. If they got hurt, no one there saw it. Descriptions have been pretty generic. I'm waiting for the test results to come back on the blood from the sidewalk to see if there are any foreign profiles."

"Guess we're waiting on Kasey," Mal murmured, almost to himself.

"She's working pretty hard on this one. Got called in early this morning. You'll know as soon as she knows." Gwen leaned back in her chair and folded her arms.

"Oh, are you two friends now?" There was a long-standing animosity between the two women. Gwen always felt threatened by their friendship, even though he assured her Kase only had room for one man in her life. Gwen resolutely held onto her belief that there were some unresolved feelings between the two. To her, it was the only way to explain why Mal always put his best friend first.

"I'm just stating the facts. We're all shocked by this double homicide. Drive-by shootings just don't happen in midtown."

"No, they don't." Mal pursed his lips and skimmed through the rest of the report.

Houston wasn't some fairytale Metropolis. It was seedy, corrupt, and violent. It was a city bursting at the proverbial seams with rage and poverty, covered by a thin veneer of superficial wealth. Areas like Uptown or the Heights were the principal attractions for investors and wealth managers. Crime statistics for the wards were artificially distributed through different law enforcement agencies to minimize their impact. The lack of zoning laws led to luxury and poverty living as neighbors. Driving down a long stretch of Montrose would show decrepit houses cowering next to stately townhomes. Houston covered such a vast area that, although there were three forensic labs within the city, a backlog persisted.

However, there was one thing all officers could agree on. Gang violence usually happened in their own territory; not less than ten minutes away from police headquarters. The shooting happened on the corner of a building owned by one of the largest real estate firms in Houston. Shots were fired at 11:45 in the morning; first responders arrived on scene at 11:51.

"Mal, what are you thinking?" Gwen knew the look. Some insignificant detail had caught Mal's attention. He ignored her question.

"What else do you know?"

"I've only started the preliminary exams by pulling some large caliber bullets out of their bodies. I'm not familiar with what they are. Firearms will have to run some tests. I haven't opened them up, so I can't tell you which were the kill shots. It was an automatic weapon, though; that was confirmed by eyewitness testimony."

"Anyone get a good look? Plates, descriptions?" Mal rubbed his chin, processing.

"Honestly, everyone was too busy ducking."

"Any chance you can give me access to their office? Have officers been over there yet?"

"Dammit, Mal! Will you please tell me what you're thinking now?" Gwen grew impatient. This was the epitome of their relationship: it was one-sided. She would talk, he would ponder and never respond.

"It's too soon to say anything, Gwen." He was pondering how much to tell her about his client. Despite their relationship, he knew she still had an obligation to her job. Anything he told her could be brought up during trial and he didn't want to risk her career over a hunch.

"But the two gangbangers–" Before she could finish protesting, there was an echo of high heels and a knock at her door.

"Well, well, Malcolm Ly. Fancy seeing you here." Both Mal and Gwen looked to see cream-colored silk shorts and slender legs. Long, jet-black hair partially concealed the full bosom peeping from under her blouse. "Forget how to use a phone?"

"Selena, what are you doing here?" How many more ghosts from his past were going to surprise him today?

"I've missed you too, darling." Her lips curled sensually as she approached him, cupping his face in her hand.

Gwen bristled. *Who the fuck is this girl?*

7

D r. Gwyneth Bixby, this is, uh–" Mal stumbled to a stop, caught in the middle of a guy's worst nightmare.

"Selena Parish, insurance investigator." Selena introduced herself, smoothly handing her business card between two polished fingers. Gwen gingerly accepted it, running her fingers through the gold embossed *Mutual Financial Protection*. Selena amused herself with Gwen's pictures and memorabilia.

"How can I help, Ms. Parish?" Gwen asked, uncomfortable with the way this *investigator* slinked around her office, touching everything on her shelf. She was more inflamed by the familiar way she caressed Mal's face.

"I'm actually looking for Malcolm. My sources told me I could find him here."

"And where is your escort?"

"The sweet girl at the front let me in, even told me where to find your office." Selena chuckled, gazing at a portrait hanging on the west wall of Gwen's office. "This is a fine copy of *La Promenade*," Selena complimented, pronouncing the title in near-perfect French.

"You know your art." Gwen begrudgingly admitted, feeling the heat rise to her face. Beautiful and sophisticated.

Nancy's either going to stop this or find another job, Gwen noted.

As if reading her mind, Selena said, "Don't blame Nancy, Doctor. Very few people can resist my charms." Her gaze stayed fixed on the Renoir as she took another jab at Gwen. "Malcolm can attest to that."

Selena was superb at reading a room, and most people were transparent to her. It made her a good grifter and an even better investigator. As soon as she knocked on the door, she felt the sexual tension between Mal and the good doctor. The poor girl was still head over heels for him, even if Mal was too blind to see.

"Selena, you said you were here to see me. You could have called first." Mal cleared his throat, trying to defuse the situation. Gwen's face had turned an unnatural red.

"I did, darling. I even left you a voicemail. Unless you changed your number and some other poor soul got the message? It wasn't particularly appropriate." She spun and smiled seductively. Mal glanced down at his phone, hoping Gwen would ignore that last comment.

Shit. She called almost a week ago. He must have been in an area with poor reception, or he might have simply ignored the call. Sometimes he would misplace his phone for days before realizing it was gone.

"Anyway, it's not just all pleasure for me this time. I'm here on business, and I hate to admit it, but I might need your help."

"Mal doesn't work insurance cases," Gwen said, realizing how defensive she sounded as the words emerged.

"Au contraire. Mal and I have worked plenty of cases together."

Gwen inhaled, incensed. This was another reason she couldn't bear to be with Mal. If they had spent so much time together, why was this the first time she heard of Selena? How many cases did they work together? Did they sleep together too? If they did, was this during their relationship?

"Last time I saw you, you were blonde. I barely recognized you walking through that door." Mal changed the subject again.

"I'm actually busy on a case right now. I don't know how much help I can offer."

"Doctor, I must have the name of the artist who painted this imitation. I want one for myself." Selena ignored Mal's comment, her focus solely on the painting. Gwen was shocked into answering by the abrupt swerve in the conversation.

"I'm sorry. I haven't been in touch with him in years. I don't have his contact information anymore," she replied honestly.

"That's a shame. A name, perhaps? I may find him through my own resources."

"Kyle Pratchett. He was a friend from Duke, but he dropped out." He had actually been enamored with Gwen from the moment they met. Hailing from a family of lawyers and politicians, Kyle was an economics major headed for law school. During his third year, he dropped out and left his family, realizing he couldn't follow a path that wasn't his. He was a gifted artist. Painting, sculpting, there was nothing he couldn't master.

On the night he left, she asked for a portrait he painted of her, but he couldn't bear to part with it. Instead, he gave her *La Promenade*, knowing her love for the Impressionists. Every birthday, she still received a hand-painted postcard with no message and no return address. She kept every single one in a wooden box hidden in her office.

"That's a start." Selena turned to Mal. "You have my number. If you change your mind, call me."

With that, Selena disappeared down the hall as mysteriously as she came, leaving behind only the soft scent of Chanel as a sign of her presence.

8

Hey Selena," Mal chimed before turning on the lamp in his darkened office. "Glad to see you haven't lost your lock-picking skills."

With Selena, everything was a game, and he learned to anticipate her moves. He first ran into her when he was investigating the bludgeoning death of an art dealer and she was attempting to recover the stolen Manet that cost him his life. They worked the case together, fell into lust, and then she stole the Manet from under him. She considered the painting "recovered". He considered it stolen evidence.

"Malcolm, darling, can I buy you a new couch? This one is breaking my heart." She pulled at the loose threads and the flaking pleather.

"I'd offer you a drink, but I don't have a fridge," he riposted. He regarded the woman on his couch, outlining her curves while his eyes adjusted to the dim lighting. She was a complete mystery to him. He suspected she had been a con artist, and Mal wondered if "Selena Parish" was just a character she played to fit her needs for the present.

As for who she was? She was a chameleon, able to speak multiple languages and switch between accents at will. When she was in character, her entire demeanor changed. In another life, she would've been a gifted actress, but she loathed the limelight, choosing to blend in with her environment. She was cunning, intelligent, and dangerous. Her background checks turned up zilch and her alias only went back about five years.

"Should we continue our banter, or do you want to tell me why you're in Houston?"

"Malcom, learn to slow down. Not everything has to be about business." Selena walked to Mal, perched on the edge of his desk. She kissed him, deep and passionate, their tongues tangling inside his mouth.

"I've missed you so," she murmured against his lips.

"Oh yeah? You tell that to all your men?" he asked before he could stop himself, his hands running down the small of her back.

"And some of my women, too." She smirked.

"I don't think this is a good idea." His protest was half-hearted, between gasps of air, but he still pushed her a few inches back. She smelled amazing and looked even better, but he couldn't get distracted by her. His life was already a hellish mess without the added Selena factor.

"Boo, you were so much more fun in New York," she lamented. But she withdrew, plopping into the tattered rolling chair facing him, and flicked her nails. "What is the biggest case of art theft happening in your city right now?"

"I had a feeling you were on the Sandoff case. Anything under fifty million wouldn't be worth your time." He estimated Selena had been in Houston for about three days. She must have caught a whiff of something, or else she wouldn't be sitting in his office seducing him for help. "What did you find?"

"I knew you couldn't say no." That damn smirk came back, the one that made her almost irresistible.

"Hold your horses. I'm not saying yes either. I'm not on the force anymore. But I'll help you." He suddenly smiled. "If you'll do two favors for me."

"Malcolm! Tit for tat. I love it." Selena was a woman who dealt in favors. It was usually some poor schmuck who owed her, but she could deal with owing Mal. If she ever let her guard down, it would be around him. He was a man with an astounding moral compass and an innate obligation to do the right thing, aside from being kicked off the force. But everyone was allowed one moment of insanity.

"Tell me." Two cases in one day. That was a record for him. He figured it wouldn't hurt to distract himself with art theft while he waited to hear from Kasey.

"I'm famished. Let's go to dinner."

He groaned impatiently. Her penchant for foreplay was great in bed. For solving crime? Not so much.

He countered. "Tell me everything and then I'll take you to dinner."

She rebuffed his offer. "Please. Malcolm, you would take me to a hot dog stand. Get changed. I'm taking you out to dinner, and don't argue with me when I'm hungry."

He yielded and took off his shirt, coyly leaned over her and grabbed what she could only assume was a fresh one from another pile. She resisted the urge to stroke his chest. He flashed her a crooked smile, highlighting the epicanthic folds of his eyes.

"God, you're such a tragedy." She tousled his hair before walking out. "Come along."

#

"I found the van." For an opener to their after-dinner conversation, it was a good start. Mal looked over from the driver's seat as she fired off a text and put her phone away.

"Do I want to ask how?" It was a rhetorical question. Selena's investigative tactics usually involved something barely this side of criminal. "You've been here three days and already found the van the thieves drove. I could've used someone like you on my team."

"Darling, blue polyester is not really my style." She shuddered. "Anyway, red tape always makes life so much more difficult for you boys in blue. Did you know that almost everyone has cameras outside their houses now? It's a new age.

Everyone is paranoid as hell."

"Getting warrants for all those cameras would have taken us months."

"Yes, well, that's why I get paid the big money." She stifled a yawn. Dinner was making her lethargic. They had indulged in duck confit, roasted pheasant, and a tower of seafood. She polished off a bottle of wine, while Mal drank diet cola. He certainly wasn't much of an eating companion, but she always enjoyed his conversation.

"I lost sight of the truck after it left the area, but I figured they would want to dispose of it, strip any identifying markers off. I thought a shady neighborhood might do, and I was right, but that's where I hit a dead end. The van's been gutted. I don't have any contacts here who would sell me stolen parts."

"I know a guy." Mal turned to her, flashing a devious smile. "But first, the favor."

He directed them into a large garage and the first spot to the right. He pointed to a tall, rundown building across the street with the words *Houston Police Department* painted in blue letters across the windows.

"On the sixth floor sits a very lazy but handsome bulldog by the name of Terrance Baker. I need you to convince him to give you copies of a file. Here's the case number." He handed her a scrap of paper.

"What kind of case is it?" She memorized the number, then tore it up.

"Something I'm looking into. A homicide. Baker and I don't get along, so he won't give me any information." Mal stopped, knowing she wouldn't need any more details; she always thought murders were messy and uncouth.

"So, you're resorting to subterfuge instead? I'm glad I'm rubbing off on you." She rolled her eyes. Men could be so insipid. "Want to make it a game and time me?"

"It's not a competition."

Selena strode smoothly towards the brightly lit building, heels clacking the whole way. Mal watched as she entered the department, catching sight of her through the window, flipping her hair and throwing her head back in enraptured laughter. Then she leaned in and whispered something in the guard's ear. He escorted her to the back doors and badged her in.

Mal drummed the steering wheel while sweating through his button down. The thick, unrelenting humidity clung to his skin, releasing a sickly-sweet mixture of body odor and deodorant. Twenty minutes later, he spied a flash of raven-colored hair and red-bottomed shoes walking back towards him. It used to take him twenty minutes just to get up to the sixth floor; even the dinky elevators cooperated with her.

9

Kasey took a drag from her cigarette while the ringing continued. Either Mal lost his phone again or he was ignoring her call. She dropped the rest of the cigarette and gagged at the bitter aftertaste as she walked back into the lab. It cost her two dinners and a round of shots, but she got one of her favorite analysts to expedite the DNA report. Perry stayed late to finish the calculations, and the report was ready for review. As suspected, the DNA couldn't tell them much.

RESULTS ARE BACK. ALL PROFILES BELONG TO VICTIMS.

She sighed as she sent the text.

CALL ME

She returned to the twenty-sixth floor and locked her bench. There was nothing more she could do for the night. She had exhaustively examined and swabbed every nook of the victim's clothes. All the evidence told her was that Levi was a devoted father who shielded his daughter until the very end. Most of his blood and contact DNA were found on her clothing. This supported the eyewitness accounts of the paramedics having to pull Levi off of his daughter.

Kasey grabbed her purse and turned off the lights, leaving only the muted overhead casting ominous shadows around the darkened room. As she locked up the lab, her phone buzzed within the front pocket of her scrubs.

"Mal, where the hell have you been?" She answered without looking at the screen.

"No, it's Gwen." She had her professional voice on, so this call wasn't about Mal. Over the years, Kase had gotten used to the drunken phone calls from Gwen, usually after some lover's quarrel. Gwen would berate their friendship, oscillating between threats and pleas for her to stay away from Mal. The girl was brilliant, but she was "enthusiastic" when it came to love.

Mal had that effect on women, though. Trish acted the same about his past relationships. She would always find the most miniscule detail from a past fling to throw in his face and start an argument. Maybe it was his lot in life to fall in love with passionate, hot-blooded women. Knowing what she knew now about Trish, she couldn't help but wonder if all those fights were only part of some elaborate escape plan.

But they got married and had a kid instead, she thought, rolling her eyes.

"Hey, what's going on?" She tried to sound casual, but she really couldn't stand the doctor and she couldn't fake it. Gwen was the opposite of everything she stood for. A privileged, silver-spoon, private-school brat who threw a tantrum every time life didn't go her way. Her parents didn't give her enough attention, so she almost threw away her medical career. Adam was too busy being a heart surgeon, so she threw him away. Mal was too closed off for her, so she threw him out, too. She was surprised Henry survived the six-month itch.

"I'm finding some anomalies in Abigail's body. I was wondering if you finished processing her clothes?"

"The report will be issued tomorrow after the technical review, but between you and me, they were all mixtures that came back to our victims."

"Was Levi the major profile?" Gwen asked.

"Looks like it. You can call Perry in the morning to confirm. She threw me out of her cubicle when I started hovering too close." Kase paused and sat back down. She might not get to go home yet after all. "Gwen, what are you thinking?"

"The clothing might be a dead end, but I'm sending some vaginal swabs over. Can you take it to DNA?"

"Vaginal swabs? It was a drive-by. There's no indication of sexual assault."

"It may be nothing, but seems our girl had sex fairly recently before her death. He may have been the last person to see her alive. If we can find him, we might get some answers."

10

What are we doing at the county hospital?" Selena looked up from her phone, her polished thumbs still sending rapid-fire texts to her assistant.

"The second favor." Mal winked as he ushered her out of the garage. "I need to talk to my client. His girlfriend hired me. Got himself into a pickle and barely survived a jailhouse shanking."

Selena's interest was piqued. The case just took an intriguing turn. "You're thinking set-up?"

Mal nodded. "The guard is a guy I don't know. He wouldn't let me in to talk to the victim earlier. I even flashed him my PI badge, told him the victim was my client. The by-the-book prick said I had to get clearance from Homicide first."

"Ah, the handsome bulldog." Selena was quick. "It's all coming together. You want me to use my feminine charms again?"

He opened the door for her. "Well, that and your investigator badge."

"He has nothing to do with art theft, Mal," Selena chuckled.

"Since when has that stopped you?" He added a smirk.

She liked him this way. Civilian Malcolm was more willing to bend the rules, lie, and do what was needed to get the job done.

Maybe one day I'll convince him to lift a few things. We would make a great team.

"Excuse me, where are you two going?" a dark-haired nurse demanded. Her blood-shot eyes watched their movements like a hawk.

"We're here to—" Mal started, but Selena smoothly cut him off.

"Selena Parish, insurance investigator." She whipped out her badge and opened it in one swift movement. "This is my associate. We need to speak to Jamal Wilson."

"Visiting hours are from 8 to 7." The nurse replied without blinking, nodding at the visitor's sign against the wall.

"I understand he was gravely injured and might not survive. He's a key witness, and I need his testimony. We need to speak to him urgently," Selena insisted.

"Then you can come back at eight tomorrow morning," the nurse sassed back without realizing she'd unwittingly started a game of chicken with Selena.

"Listen, Nurse—" Selena glanced at her name badge. "Logan. That man in there is a key witness against an enormous art smuggling ring that we have been chasing for months. Why do you think he's lying there with stab wounds? We believe the people who want him dead are going to try again. If I don't get to talk to him before that happens, I'm sure you can tell my employer that you'll be responsible for the $50 million payout." Selena glared, not blinking even once.

Nurse Logan blinked, but she wasn't giving in just yet.

"Fine, but if his blood pressure rises two points, you can tell *my* employer you'll be responsible for his life."

Victory in hand, Selena tossed her hair and walked toward the corridor, a smug smile Mona Lisa'd across her face. Mal mouthed an apology to the nurse and followed silently, feeling her death gaze on the back of his head.

"That was great," he whispered, pinching her arm to hide his discomfort. The sound of heart machines whirring and beeping made his hairs stand on end. The only memories hospitals evoked were bad: his last visit ended with the loss of his only child. Malcolm and Trish had one child in their marriage, a Hail Mary to save a doomed relationship, and it failed. Trish abandoned them after his son turned two. For five years, he raised him as a single dad, balancing stake outs and late nights with soccer games and school plays. Georgie seldom asked about his mom, and Mal wondered if he even remembered her.

"I hope you got clearance from Homicide, Mr. Ly." The guard declared when he spotted them. "Otherwise, you wasted another trip."

"Listen, officer…" Selena took the lead again.

"Hamill," the guard replied curtly.

"Officer Hamill, I was at the precinct speaking to Detective Baker not twenty minutes ago. We need to talk to Jamal urgently. Would that be a problem?" She batted her eyes hopefully, her voice no louder than a subdued whisper.

"No ma'am. Not without clearance." Hamill had no give to his staunch demeanor.

Shit. She pulled Mal aside; she should've seen it sooner, but her charm wasn't going to work on this guy.

"Malcolm. I can't do it," she muttered.

"Selena, now is not the time to develop performance anxiety."

"It's not that, you colossal idiot. He's gay!" Selena hissed, exasperated. "I can't charm a man who isn't attracted to women."

Mal stood dumbfounded, without a contingency plan.

"How about we just knock him out?"

"Are you crazy? Forgetting that he's taller than either of us and looks like he could bench press a Buick, he's a police officer *and* he knows both our names. We'll be sitting in jail right next to my client," Mal hissed.

They stood there arguing under their breaths about their next course of action, with Selena suggesting several highly illegal maneuvers.

"Detective Baker," Hamill announced. Both Selena and Mal groaned. "These two said you gave them clearance to talk to

Wilson."

Baker looked up from his phone and immediately went red.

"What the actual fuck? I should have known it was you, Ly."

"Look, Baker, I really need to talk to your suspect. It's important. I think he's being set up." Mal tried to explain.

"I don't care what you need. You're a real sonofabitch for sending this tart in to blackmail me for a damn file." Baker spat as he talked, his agitation growing.

"Blackmail?" Mal turned to Selena, hissing, "What did you do?"

"Now's not the time to talk about that," she whispered through gritted teeth, pulling Mal toward the exit. "Nice to see you, Detective. See you later!"

"That's right, you better run. Next time I see you anywhere near this suspect *or* the precinct, I'll have you both arrested," Baker shouted after them.

#

"What the fuck did you do?" he shouted, slamming the car door. "Why is he talking about blackmail?"

"Calm down, Malcolm. You didn't tell me I had to play nice." She almost sounded defensive. "I just walked in and kissed him; took a picture of it and said I was going to send it to his wife if he didn't give me the file."

"Oh. My. God. You blackmailed an officer in his own office?!" Mal bellowed, incredulous. "Does your depravity know no bounds?"

"Hey! You asked for my help. You knew who you were getting into bed with." Selena shouted back, then turned away. The hurt in her voice startled him.

"I'm sorry. I didn't mean what I said." Her face was turned towards the window; an uncomfortable silence lingered after his apology.

"I'm really sorry," he repeated. "What you did wouldn't have been so bad if Baker wasn't going through a nasty divorce. He stepped out on her, and that picture? Well, she's already getting his pension. Who knows what else her lawyers would grab with that photo as evidence? No wonder he caved, and small wonder he didn't throw you in jail. But there's no way you could have known," he finished, sounding lame to his own ears. Much as Mal disliked Baker, he wouldn't knowingly set him up.

Hell, she probably would have asked for a kidney out of spite.

The uncomfortable silence was broken by the small buzz of his phone.

Joe, thank God.

"Hey man, where have you been?"

"Sorry boss. It's been crazy around here." Joe said, out of habit.

"I'm not your boss anymore," Mal corrected. "Did you get my message?"

"Sorry boss—I mean, sorry Mal. Yeah, I can get you in tomorrow. Let me text you a time when I figure out my schedule."

"Thanks man, that's great. In the meantime, can you put extra security on Wilson? Just call it a hunch, but I think he's still in danger."

"I'll see what I can do." Joe paused, a world of meaning unsaid. "Good hearing your voice, Mal. We've been really worried about you over here."

"Yeah, well, you know me. Still breathing. I'll see you soon."

He hung up quickly and looked over at Selena, still facing the window. "My buddy from the force says he can get me in tomorrow." More silence. "I should take you home. Where are you staying?"

That finally provoked a response.

"Hotel Alessandra."

11

Bethany Tremel wiped a stray tear from her cheek.

It had been a trying few days as news of the Stevensons' murders spread. Levi and his daughter were tremendous contributors to the charity circuit in Houston. They were magnanimous in their donations of both money and time to various causes, many of which were spearheaded by Bethany. More than that, Abigail had become a close friend. Petite and ghostly pale, the heiress lived a lonely life of boardroom meetings and late-night dinners in the office. She was constantly overshadowed by her father's successes and the memory of her mother's beauty.

Jeanette Tremel was a Southern Belle-turned-model turned billionaire's wife before her untimely death in a car accident when Bethany was still in high school. The teenaged heiress was in the passenger seat and barely survived. No amount of laser treatment could erase the physical reminders of that fateful afternoon. The jagged wounds left garish outlines wrapping from her left cheek down to her neck and shoulders. During times of enormous stress, she absentmindedly picked at the dried flakes of skin that never healed.

"Ms. Tremel?" The mousey secretary poked her head through the door. She sucked in air through the tiny gap in her front teeth, waiting to be berated for interrupting.

"Yes?" Bethany asked, not turning her chair away from the panoramic windows overlooking the downtown skyline. She wiped away another tear, cleared her throat, and faced the door.

"I'm sorry to interrupt—" The girl started meekly.

"What is it, Stacy?"

"You have a letter." Her body was wedged between the large oak doors, one foot in the office, the other outside, poised to run away. *Seems all my employees have one foot out the door*, Bethany noted absentmindedly.

"It's from Ms. Stevenson. I just thought…"

"Bring it here." Stacy did, and Bethany pounced on it. "Thank you, you can go."

Stacy fled. Bethany tore open the envelope as the door closed behind the secretary. It was a plain, tan envelope made from recyclable cotton, addressed in a familiar, neat, square print. Typical Abigail.

My dearest Bethany,

Firstly, I want to thank you for your wonderful friendship…

Bethany clutched the letter to her chest and sobbed.

#

Mal read the text message from Kacey, then placed it face down on the nightstand.

He didn't expect a different outcome. No foreign DNA was a positive for his client. It meant they couldn't place him at the scene, but it also meant the actual killer was getting away with murder. Kase had called him a few more times last night, but they all went to voicemail. He didn't feel like being mothered; besides, he had been busy.

Mal felt guilty. He admitted it. So, to atone for chastising her, Mal spent the better portion of the night satiating Selena's appetite. As soon as they crossed the threshold of her suite, his former lover ripped apart his only good button-down and clamored at his belt, her nails digging into his abdomen. She nipped at his lips and kissed his chest, making her way down to his groin. He stood awkwardly behind the hotel door with his pants around his ankles, huffing as he felt her warm tongue taking him in. They finally made their way to the bed. After hours of bodies writhing and moaning, they wrapped each other in one last embrace before falling into a deep, exhausted sleep.

He awoke to a blurred outline of Selena's bare back, soft tresses curled and swept to the side. He kissed her warm, soft shoulder, taking in subtle hints of lilac. Her body stiffened.

"You're not getting sentimental on me now, are you?"

"You and I aren't like that. Besides, I haven't forgotten about that Manet. You're a glorified art thief." He lashed out more harshly than he intended, embarrassed by her comment.

She whipped around and glared. "I was doing my job. I can't help it if I do it better than you do yours."

There was a brief pause, as if she were considering her next words. "If I'm an art thief, then what does that make you? You beat a man half to death!"

It was hitting below the belt, but this was the epitome of their relationship: a passionate wildfire that left nothing but destruction in its path. Mal's eyes narrowed as he stomped to the bathroom.

"I'm going to take a shower. We have a lot of work to do today."

"I sent out for fresh clothes. They're hanging by the door." That was as close to an apology as he was going to get.

12

You should probably wait here." Mal unbuckled his seat belt and slipped out. The silence on the ride to Chinatown was uncomfortable, and he was grateful for the reprieve.

"I'm coming with you. Hey!" She protested as Mal refastened her seat belt. She shot him a dirty look, insisting, "I can handle myself."

"I know you can. But Madame Moua doesn't trust anyone, and that includes me. She barely tolerates me. If she sees you, she'll clam up and give us bullshit info. She won't believe you're not a cop, even with the way you dress."

"Madame? I thought you said you knew a guy?"

"Yeah, she's my guy." Mal closed the car door and signaled for her to stay put.

The poker club was only half lit, bar chairs rested upside down on the counters, and the smell of stale beer and desperation lingered in the air.

Must have been a helluva fight last night. He surveyed the broken chairs piled to the side where Tiny was meticulously sweeping up broken glass. He glanced up when the door chimed, realized it was Mal, and gave a slow nod before going back to his task.

"She in?"

Tiny pointed a single sausage finger towards the poorly lit

office. Mal always thought it was fitting, in a backwards way, that they called him Tiny. After all, at 6'6" and thick as a bear, he towered over most of the patrons at the club.

"We're not open yet, unless you're here to pay me." A throaty voice grumbled from within the murky room.

"Not even for a friend?" He casually leaned in the doorway, folding his arms across his chest.

"You're no friend of mine." Madame Moua expertly shuffled through a stack of bills, flipping each so they faced the same way. The shrewd loan shark didn't need to look up to recognize the lilt in his voice. "Or have you forgotten all the furniture you broke the last time you flew through here?"

"Hey, that guy attacked me." Mal smiled, raising his hands defensively. "Someone should have cut him off."

Madame Moua finally glanced up at him through her horn-rimmed reading glasses. She was in a terrible mood; her nightly profits were off by twenty percent. Five of that, she anticipated and allowed. Her waitresses made the bulk of their money through tips. She knew they skimmed off the till, but considered it hazard pay for the groping and propositions of slimy, stinking, drunken patrons. The remaining percentage was an unpleasant surprise. Now she would have to shoulder the burden of figuring out which of her dealers were cheating. No one stole from her unless she allowed it.

"What do you want, Malcom? I have no patience for your nonsense right now." She narrowed her good eye and glared at him suspiciously.

Despite her appearance, Madame Moua was only in her late forties. A traumatic youth and an arduous journey on a boat to America had left her aged and calloused. At six years old, her father sold her to a local gangster to pay off a gambling debt. When she tried to fend off a rapist, he threw acid in her face to set an example. During a period of political turmoil in Laos, she made her escape into Vietnam and was smuggled out in a small boat by a kind-hearted fisherman in 1975. Stranded at sea for nearly forty days, they were rescued by an American naval ship hours before the harsh sun would have finished them both. Moua was a survivor, and she let no one forget it.

Mal crossed paths with her when a more experienced Moua distinguished herself as a discreet and shrewd businesswoman in Chinatown. Some of the most powerful and corrupt politicos and entrepreneurs ran their dirty money through her business. It was rumored she held a ledger that could burn most of Houston's elite. Local and federal law enforcement tried every way to shake her down, from weekly raids of her club to bribes to outright begging for information. It was fate that a young Detective Ly stopped by one night to do some surveillance and pulled her and one of her bodyguards out of the burning game room. Feeling she owed him a life debt, one she was unlikely to repay any other way, Moua and Mal formed a tenuous relationship. She became his unofficial and very off-the-books informant.

"I want the same thing I always want. Information." He threw a roll of cash on the table. She grabbed the wad and leafed through each bill, appreciating that he never tried to haggle.

"This is more than my usual fee. This information must be valuable to you?"

"Not really." He tried to sound disinterested. "A theft. Stolen art. The rest of that is for the broken chairs."

"Ah, the Marc Sandoff case." She smiled mischievously, playing coy. "Isn't burglary a little beneath you?"

"Tell me what you know."

Without a word, she slid a sliver of notebook paper across the desk towards him. The hazy desk lamp illuminated a series of hastily scratched numbers and letters.

VIN numbers. I could run these and—

"It won't do you any good," she remarked, as if reading his mind. "The van goes back to a small rental company. The renter paid in cash and used a fake ID."

"So, I'm buying useless information?" Mal scoffed.

"Malcolm, how long have we known each other? Do you think I would ever sell you anything 'useless'?" Moua pretended to be offended.

"I've known you long enough to know you're playing coy on purpose. What are you planning, Noy?"

She shot him a vitriolic glare. Most people didn't know she had a first name, let alone dared to use it.

"You're playing with fire. This information is worth so much more than that sad roll of bills you threw at me, I can't begin to tell you."

"How much?" he interrupted, impatient. Selena was probably outside slashing his tires out of boredom and spite.

"A small favor." She didn't look at him, her response sour in her throat.

"What kind of trouble are you in, Noy?" Eye contact was everything to her. It was her way of instilling fear and respect in a business where a limp and acid scars were a sign of weakness. She hadn't looked him in the eyes since he walked in.

The scarred crone ignored his question. "Do the job and I'll give you the information. Simple as that."

"Is it legal?"

"It's a simple exchange. You drop off a duffel and you count the containers. If it equals ten, you call a number and then walk off. Someone will come by to pick them up. Even you can't mess this up."

He weighed the options, knowing there was no such thing as a 'simple exchange.' He, they, needed the information, but the smart thing to do was walk away. However, Selena would ask him, get the drop location, and do it herself. They were most likely walking into an ambush; he couldn't let Selena walk into it alone.

"You don't want me to check what's in the containers?"

"That's none of your concern."

"Alright, but I want the information up front. If something goes wrong, I want my people to continue the investigation."

"That's a fair request, but I respectfully decline. I've learned my lesson with you cops. Half of the information now, half upon completion. *If* something happens to you, you can send Kasey to retrieve the rest of it." Mal froze, locking eyes with Moua. He wasn't comfortable putting Selena in jeopardy, but Kasey was out of the question. He didn't want her involved at all. If she got dragged into it, got hurt? He would never forgive himself.

"No. If something happens to me, Selena Parish will retrieve the information." He handed her a card swiped from Selena's purse earlier. "She's not a cop; she doesn't care what you do here. Noy, you leave Kase out of this."

"Fine." She handed him a cell phone. "Pre-paid, GPS disabled. The number you need is programmed in; push 1 and dial. Once you're done, throw it away. The drop is tomorrow night, at midnight, in Galveston. Tiny will drop off the bag at your office tomorrow morning with the address."

Moua handed him an envelope and dismissed him with a wave. "Now go away Mal, you're exhausting."

13

"Hey boss, you have some time right now?" Joe chirped through the phone. "I can be at the hospital in 30 mins."

Finally, some good news.

"Yeah, I'll see you there." Mal exclaimed. "And Joe, Selena's coming too."

"Shit. I didn't know she was in town." Joe chuckled. "That's who Baker's been ranting about all morning."

"What's he been saying?" Mal didn't think Baker wanted anyone to know he had been bested by a slim, seemingly harmless "wannabe detective", a moniker he condescendingly bestowed on anyone who wasn't law enforcement.

"You brought some cheap hooker with you to the hospital to seduce Hamill, and that luckily, Baker was there to stop the whole thing." Joe chortled, amused by the spin Baker put on the story.

"Yeesh. Whatever you do, don't tell Selena that. She might hurt him for real."

"No problem, boss. We all know Baker exaggerates."

Mal chuckled as they sketched out plans to meet in front of the hospital. Selena was thumbing a photograph with a puckish grin across her face as he plopped into the driver's seat. It was a polaroid of him embracing Gwen from behind as they both stared blissfully into the camera. The sultry investigator was fanning herself with the photo, her dark hair sloppily held up by a pen she found between the seats.

"The good news is I have some information for you." He cleared his throat, trying to ignore the photo in her hand. "The bad news is, it's only half the information."

"We'll get to that in a minute. Want to tell me about this?" She waved the yellowed photo in his face.

"It's a picture of me and Dr. Bixby." He tried to sound casual and unconcerned.

"Dr. Bixby! Malcolm, anyone who sat in that office with you two for five seconds would pick up on the sexual tension," she exclaimed. "Now tell me, darling, do you still have feelings for her?"

"That's none of your business! How do you even have that photo?" He started the car, ready to change the subject.

"I got bored. You left me in this car to die!" She retorted with only slight exaggeration, yanking on the emergency brake. "And we're not going anywhere until you tell me. You didn't cheat on her last night, did you?"

"Oh my god Selena, who do you think I am?" Mal threw up his hands. "She and I had a thing for a while. I was messed up and couldn't commit, so she left. She's over it. She has a serious boyfriend now; they've moved in together. Anything else you want to know, Dick Tracy?"

"Are you over it?"

Why did every woman in his life insisted on talking about his feelings? Of all people, he would expect Selena to understand he wanted to keep some things private. Her life was shrouded in mystery.

"If I tell you, will you stop badgering me about this?" She nodded enthusiastically, as if he just offered her a Matisse.

"Promise?"

Selena made the ancient childhood gesture. "Cross my heart."

"From time to time, she and I --"

"Hook up?" Selena offered. He shot her an icy glare. She

smiled unapologetically.

"We let off some steam. Then we always regret it, and always for the same reason. She gets melodramatic and wants to leave whoever she's with to run off with me, and I can't. I care for her, but I can't give her what she wants. She's perfect, and she deserves a perfect life. You know, a great husband, two point five kids, white picket fence, the works. I'm not any of that." He gripped the steering wheel and sighed. "She has a very idealistic view of the world, so she has a hard time empathizing. Every time she looks at me, all I see is pity."

She gently stroked his knee. There was something comforting about Selena's sudden shortage of words.

"Courtesy of Madame Moua." He tossed the wrinkled manila envelope on her lap and hoped that would change the subject. She opened it and dove in. On the way to the hospital, he brought her up to speed. "She's holding out on me. She knows who forged those IDs. We track the fucker down and squeeze him for everything he's got. If things break bad tomorrow night, I told Moua you would come for that information."

He squeezed her hand.

She pulled it back, appalled. "You're kidding me, right? You think I'm going to let you walk into that death trap by yourself? We both know she's setting you up. It's my case, Mal. I can figure out another way to find this guy. Forging is still an art crime, which means my sources will have something."

"Alright!"

"What?" Selena stopped arguing, stunned that he agreed so quickly.

"I'm depressed, Selena, but I'm way past suicidal. We'll do it your way." He gave her hand another squeeze and flashed a toothy grin.

"You're messing with me again, right?" She looked around. "Am I on camera?"

"You're right. Of course it's a setup. Moua wouldn't have sent me if she didn't expect *some* backstabbing. She's probably trying to suss out a leak in her organization and she's using me as a patsy. I'm not stupid, but I needed her." He waved at the envelope. "Look at the documents. If you can figure out the forger before tomorrow night, then we leave the Madame to her own dealings. She probably has five contingency plans for tomorrow night, anyway."

"Thanks for sharing your plan with me." Her voice still dripped sarcasm, but her breathing leveled off.

"Besides, Kasey would kill me if she found out I knowingly walked into a death trap." He smirked.

"That's who scares you?"

"She's all I have left," he confided.

"Do you want to talk about it?"

"Nope." He flipped on the radio. "Some things are private."

#

Joe met them at the front entrance wearing a black muscle shirt and stained khakis. He wiped sweat off a forehead crowned by slick, gelled black hair and pulled uncomfortably at a gold chain dangling from his neck. Mal noticed two new tattoos since the last time they saw each other.

"You look like hell. Another all-nighter?" He shook Joe's hand.

"Yeah boss, sorry about not calling you back right away. I've been undercover for the last two weeks." He nodded at Mal's companion. "Selena."

"Detective Sanchez, always a pleasure." She extended her hand.

"It's Sergeant." He corrected. "And the pleasure's all yours."

Guess he hasn't gotten over that Manet. When Selena recovered the missing painting for her client, it almost destroyed the case Mal built against Patrick Soren, a known art thief and murderer. Mal took the heat for the missing evidence, but a fiercely loyal Joe could never let it go. In his mind, any time the insurance investigator was in town, trouble followed.

"I spoke to Baker and smoothed out the situation as much as I could," Joe started. "Did she really try to blackmail him?"

"It was a misunderstanding." Mal glanced at Selena, who was chuckling to herself. "My fault, really. I asked her to get me a copy of the file without specifying not to do anything illegal."

"Well, he's still in a tizzy about it, but I talked him off the ledge. Told him I would 'supervise' you and Brigid O'Shaughnessy here. Hamill is upset you guys lied to him, but he's a good kid. He's on watch duty again today, so maybe apologize and be nice." He eyed Selena. She gave an unrepentant shrug as they made their way towards the ICU. Officer Hamill stood in a neatly pressed uniform by the door. He gave the trio an expressionless nod as they approached him.

"Hey Josh, I'm here to see the suspect. These two are with me."

"Detective Baker called ahead. I can't let them into the room unsupervised. Either you or I have to be in the room with them."

"Oh, come on, you know he won't tell me anything with a cop in the room," Mal protested. Joe shot him a look to say, *I've got this*, and Mal shut up.

Joe placed his hand on Hamill's shoulder and squeezed firmly. "Look, why don't you take a ten-minute coffee break, grab lunch, something? Do me this solid and I'll consider your transfer to Organized Crimes."

Hamill's eyes widened, and he nodded excitedly.

"I guess I need to go to the bathroom and could eat something. I'll be back in *ten minutes*." As he rounded the corner, Joe opened the door and signaled for Mal and Selena to slip inside.

"You know the drill boss; you've got ten minutes. Make them count."

14

Terrible news about Levi," Bill Stanton lamented as he sliced into a slightly overcooked pork tenderloin. "And his poor daughter. She was so young! What was her name?"

"Abigail, dear," Stanton's wife reminded him.

Bethany watched as she cut a strand of haricot vert into five smaller pieces and rearranged them on her plate. Barbara Stanton was a notorious bulimic whose infamous stints in rehab cost almost as much as the annual salary of Bill's employees. She rarely made public appearances since she started losing her hair and some of her teeth. Her illness started after she caught Stanton in bed with a skinny blonde the same age as their youngest daughter. His constant gas-lighting slowly destroyed her, leaving Barbara a shell of the woman she used to be.

So, the dinner guests were all surprised when she turned up in the Sandoffs' foyer, dressed from head to toe in Chanel, her pasty face adorned with an expensive new wig.

"Did you know her well, Marc?" Bill asked absently, the tenderloin shearing under his knife.

"No, I mainly worked with her father." Marc cleared his throat. "I believe Bethany was fairly close to her, though."

Bethany shifted uncomfortably in her seat. She hated the situation. First, he lured her best friend into a sordid affair before discarding her as one might dispose of a broken toy. Now he sat, feigning ignorance, as if a month ago, he wasn't mounting Abby in that smutty downtown condo he keeps for his mistresses. Worse, he depended on Bethany to keep his name clean.

"We were as close as colleagues could be." Bethany dabbed her lips with an embroidered napkin and motioned for the maid to refill her wine glass. She hated downplaying their friendship, but she couldn't afford an emotional breakdown at the dinner table.

Every month, the Tremels gathered with their associates to go over asset holdings and investment decisions. It was always the same. It would begin with a tedious dinner where they pretended to care about each other's personal lives. After dessert, the men would "retreat to the drawing room" for cigars and brandy, while the women were left to muse over next month's charity project or the latest gossip. Bethany found it dreadfully Victorian. However, since her father's semi-retirement, she found herself in that same drawing room sipping brandy while trying to prove to "daddy's friends" that she was worthy of her expensive executive office. Any kind of tearful breakdown would obliterate all the respect she may have wrested from them.

"Please Marc, Bethany doesn't have time to socialize with nobodies like that. She's much too important inheriting daddy's company," Lenore sneered. Bethany hid a small smile between sips of wine. The bitch was especially vicious tonight, and she wondered what might have set her off. A single hair out of place made her ass cheeks clench.

"You know Lenore, last month Marc was talking about his company's profit and loss, and it seemed like you caused much of that loss. Do you need a job? I would be happy to offer you one if you know how to make a good pot of coffee." Bethany cleared her throat as Lenore's face turned a bright red.

"Excuse me, I have to go to the ladies' room." Barbara

whispered. "Where is it again?"

She directed her question at a bristling Lenore, hoping to defuse the situation. Tension filled the intricately decorated dining room as she made her way down the hall. Pretty soon, they would all pretend not to hear the hacking and vomiting that followed every one of the poor woman's meals.

Talk of the tragedy droned on, with each of the guests remarking on the increase in gang violence in Houston. The discussion quickly turned to the recent burglary at the Sandoff residence. Marc pushed for a quick investigation and got one. CSI, both day and night shifts, worked tirelessly to collect evidence and clear out before his next dinner party. Despite this effort, the maids could not wash off all the evidence that a crime had been committed.

Smudges of fingerprint powder could be found within the crevices of the door panels. Areas where paintings used to hang were highlighted by the sharp contrast between dull, exposed hues of eggshell and what was a more tinted alabaster. Marc did not hide the crime, either. He advocated stricter zoning laws and tougher penalties for repeat offenders for years, and a high-profile burglary would only help his case. His sprawling manor in Rice Military was a mere fifteen minutes away from the freeway overpass, a respite for kush addicts. Any habitual drunk or convict out on parole could have wandered to his neighborhood looking for their next payday.

As the night wore on, Bethany traded her wine chalice for a Glencairn whiskey glass. The combination of whiskey and boredom slowly weighed her down as she listened to Bill's warnings against aggressive investments in tech companies. He believed larger companies would be usurped by start-ups that required low overheads, had higher turnovers, and yielded larger returns in short spans. Her eyelids drooped, and she suddenly realized how emotionally exhausting the last few days had been.

"Pardon me, Bill, but I think the whiskey was a bit much for me today. I'm going to call it a night." She excused herself. They all bid her goodnight as Marc escorted her to the foyer.

"I hope you're alright, Bethany. I know it's been hard for you." Marc said, his voice barely above a whisper.

"Yes. It's almost a relief." He looked shocked, and she continued pointedly. "It's been maddening for much longer than that. She's been upset for a while. You broke her heart."

"She put me in a weird position," he defended weakly.

"Don't they all, Marc? What did you think was going to happen?" She didn't know if it was the whiskey or the anger, but she could feel the heat rising to her face. Tears welled up in her eyes and she swallowed hard, fighting them back.

"You took an innocent girl, a child, broke her in every way possible, and now that she's dead, you sound positively relieved. Like it's one less problem for you to worry about."

"Please keep your voice down."

He has the audacity to shush me?

"I don't want to talk about this now. It's not the place. Get some rest Bethany. Perhaps another time." He ushered her out the door and fastened it behind her. She knew there wasn't going to be another time. Unless he could make political points from her death, Abigail had been all but completely erased from his mind.

#

Marc found Lenore in the library by the window, her gaze fixed on nothing in particular. A sconce on the adjacent wall cast a dim beam of light in her direction, softening her features and giving her profile an almost angelic glow. In that light, he could almost believe she wasn't a caustic bitch out to ruin his life. In their twelve years of marriage, the only joy she brought to his life were their children, fraternal twins she brought into the world, and then promptly sent off to boarding school.

She never wanted children, but when he expressed his reservations about marriage? Suddenly she was with child. Not wanting to taint his future political aspirations with a messy personal life, Marc proposed to her with the biggest diamond he could find in the hopes it was enough to shut her up for the rest of their marriage. He was wrong, and now, leaving her would cost so much more than having to endure her vitriolic abuse day after day. Eventually, he would die and be released from her.

"Slinking off to see a new blonde?" Lenore rasped without turning around. "How old is she this time, Marc? Twenty-two, twenty-three?"

"Twenty-six," he replied coolly. He had hoped to grab the documents off his desk and sidle off without getting into another sparring match with her, but at the sound of her grating voice, he couldn't help taking a jab at her.

"You piece of shit." Lenore whipped around, the flickering lamps lighting her eyes on fire, Chopin's nocturne reaching its climax in the background. "Why can't you be a decent human being for once in your life?"

"I don't know what you're talking about. I am a decent human being. I pay for everything, the cars, the clothes, the children I never see. Everything I've ever given you just goes up your nose, so why don't you just shut up and appreciate it?"

"Were you going to leave me for that whore?" She was in one of her moods.

How many glasses of wine did she have at dinner? He could see the familiar patches of white powder lingering beneath her nostrils. He walked away, shaking his head in disgust.

"You were different with her; I could feel it. Did you love her? Why can't you love me?" she shrieked wildly at his back.

Marc let out a slow breath, his voice threatening. "If you throw another whiskey glass, I'm taking you back to rehab."

I'm out of here. Crazy bitch. He dialed Tessa's number as he galloped down the stairs. *Time for another late night at the office.*

15

The room in the ICU was almost completely dark, lit only by a fluorescent bar lamp hanging at the head of the bed. Jamal Wilson laid with his back to the door, semi-conscious, his face scarred and bandaged, half-hidden under the thin polyester blanket. He looked cadaverous beneath the garish light, his breathing light and uneven.

"Jamal?" Mal whispered. The man stirred slightly. "Jamal, my name is Malcolm Ly. I'm here to help you."

"You're Officer Ly?" Jamal asked breathily, struggling to turn onto his back. Mal reached for his arm to help, but Jamal swatted him off.

"I'm not an officer anymore, but I was hired to help you." The young man rolled over, grimacing at the pain. The flimsy hospital robe fell off, revealing bandages stained a dark red, wrapped around a bruised abdomen. He adjusted the cotton around his face, lifting the eyepatch to get a better look at his champion.

"You're shorter than I remember," he joked, his lips curling into a half smile. "You probably don't remember me though, do you?"

Mal shook his head. It was hard enough to place him without all the lacerations. "Were you one of my CIs?"

"Nah man, I ain't no snitch." Jamal's frail laughter ended in a coughing fit. "It's okay if you don't remember me. I was only ten years old when I got pinched." Mal did a double-take. He remembered chasing down a mouthy kid once as an officer. They were called as back-up to a double homicide; gang violence in a dangerous neighborhood. The kid had blood all over him. It was his brother who had been shot, and he was running away with the pistol that was in his brother's waistband.

"Any other officer and I would have been in a grave next to my brother. But you listened and you let me go," the kid continued, struggling with each inhale.

"I hate to break up this touching reunion, but Mal, you need to see something." Selena handed him an item from Moua's envelope: a masterful fake driver's license belonging to one Jamarcus Simms. The photo on the ID resembled the kid lying in front of him.

"Jamal, Ericka hired me to help you, so I'm on your side." He held the driver's license up to the light near Jamal's good eye. "But you have some explaining to do and you better tell me the truth."

"I'll only talk to you. I don't know her."

"No deal. You'll talk to the both of us. This is Selena Parish, an insurance investigator, and I trust her." *At least I think I do.* "You need to tell us why the evidence we gathered for her case is linked to you, and how it's connected to the double homicide you're implicated in."

Beads of cold sweat formed on the open areas of Jamal's forehead.

"Look man, we were hired for the art theft." He lowered his voice to a raspy whisper. "But that was it! We weren't told to off nobody."

"By whom?" Selena pushed.

"Some Darth Vader-sounding dude. I don't know. I wasn't even supposed to know about him. Tory was the one who got the phone calls. He just let me listen in once." He started whimpering. "It was supposed to be simple. Steal some expensive shit, stash it, get rid of the van, and wait to get paid." Tears were streaming freely from his eye now.

"Next thing you know, Tory and I are being picked up for murder. We weren't even near that area when the white chick and her pops got knocked off. Then he didn't even make it. They got him, man." His voice cracked. "This wasn't supposed to happen. We were supposed to get away clean, man."

Selena stood near the door, unmoved by the kid's bawling. She picked up on the detail that they were ordered to stash the stolen art, meaning it was still somewhere in the city. To her investigator's senses, that suggested it was fraud. Marc Sandoff arranged the burglary of his own home in order to claim the insurance money and possibly to further his political agenda. She was tired of the corrupt and dirty side of Houston and wanted nothing more than to recover the property and be on the next plane back.

"Where did you hide the art?" Selena asked as Mal simultaneously questioned if Jamal knew the forger.

"I don't know who made the IDs. Tory picked them up." He looked at the pair. They looked defeated. Tracing the forger was the only way Mal was getting out of making the drop for Moua. He glanced at Selena, only to see the small creases around her deep-set eyes. She was thinking the same thing. She shook her head as if to tell him that her contacts did not come through either.

"I can tell you where the storage space is, though. I wasn't s'posed to know. The instructions were for Tory to hide the art alone, but he didn't want to do all the heavy lifting."

It's probably the only reason you're alive right now, Jamal. It didn't take long to get the location, and as he finished giving them directions, Joe knocked on the door and motioned at his watch. Mal's client pulled him towards the bed and whispered one last thing in his ear. Mal didn't react, other than a nod and clasp to Jamal's arm in reassurance.

"What did he whisper to you?" Selena wondered, as the trio walked away from Hamill.

"Put Jamal in protective custody, Joe. He can't go back to jail. He'll be dead in a day," Mal urged, ignoring Selena's question.

"I'll try, boss. He has a few more days in the hospital, at least. I'll see what I can do." They shook hands before going their separate ways.

The semi-couple headed for the exit in silence, Selena's heels adding to the rhythmic beeping of the machines. She looked at her companion, his brow furrowed, nostrils flared, face twisted in a contemplative expression.

She could see Mal deciding what to reveal to her. Their cases were linked, so they would work together until it got resolved, and yet… he still couldn't trust her Not wholly. She couldn't blame him. She used her job as an excuse for stealing off in the middle of the night with the Manet. If she was honest with herself, she simply could have told Bausch it was in police custody. The lackeys would have taken care of the paperwork, declined the payout, and the painting eventually returned after some minor abuse by the indelicate hands of Houston's forensics personnel. She took off because she shared an unprecedented intimacy with Malcolm Ly, because their last night together a few years ago made her think about leaving New York to be closer to him. She couldn't afford to have thoughts like that; they were a hazard to her occupation and a danger to her personal life.

"I wasn't trying to ignore you. I just didn't want to discuss the case in front of Joe. I owe him enough." Mal broke the silence, meeting her gaze. Her eyes were now a deep hazel with a touch of caramel. "We need to set up some ground rules. I'm no longer helping you and vice versa. We're in this together. If we do this, you can't hide anything from me, and you can't run off in the middle of the night again."

"You're one to talk—"

"I'm not done, Selena." He gently tipped her chin, pulling it upwards. "Complete honesty between you and me. I tell you everything, and you do the same."

"What, you don't trust me?" she quipped.

He raised his brow. "No."

She hadn't expected his answer to be so definitive.

"You make it hard for me. If you don't agree to this, then we go our separate ways."

"Fine. Complete honesty." She flashed him a bitter smile and climbed into the truck.

Here goes nothing. He hoped this new lead wasn't another dead end.

16

K asey flicked the light on in the mudroom. The house was still, save for the incessant barking and tail thumping of her giant Labrador mix. She absentmindedly called out to Bruce, dropping a trail of keys, bag, and sweater all the way to the bedroom. Calling out to him in the silence was a safety precaution she's used since college and it was a way to still her grief.

She flicked on the television, and the sound of a random show filled the quiet. A mixed bag of curiosities. She didn't mind being alone, but needed noise to not feel alone. She needed the sound of people conversing, doing inane chores, running around on busy city streets to comfort her, but if someone were to call or drop by unannounced, she would grow bilious at their intrusion.

She clamored out of her scrubs, the dented phone vibrating on her night stand. Half-dressed, she picked it up.

Mal.

Kase debated for a moment whether to reject the call, but then thumbed the line open. "Oh good, you're alive. Bye now. I'm busy too."

"I'm sorry." The voice on the other line didn't sound apologetic; he sounded annoyed. "Are you still at work?"

Mal didn't think she was. The shuffling meant she was

probably home, changing, and on her third drink.

"If you're calling about the case, I don't have anything new for you."

That was a lie. She ran the vaginal swabs from Abigail Stevenson's morgue kit earlier today, and it was positive for semen. There was a partial unknown male profile in the sample. On a hunch, she went back and tested Abigail's panties, which also tested positive for semen. A microscopic sperm search revealed only a few remaining acrosomes; the profile was weak, but it was a partial match to the swab sample. What it meant was Abigail Stevenson had sex recently, within the three days before her death. The panties confirmed this. She had a boyfriend, or at the very least, a consensual sex partner.

Though the police were trying to write off the shooting as random gang violence, that urgent phone call from Gwen gave her an unshakeable feeling there was something more to it. They don't test vaginal swabs on drive-by shootings; it wasn't protocol. What prompted Gwen to collect such intimate samples?

"Kase, don't start this. I was calling to check up on you. And yes, to follow up on the case. I'm sorry I hung up on you the other day." He tried to lighten the mood. "I'm allowed to be frustrated too, I think."

"I know. Sorry, it's been a long week." The flat tone of her answer gave the lie to her words. He could hear the clink of the scotch bottle against glass.

"Have you had dinner?" A tinge of worry in his voice.

"Microwaving it now," she lied. Most nights she munched on popcorn or ham and completed her dinner with two or three glasses of scotch before blacking out on the couch. She couldn't remember the last time she cooked a full meal.

"We haven't had any luck with the databases. No hits so far." She tried to get him off her non-dining habits and back on to the case.

"I think I might know who it is. We're about to pull up to

your house. Open the door." She could hear a female voice in the background.

"We?" Before she could ask any more questions, her giant beast dog howled and ran towards the front door. "Appa, quiet!"

Heels. *I should have guessed Selena was in town.*

"No, I can't deal with dogs." Selena's nervous voice resounded through the door.

Well, then you can wait outside.

Kasey took in a breath before yanking at the nickel-plated knob, Appa lapping her left hand. Mal stood in the doorway with a pizza and a case of beer. Appa lunged for the pizza box and Selena flew back, almost tripping on the porch steps. Mal adroitly dodged the dog.

"I knew you weren't microwaving anything. Appa, sit," Mal commanded, turning to check on his frightened companion. Even under the dim porch lights, her complexion had turned a deathly pallor. "You'll be alright. Just let him sniff you for a bit."

He once saw Selena take down two burly security guards without breaking a sweat. It took a third guy tackling her from behind before they made the arrest. He never imagined a ninety-pound furball would be her kryptonite. Appa let out a soft growl as Selena tiptoed past him.

"Good boy," Kasey whispered, patting him on the head and scratching behind his ears. Like most dogs, Appa instinctively recognized trouble when it was near, and trouble was standing there in silk shorts and open-toed Manolo Blahniks.

"Shoes off." She directed her command at the wily con artist. Mal was already trotting towards the couch in his socks.

"Do you have slippers?" Selena grunted, begrudgingly unclasping the straps.

"I don't wear slippers."

Selena snapped, "I meant for me."

"Oh, right." Kase shook her head as if realizing what Selena meant. "I'll see what I can dig up for you." Kasey walked into her bedroom and came out with a pair of dinosaur socks.

"Seriously?"

"Take 'em or leave 'em." Kasey wiggled her toes, showing off her own furry colored socks.

The headstrong analyst ambled to the kitchen with her colossal slobbering beast following close behind. She re-emerged with paper plates and napkins. Selena could see her thin, lithe figure even through the billowing pajama pants and oversized t-shirt.

To Selena, it was interesting to consider the women in Mal's life. She didn't know his ex-wife, but from the looks of it, he didn't really have a type.

The doctor was conventionally beautiful, buxom, with an elegant optimism that radiated through the room. He probably found solace and warmth in her arms. The scientist, in contrast, had a sharp nose, a slight overbite, and a sarcastic tongue. Her words penetrated the soul, as if it were a common and transparent thing. Broken down, her features were masculine and didn't quite make sense on her face, but as a whole, with her hair down, they made for a deeply expressive and intensely attractive composition. The only things these women had in common were their intelligence and the mayhem it stirred in Mal's life.

Selena sipped her beer quietly as Mal recounted their adventures over the last few days. She suddenly understood Gwen's jealousy; he was an open book with Kasey. They finished each other's thoughts and spoke with their eyes. She also stared in muted amazement and disgust as Kasey inhaled a slice of pizza, with bits of cheese and toppings falling onto the ground to be vacuumed up by a patiently waiting Appa. The loyal creature draped himself over Kasey's feet, knowing he would be rewarded with her leftover garlic bread crusts.

"We were at the storage space…"

"But you didn't have a warrant," Kasey completed the thought for him.

"Yeah, they wouldn't open it for us. But Selena convinced the guy to let us look at the rental documents."

"Forged?"

"I only saw a copy, but I can guarantee it was the same guy." Selena interjected. "His work is impeccable. I could discern a small marking in the corner of this copy and Jamal's and Tory's fake IDs. It was the only thing that ties the three together. It may be a signature, or maybe his printer is defective."

"Can you trace it?" This time, Kasey's questions were directed at Selena.

"No, my people can't tell me anything. This guy is good if he's been able to stay under the radar for this long," Selena replied. "It's strange. Guys like these *always* sign their work. It's like not wanting to sign a Picasso. It's so uncommon."

"It means he's smart enough not to let his hubris get in the way. If I were a criminal, I would be this guy." Kase took a bite of another slice.

She has the table manners of a five-year-old.

"He gave us a copy." Mal unfolded a sheet of paper. "Kase, I recognize him. He was on trial, one of the shooters in a gang shooting."

"Wait, you know his name?"

"No, I was only an auxiliary to that case. I wasn't even the first on scene. I only testified to finding the victim's gun. A gun that his 10-year-old brother was trying to hide. But I remember who they hired to defend them." He paused, then said, "Marc Sandoff's law firm."

17

By the end of their strategy session, they had a plan. Their conjectures were tenuous and the evidence laughable, but the common denominator in both cases was Marc Sandoff. Someone at Marc's firm had a relationship with Abigail. Maybe she discovered something about the theft that made her a liability to his campaign. Maybe Abigail discovered the insurance fraud. Whatever the cause, Abigail had become a liability to someone.

They also agreed, after vehement protests from Selena, that it was time to bring in the cavalry, or at least someone with authority to flash his badge and open doors for them. And by someone, Mal meant Terrance Baker.

The problem was deciding how much to tell Baker. He was jealous and petty, yes. In his favor, as far as Mal could tell he was straight as an arrow, a by-the-book bastard that wasn't as inept as he seemed. He also carried a torch for Kasey and had been subtly hinting he'd like to have drinks with her for a year now. If anyone could convince him to hear Mal out, it would be her. Of course, he was going to be livid when Mal ambushed him on their date, but Mal could deal with that.

"Why didn't you tell her about the meet tomorrow night?" Selena asked as they backed out of the dimly lit driveway. Mal made a note to change the bulb above the garage next time he came over.

"Because if I told her what I was doing for Moua, she would have refused to talk to Baker until I promised not to go," he replied. "She's a smart girl. She'll figure out the same thing we did."

"So much for complete honesty. You could just promise her and then go, anyway," she sneered.

He slammed on the brakes and shifted into park. "Selena, I don't go around making empty promises because it suits me. I'm not you." There was an edge to his soft, but firm, tone that silenced her immediately. "Let's get some rest. We have to meet Tiny tomorrow morning."

They drove the rest of the way without another word. Once they arrived, Mal instructed her to be ready by eight, and the truck sputtered off, much to Selena's dismay.

#

Gwen stared at the brightly lit face of her phone, idly swiping back and forth at the apps on the screen. It was the third time she tried to read this Reddit thread, but she couldn't concentrate. Usually, mindless reading provided comic relief and helped her relax, but not tonight, even combined with a valium and two glasses of wine. It wasn't the untimely deaths of the Stevensons that nagged at her. It was the entire case and everyone investigating it.

It was Mal. It always came back to Mal.

Are you up? A text was safer since she wouldn't have to hear his voice.

Always. You ok?

Yes, just lonely.

Where is He? Mal never mentioned Henry by name. Did it pain him to do so? Did he expect her to wait for him forever?

San Francisco. Business trip. You alone?

She hesitated before typing that last line, realizing ignorance was bliss. What if he was with that Parish girl? It was silly of her to hope that they were keeping things platonic, even though she had Henry.

Yeah.

Her heart skipped a beat. *Want me to come over?*

No answer. It seemed like an eternity as the numbers on her phone changed from 12:39 to 12:40 and to 12:41.

Probably not a good idea. Get some sleep. Good night sweets.

Her lower lip trembled at the thought that he might not be alone. It wouldn't be too crazy for her to casually drive by, would it? She wished she could text one of her girlfriends to talk her out of it, but after her last stunt with Mal, they all cut her off. He was no good for her, despite his best intentions. Wrapping a cream-colored coat over her silk nightie, she clamored for the door and ran smack into Henry.

"Whoa, hey baby." She looked up to see his luggage in one hand and a bouquet of roses in the other. "Where are you going?" He searched her face for an answer.

"Henry! I thought you were going away until the weekend?"

"Well, our deal wrapped early, and I missed you." He held her close and planted a gentle kiss on her cheek. "Can I come in?"

"Oh yeah, I was just... going to get some ice cream. Had a craving." She stepped sideways from the door, hoping he couldn't see the guilt.

"We bought some on Monday. Did we run out already?"

"No, uh... I forgot," she stammered, her cheeks turning pink. Henry gazed at his fiancée standing in the middle of their high-rise, the city lights illuminating her silhouette. Gentle fingers stroked her auburn hair; his blue eyes pierced her gaze.

"Gwen." He stood in the same gray suit, wrinkled from travel, and she was shamelessly planning a surprise tryst with a man who could never love her back. "Are you using again?"

On the night Gwen met him at a speakeasy in Montrose, Henry Kingman was a junior consultant at one of Houston's top financial firms. She was bored to tears at another bachelorette party for a sorority sister. The bride-to-be pretended to be uptight and classy, while the bridesmaids ignored the key bumps she was shoveling up her nose in between bathroom breaks. He offered to buy her a drink when one of his drunk colleagues spilled the last of his Old-Fashioned on her Balenciaga flapper-style dress. That he was tall, handsome, and polite played into her acceptance, and Henry had saved her from another hour of shrieking girls as he regaled her with stories of his trip across Europe before graduate school.

By the end of the month, Gwen had fallen madly in love with his laugh and the way he leaned towards her when they talked, as if to reveal a secret only she was privy to. By the following month, to gain even more intimacy, she confessed all her wildest sins to him, including her well-hidden former drug addiction. What she neglected to tell him was that she simply replaced one addiction with another. And she was still on the mend from a soul-crushing break-up.

"Gwen, are you?" Henry asked again.

She stammered, "N-n-no! I was just caught by surprise, that's all. Just don't do that again. You scared me!"

Henry took a step back. He thought it would be a delightful surprise to come back early, but he had interrupted something. Not wanting to provoke another fight, he dropped the subject.

Since the move, it seems all we do is fight.

"I'm going to shower and go to bed. I missed you." He gave her a small peck on the lips and sulked off.

Damn it!

Why couldn't she stop chasing after a shadow, sabotaging her own happiness? She looked longingly at the half empty glass of wine and chased Henry to apologize.

18

Kasey woke up the following morning with a knot in her stomach. It could either be from the entire pizza she consumed last night. More likely it was her date tonight, her first in a decade. Assuming she could set it up, but she didn't anticipate a problem.

There was also a genuine possibility Baker wouldn't speak to her again after Mal shows up. Terrance and Mal never got along, but it was hard living in the shadows of one of the best detectives on the force. Baker wasn't incompetent, but compared to someone who spent twenty-three hours a day on the job, he seemed lazy and narrow-minded. However, their animosity towards each other did nothing to hinder Terrance and Kasey's friendship. In fact, Baker and his wife had gone on a few double dates with Kasey and Bruce.

The night Bruce and her parents died, it was Terry and Mal who came to her door to deliver the news. Bruce had driven her parents to a wedding while she stayed home nursing an especially virulent case of the flu. "Drunk driver" was the last thing she heard before she collapsed into Mal's arms. For the next three years, while her best friend nursed her back to sanity outside of work, it was Terry who brought her back to life at the lab.

During their many lunches, he confided that he and Amanda

had been trying to conceive, but it wasn't working. Finally, he convinced her adoption was a worthy alternative. They spent two nights with the infant before the birth mother changed her mind. After that, Amanda shut down and any talk of starting a family was unequivocally dismissed. One morning in June, during one of their coffee breaks, Terry revealed Amanda had filed for divorce, and that she was taking him to the cleaners.

"Morning Chris, I forgot my badge again. Can you let me in?" The portly cop shook his head in resignation and annoyance, wiping a coffee stain from his rumpled uniform. She wouldn't admit it, but she couldn't remember where she shed the lanyard and was too hungover to search for it this morning.

"Just glue it to your scrubs, Khuu." He pushed a button, lowering the bars, allowing her to walk into the inner sanctum. The prehistoric elevator creaked its way up twenty-six stories, stopping every few floors. At one point, the lights flickered and the doors wouldn't open.

Not today, sir, not today. She shuddered at the thought of getting stuck in an HPD elevator with twenty other people in late June.

Coffee later? She texted Baker.

He immediately confirmed.

"Kase." A voice called out as she set her bag down amongst the mountain of folders. "I need you to initial this page before it's complete," Perry chirped.

Sunlight glared through the vertical blinds, illuminating her desk in bright bars. Thank you cards, birthday cards, and group photos were pinned haphazardly around the walls of her cubicle; a historical record of her years at the lab. She looked around the foliage of papers for her favorite pen. Ten of its identical brothers sat in a cup by her monitor, but this one was her favorite at the moment.

"Thank you! You want to get coffee later?" the affable lab analyst asked. Her periwinkle eyes were a hint bluer under the fluorescent light. A golden braid crown surrounded her head, accentuating her pointed chin and slender neck.

"I already promised Baker. Want to grab lunch later, though?" Typical day at the lab, making lunch plans before the morning even started.

"You guys should just date already. He's cute." Perry's thin lips curled into a teasing smile. "He's so into you."

Not after tonight, he won't be. Kasey rolled her eyes at her colleague. The girl was sweet with a strong streak of naivete; she thought most of the guys on the force were cute and that Kasey should date all of them.

"You're crazy. He's still married."

"*Separated*, and about to be divorced. *And* I talked to Rachel in Accounting; he's ended things with the other girl."

"You're really invested in this. Why don't you date him?" Kase teased back. Like Perry, most of the analysts thought Baker was *hot*. Every time he met her outside the lab for coffee, the girls would huddle by the door to greet him like schoolgirls swooning over their favorite teacher. They would do the same today.

"I would date him if he were interested in me," Perry interjected. "Unless you're holding out for someone else? Is it finally coming true? Are you and Mal getting together?" Perry was slightly envious that her friend always befriended the good-looking men at work. Perhaps broadcasting emotional unavailability was the way to go.

"Okay, now I know you're out of your mind." Amusement unfurled in her eyes. "He's my best friend, and he's like a brother to me. Go back to your desk, you crazy person. Let me work." Perry laughed and jumped from her perch. Kasey smacked her lightly on the ass, shooing her, before turning her attention to the mountain of casework on her desk.

Halfway through an especially tedious report, her pocket buzzed. Baker was on his way up, prompt as usual. He always insisted on meeting her outside the lab, even though it was twenty stories out of his way. Maybe he liked all the attention the analysts gave him. The soft dinging of the interoffice group chat alerted Kasey that the cute detective was outside. That was her cue to leave.

"Hey." She greeted him without looking up, both thumbs tapping at the coffee app. "Do you want your usual? I'm going to order ahead of time."

"How about we stand in line?" he asked, waving at Jen peeking out from the double doors. Kasey glanced up from her phone, eyebrows raised in confusion.

"Sure?" Maybe Baker needed a few extra minutes away from his office. Homicide was usually buzzing with frantic energy. Everyone on the sixth floor ran on Red Bull and fear: fear of the next dead body dropping too soon, fear of losing their jobs, fear of losing their marriages. "Are you ok, Terry?"

"Huh, yeah. Just a little distracted, I guess." The usually suave detective ran his hand through a wave of sand-colored hair, subtly wiping beads of sweat from his forehead. He nervously shifted his weight from one foot to the other, then stuck both hands in his pockets.

"Dude, you don't look so good. Are you sick?" His knitted brows reminded her of an adorable Scott Caan.

"I'm okay. Didn't get much sleep last night."

"Did you finalize your divorce? Did Amanda let up a little?"

"The divorce is being finalized next week. She's gonna take everything, but I deserve it, I guess," he replied. Kase didn't believe it for a second. After repeatedly reassuring him it takes two to break a marriage, Kasey bristled at his standard response. She didn't condone his affair, but Amanda had checked out of that relationship way before his indiscretion.

"So, what are your plans for this weekend? Besides hiding all your assets from your soon-to-be ex-wife," Kase joked, trying to lighten the mood. The line at the coffee shop was unrelenting, and the guy at the counter was the slowest cashier *ever*.

"No plans. I might have a date Saturday night, but she's already canceled once." Baker replied, gauging his companion's reaction. He had been dropping subtle hints at her for a year, but there didn't seem to be a spark of interest.

Today, though. Today was the day he was going to drop a very non-subtle hint her way. He didn't know when his feelings for her transformed from a platonic friendship to something more, or why he even liked her. Her hair was always swept up in an unbrushed bun and she wore the same five scrubs to work every week. She cursed way too much, was quick to judge, and used her biting wit to be as condescending as possible. In all regards, Baker was in love with an asshole.

Before he could gather his courage to use his planned line, Kase spoke.

"You have any plans tonight?" Kasey broached the subject cautiously.

Excitement stirred in his chest, and he bit his lip. "Besides working late and eating bad Chinese takeout? Nah."

"You want to have dinner, then?" All the blenders turned on at once. Kase swore softly; this mating dance was quickly turning into an exhausting ritual. Especially for a fake date.

"What?" Baker leaned closer, looking confused. Did he hear right?

"Do you want to have dinner tonight?" She slowed her speech. "With me. At a restaurant." Baker stared at her, stunned into silence. "Close your mouth. It's only dinner."

"Yeah, sure." He snapped back to reality, tugging nervously at his tie. "Where at?"

"I don't know. Meet me downstairs after work. We'll walk somewhere." She smirked and turned towards the counter to order. "I'm not changing out of my scrubs, by the way. Take it or leave it."

#

The black truck puttered into the rounded driveway of Hotel Alessandra exactly at eight. Waiting by the curb was a statuesque figure in dark green chiffon slacks and a mustard-colored halter.

"Good morning," Mal greeted cheerfully as she climbed in. He noticed her signature heels had been replaced by pointed, cream-colored snake-skin flats. "How many snakes had to die for those shoes of yours? And were they venomous?"

"Only ones that deserved it, and wouldn't you like to know?" she quipped, giving him a quick peck on the cheek. Without missing a beat, he jumped into their itinerary for the day, beginning with their meeting with Tiny and ending with the drop at midnight. He seemed in a better mood today, probably because Selena wasn't there last night to keep him up.

"All work and no play, Malcolm?" She groaned. "Can we at least get breakfast first?"

He pointed to a rumpled paper bag dotted with grease marks in the center console.

"The best kolaches in town. I got it from the Korean lady down the street." As if there were only one Korean lady selling kolaches in all of Houston.

"That is not breakfast, Malcolm." The thought of calling synthetic pork encased in dough a meal made her indignant.

"It is to eighty percent of the population. Besides, we don't have time for a sit-down breakfast. We have a busy day before we crash Baker's date," he retorted, while tearing at the doughy flesh of a rounded pastry. "I got sausage, cheese, and jalapeno. All the good stuff."

Selena's stomach churned as he listed the ingredients. She never understood the obsession Southerners had with jalapenos, but it appeared in all kinds of random dishes.

Confronted with another out-of-order sign by the elevator, the pair trudged up the five floors to Mal's office. The hallway reeked of cheap disinfectant and cigarette smoke. Selena ascended each step with a determined tread, trying her best to avoid touching anything, from the peeling handrail and yellowed walls to the floor itself. Her partner seemed unfazed by the condition of the stairwell or the smells emanating from each floor they passed. They found Tiny leaning against the wall opposite the office door, thumbs flying across the pad of his cell phone.

"You're late," he muttered, holding out a black, scuffled duffel bag.

"I always want to make a fashionable entrance," Mal joked. "Can you at least wait until we're inside?" Tiny thrust the bag towards him, this time with more urgency, as if it were a bomb that could detonate at any moment. Mal busied himself with the lock. Once inside, he threw the bag at Mal's feet.

"I texted you the address for the drop. There's a quarter of a million in there. It better all be there tonight. Dial one when you're done," he instructed, disappearing down the corridor before Mal could ask questions.

The pair walked to his inner office, where they examined the ratty duffel. The bag seemed well-used, with the corners scratched and unraveling. The white logo advertising the Tae Kwon Do dojo where it originated was almost peeled off, leaving behind the adhesive shadow. Mal unzipped the bag, the slider moving bumpily down the tracks, catching on to some of the melted teeth.

"Two hundred and fifty thousand? I don't know. Seems awfully light," Selena commented as she thumbed the neatly packed bills.

"Not when they're all in hundreds." He made a quick mental check of the quantity before looking around the office. "We need a place to stash this. We can't walk around with this kind of cash in the car." His eyes caught the moldy ceiling tiles, some rotten through and others stained yellow with age. He picked the least rotten tiles out of the bunch and dragged a chair towards it, hoping the tiles wouldn't give out with the cash tucked precariously on a ledge.

"Why aren't I all warm and fuzzy about this brilliant plan, Malcolm?" The raven-haired sleuth pointed out sarcastically as she handed him the duffel.

"Well, unless you have a better suggestion, we're flying by the seat of our pants right now, Selena."

He grunted, feeling for a sturdy cross bar to plant the bag.

"Your contacts were supposed to come through, and they didn't. Right now, we have an untouchable warehouse hiding millions in art, a corrupt politician, two murdered bystanders who might not be so innocent, and no substantial way to link them all. So here we are."

He hopped off the chair and touched her face gingerly, tracing her lips with his thumb, and then pointed to the ceiling. "I can trust it won't disappear, right?"

"Fuck off." Selena pushed him, disgusted by his accusation.

"I had to ask." His charming smile bared half-truths that simultaneously captivated and exasperated her. He grabbed her by the waist and pulled, wrapping her in a tight embrace. Her warmth against his skin was punctuated by their hearts beating in unison.

"I know this isn't ideal, but remember our plan. If something happens, grab the evidence from Moua and get out of town." He kissed her softly, brown eyes pleading under heavy lids. "And whatever happens, please leave Kasey out of it."

Her heart flipped.

"I promise." One more thing his women had in common: they always came second to Kasey Khuu.

19

The humidity had risen to a new high by the time they left the decrepit office. Selena walked a step behind Mal, contemplating the information he just revealed to her about where they were going next. A V-shaped sweat stain was slowly forming through Mal's gray cotton polo, and she could feel her own blouse clinging to her back. Even on its hottest day, New York City felt like an eternal spring compared to this inferno.

"At the hospital, Jamal told you to check out Tory's apartment?" Hot air blasted through the truck's vent, causing thick strands of hair to stick to her sweaty neck.

"Tory wasn't an idiot. Well, he was for taking this job, but he was a professional criminal. Bringing Jamal along to unload the art wasn't out of pure laziness."

"He wouldn't have told you where this 'secret compartment' might be? And what are we going to do, break into his apartment? Do you even remember how to pick a lock?"

"Yes, I remember how to pick a lock, but luckily, we won't need to do that." The ex-cop eyed her, his lips curled into a devious smile.

"Mal, I'm tired of sweet-talking people into doing things. I want to kick the door down."

"Sorry to disappoint you, Selena. As much as I appreciate

your womanly wiles, we can do without them this time. We're going to go pick up the key." His face grew solemn. "Besides, I think my client deserves an explanation."

"How much are you going to tell her?"

"She's right. The man she loves isn't a murderer. It's too dangerous to tell her more than that." There was one other concern Mal didn't voice to Selena, but he knew she was thinking about it, too. What if they were too late and Sandoff's hired guns had gotten to the evidence first?

#

Houston's landscape changed swiftly through the tinted window. In ten minutes, they had driven through a posh upscale neighborhood near Rice University, where real estate cost millions and peace of mind cost more, past the bustling, pocked streets of the Medical Center, where white coats and blue scrubs filled the sidewalks, and finally to a dilapidated condominium complex where a warped gate and smashed code box showed its state of disrepair.

Mal waved to a group of teenagers smoking by the carport, sharing sips from a bottle wrapped in a brown paper bag. The oldest in the group, a boy who looked about fifteen, was fitting a bright red do-rag on his head when his young sidekick pointed at the beat-up pickup. He took a hit from the passing blunt before punching a code into the box. He nodded tersely as Mal gave an appreciative wave.

"I guess school's out for the day," Selena remarked, as four sets of beady eyes followed the truck into the open parking lot.

"Sadly, these kids probably only show up enough to move on to the next grade level."

"No child left behind, right?" They scanned the sides of the buildings for any signs pointing to 8425. The red do-rag rapped on Mal's window, his eyes bloodshot from the kush.

"You guys lost?"

"I'm looking for 8425, number twenty-nine." Mal responded calmly.

"You po-po?"

"Do I look like a cop?"

"Yeah, kinda."

Selena stifled a chuckle. Years away from the force and Mal still carried himself like an officer. Even as he calmly spoke to the kid, he was scanning the parking lot with his peripheral vision, his right hand resting on the butt of his pistol.

"Fine. I was, I'm not anymore. Besides, does she look like a cop to you?" Do-rag leered at Selena's chest. "Hey, eyes in front. You know where it is or not?" Mal snapped.

"That's Ericka's place."

"You know her?"

"Yeah, that's my girl!" He replied drowsily.

"What, like your girlfriend?"

"Nah, man, it ain't like that. She's righteous. Lets us hang out sometimes. She's got cable and air conditioning."

That's more than I have. "Can you show us where it is?"

"I can. For five bucks."

"Tell you what, how about I give you ten bucks and you throw in a little information?"

"Make it fifty, old man, and I'll tell you anything you want."

Selena snorted. The kid had guts.

"Twenty."

"Forty."

"Twenty-five, my last offer. I'm sure I can find this place on my own."

"Alright, alright."

Mal pulled out his wallet and counted the bills. "You know Jamal and Tory?"

"Yeah, Jamal is Ericka's baby daddy. He cool too. Used to buy us MDs from the corner store. Sad what happened to Tory, though. I heard he got jumped in jail for being a snitch."

"What did he snitch about?"

"I don't know. Do I look like a snitch?"

"For twenty-five bucks, you better know something."

Do-rag's eyes flashed before he spoke. "Look, all I know is before the two of them got picked up by five-o, Tory was out here smoking a joint with us, bragging about how he and Jamal were about to score big and move out of here. He said something about how he got the drop on some rich dude, got him on tape or something. But that's all I know. I swear."

There was a tape. Mal hoped even more now that they weren't too late, and the tape was hidden in Tory's apartment.

"Alright, here's an extra five. This conversation never happened."

The kid's face spread into a wide grin, reducing his drowsy eyes into mere slits. "You got it, boss. Pleasure doin' business with you both."

As he walked off, Mal yanked his arm and gave him a stern look.

"Oh yeah, Ericka's is that way. Follow the walkway through the metal arch. Door to the lobby is in the back. Code is five-five-two-two. You should take the stairs. Somebody took a shit in the elevator and no one's cleaned it yet." The kid laughed sheepishly and walked away.

"Lovely," Selena murmured as she unbuckled. They followed the broken walkway towards the back of the building. She judged from the skywalk and rectangular architecture that the complex was built in the seventies and was probably one of the more modern designs of that era before it was ravaged by time and weather erosion. The property manager tried to maintain the grounds, but their best efforts were thwarted by trash bags, diapers, and random toiletries dumped from the balconies.

The flax-colored door creaked open to reveal an unkempt toddler in a much too small t-shirt and underwear. She gazed at Mal and Selena with large, round eyes sunken in an emaciated face, thumb still in her mouth.

"Is your mom home?"

"Mr. Ly!" The young mother seemed haggard and bereft, unchanged since the moment she left his office. "Were you able to see Jamal?"

Mal put a finger to his mouth, motioning for her to stay quiet until they were inside. She stepped aside, regarding his companion with both amazement and confusion. Selena seemed out of place in the cramped apartment, like a stroke of Caravaggio in the center of a child's finger painting.

"This is my associate, Selena Parish. She's an insurance investigator."

"Insurance?"

"She's here to investigate the art theft from this past week."

"I knew it. Those two idiots did it, didn't they?" Ericka's voice cracked as she slumped onto the ragged couch. She swatted at the toddler, who had replaced the thumb in her mouth with a small toy. The sophisticated investigator shifted uncomfortably as the child came near her, offering her the slobbery toy.

"When was the last time you guys ate anything?" Selena asked. Before Ericka could answer her seemingly irrelevant question, she headed towards the door, muttering she would be right back. Unconcerned with Selena's sudden departure, Mal lowered himself into an armchair opposite the weeping mother.

"Ericka, Jamal got himself into a pickle," he started. "And I'm trying to get him out, but I need your help."

She nodded, the head movement causing more wet stains on her blouse. "What do you need me to do?"

"Jamal says you have an extra key to Tory's place?"

She pointed towards the outermost drawer in the narrow kitchenette. "It's under the liner. That's where he hid it." Ericka explained in between sobs.

Mal dug through a slew of screws, nails, and batteries until he reached the liner. He caught a glint of brass between the mesh. He pocketed the key as Selena quietly stepped back inside the apartment.

"I want you to know that you're right. Jamal is not a killer. He was set up and I'm going to sort this out." Mal clasped both her hands in his as she looked down, tears streaming freely from her face.

"Oh god. Stupid, stupid."

"If we can, we're going to get him out of this. Alive. Both of us." He glanced at Selena, who was picking imaginary cotton balls off her pants. He had never seen her so uncomfortable. Maybe Ericka's tears were too much for her.

"Ericka, is there someone you could stay with? A relative? A friend?" Selena spoke up, her caramel eyes glistening.

"No, I haven't spoken to my parents in years."

"You need to be careful," Mal cautioned gently. "In the meantime, we're going to get you some police protection."

"No police!" She grasped at Mal's arms, pleading. "They can't be trusted. Look at what they did to Tory!"

"Not these guys. I trust them with my life," he insisted.

"We can take care of ourselves. Just solve this." The quiet determination in her voice told Mal there was no point in arguing. He needed to finish this, and he needed to finish it quickly. However, her resolve wasn't going to deter him from requesting Baker put a few patrol units outside her place. She wouldn't have to know.

They left Ericka in a state worse than when she first appeared outside his office. Mal hoped the news that her boyfriend had been set up would comfort her, yet she seemed more agitated at his incessant stupidity and bad choices. As they closed the flaking flax-colored door, Do-rag came running down the corridor carrying a bag of groceries in one arm and a gallon of milk in the other.

"Good timing. I thought you ran off with my money." Selena commented.

"Thought about it," the boy said, a crisp smile across his face. He kicked at the door and shouted the young mother's name with familiarity. "Got somethin' for you."

"Where did you–" Ericka swung the door open, stunned.

"Seems you got some good folks lookin' out for you," he said as he dropped the bags at her feet. She flashed the couple a silent look of gratitude and gathered the groceries inside.

"Good job, kid," Selena complimented as she passed him another twenty.

"Pleasure doin' business with y'all." He laughed as he ran off to the other end of the corridor.

"That was decent of you."

"I can be decent," she replied, walking towards the skywalk to the staircase, secretly dabbing the tears rimming her eyes.

#

"Your friends just left Ericka Thomas's place."

Anthony Rizzo reported in while chomping hungrily at a cheeseburger. These mid-day stakeouts were a burden in the sweltering heat. He had been tailing Malcom Ly for days, ever since his bosses caught that Ericka, the nosy bitch, hired a private investigator to launch her own inquiry.

It was hard trailing someone as cautious as Mal. He lost him a few times, having to sit across the street from the Hotel Alessandra or outside that sad, rundown office until his target reappeared. He would have walked away sooner, but the bosses paid handsomely and he owed a loan shark named Side-Eye too much money from his last unfortunate run at the tables. Rizzo's game was craps and his large, calloused hands have been rolling nothing but crap on his last few visits to Louisiana.

"Were you able to get ears inside?" the Darth Vader voice boomed.

"No, the bitch never leaves her house."

"So, you don't know what the visit was about?"

"Neither of them was carrying anything, so they weren't there for a pickup. Maybe he wanted to update her," Rizzo replied flippantly.

"What does he know?" The voice sounded nervous, taking in deep breaths with every sentence.

"He's been driving around a lot. Making some visits, talking to people. I don't really think he has anything. I tracked him to a storage space in the Woodlands, but he wasn't able to get in."

"You sure?" There was an edge of panic in the question.

"Yes, I was right outside. The clerk kept shaking his head, then they drove off." He could hear a sigh of relief through the distortion. It sounded almost comical.

"And you went through that rat's apartment? You're sure you didn't find anything?"

"I was thorough. He was fucking with you. He didn't keep anything."

"I don't want any loose ends. This is getting too complicated."

Rizzo assured the boss it wasn't that complicated. He had been careful about compartmentalizing everything and there's no way anyone knew enough for it to lead back to him. That seemed to be his job nowadays, part spy, part therapist.

He was only half-assured by his own comforting words. They were true; the boss had been careful about compartmentalizing each element—even he didn't know what was in that warehouse, though he could guess—but he felt like mistakes had been made throughout the entire operation. Malcolm Ly's involvement was a definite surprise.

"I don't care. I want this wrapped neatly with a bow," the voice demanded, sounding a little more reassured. "If there's no physical evidence like you said, then the next step is to get rid of anyone who can be a witness."

"Alright boss. I'll take care of it."

Rizzo swore softly after the click. He was hired to set up two separate jobs, which he easily delegated to some ex-cons. All he had to do was set things in motion. Those two "simple" jobs were slowly becoming a train wreck of epic proportions. The other red flag that should have sent him running? The anonymity of his employers. He knew there were at least two, though he only ever talked to that vaudeville Darth Vader.

He wasn't the mastermind; he was quick to panic, and Rizzo could almost hear him hyperventilating over the line. Rizzo had always made it a rule to know who he was dealing with, do research on his employers and make sure they were good for the price they offered, but the pay was too good and he was desperate. When he asked for a hundred grand up front so he could buy a little time with Side-Eye, the money appeared the next day in his usual drop-off location.

In the world of wealthy entrepreneurs and politicos, Anthony Rizzo was known as the "fixer". An ex-con with an even more questionable background, a gambling problem, and no moral compass, he was the go-to if they needed to make a problem disappear. His ingenuity and discretion made him a valuable asset, and his fees were nominal compared to what it would cost these men in their careers or marriages. Over the years, he gained invaluable information which could have toppled local governments and damned city officials.

Yet, as he depleted his little nest egg with every trip to L'auberge, he desperately sold these golden nuggets to a Laotian bottom-feeder in Chinatown. The juicy morsels she bought elevated her into one of the largest players in the game of illicit activity in Houston. She dabbled in everything from drugs to guns to knock-off designer items, and laundered her dirty money through the multiple game rooms in town. She wielded a burn book so powerful she was virtually untouchable.

Rizzo inhaled the last of his cigarette as he watched the rusted pickup turn out of the complex and drive towards the highway. He flicked the butt and drove in the other direction. There would be no more tailing today. He had to go home and prepare. Tonight's work was delicate and would require precision planning. Even if he downplayed everything to the bosses, he knew Malcolm Ly was no idiot. In case he was really on to something, Rizzo wasn't going to leave it up to chance.

20

Kasey just texted. They're going to McCormick's tonight for happy hour drinks and dinner." Mal showed Selena the message.

"Are you going to let them make it to dinner?" his raven-haired companion scoffed.

"Probably not. Homicide takes precedence."

"Since they're eating near the hotel, any chance we can make a stop so I can change?"

"What's wrong with what you're wearing?"

"It's drenched in sweat. I smell like garbage," she complained. "Houston is dreadful. When are you going to move to New York already?"

"Is that an invitation?"

"Is that all it takes? Here I thought I would have to kill someone and steal a painting to get you to New York."

"Not my jurisdiction, *darling*," he retorted. "Besides, Houston's my home."

"Yes, but I suspect you would be so much more fun in New York," she teased, gently dabbing her face with an oil blotting sheet.

"We have to get to Tory's before someone else does, then I'll take you home. It'll be best if I go to McCormick's alone. Baker might get riled up seeing you again."

Tory's apartment was nestled farther in a rundown, derelict part of town. It was the hidden part of Houston city officials would like everyone to believe doesn't exist, where the crimes run deep and the poverty even deeper. Kasey's parents owned a convenience store amidst the squalor once upon a time. Every month, when they came home to load up on supplies, her mom would entertain them with the latest gossip about their regulars. In this part of town, mothers sold themselves, their government subsidies, and sometimes even their daughters for the next fix. In order to survive, girls would get pregnant early because the more children you had, the more welfare you received. No one was free from the pipe, from the most innocuous school teacher to the retired professional baseball player who now cleaned floors and stocked shelves for a living. The only well-to-dos were the drug dealers and gang bangers who kept their people contained with a whiff of the "good stuff".

Mal felt a sense of foreboding as he searched the street numbers for the right apartment complex. Police activity fluctuated in this area, but it wasn't surprising. When he was working narcotics, they left instructions for patrols to lay dormant for months until it was time to take out the players in a heavy raid. They would swarm the apartment, snatch up as many guns and kilos as they could find, and then disappear the way sea foam dissipates as the waves recede. However, the activity surrounding their destination looked different. Crime scene tape blocked off a perimeter by a broken door. He had a sinking feeling that the key burning a hole in his pocket was going to fit in that door.

"Doesn't look like we're going near that apartment right now," Selena commented.

"Nope." Unbroken tape meant that there'd be an active presence monitoring the scene. "Let's just hope the cops don't find what we're looking for, either."

#

Selena ordered steaks and a bottle of Cote du Rhône for a late lunch. She couldn't risk another meal of kolaches or whatever leftovers Mal might feed her. The hotel's air conditioning was a godsend after spending hours on cracked leather in a barely operational vehicle.

Now they were in her room, her partner hovering by the narrow, oaken desk, drumming his long fingers across the shellacked surface while he whispered into his cell phone. His furrowed brows and sculpted jawline made for a disheveled and brooding Adonis; a painting brought to life by Titian himself.

She shed her clothes and let the steam from the shower soak through her. Undoing the thick, gossamer bun, she stepped gingerly into the glass case, testing the spiraling water, first with one foot and then the other. Despite the Southern heat, Selena basked in a scorching torrent as it rained down her face and across her chest. She thought putting three years and a thousand miles between her and Malcolm would have purged any residual feelings from their history, yet here they were. She felt a soft, breathy kiss on her neck and the gentle embrace of muscular, tattooed arms around her waist.

"We haven't done this in a while." Selena leaned into his embrace.

"You haven't given me the opportunity." He kissed her shoulders. "Last time we did this, you ran away in the middle of the night. Remember?"

She turned around, staring into his russet-colored eyes, pulling his face closer until her lips grazed his ear. "You could've followed me."

"I didn't know you wanted me to." Remorse clung to each word.

"It would never have worked, you know." She tried to sound indifferent. "We're two sides of the same coin, fated to play cops and robbers."

"Maybe that's why it would've worked." He pressed her back against the tile. It felt cool amidst the rising humidity. Her heart swelled as he pressed his lips against hers, passionate, painful, fleeting, just like their relationship. "I would have moved to New York, you know, if you asked me."

"No, you wouldn't have. Houston is your home," she repeated woefully. This time, she kissed him, her tongue desperately searching for his, taking in every breath earnestly. They made love with a frantic sense of hopelessness, the only kind she ever had with the only man she ever loved.

21

aker did a double-take as Kasey walked out of the elevators. Not only had she changed, her signature bun was gone and there was a touch of gloss on her thin lips. The flowing, printed dress stopped short of her knees, cinched at the waist by an ochre, braided belt. Her voluminous hair was swept to the side and held in place by a long, black barrette. The work bag by her side flapped with each movement of her hips.

"Baker, you ready?"

He snapped back to reality. "Sorry. I thought you weren't going to change."

"Yeah, well, the girls in the office didn't think it was good form to go out in my scrubs." She pulled nervously at the skirt. "What do I know? I haven't been on a date in almost a decade."

Baker's chest swelled. He had spent the entire day pondering if he should be Detective Terrance Baker or Terry, the-lunch-buddy-slash-quasi-friend. Hearing her say "date" made it easier to decide.

"Where are we going?" He held the door open, remembering his manners.

"Happy hour at McCormick's?" It was more of a demand than a question. Kasey was never one to dawdle over trivial decisions. Her stomach churned as they walked the five blocks to the restaurant. He was more nervous than usual, bumbling his way through their conversation, and Kasey felt a twinge of guilt. Her friend was going to be irate once he realized why she invited him out.

"Inside or out?"

She pointed to the patio, noting it would be easier to have a quiet conversation without having to talk over blaring music and drunk bankers. He ordered a draft beer from the bubbly brunette, while Kasey ordered a double gin and tonic. She looked up, hoping to spot Mal's faded jeans and uneven gait strutting around the corner. No such luck.

Sonofabitch better not wait until dinner. There was no quick exit once you order dinner.

"I'm glad you wanted to grab drinks tonight. I feel like I haven't hung out with you in a while," Baker started.

"What are you talking about? I see you every day." Kasey pretended to be oblivious.

"I mean, we've been busy with work. We haven't had lunch or caught up in a few weeks."

"Yeah, I guess you're right. Sorry, business is booming, and this double homicide has me working a lot of overtime."

"Same, I have that on top of all my other cases. Hey, you wouldn't have the results for the swinger's murder, do you?" Baker mentally slapped himself; he didn't want to talk shop on their date.

"The serology report is done. No surprise there, lots of presumptive blood stains. You'll have to wait for the writer to finish the comparisons, though. I think Katelyn is on that case. I can ask her for you tomorrow."

"Thanks, that'll be great." Awkward silence. They had fantastic conversations, as friends. Could it really be possible that they had zero romantic chemistry? Baker noticed she seemed a little off tonight. Maybe she was nervous too.

"So how are things with what's-her-name in accounting?"

Another topic of conversation he wanted to avoid. "We broke up."

"Oh, why? You're about to be divorced. You can technically date her now."

"It was a lapse in judgement. She's too young for me."

"Dude, you got married at nineteen," Kasey teased, feeling more at ease.

"That was also a lapse in judgement," he quipped. "No, she's a sweet girl, but she wanted too many things too fast, if that makes sense."

"She wanted you to marry her?"

He took a gulp of his pilsner. "Let's say it was headed in that direction."

"Yikes." She palmed her face. "You have a knack for messy relationships."

"I'm trying to change that now." He chuckled, throwing a meaningful glance at her. "In all fairness, Amanda wasn't crazy or anything. Not at first. She was sweet, patient, and kind. She just went through a lot and couldn't deal with it. It wasn't like I made things easy either."

"Fair. I would be crazy too if my husband slept with a girl ten years younger than me." Kasey didn't want to point out that what's-her-name in accounting could pass for Amanda's younger sister. That made things even more. "Don't be too hard on yourself, Terry." She consoled him. "It was a difficult situation all around."

"Thanks, Kase."

"Just don't do that again or the next girl might not be so nice. I don't want to be swabbing your blood off some jealous girlfriend's kitchen floor."

Baker laughed, quietly acknowledging that he must really like crazy, because if Kasey were that girlfriend, there would be no blood to swab up; there wouldn't even be a body. The bubbly brunette came back for a round of appetizers, and then again for another round of drinks. Every time she came to their table, she would cock her head towards Baker, flip her hair, and giggle.

"Dude, she's totally into you," the analyst whispered as the server sauntered off with their order.

"What? No. Stop it." He could tell she was a little tipsy. Somewhere along the date, he had returned to being Terry the lunch buddy.

"Oh my god, she's totally flirting with you. That's kind of rude. You're on a date!" she exclaimed with mock indignance.

"Are you jealous?" He took a chance and grabbed her hand from across the table. Stunned, her initial instinct was to pull back. Instead she laced her fingers with his, locking eyes with him, as if to ask whether she needed to be jealous. Her phone's sudden vibrations shook the wrought-iron table, jolting them from their flirtatious haze. Baker's face wilted into a crooked grimace as he glanced at the caller ID. She double-tapped the side bar, and the screen went dark.

"Terry, I have a confession to make." He braced himself. "I had another reason for asking you out tonight, and you won't like it.

22

That was a shitty thing to do, Khuu," Baker sputtered. "You could have told me. You tricked me. You lied to me!"

"I know. I'm sorry. But if I told you the truth, would you have agreed to listen to Mal?" She argued, guilt-ridden.

"That's beside the point, goddamn it." He raised his voice, the setting sun intensifying his anger with rays of red and amber. She could feel his ire slice through the still dampness like a cyclist through traffic.

"Baker, please. Lower your voice." Kasey winced, embarrassed. A group of girls dressed in casual business attire were stealing curious glances at them. She couldn't blame him. She had taken advantage of his feelings for her; they all did.

"Did I come at a bad time?"

Kasey exhaled, thankful for the save.

"I should have known." Baker shot up, indignant. "Look, Ly, this is the second time this week you've manipulated me. I don't have to take this. I'm leaving."

"You gonna let the lady pay for her own drinks?" Mal asked coolly, while his best friend covered her face.

Way to poke the bear, Mal.

"Why not? It wasn't a date." Baker spit.

Kase mustered the best "mom voice" she could manage, drawing on a lifetime of RomComs and made-for-tv movies.

"Alright, stop it, both of you. Sit down and stop acting like children." Stunned, the handsome bulldog slinked stiffly into his seat while his lanky counterpart dragged an identical chair over from the next table.

"I know I'm a shitty person and I did a shitty thing." She gazed at Baker apologetically. "But Terry, this is bigger than us; it's bigger than any petty differences you might have with this asshole." She flicked her thumb towards her best friend.

Mal shrugged and nodded in agreement. "This was my idea. I talked Kase into it. You can be mad at me later, but I need you to listen to me now. A man's life, his family's life, is on the line."

As if to prove it could get worse, Kasey saw the flirty waitress coming towards them out of the corner of her eye.

"Hi, can I get you a drink?" She flirted at Mal, hips swaying to the distant music.

"I'll have whatever he's having."

Baker's shoulders tensed. Whatever Mal had to say must be serious for him to actually have a drink.

Mal downed half his beer in a single pull before he began his story.

23

"Jesus Christ Mal, do you hear yourself? You're telling me that the wealthiest, most charming man on the ballot is using old defendants to pull off insurance fraud and murder? To what end? Where's your evidence?" Baker grew more animated.

"It sounds unlikely when you put it like that," Kasey muttered, sipping from a quickly defrosting glass. Her eyes were glazing over as she requested less tonic and more gin.

"You can't possibly be that dense," Mal exclaimed. "You're telling me none of this sounds fishy to you? Even if it's tenuous, we have to start somewhere. We can gather the evidence."

Kase winced as Mal continued to berate Baker. They needed someone on their side with a badge, and he wasn't making it easy for Baker to lay down his pride and help them.

Mal's gonna screw this up if I don't step in.

She broke in. "What Mal means to say is we have some proof, but we lack the resources to run an investigation that could gather substantial evidence for our *theories*." She glared at her best friend. "We need your help, Terry. You can't tell me that everything we've surmised is completely ludicrous."

Baker dropped his shoulders. He had to admit the double homicide never sat well with him. From the moment the case hit his desk, he had an uneasy feeling that things were just too neat. As much as he hated Mal, he never pegged him as a conspiracy theorist.

"I can't believe I'm saying this," he murmured. "Let's suspend reality for a minute and say that your *theory* is correct. We would need hard, tangible evidence to nail this sonofabitch— and I mean irrefutable proof. What exactly are we looking for?"

Kasey breathed a sigh of relief. He may be furious with her, but he was ready to listen.

Mal pulled an envelope from his back pocket.

"I wasn't going to show you this until I knew you were really going to listen." The creases on his forehead relaxed as he pulled out one of the driver's licenses. "Does he look familiar to you?"

"That's my suspect!" Baker examined the impeccable forgery. "That's not his name. Where did you get this?"

"Confidential informant."

"You're not a cop anymore. You can't have confidential informants without obstructing justice," Baker pointed out flatly.

"Protected source." Mal shrugged. "I'm not telling you. Or anyone. All you need to know is it's a very reliable source. These IDs were used to rent a van."

"You're kidding." Baker connected the dots.

"The van was abandoned and stripped for parts. My source got the VIN and traced it back to the rental company. Don't ask me how they obtained the actual drivers' licenses, even I don't know."

"So, you find the forger and you might find who hired him."

"Right, we're working on that part."

"What do you need from me?"

Mal pulled out a sheet of paper with the rental documents from the storage space. As he carefully laid out their investigation from the last few days, Baker leaned forward, unable to resist the lure of a puzzle. And this one was a whopper. He might never admit it, but he was glad Kasey tricked him into coming out tonight.

"Terry, I recognize this kid." Mal tapped the photocopy of the

ID from the storage rental agreement. "Sandoff defended him in a murder trial, but I never knew his name. I don't have access to those files anymore, but you want to look for a gang shooting that occurred about fifteen years ago."

"Shit, Mal, do you know how many cases you're talking about? Not to mention we didn't start digitally archiving anything until five years ago. I might have to pore over actual folders; it could take months!"

"I can help you." Kasey slurred. She immediately regretted volunteering, but in her drunken state, she couldn't bear Baker staying mad at her forever.

"This next part, Kasey will have to explain to you… if she still can." Mal shot his best friend an uneasy glance. "Take a gulp of that water, will ya?"

"I'm fine." He kicked her under the table as her volume rose. She kicked him back.

"If you two are done playing footsie…" Baker cleared his throat.

"We found semen in Abigail Stevenson."

"So?"

Kasey explained the match between the vaginal swabs and the samples from the panties. "Does she strike you like the type to sleep around?"

"She has a boyfriend? Had?"

"If she did, why hasn't he openly mourned her death? Has anyone you talked to in your investigation mentioned if she were seeing someone? Dating?"

Mal added, "She has a point. Why hide your relationship unless there's something else to hide?"

Baker rubbed his stubble absentmindedly. "Let me guess, you didn't get a match for that semen?"

"Not in CODIS." The Combined DNA Index System, the files the FBI provided to support local law enforcement.

"You think there's a connection to Sandoff? Someone at his firm?"

"We already know he committed insurance fraud. The evidence is sitting in a storage container in the Woodlands. If Abigail was seeing someone at the firm and she found out about the fraud, would you put it past them to shut her up?"

"Someone's cleaning house," Baker agreed. "She must have been dating someone important, though. Law firm that size? If she was dating some lackey associate, they wouldn't give two shits about her."

"Problem is, how do we suss out this mystery man to get a DNA comparison?" Mal lamented.

"Look into the married men first," Kase blurted. "That's what they're hiding. Abigail's man was probably having an affair."

"Kase, you're a drunken genius." Baker was impressed. Half-pickled and the brain still worked. He ignored the similarities to his own difficulties.

She beamed.

"A married man who is high on the totem pole. That's going to be difficult to nail," Baker pondered, more to himself than to the group. The investigation was already becoming a logistical nightmare.

"I hate to throw another log into the fire," Mal said haltingly, his brow furrowed. "We can't access that storage container without a warrant and time is running out. They could move that evidence at any moment."

"I can send some guys over to watch the place in case they make a move, rotate some black and whites through the area. I know the district, and nobody's going to notice a few extra badges hanging around. No judge is going to sign off on a warrant with what we have. Even if I could convince one of them to throw ethics out the window and sign it, we risk tipping off Sandoff. His pockets run deep and district clerks make beans."

"Now that you're on our side, could you spare some guys for protection detail?" Mal pleaded. "Jamal and his family need protection. He's our only witness."

"I can put a protection detail on Jamal since he's in police custody. I can't justify sending someone over to protect his family. Besides, from what you told me, Ericka doesn't know anything anyway. She'll be safe."

Mal doubted this, but knew better than to argue with Baker at this point. The detective had far exceeded his expectations. He came to McCormick's expecting a throw down and instead got a brainstorming session out of a drunken scientist and compliance out of a bullheaded jackass. He considered that a win at this point.

"Well, if you change your mind, here's her address." He texted Baker's personal cell.

"I'm not even going to ask how you got this number." He shot Kasey a dirty look and signaled for the check. "As much as I enjoy your company, you guys have given me a ton of work to do tomorrow. Kase, don't drive home. Night."

Kasey's heart sank as she watched Baker saunter off.

"Don't worry, he'll get over it in a few days." Mal comforted.

She hoped Mal was right because she felt like she just lost a friend for good.

24

Rizzo traversed the living room and hesitated as he felt a toy under his shoe. It shattered with an inaudible crunch under the thick rubber sole. The room was dark save for a muted night light flickering in the kitchen. He had pulled up photos of a similar unit on the Houston realty website, but those plans showed the master bedroom on the opposite end of the living room. He walked into the dimly lit bedroom and almost kicked the baby's crib. He held his breath as the toddler stirred and backed out slowly only when the child's breathing evened out.

"Make a sound and I'll shoot those brats."

Ericka had been fast asleep with her back to the door. The dark figure had his hand clamped tightly around her mouth and nose. She struggled to breathe; hot tears streamed down her face, turning cold in his palm. He deftly set aside the pistol and wrapped a cloth gag around her mouth with his knee planted firmly on her back. Her eyes struggled to adjust to the darkness, realizing the night light in her room had been unplugged. Searching for her phone, her eyes darted from side to side. Her heart sank when she realized she left it on the kitchen counter earlier.

"Now you're going to bring those brats out to the living room one by one so I can keep an eye on all three of you. Got it?"

She nodded as he snatched her t-shirt, pulling her backwards out of bed. She felt a barrel digging into her back as she carried each child out. The toddler, sensing her mother's panic, whimpered.

"Shut her up." The pistol ground deeper into her back. She tried her best to rock the child back to sleep, gently laying them both on the tattered couch. The figure draped a blanket over both children. She let out a small breath of relief hitched between gasps, a gleam of hope tight in her chest.

Maybe he isn't a complete monster, maybe he'll spare them.

He motioned for her to sit and to switch on the living room lamp, then blindfolded her. Enveloped in darkness, she could hear him shuffling around the frayed rug as he tied her hands behind her back with some kind of soft fabric. Silk?

"I'm going to ask you a series of questions." The acrid smell of cigarettes filled the room. "Any squeak other than answers to my questions, and I put a bullet through the baby's skull. I know you can't see me, but this is a Walther .22; it'll play pinball inside your kid's brain before it comes back out. You understand?" She shivered and nodded as he lifted her feet and placed them on an icy surface.

Rizzo pulled an amber bottle out of his jacket pocket and placed a few drops in each child's mouth. The toddler suckled at the tip as if nuzzling at her mother's breast. The older girl opened her mouth to cry, but he quickly squeezed a dropper-full down her throat. She coughed, then smacked her lips, swallowing the last of the grape-flavored liquid. He needed them sedated for this next part.

It was a risk, launching a lone assault with three subjects in the house. There were too many variables out of his control. Even though it would be easy to subdue Ericka by using her children against her, it was that same motherly instinct that could will her to fight him and ruin his plans to make her death look like an accidental overdose.

He had returned earlier in the evening under the pretense

Malcolm had ordered food for them. He looked innocent enough with his nondescript jacket and khakis, carrying a large GHB-laced pizza by his side. He was careful only to use enough to knock the fight out of her. She had to be conscious and able to panic a little for the next part of his plan.

"Who did you tell about Jamal's arrest?" It was a test question. He already knew about the private investigator, but he wanted to know if she would need some motivation to be honest. A line of drool followed the gag to her chin.

"No one, I swear. Please, everyone in this complex already knew. I didn't tell them!" She felt a crack as her feet burst with unbearable pain. A hand slammed across her mouth as she let out a shriek.

"Don't lie to me, bitch. Think of your children," he hissed, hot breath and spit landing on her earlobe. He let go of her mouth as her cries fell into small whimpers. "Try again. Who did you contact regarding Jamal's arrest?"

"I- I hired a private investigator. An ex-cop. Ly," she replied, in between sobs.

"And the girl? Who is she?"

"His partner." Another crack and searing pain. "I don't know, I swear. He introduced her as his associate."

"What's the bitch's name?"

"Selena. That's all I know, I swear." It took her a minute to recall the name. Her senses felt dull, and the room was fuzzy. "Please let my kids go. I'll tell you everything I know. Please."

"Apparently you don't know shit," he growled. "They came to see you this afternoon. What does he know? What did he tell you?"

In a moment of clarity, Ericka realized her life was over; she had stumbled upon something far more sinister than any of them expected. "Jamal was going to be convicted for both murders and that he couldn't help. He wanted me to take the kids and leave. He felt bad. That's why he bought us groceries."

She prayed her lie would buy the detective some time to save

Jamal and her kids. The young mother strained to see through the black cloth as a silence fell over the room. Suddenly, there was a pinching between her toes before a warm feeling draped over her.

"You're a nice girl," the voice lamented as he untied her blindfold. "It's too bad you got involved with such a cocksucker."

"W—what did you do to me?" She rasped.

"It's insulin." He clucked. "Consider yourself lucky. It's a great way to go. First you feel sleepy, then?" He opened his arms in emphasis. "You feel nothing at all."

"But m—my kids?" she protested meekly.

"Are no longer your concern." Two calloused fingers press against her eyelids. "Shhh, just sleep."

She cried the last few tears of anguish, limbs limp, and then nothing.

Rizzo rustled through the small kitchen searching for a metal spoon. Almost all the utensils in the drawers were plastic. He cursed himself for not being more prepared, but he needed the spoon to look used and rusted. Finally, he caught a glint of metal in the bottom drawer.

He gently cooked the crystals while watching Ericka's chest rise and fall until the movement was almost indiscernible. Drawing the brown liquid through the same syringe, he hoped she still had enough of a pulse to push the heroine through her system.

Finally, the scene was set. Now the actual work began. He had to look for this evidence the boss was convinced existed. There was an hour before sunrise and then it would be too risky to leave the complex without being seen. If only he knew what the fuck he was looking for.

25

"Y ou're late." Selena grumbled. "We said ten, right?"

"You really like to sit in the dark, don't you?" Mal turned on the desk lamp, sending dull beams to the corner where his accomplice sat, outstretched.

"Are you afraid of the dark?" she teased. "Your meeting with Baker run longer than expected?"

"Yes and no." He sighed, collapsing onto the squeaky swivel chair. "Kase got pretty wasted. I had to drive her home."

"Why didn't you just call her a rideshare?"

He stopped rubbing his eyes and shot her a *look*.

"Alright, dumb question." She put her hands up defensively. "You ready for tonight?"

"Do I have a choice?" Mal slid his pistol from its holster, released the magazine, and pulled back the slide in one swift movement. He grabbed another clip from the drawer and deftly inserted cartridges. "Remember, if you don't hear from me an hour after the drop, lie low and go find Moua in the morning."

"Like hell I'm going to let you go alone."

"This is not a discussion, Selena. We could be dealing with drug dealers, gun runners, scum like that. These aren't your usual white-collar criminals."

"All the more reason you should have back-up."

"I don't think your taser and jiu-jitsu would help me in this case. Stay here in the dark and meditate or something. I'll be fine." He moved towards the couch, planted a soft kiss on her down-turned lips, and flashed her a wry smile.

"You better be."

"Always am."

"Misogynist." She smiled half-heartedly.

"Still a better person than you." Another goofy smile and he was gone.

As the heavy wooden door whined to a close, Selena picked up her phone.

"Time to quit your drunken act," she murmured. "Come pick me up at his office. And Kasey, hurry."

#

"God, you smell like alcohol!" Selena wrinkled her nose, covering her face with her hand. "Are you sure you're not drunk?"

"I had to pour some on my clothes when Mal wasn't looking," Kasey defended herself. "It's difficult fooling him; he knows what I look *and* smell like when I'm wasted."

"Like a pig, apparently."

"Do you want to get kicked out? Cause I'm about to kick your ass out of this car."

"I'd like to see you try," Selena dared as her companion rolled her eyes and jerked the shift into drive. It was going to be a long hour and a half. She didn't know which was worse, Mal bumping uglies with Gwen or with this chick.

God, he has terrible taste in women.

Like most of his colleagues, Kasey didn't have the best impression of the insurance investigator, especially after the Manet debacle. However, she understood his attraction to Selena. She was his desire to throw caution to the wind, his liberation from a life of discipline and restraint. For all her past treachery, she must care for Mal deeply to be sitting in a smelly, outdated Camry with someone she barely tolerated, on a two-woman rescue mission. She could've left Mal to his fate and absconded with the information from Madame Moua.

"I appreciate you telling me about the drop."

Crickets.

"I'm going to kick Mal's ass for trying to keep this from me," Kasey proclaimed, mainly to herself. "Typical Mal. Trying to save everyone but himself. Who does he think he is?"

"He's concerned about you. That's all." Selena tried to change the subject. "We should really come up with a plan for later. The drop is taking place at the port."

"That narrows it down to about ten miles. Do you know where, which wharf?"

Selena produced a satellite image with a large circle near the center right. "I pulled this off of Mal when he wasn't looking and made a copy."

"Well, I can't read maps, so you're giving me directions."

"Jesus. Can you handle a gun?"

"Of course I can!" Kasey scoffed. "This is Texas. Everybody has a gun."

"Good, because I hate guns."

"Great, so we're going to save Mal with one gun and your rapier wit?"

"Hopefully, Mal won't need saving," Selena murmured, but nothing else had gone their way the entire investigation. Why would it start now?

#

Mal's pickup puttered through the open chain-link fence towards dock number twelve. As promised, the security guard had abandoned his station and there was no one to greet him but seagulls. Algae-covered water quietly lapped against the pier while a gentle breeze carried its natural stink inland.

Mal wrinkled his nose as he navigated through the maze of colorful containers with only the beam of his flashlight to lead the way. He had arrived a half hour early to do some reconnaissance, hoping to find at least one easy exit in case things went wrong. A dark warehouse jutted from the corner, its single bulb casting eerie shadows in an empty clearing.

This must be the spot.

It was difficult to get here, but the containers would certainly provide some cover.

He discovered some discarded wooden crates near the warehouse and lifted the lid to make sure they weren't filled with anything that went *boom*. Satisfied they were empty, he pushed them closer to his chosen fallback position. Whoever he was meeting would have to come in from the north, since there was nothing behind him but water. His watch glowed.

11:50.

He wasn't going to leave himself exposed; it was time to hide.

"Hey boss, how many of these do you want out here?" a voice shouted at exactly midnight.

"Bring out five. Once he shows us the money, we'll carry out the rest." A deeper voice commanded. From his hiding place, he made out four guys; two doing the grunt work, one standing guard, and the boss man himself barking orders and sweating bullets through his thick trench coat.

Great, a 1950s gumshoe. Is this guy kidding? It's 100 degrees out here.

"Looks like this asshole's late boss," the guard complained, stomping out his cigarette.

He waited another five minutes before shuffling out from the nook to make sure there weren't any more surprise henchmen hiding in the van.

"Sorry, this place is a maze. I got lost." He flashed a quick smile, trying to sound like an idiot.

"Who's there?"

He rolled his eyes.

Who else, stupid?

A MAC 10 swung from the guard's shoulder as he turned. Both grunts were carrying semi-automatics, and the bulge underneath the boss-man's coat suggested a bulletproof vest.

Fuck. He was out-manned and outgunned. A bulletproof vest

would have been too hot and bulky underneath his crew neck. *Let's hope this doesn't turn into a shoot-out.*

"Madame Moua sent me. I'm supposed to drop off a duffel." The guard loosened his grip on the weapon and boss-man squinted at the figure closing on them. Mal walked in front of the light, making his face invisible to the thugs in front of him.

"What's your name?"

"No names."

Boss-man looked slightly agitated.

"I'm only following instructions," he lied.

"Where's Moua? I'm not dealing with some two-bit thug I don't know."

"Look man, don't make my job harder, okay? This is my last chance to prove myself. She's going to kick my ass all over Houston if I mess this up." Boss-man seemed to relax a little, and the grunts started chuckling. At a towering six feet, they found it hilarious that he was terrified of tiny, scarred Moua.

"Where's the money?"

Mal lifted the duffel. *God, these guys are idiots.*

"Hand it over."

"No, I was told there would be ten containers. I count only five. I'm dumb, but I'm not that dumb," he argued.

"The other five are in the van. We'll bring them out once we make sure the money is there. *All* of it."

"That's not the deal. I count to ten and then I hand you the bag."

"No bullshit. You know we're good for it. You can see the van right there!"

"Don't bullshit me! I count to ten or I walk. This is a quarter-million dollars, guys. It's not chump change."

"Two-fifty? The deal was for five."

Fuck fuck fuck.

#

"I can't hear anything, can you?" Kasey whispered as Selena shushed her.

They made it just in time to see Mal disappear between the containers. Trailing the beam of light and his footsteps, they made it halfway through before they lost him. Now they were watching the drop from between two smaller containers, and it didn't look good. Body languages were tense all around, and Mal was definitely out-manned.

Suddenly, they made out a flash of light and then shouting. The lanky silhouette dashed towards a row of wooden crates curiously laid out in proximity to the containers. Loud, white flashes popped off as the squat, muscular one carrying the automatic opened fire. They saw the detective's shoulder snap before he dove into the tumbling cascade of crates.

"Kasey, he's hit!" Selena yelled. An explosion of rapid gunfire sliced through the stillness, lighting up the somber sky. Selena could see yellow flashes coming from Mal's side. He was returning fire, but he was going to run out of bullets soon. More flashes and shouting from the gangsters' direction. It sounded like more than four voices.

Maybe Mal had been able to dial one before chaos broke out.

Maybe Moua's backup had arrived.

"Cover me," Selena instructed. Taking advantage of the confusion, Kasey opened fire towards the group. There were definitely over four guys now, and they looked like they were fighting amongst themselves. Selena raced towards the crumbling boxes, where Mal was slumped over, bleeding.

"Mal, talk to me!" She slapped his face.

"Is he okay?" Kasey shouted, firing sporadic shots at nothing at all. She didn't want to hit anyone, but she wanted them ducking, distracted.

"Now's not the time, Kasey," Selena shouted back, wood chips flying towards her face. "Malcolm, honey. Do me a favor and wake up, okay?"

"Selena, what are you doing here?" he rasped, barely conscious.

"Saving your ass, love." She ducked, grabbing the pistol from his motionless right hand, expertly ejecting the magazine. Three cartridges left. "Please tell me you have another magazine, or we're not making it out of here."

"Revolver," he sputtered. "Left ankle."

"I'm so glad you're such a boy scout." She pulled the revolver from the ankle holster under his jeans. "Can you walk at all?"

Kasey continued to pop off rounds in the distance. More shouting echoed from directly in front of them, but it seemed the gunfire had halted. Then she heard the screech of a van. More men.

Without thinking, Selena threw his arm around her shoulder.

"I'm going to need you to help me. I can't carry you alone." She pointed towards Kasey with the revolver. "The goal is that container right there, okay?"

He gave a solemn nod. His eyes were blurring.

"Kase, cover!"

Kasey ejected the magazine and quickly slapped another one in place, firing at anything facing their way. Selena lead a hobbling Mal towards them, praying the men on the other side were the worst shots in henchmen history. As soon as they broke the container's threshold, Kasey threw Mal's other arm onto her shoulder and they took off.

"I hope you remember the way out!"

"M&Ms, follow the M&Ms!" Kasey screeched.

"What?"

"I dropped M&Ms on the way in."

"Where did you get M&Ms?"

"I was eating them the entire ride here!"

"You drunken genius. I'm going to kiss you." Selena searched the ground using the beam of light coming from Kasey's forehead. Sure enough, there was a trail of multi-colored M&Ms leading towards their exit. She had to admit Mal definitely underestimated his best friend.

"Now's not the time. I'll let you kiss Mal later." A wave of relief washed over Selena when she spotted the white Camry behind Mal's beat up truck. "Hurry, push him in." The girls shoved their bleeding companion into the back before Selena followed, cradling his head.

"What about his truck?" Kasey asked, rounding the car to the driver's side.

"Leave it, maybe someone can tow it for junk metal. I'll buy him a new car. Just drive!" They screeched onto the road as the shouting grew louder and bullets ricocheted off the fence and Mal's truck.

The Camry squealed around a corner, smashing against a curb before leveling out along the seawall. Kasey prayed silently they would make it to the freeway without getting pulled over by Galveston PD. Even with her forensics badge, it would be hard to explain the bloodbath in her backseat.

"Kase, it's not looking good." Still cradling his head, Selena counted a gunshot wound on his shoulder and two more on his right thigh. Dark, thick liquid poured from the holes, seeping into her pants and the floor mat.

"He needs a hospital. The medical school is ten minutes away."

"No hospital," Mal gasped in between breaths.

"He's right. They would have to report the GSWs. If we get Galveston PD involved, then Port Authority will follow. At that point, even Baker won't be able to get us out of this mess." Kasey whipped out her phone and dialed with one hand. "Can you stop the bleeding? Make a tourniquet?"

"I can hold it for now. But we need to hurry."

"Hey, it's Kasey. We have an emergency. It's Mal." She slammed on the gas pedal, flying up the ramp onto the freeway.

26

"Christ, Malcolm!" Gwen exclaimed, studying the trio drenched in blood, standing at the back door of her building. She was glad she told them to use the freight entrance. "What the hell happened?"

"Now's not the time, Gwen. We drove here from Galveston. He needs treatment."

"Henry, we need towels!" she shouted as they whipped through her front door. A befuddled Henry walked out of the bedroom, yawning, still in sweats and a muscle shirt. His eyes widened as he noticed the bloody group rushing through his living room.

Gwen cleared the dining room table, swiping the décor to the ground and ripping out the table runner.

"Lay him here. Flat out. Kasey, put this under his head." Now the redhead's tone was that of Harris County's Chief Medical Examiner.

"Selena, my medical bag. Closet by the front door. Henry, hot water," she barked, doing a cursory exam. "Where are his wounds?"

Using medical shears on his pant leg, she located two on his thigh; not exactly flesh wounds, but the bullets definitely missed the femoral artery.

"What the hell?" Kasey furrowed her brows as Gwen worked

around two dark red cotton pieces with strings jutting out from the leg wounds. "Did you put tampons in there?"

"That was all you had in the car," Selena defended.

"Guys, now's not the time," Gwen barked. Mal's black shirt was drenched, but she couldn't find the entry wound. "Do you know where he was hit in the torso?"

"Left shoulder, from the back." Selena stated, wiping sweat from her forehead, leaving a smear of Mal's blood in its place. A mix of mascara and tears stained her normally composed face.

"Could've used a tampon there," Kase murmured.

"Henry, I need you to cradle his neck and back. We're going to flip him on his side. On three!"

After Mal was on his stomach, Gwen ripped through the collar down the back to find a small hole by the shoulder blade. After determining the bullets all narrowly missed major arteries, she got to work extracting each one and carefully stitched the wounds. "He should still go to the hospital. He lost a lot of blood."

"We can't." Kasey's declaration left no room for argument.

"What kind of shit did you guys get into?" Gwen demanded. "I think I've earned it."

"It's complicated."

"Damn you and your secrets, Kasey. I'm tired of you and Mal hiding things from me," Gwen berated.

"She's not lying, Gwen. It *is* complicated," Selena tried to help.

"I need to make a phone call." Gwen yanked off the gloves with a smack and glared at Kasey.

"Well, if you won't tell Gwen anything, can one of you at least tell me if you committed a crime? Should I call you guys a lawyer?" Henry's blue eyes rounded with concern.

"No, thank you. We just need to sit for a minute." Kasey's legs felt flimsy and her shoulder and neck ached. She felt like she was breathing for the first time in an hour. "I'm Kasey, by the way. This is Selena. We're… friends of Gwen."

Selena gave a small wave and a curt smile. Henry's eyes darted from the short, slim girl with the thin lips and wide eyes to her tall, slender counterpart. They looked like they had battled it out with both Alien and Predator: blood, sweat, and tears dripping onto the hardwood floor, clothes torn, cuts and bruises on their arms and legs.

"Would you like a shower? I can grab some of Gwen's scrubs…"

"They can shower somewhere else," Gwen snapped, returning to the dining room. "I need your help with one more thing."

An eternity later, the doorbell rang. The medical examiner motioned for them to stay in the dining room, invisible to any guests in the foyer. Pulling on her robe, she slapped a fake smile on her face before greeting the person at the door.

"Thanks so much for this, Parker. I owe you one," they heard her say.

"No problem, Gwen. Just let me know if you need anything else. When Henry is all better, you guys need to come over for dinner," a male voice boomed.

"Of course. And sorry to bother you so late. Good night!" Gwen traipsed back into the dining room with two bags of saline and some tubes.

"What's all this?" Selena questioned.

"Well, he needs fluids, and since you guys won't take him to the hospital, I had to call in a favor," Gwen explained, motioning for Kasey to hold one of the clear plastic bags up above her head. "Parker is a trauma surgeon that just got off shift. I asked him to grab some supplies for me."

"Shouldn't we move him to the couch or something?"

"I don't want to risk ripping the stitches. Once his pulse stabilizes, we can move him." Gwen eyed the pair, relenting on her earlier proclamation. "You two should go shower. Guest bathroom is to the left."

#

Detective Langstrom knelt beside the corpse spread out on the concrete. He examined what was left of the blood encrusted face before pulling open the trench coat and searching the pockets for identification. *Guess this vest wasn't bulletproof after all.*

"How can you tell he was shot execution-style?" he asked the medical examiner's assistant.

"This guy, the squat fatty over there, and those two in the back were all shot in the face from an upward angle. Close range. Trench coat guy showed visible stippling on the forehead wound. Someone put a gun right up to his head." The assistant looked up from his clipboard and adjusted his glasses, forgetting he had gloves on. "Check out the dirt stains on their knees."

"And they all had weapons?"

"Bodies were found within proximity to an automatic weapon and three semi-automatic pistols. We would have to test for gunshot residue to be sure they were firing, but from the looks of those crates, either they were using them for target practice, or someone's in the hospital with a bunch of holes in them."

"McGregor—"

"I'm on it," his partner interrupted, cradling the phone on his neck while pulling out his notepad. "Tracy, call local hospitals. See if they've received any GSWs within the last few hours. I also need you to run a trace on this license plate."

Langstrom had to admit his rookie partner was a quick study. A few more crime scenes and he would be happy to pass the torch and make the lateral move into recreational fishing. Peter McGregor spent three years undercover in Narcotics in LA before the job took its toll on his marriage. His ex-wife then remarried and moved their son to Seattle, where he soon followed, working sex crimes at Seattle PD for some time before again following his son to Galveston. He wasn't exactly a rookie on the force, but to Langstrom, anyone who has never worked Homicide was a rookie.

"So, what do you think?" The weathered detective tested his

partner.

"Definitely some kind of deal gone bad," McGregor started.

"How do you figure?"

"Place like this, dark, secluded? It's a suitable setting for a drop. Multiple sets of tire tracks. They might have been ambushed. We would have to wait for ballistics to confirm, but I examined the crates earlier and saw cartridges that could have been from the MAC 10. I'm guessing these four were focused on shooting at somebody or multiple somebodies behind those crates. Ended up getting flanked and overpowered."

"But why the execution?"

"I don't know, partner. Seems personal. Some kind of vendetta? Message?"

"What about that truck out front?"

"Plenty of trash. No personal items inside, though. I'm still waiting for Tracy to call me back with the registration."

McGregor hesitated.

"Spit it out, kid."

"Does something feel off to you?" Langstrom could see the kid's gears turning.

"Smells like a trap. Something tells me no matter the outcome of the deal, bodies were gonna drop tonight."

Just then McGregor's phone let out a soft chirp. "Tracy just emailed me. Truck is registered to a Malcolm Ly, private investigator. Ex-HPD. I have his home and office address."

"Stolen?"

"Wasn't reported." McGregor shook his head. It was Langstrom's turn to pull out his phone. "Who are you calling?"

"Waking up some friends at HPD." He clucked. "It's time we pay Mr. Ly a visit."

27

Selena sank into the velvet loveseat, leaning against its oversized arm while rubbing her temples. The overhead lights were suddenly overcast by a shadow. She looked up to see the exquisite doctor handing her two fingers of whiskey.

"Thank you." She raised the glass. "A tad foreboding, don't you think?"

"Depends. Are you a glass-half-full or glass-half-empty kind of person?"

Selena studied the picturesque figure perched across from her, dressed in an emerald silk robe which perfectly accentuated the fiery mane flowing wildly over her shoulders. She had a feeling Gwen was studying her equally intently.

"I'm neither." She downed the whiskey. It was quality stuff. "I'm a realist."

Gwen placed the decanter on the marble coffee table and motioned for her to help herself. "I'm more of a Scotch girl myself, but Henry loves whiskey." She took a sip, her eyes never straying from the olive-skinned beauty in front of her. It was hard to be poised and sophisticated in someone else's cotton scrubs, but somehow Selena pulled it off. She felt more than a twinge of jealousy that this was who Mal had been gallivanting around town with.

"Mal is a Scotch drinker," Selena mused, twirling her hair.

"You guys must have so much in common."

"We share quite a few… *passions*." Gwen emphasized. "More than you and he shared, I'm sure. Seeing as how he never mentioned you until a few days ago."

"Oh, dear girl, men rarely share their deepest, darkest secrets. Take it from someone who knows."

"What are you saying?"

"That I'm Malcolm's darkest secret." Selena leaned forward, her lips twisting into a smug grin. Gwen's face turned an unnatural vermillion.

"For God's sake, why don't you two just whip it out and measure already?" Kasey shuffled in, dragging the long pant legs across the rug. She continued to towel dry her hair while eyeing the decanter. Gwen knowingly handed her an already filled glass from the end table as Kase dropped next to Selena.

"I was just having a little fun with the good doctor."

"Well, stop it. You're upsetting her, and she saved our asses," Kasey chastised after taking a long swig of whiskey. "He loves you both, so you can stop competing."

"Shh! Keep your voice down." Gwen winced, looking towards her bedroom door.

"Wait, how much does Henry know about Mal?" Kasey lowered her voice, surprised by Gwen's request for discretion.

"Just that he's a friend and former colleague." She wrung her hands. "He doesn't need to know any more than that."

"What a healthy relationship," Selena chimed in.

"My relationship is nobody's concern except mine." Gwen glared at Selena. "What happened tonight is the actual issue. You two better talk."

"Gwen, it's not like we don't want to tell you, but the stuff we've done isn't exactly the most legitimate," Kasey started. "Mal doesn't want to put your career on the line, and frankly, neither do I. You have a lot more to lose than we do."

"To hell with Mal," Gwen snapped, pointing a slender finger at Selena. "Beyond the fact that I just stitched him up on my fucking dining room table? Knowing him, he told *this* one to keep you out of it and she still pulled you into it, so fuck what he wants."

Kasey shared a knowing glance with the insurance investigator. Despite her friend's adamant requests Gwen be kept in the dark, she always knew their inquiry would lead to the doctor's involvement.

"I don't even know where to begin." Selena relented first, leaning forward for a refill.

"The beginning would be nice."

Selena recounted her adventures from the last few days, explaining how Mal's case became intertwined with hers. She chronicled their interactions with Jamal and Ericka, and how they eventually pulled Baker into the mix.

"Great, so Terrence Baker knew about this before me?" Gwen scoffed, incredulous.

"We needed his resources." Kasey interjected. "We didn't tell him everything." She furrowed her brows as she remembered they would have to tell Baker about tonight. She hoped no one would find Mal's blood and his bullet-ridden truck until morning, giving her a few more hours before she had to ruin Baker's day.

"Something went wrong tonight, but we're not sure what. According to Moua, it should have been an easy drop. We couldn't hear what they were saying, but then one guy shined his flashlight on Mal's face. Next thing we knew, they were shooting at Mal and he was sprinting away and shooting back."

"And you guys..." Gwen realized what happened next. It definitely was not legal for Kasey to be involved in a shootout with gang members, but it wasn't illegal either. And she did it to save her best friend. Selena ran into the line of fire to carry him out because he was her lover. And Gwen? She secretly stitched him up, because he was her... she didn't even know anymore. She glanced at the bedroom door. Henry proposed tonight, but she had taken off the ring as soon as she heard Mal was in trouble.

"We're going to have to report this in the morning."

"Just leave that to me. I'll call Baker in a few hours." Kasey volunteered. "What do we do next, guys? Who knows when Mal will wake up and we're in too deep to wait around for him."

"I'll go to Moua tomorrow to collect the rest of the information. A deal's a deal. Mal almost lost his life for her bullshit. I'll be damned if I let her renege on her end," Selena exclaimed, and neither of the other women doubted that the formidable Moua would meet her match. "Kasey, see if Baker will go with you to Tory's apartment. We need to find that evidence before anyone else does."

Selena handed Kasey the key, then hesitated. "You're going to need Baker's badge in case you get caught behind the crime scene tape. And you probably shouldn't go alone."

"Where were you hiding this key?" Kasey asked, wiping the damp brass on her leg.

"You don't want to know."

"Gross."

"Why haven't we searched Abigail's apartment and office yet?" Gwen asked.

"Baker did a cursory search when he caught the case, but I don't think he knew what he was looking for. He definitely didn't pick up that she had a boyfriend, though." Kasey explained, walking towards the kitchen. "Do you have food? I'm starving."

"There's leftovers in the fridge."

Selena smiled at Kasey's ease and familiarity. She could never imagine herself standing in the middle of a jealous rival's kitchen, digging through her refrigerator, and eating her leftovers. She spoke over the microwave, detailing a plan for Gwen and Selena to go to Abigail's apartment the next day. She could easily have gone with Gwen, but Selena had a feeling she was trying to avoid any more uncomfortable confrontations with the doctor.

"I guess we have a plan, sort of. We should get some sleep. Selena, you can take the guest bedroom. I'll sleep on the couch in case Mal wakes up."

"I don't think we're getting any sleep tonight. I know I'm not tired." Gwen couldn't lie next to Henry while tossing and turning over Mal. "I have something else I want to ask you, Kasey. Did he really tell you he loved me?" Desperate eyes searched Kasey's face.

Selena groaned. "Are we really back here, again? Kase, can you please just tell her what she wants to hear so we can all get some rest?"

Kasey rolled her eyes, speaking while shoveling bits of chicken and broccoli into her mouth. "If you must know, you *crushed* him when you walked off in the middle of the night with the Manet."

"I did?" Selena uncrossed her long legs and sat up straight.

"Well yeah, he jumped on that sword for you, almost lost his job. He said nothing, but he couldn't mention you by name for weeks."

She then turned to Gwen. "And you, well, everyone, including blind Martians, knew he was head over heels for you."

Gwen's lips trembled, and tears gathered in her eyes. "But he *left* me. I loved him, and all he could say was that we weren't a good fit. I still love him."

"Because you were jealous and suffocating!" Kasey raised her hands, exasperated. "Think about it. In the time that you were together, how many drunken, accusatory phone calls did I get? You cheated *with* him and then you started projecting your insecurities. It was insane!"

"I—" Gwen bit her lip; she couldn't deny that the relationship between Mal and Kasey brought out some deep-seated insecurities within her, but they were her own. She had no reason to believe there was anything more than friendship between the two of them.

"Not that I care about his sexual history," Selena lied. "But what about you?"

"What about me?" Kasey shot back. People commonly misconstrued their closeness as sexual intimacy, but the truth was they shared one kiss long before she met Bruce and she never thought about it again, a kiss that Kasey initiated in self-defense against her parents' expectations.

It was difficult for the Khuus to justify having more than one child when they were barely scraping by. Being an only child of immigrants, Kasey became the center of all their displaced hopes and dreams. They dragged her from piano lessons to spelling bees, from ballet classes to decathlons. It was a great relief when Mal showed up for dinner on Christmas Day their freshmen year and Mr. Khuu realized how much he wanted a son. Mal became the older brother she needed to deflect uncomfortable conversations with her parents. He was also the late-night study buddy, the perpetual designated driver, and as they got older, her emotional crutch. It was easy to misunderstand their relationship when there was so much history there.

"I think inquiring minds want to know if you and Mal ever slept together," Selena spelled out, nodding towards Gwen.

"It's a question I've answered repeatedly," Kase replied. "It's not my fault she refuses to believe it."

"How can I when she won't even give me a straight answer?" Gwen protested.

"Are you really that childish? I'm done discussing this. You don't see Selena throwing a tantrum over it."

Selena chuckled as the two continued arguing. She wasn't being hyperbolic when she described herself as a realist. She and Mal led vastly different lives; she was secretive, almost protective of her past and despite his best efforts, his past was a tragic art exhibit constantly on display. Reveal her demons? Open up emotionally? It was impossible for her, even to Mal. In contrast, he already had someone who could read him like an open book and that someone wasn't her.

"Shh. Do you guys hear that?" The raised voices suddenly subsided. They were dispatched from the living room by a soft rustling nestled in heavy breathing.

"Mal?" Gwen whispered, flicking on the chandelier.

"Kase."

"What?" Gwen checked his pulse and leaned towards his mouth and chest.

"Kasey." He whispered through painful breaths.

The doctor pursed her lips. "He's asking for you."

Selena crossed her arms and leaned against the wall, watching as the obdurate analyst clasped her best friend's hand.

"I'm here, dude." He opened his eyes long enough to glimpse the mass of unruly curls on her tiny figure, smiled with relief, and went back to sleep. Dejected, Gwen quietly slinked off to bed.

28

The obnoxious ringing of an old rotary phone jolted Baker awake. Dazed, he adjusted his eyes to the blurred sight of his desk and television. He stared at his phone, realizing the sound wasn't his alarm, but a ring tone that was usually put on "silent". The bright screen showed five am and a missed call from an unknown number. He cursed the spam caller and rolled over, knowing sleep would completely evade him.

Absentmindedly, he threw his arm over the space to his left. No Amanda, no girl-from-accounting, and now he knew for sure no Kasey. Seems she only had room for one man in her life at a time. Sighing, he threw back the tan-colored flat sheet and walked to the kitchen.

Might as well start the coffee and catch up on some reports.

The best part of getting divorced was the thermostat stayed set at a cool sixty-five degrees, no more fluffy comforters or sweaty sheets. The second-best part was being able to walk around in his underwear. Amanda never liked his bare skin touching the expensive furniture, furniture he paid for, furniture she eventually demanded in the divorce settlement. An almost inaudible *plink* caused Baker to look down at his phone again.

Voicemail.

"This is Ian Langstrom from Galveston PD. Call me back. It's urgent."

Baker took a moment to recall the name. Ian Langstrom was the no-nonsense detective he crossed paths with chasing down a double murder a few years ago. They begrudgingly agreed to work together when it became apparent they were chasing the same suspect and eventually bonded over their shared military background. After they closed the case, Langstrom gave him a firm handshake and a grunt, the only approval a man like him could muster. They shared a few emails, and when Langstrom's wife Anita died, Baker attended the funeral. Afterward, Langstrom withdrew further, and the emails stopped completely. It was a surprise he hadn't retired yet and even more of a surprise he was reaching out.

"Hello," a gruff voice answered almost immediately.

"Ian? It's Terry."

"Sorry to wake you." He didn't sound sorry at all.

"I was already awake. What's going on?"

"I've got four dead bodies and a name in your jurisdiction." Langstrom was never one for small talk. "Malcolm Ly. Computer says he was one of yours?"

Fuck. What did you do now, Mal?

"He was. He left the force a few years ago." Baker cleared his throat, crafting his replies carefully.

"I'm almost at your house. Mind showing an old-timer around Houston?" Baker understood this was merely a courtesy call.

"I don't live there anymore. Divorce."

"Sorry to hear."

"Just give me an hour and meet me at the coffee shop across from the station?"

"An hour."

Baker hurriedly dialed Mal's number. Straight to voicemail.

Dammit, Mal, pick up.

He dialed and got voicemail again. He tried Kasey's phone.

"Hello?" Kasey's voice was dull and small, not the upbeat greeting he was used to whenever he called her. She was probably still sleeping off her hangover.

"Kase, where is Mal? He's not answering his phone."

"Uh… he's here."

"He's there, with you? Like at your house?"

"Not exactly." Kase hesitated. "Are you sitting down?"

Baker braced himself. "What happened?"

"We did something yesterday, and you won't be happy about it."

"You slept with him?"

"What the fuck? No!" Kase's voice grew louder. Baker bit his lip, feeling foolish for letting that slip. "We sort of made a mess in Galveston."

"A mess? That's the understatement of the year." Baker pushed back. "I would call four dead bodies a bit more than a mess."

"Wait, what dead bodies? I'm a good shot, but I'm not *that* good."

"Are we talking about the same thing here?"

"Are you talking about the shooting at the docks?"

"Yes! Kasey, there are four dead bodies down there. Galveston PD just called me. What did you and Mal do?"

"We didn't kill anybody! At least I don't think so." Her voice sounded meek, almost scared. He sighed.

"Where are you right now?"

"Gwen's apartment."

"Oh great, so you got the doc involved. It's a conspiracy now?"

"And Selena too." She gulped.

"Fan-fucking-tastic. I'm picking you up in fifteen."

#

Henry fidgeted with his tie, undoing and retying the knot; this time, it landed too short on his torso. Maybe he was unhappy with the color. Or maybe it was the fact that the apartment was feeling a little crowded. Early this morning, they received a call from the concierge that a Detective Baker was waiting for them downstairs. Even with the bedroom door closed, Henry tossed and turned to the muffled exchange outside and eventually gave up. He would make it to the office right before the New York market opened.

"Hey, I'm sorry, are we being too loud?" Gwen asked, closing the bedroom door behind her.

"It's alright. I'm going to go to the office. I have some work to catch up on anyway," Henry replied coldly, concentrating harder on his Windsor knot.

"I'm sorry for all the commotion. This case is…"

"Don't worry about it." Henry cut her off and pointed to the dresser. "I found this on your night table. You should put it away if you're not going to wear it."

Gwen looked down at the flawless marquise cut engagement ring she had hurriedly flung off her finger last night. She meant to put it back on before he noticed, but Baker had woken them, and thus Henry, earlier than she expected.

"Let me explain—"

Henry held up his hand. "Gwen, I heard everything last night. We need to talk, but I wasn't going to bring it up until your friends were gone. I don't want to add to your distress, but I really don't want to hear it right now." He stared down at her with vacant, icy eyes. "I'll probably work late tonight. Call me if you or your friends need anything."

"Henry, I do love you."

He paused for a moment, then walked out without looking back.

29

I an." Baker nodded. The boorish detective let out a grunt while sipping what Baker could only presume to be the darkest roast Starbucks could brew: no cream, no sugar, and scalding hot.

"You're late."

By two minutes.

"This the reason for your divorce?" Langstrom tilted his head towards Kasey. The analyst blushed as she realized how it must look. Baker didn't have time to take her home to change. She was still in the wrinkled green scrubs she slept in, hair tousled in a messy bun, all the dirt and stress from last night lingering in her bones and prominently displayed on her face.

"No. This is Kasey Khuu, she's a forensic analyst in the lab. We carpool sometimes." Langstrom narrowed his eyes, not knowing if he really believed Baker would so casually bring an outsider to such an important meeting.

"You look like you've been through hell, kid." He examined her ill-fitting scrubs and the scratches on her arm.

"Wow, you sure know how to make a girl feel special." Kasey retorted. She felt a jab in her ribs and glared at her companion. "I'm just going to get a coffee and walk to work. Nice to meet you." *Jerk.*

Baker wanted Kasey to wait for him across the street, but she

142

insisted on being within earshot of the meeting so she could hear what Langstrom had to say. Now she was standing by the glass case, not-so-subtly staring at pastries and sandwiches she was in no mood to eat.

"What's going on Ian? Why the early wake-up call?"

"Thought you said you were already awake?"

"Get to the point, Ian."

"Four bodies shot execution-style down by the docks. Know anything about that? Looked like they'd been through hell too."

Langstrom was sharp; Baker always thought his skills were wasted in Galveston. He should've been in Houston solving homicides and gang shootings, not the occasional fishing accident or spring break overdose.

"Only what you've told me. How is Mal involved?"

"So, you're on a nickname basis with this guy?"

"We worked homicide together. All the guys called him that."

"We found his truck shot to hell, but no person. No one by that name or matching his description has checked into any hospitals in Galveston or Houston."

"You can't possibly believe Mal could subdue four guys and shoot each in the head one by one?"

"I don't know what to believe, but I know he's a witness at the very least and maybe even a person of interest, so I want to talk to him." Langstrom intertwined his large, dark hands and gave Baker a hard stare. "Do you want to come with me to his house? I'm extending a professional courtesy to the both of you."

Langstrom turned to Kasey, who had changed her gaze to the coffee mugs and tumblers, and addressed her in the same breath. "You might as well come sit down with us, sweetie. You can't be hearing me that well from over there."

The analyst sheepishly pulled another chair towards the round high-top and sat down.

"I'm old, but I'm not stupid. How do you factor into all of this?" Langstrom asked.

"I'm only here as a second set of ears," she fibbed.

"I don't buy that. Now either you two shoot it straight with me, or I'm going over your head and putting a BOLO out on your buddy."

Baker and Kasey glanced at each other. A "Be On the Lookout" would be a pain, and almost impossible for Mal to dodge. Thankfully, they had rehearsed a believable narrative for Langstrom on the way over. They were going to tell him parts of the truth and leave Sandoff's name out. Baker quietly thanked the stars that Mal was recovering at Gwen's apartment. There was no way he was going to talk Ian out of going to his house or his office.

"I don't have all the details. I just know Mal was hired as a PI to look into a theft. I guess he was chasing a lead, and it led him to Galveston. He brought Kasey with him and they got out when the shooting started."

"Why do I find it hard to believe that he brought you as backup? You're a hundred pounds soaking wet. If this Malcolm is any bit the man I've read in his file, then that is one big tactical error."

"He needed a civilian with him, someone who wasn't bound by law to make arrests when they see something untoward." Beads of sweat pebbled on her skin as she tried to sound nonchalant.

"And what were you supposed to do if there was trouble?"

"Getaway driver."

"His truck is still there, so you failed at that."

"We took separate cars. Mal was taking fire, so he jumped into my car and we took off."

"You saw nothing then?"

"I was in the car the whole time."

"Then you can't be sure if Mal killed those men or not?"

"If Mal killed those men, then who was firing at us?" Kase shot back. The detective looked stumped. He let out a soft growl and nodded, satisfied for the time being. He knew there was more to the story, but he would have to bully it out of Malcolm.

"Look, Ian, I would love to sit here and let you interrogate Kase some more, but I just got a ping." Baker held out his phone to show the notice he just received. "Fresh homicide. How about we meet at Mal's house later today and you can ask him all the questions you want?"

"You know what I find funny?" Langstrom was unrelenting. "That we've been sitting here the whole time and you haven't called him once or even offered to give me his phone number. What are you hiding from me?"

"What makes you think I haven't called him?" He showed Langstrom his call history, marking the two calls he made right after he got Ian's message. "It went straight to voicemail. Mal does that sometimes. He's not exactly the most "plugged in" person; he'll lose his phone for days or just let his battery die. If you want to talk to him, we'll go see him in person."

He yanked on Kasey's sleeve and headed towards the door, hoping the explanation would quell the tenacious bulldog for now.

"Three o'clock Terrence." The husky voice yelled after the pair. Baker raised his hand in acknowledgement while hustling his companion out the door.

#

Sergeant Malcolm Ly had always been a rule follower. A hard worker with no ambition other than doing his job to the best of his abilities. To his trainees, he was stern, but compassionate. To his colleagues, he was driven, a force to be reckoned with, too good to be true. Some on the force hated him and were envious of his skills, while others were just glad he was on their side. No cop should really be that virtuous; which was why everyone on six remembers the day he fell from grace.

Malcolm had spent years chasing the local chapter of a gang suspected of working with sex traffickers. Once they smuggled their victims to the border or to the port, those victims were lost forever. The FBI Organized Crime Task Force was recruiting talented officers from local law enforcement to do their fieldwork, and the fresh-faced sergeant with a spotless record and multiple recommendations was their first choice. Mal spent countless hours on the wire and on stakeouts, working the case on weekends and during his free time. During those years, he rarely interacted with anyone, including his family, afraid of bringing the worst elements of his job home to them.

As Mal got closer to breaking the case open, his life became increasingly dangerous. After an attempted break-in caused Georgie to suffer night terrors, he moved his ex-wife and child to a safe house and begin working overtime to make arrests. On the night he was to make the final bust, he received two phone calls that forever changed his life. A panicked Trish called to tell him Georgie wasn't in bed. A few minutes later, a gravelly male voice called, demanding he call off the raid, or else. But the decision wasn't up to him, and the raid proceeded. Forty women and children were liberated from industrial warehouses, where they were awaiting transport across the border.

Five days later, the bloodied body of a seven-year-old was found in a culvert, barely breathing, left alive enough for Mal to see his son take his last breath. The bayou had claimed another victim.

The case unraveled without Mal to helm the investigation or testify, as he unraveled mentally. On his last day as a cop, Sanders and Polk raced into interrogation to stop a frenzied Mal from beating a suspect unconscious. The bastard was withholding information and taunted Mal with the prospect of never finding his son's killer. On that day, everyone realized Malcolm Ly was merely human.

"Mal! Malcolm!" Gwen's gentle voice wrenched him from his feverish nightmare. There is nothing like waking up to your ex-lover crouching by your side, a vision in her beige-striped summer dress and that rose-gold locket he gave her resting on the curves of her collarbone. "Hey sleepyhead. I'm glad you're awake."

"How long was I out?" He shifted uncomfortably, the hard, wooden dining table digging into his spine.

"Not as long as I thought you would be," Gwen replied, checking his pulse. He grabbed her alabaster hand, her skin soft and warm to the touch.

"Thank you."

She managed a weak smile before collapsing into a high-backed dining chair. "I thought I'd lost you."

She cried, the restraint from last night gone, washed away by the stress and fear of losing him.

"I'm sorry, Gwen." His heart broke to see her in tears. "I'm alright. Besides, it's not that easy to kill me." He flashed her a crooked smile.

She chuckled through the tears and playfully smacked his arm. "Shut up, you jerk. You had us all worried."

He tried to pull himself up, but could only manage a weak lift onto his elbows. The plush blanket fell towards his stomach, revealing his heavily bandaged chest and shoulders. Cuts and bruises marred a well-defined torso.

"Will you help me up?"

"Be careful. Don't rip your stitches." She helped him into a sitting position as he studied his surroundings. He had never been to her new place. It was posh, classic, something he envisioned a stylish couple like Gwen and Henry would own. An avid nester, she had turned their apartment into a home, from the elegant pieces displayed in the foyer and kitchen to the framed professional photos of the happy couple on the walls.

"How are you feeling?" she asked as he got to his feet.

"Like I've been shot."

"Do you want to go to the bedroom?"

"Is that an offer?" He smirked, turning the proposition into an attempt at humor.

"The *guest* bedroom, you idiot."

"How about somewhere I can't bleed all over your fancy furniture?"

"That would be the hallway. It's fine. I bandaged you up well."

"My hero," he teased.

"It's all that fancy medical school training. First time I've saved a patient in a while. Usually, I'm just cutting them open." She led him to the living room, gently lowering him onto the couch.

"That's reassuring, considering you operated on me."

"I pulled a bullet out of you Mal. Huge leap from that to surgery." She handed him a glass of water.

"I have another question. Whose pants am I wearing?"

30

The wily young blonde stared into his rearview mirror for the second time since he picked up his fare. Passengers had been scarce this morning in Sugar Land, but as soon as he arrived downtown, his phone buzzed nonstop. The raven-haired beauty from Hotel Alessandra was his fourth fare for the morning.

Armed with an MBA from Stanford, he thought he would have his pick of the top oil and gas companies when he returned home. Instead, he was living with his parents and picking up rideshares as his principal source of income. The money he made barely covered gas, with a bit left over for his weed habit, but he didn't mind it much. It got him out of the house and away from his critical old man, who was constantly sneering at his failure.

"Spit it out already." She didn't look up from her phone, tapping furiously. Her voice carried a low rasp that reminded him of sultry smoke rings and dim jazz lounges.

"You must not be from around here."

"Gee, how did you guess?" Selena replied flatly, uncrossing her lean, sun-kissed legs. After they debriefed Baker this morning, she returned to her hotel and ordered a massage from their in-house masseuse. Feeling refreshed and dressed in her own clothes, she decided it was time to confront Moua.

"Well, you're way posher than any of the girls from Houston." The kid leered at her black lace shorts and matching one-shouldered peplum top. "And your destination is in a pretty shady part of town. No one that looks like you would knowingly go there."

"And I suppose you're going to be my knight in shining armor?" She wondered sardonically. The tone of her comment was lost on him.

"I don't know about all that." He puffed out his chest. "But I can show you around after I'm done for the day."

"You're a sweet kid." She finally looked up from her phone. "But you wouldn't be able to afford the shoe bag for these Ferragamos, so how about you just concentrate on driving so I can work, please?"

"As you wish." He shot her a smile, unfettered by her rejection.

The kid has balls, that's for sure. She checked in with Gia and emailed her a set of instructions for the next few days before they pulled into the familiar decrepit shopping center that held a small smoke shop and Moua's game room.

"What's your name, kid?"

"Miles."

"How much do you make per fare, Miles?"

"It depends—"

"Ballpark it for me."

"About twenty bucks?" It was an overestimation, but he could see where this conversation was going.

"I'm a busy woman and I don't have all day to wait for drivers to come pick me up. How about I give you fifty bucks for every destination and another fifty bucks every time you have to wait for me?"

"What are you saying?"

"I'm saying turn off your app, be my driver for the day, and make a few hundred bucks easy. Buy yourself a haircut." She stared at the mop on his head and his dirty sweatshirt.

"Done." A short, dirty thumb reached out to deactivate the app.

"Great. Wait here for me and keep the engine running. Be ready to drive if you see me sprinting out of here." She opened the back door. "And Miles?"

"Yeah?" He asked, suddenly dubious of the deal he was happy with seconds earlier.

"Everything that goes on in this car is confidential. Speak a word of it to anyone and I will have my people hunt you down." She snapped a photo of him with her phone and threw a fifty on his lap. He quickly nodded and gulped, not doubting her threat for a minute.

Moments later, Selena was yanking at the tinted metal door. She violently fell back at the strength of Tiny's push. His arm was on the door, a trash bag dangling from the other hand.

"Where is she?" Selena demanded. Tiny pointed to the dusty room in the back, unfazed by the anger in her voice.

"Here for the rest of the information, Ms. Parish?"

Selena stomped towards the voice, following the low whir of the cash counting machine into a small office hidden by the bar.

"You treacherous bitch," she snarled. "You knew it was a trap, and you left him to die." She didn't realize the amount of rage bubbling beneath the surface until she saw Moua's shadowy figure at her desk, counting her cash, business-as-usual.

Moua looked up, unfazed. "I told him to dial one."

"No, something happened before that. You set him up." Selena accused. "To think he trusted you."

"There is no trust in this business." Moua looked up, her lips flat and straight, a glint of viciousness in her eyes. "Malcolm and I have a business relationship. He pays for information, and I deliver. This time, the information he tried to buy was worth more than what he had. He knew what he was getting into and agreed to it. I did not force him."

"You didn't give him a choice, either."

"It's just business." Moua shrugged. "Do you want the information or not?"

Selena's anger flared at Moua's indifference, but she swallowed her pride, taking the envelope Moua slid across the desk. If she had the information ready, it meant things went as planned last night. She got what she needed from the drop and she hung Mal out to dry.

"This guy? Really?" she exclaimed, surprised.

"Did you really expect anyone less for such exquisite work?" Moua smiled, her milky eye never straying from the mound of cash.

"For how long now?"

"Ask him yourself." Selena took that as her cue to leave. "And Ms. Parish, I will forgive you for your outburst this time because Malcolm means a lot to you, but never speak to me like that again. I didn't get to where I am by allowing such insolence. You will do well to remember that."

31

Baker drove through the broken gates of a rundown complex, flashing his badge at the officer in front. Flashing lights from squad cars, fire trucks, and ambulances filled the morning sky. It was early, yet the Texas heat was already setting a blanket of humidity on the city. Kasey noticed the coroner's van parked next to a CSU van from her lab. As a bench analyst, she almost never went to crime scenes and hoped the crime scene techs on duty wouldn't recognize her. Her heart sank as she walked down the hall towards the unit. Standing by the door was Cherise, crime scene day shift supervisor and best friends with her production lead.

"Kasey!" Cherise's warm brown eyes lit up. "What are you doing at a crime scene?"

"She's with me. I requested her presence for a consultation." Baker piped up.

"That's not protocol." Cherise responded, taking off her glove to wipe the sweat from her mocha-colored face. "She's not trained on how to preserve a crime scene."

"Well, you guys are, and I take it you've already secured the scene and taken photos?" Baker asked flatly.

"Yes we have. The coroner is examining the body."

"Just treat her like she's another detective. If she fucks anything up, I'll take responsibility for it." Cherise's eyes flashed from Baker to Kasey, suspicious, but not ready to get into an argument with the lead detective. Kasey blushed, realizing again how bad it looked for her.

"Fine, but you're both wearing PPE so you don't contaminate my scene and don't touch *anything*." Terrence waved off her instructions as he began slipping on shoe covers. Kasey followed suit.

"Just fill me in."

"Victim is Ericka Thomas."

Shit.

"Neighbors kicked down her door after hearing the babies cry for hours. She was found on a chair, a needle in her arm. Looks like an overdose, but the medical examiner will do a full autopsy."

The pair froze in their tracks at the sound of the victim's name. Baker knew the address was familiar, but he couldn't quite place it. Now he realized it was the address Mal texted him last night. He was wrong. Ericka was in trouble and he didn't do all he could to protect her.

Mal was going to be pissed.

Ericka's motionless face seemed peaceful, almost as if she were just asleep. Moving closer, Baker observed discoloration around her cheeks and eyes. Her body was positioned in a relaxed manner, but there was something off about the entire scene. Ericka seemed clean and well-groomed, but her apartment was a mess. It seemed superficial somehow, like the items were thrown around to mimic the life of a long-term drug user, but there were no genuine signs of decay. The home lacked a putrid stink distinct in unsanitary hygiene—the signs of a real junkie.

"Talk to me, doc." Baker turned to the assistant medical examiner, a middle-aged heavy-set man with large, coke-bottle glasses and a full head of dark curls.

"It's not suicide." He murmured, engrossed in his examination of her arms. "No new track marks on her arms. It's pointing to an accidental overdose. Unfortunately, some users, when they relapse, they forget how much their bodies can take. They take a little too much and, bam. I've seen it a million times before."

Baker couldn't believe Malcolm forgot to mention that Ericka was a junkie. Why would he go out on a limb on the words of an addict?

"Any way you can speed up the autopsy on this one?" Baker asked, knowing it was a futile request. Unlike Gwen, this guy was a real by-the-book sonofabitch.

"No promises, but I am going to put a rush on the toxicology report for you."

"You think you'll find something other than heroin in her system?"

"I don't know, but something doesn't sit right with me. I know you're feeling the same."

Baker was stunned by his sudden helpfulness, but not so stunned as to let the opportunity slip away.

"What's this discoloration on her face?" Baker observed.

"Tears. She was crying. Could be she had guilt and self-loathing for starting up again, or could be she was scared."

"You'll let me know as soon as the autopsy is done?"

"I'll call you if I see anything weird."

"Good man." Baker patted him on the shoulder and motioned for Kasey to follow him to the door.

"I need you to call my boss, Terrence. Cherise called the production lead and told her I was here. She tried to cover for me, but my supervisor found out and has been blowing up my phone." Kasey whispered. They were huddled in the hallway's corner, leaning against the yellowed, chipping paint.

"I'll take care of it. You probably should've just called in sick today, though."

"That's the problem. I did. I didn't think Cherise was going to be at the scene. I was hoping the day shift wouldn't recognize me."

"It's okay." He took her hand, trying to comfort her. "I'll take care of it."

She jerked it back as one of the CSIs walked by, not wanting to give anyone the wrong impression. Baker flinched, but remained composed.

"Why didn't you guys tell me Ericka was a drug addict?"

"She isn't," Kasey protested.

"How do you know? Did you ever meet her?"

"No, but I trust Mal and I even trust Selena on this. Their instincts would have gone haywire if they thought Ericka wasn't trustworthy. Something is going on here, Terry. Don't you see?"

"Yeah, I see, but there's nothing we can do about it right now. Come on, this shit is getting crazy. We need to get to Tory's apartment. Now." He grabbed her hand for the second time and lead her to the car. This time, she didn't pull back.

#

"Mal's awake," Kasey remarked, putting the phone back in her pocket as she climbed through the crime scene tape.

"That was Gwen?"

"Yeah, she's with him. She's trying to see if he can remember anything that happened last night, but he's pretty hazy."

"When should we tell him about Ericka?"

"Let's accomplish this first. Then we can share good news, bad news with the entire class."

"You know, I'm impressed." Baker sifted through overturned ashtrays and drug paraphernalia littering the living room floor. Couch cushions were shredded, cabinets and drawers opened, papers strewn across the room. Someone had definitely looked for something.

"About what?"

"I'm impressed Mal got all three of you ladies to work together peacefully on this. He must have some power of seduction."

Kasey rolled her eyes. "We're not all pining for him, you know."

"Or maybe you don't know that you are," Baker muttered.

"What is your deal, Terry? Are you still mad I tricked you yesterday? Should we talk about it?"

"Not here." He stole a glance at her; the color rising in her cheeks only made him want her more. Walking towards the bedroom to distract himself, he found the bathroom Selena described, nestled in the corner, dark and windowless. He flicked on the lights, but the room was still bathed in darkness. Kasey turned on the flashlight app on her phone.

"Good thinking."

"I don't see the compartment Selena was talking about." She scanned the room, the beam of LED light illuminating it all.

Baker pulled out his pocketknife.

"These buildings were built in the seventies, right?" He started towards the wall between the toilet and the tub. "Back then, they built compartments right in the wall where the standing pipes are. You pulled open the door and there would be a small valve that you could turn to cut off the water to your tub." He traced a finger around a part of the same wall, slowly pushing until there was a softness in the sheetrock. The tip of his knife sliced through like butter.

"Tory did pretty well with this patch job, but you can see a silhouette of where the paint overlapped." Baker explained. "He took out the bulb in this room on purpose. He may be a paranoid sonofabitch, but he wasn't dumb."

The detective made a rectangular cut through the wall, slowly peeling it backwards to reveal a rusted metal valve and a small cardboard box embedded between the pipes.

"Were you a plumber in your past life? How do you know so much about this stuff?" Kasey joked.

"Not a plumber, but I've fixed a few leaks in my life." Her partner chuckled, dragging the box out. They moved towards the bedroom, squinting from the natural light coming through the balcony door.

"I'm not oblivious to the fact that you like me." She sat on the bed, smoothing out the rumpled sheets, avoiding Terry's eyes.

He sighed and sat down next to her, cradling the box on his lap. "Then why pretend?"

"Because I feel guilt and confusion all the time." She broke down. "If I like you back, it's real and Bruce is really gone. And if he's really gone, then am I being unfaithful for wanting to have another relationship?"

"I think the vows only extend 'til death do you part'." Baker tried to cheer her up.

"Not our vows," she whispered. Baker placed his large, calloused hand over hers, clasping it gently.

"He's been gone for years now, Kase. I was there. I think he would want you to move on and be happy, as cliché as that sounds. And it doesn't have to be with me, but I hate seeing you so hollow. You're like a ghost walking through the lab."

He reached for her chin, turning her face towards him, searching her expression. "Am I wrong?"

She threw her arms around his neck and kissed him—a deep, penetrating kiss. His heart skipped a beat from the initial surprise, then he leaned into it and kissed her back.

32

Avengers assemble!

Selena rolled her eyes at Kasey's group text. She could be so childish, but they must have gotten some good news, or else she wouldn't have texted everyone to return to Gwen's apartment.

"Miles, this will be my last stop for today." She gave him the address to the Hanover.

"Yes, ma'am." He sounded almost disappointed. He made over three hundred dollars by chauffeuring this mysterious beauty around. After this stop, he could quit for the day and smoke a bowl before meeting up with the boys for drinks. Maybe he'd get lucky tonight and release some of this tension that's been building up. As he pulled up to the fancy high rise, a gloved attendant opened the door, greeting Selena.

"Thanks for all your help." She tossed another hundred-dollar bill on his lap and winked. "Keep the change."

"Hey."

She turned around to a boyish smile and a card thrust in her face. "If you ever need a chauffeur, or anything else. Call me."

The balls on this kid. She took the card and folded it into her bra.

Gwen opened the door in a wispy summer dress that highlighted her neckline and her silhouette. In the light of day, the apartment was warm and classic, a home built for two wealthy, idealistic people, ready to start a life together. Mal was perched on the couch, still shirtless and bandaged, but with a little more color on his face.

"Now we're all here, we can start sharing." Kase spoke from the kitchen, digging through Gwen's refrigerator again. She pulled out a plastic container. "You don't mind, do you? I haven't eaten lunch yet."

Not waiting for a reply, she tossed the container in the microwave.

"Mal, why don't you start first? What happened last night and why didn't you tell me you were going to Galveston?"

"Because you're still a cop." He looked up at Terry.

"That's not fair. You know you can trust me."

"It's not about trust, Terry. I didn't want you involved. You still have something to lose. And you take your oath seriously."

"Let's get something straight right now." Gwen chimed in, folding her arms across her chest. "We all have something to lose, even you, Mal. How about we stop all of this over-protective big brother bullshit and be straight with each other from now on?"

Everyone grew silent and nodded in agreement.

"There is a bull-headed Galveston PD detective out there gunning for you, Mal. They ran the plates on your truck. Tell me everything, or I can't help you." Baker's tone was matter-of-fact, neither accusing nor harsh.

"Is it too late to report it stolen?" Mal winced at the dull ache in his shoulder. Kasey and Selena shrank sheepishly in their seats. They didn't think about that while running away from gunfire.

"Only by about ten hours," Baker replied sarcastically. Mal sighed. It had been worth a try.

"I have an informant from the old days, Moua. She runs a game room out in Chinatown."

"I know who she is. We've been trying to flip her for a while now. How did you do it?"

"Pure dumb luck." Mal shrugged. "We were trying to buy some information from her, but she wanted more than what I could pay. She wanted a favor. It was a setup. We both knew it, but it was the only way."

"Then what happened at the docks?"

"She told me to deliver money for some crates. I wasn't supposed to look in the crates, but I had an idea they were weapons. Anyway, they were smart and only delivered half the shipment. She was smarter and only delivered half the money. I was already caught in the middle and ready to run when one of the bastards recognized me. Suddenly, they were screaming it was a police raid and I'm running for my life."

"They're dead, Mal. How did it happen?"

"I don't know for sure, but I can tell you it's Moua's doing. I never had time to dial one on the burner phone she gave me, but I could hear tires screeching and more shouting while I took cover. She had her men flank the place. Were there any weapons at the scene?"

"Besides the ones found near the bodies, no weapons, no crates."

"Then she won. She took the guns, she took the cash, and she almost took my life. How are we going to fix this?" Baker listened intently. It was like studying a game of chess, and Moua was a master.

"I don't know, but you need to stay out of sight for now. I'm meeting with Langstrom at three to go to your place for an 'interview'. Don't go to your office either," Baker instructed.

"Shit." Mal cursed under his breath.

"That's not all." Baker shared a knowing glance with Kasey. "There's more bad news."

"What is it?" Selena asked warily.

"Ericka's dead." Kasey's voice was quiet and grave. A small gasp escaped Selena's lips.

"What the fuck?" Mal exclaimed in disbelief. "Baker, I told

you to protect her!"

"And I told you I had no justification for doing so."

"Well, do you have enough justification now?"

Terry went quiet. He knew Mal was right, but so was he. HPD didn't have enough resources to send patrol units everywhere because a detective had a hunch someone might be in trouble. Mal knew this too, but he was feeling the guilt of not being able to protect his client. Then another thought occurred to Baker. They might have a leak in the department as well. It seemed this shadowy figure was always two steps ahead of them. That wasn't a coincidence.

"What about the kids?" Selena asked.

"CPS has them for now. Besides being hungry, they're alright. They're going to contact Ericka's parents. More than likely, the kids will be released to their grandparents," Baker explained.

Kasey hesitated before piping up. "Are we ready for some good news?"

"Is there any good news?" Gwen replied sardonically.

"We found a tape in the hiding place you described." Kasey looked over at Selena. "Did you buy the tape player?"

"It wasn't easy to find." Selena pulled a mini-cassette recorder from her bag. "Why couldn't these guys have gone digital like everyone else?"

Kasey placed the cassette in the archaic player and turned up the volume. The team collectively held their breaths, hoping that this might bring some vindication for everything they've been through these last few days.

"Check-check." A voice rang clear. "This is Tory Evans. A few weeks ago, I received a cellphone in the mail. Yesterday, it rang. I didn't record the first conversation because I didn't know what to expect, but hopefully I'll be able to record everything from now on. If something happens to me, hopefully y'all will find this shit."

There was some stifled laughter, as if someone was in the background with him.

"You sound like a damn fool," the other voice said. Mal thought it was Jamal. "Don't be trusting no popo to investigate your shit if you die."

"Better safe than sorry." More stifled giggles. They sounded high. Both sides of the tape were filled with recorded conversations. The team listened, hanging on to every word, to the instructions, up to the last threats Tory exchanged with the voice, the man behind the curtain.

"What in the actual Cartoon-Network-sounding fuck?" Kasey spoke up as the tape player clicked to a stop. "Is this guy for real?"

"It may be cartoon-y, but it's effective." Mal responded. "Anyone have an idea who it is?"

They all shook their heads.

"Play that last part again. The part where Tory threatens him." Selena hung on to every breathy gasp and stutter. "This guy is not our mastermind."

"He's too nervous." Gwen agreed. "I could practically hear him sweat when Tory revealed he kept evidence."

"We're looking at a two-man team at least." Selena concluded.

"Maybe more. It could be the whole firm is in on it, or at least the top guys," Kasey expounded. "It would make sense. They have a lot of money and resources; they could definitely keep one step ahead of us."

"Was there anything else in the box?" Mal contemplated, lost in his own thoughts.

"An envelope, probably the one the cell phone came in and the cell phone itself." Baker pulled out two evidence baggies. "Burner phone. It's already been deactivated. The recipient address on the envelope was printed, so no handwriting analysis there. I'm going to send it to DNA and Latents. The nervous one might have licked the envelope or forgot to wear gloves."

"Digital media might pull some information from the burner." Mal conceded.

"Here's hoping." Baker shrugged. At least they confirmed that the theft was a huge ploy and Baker could open an investigation into suspected fraud, pull Selena legitimately into the fold, and avoid more of this sneaking around business. He would have to be careful; he didn't know how many people were in Sandoff's pockets and he didn't want to tip them off yet.

"Was Moua forthcoming with the information she promised? Did she threaten you or hurt you?" Gwen bristled at the sight of Mal tenderly brushing Selena's arm.

"It was fine. She kept up her end of the bargain. She didn't seem surprised or too worried that you were hurt, though."

"I expected nothing less."

"You'll never guess who our forger is." Selena pulled out a packet with a black-and-white photo sitting at the top of the stack. "Greg Scott aka Greg Scott Lindon."

"The photographer?" Gwen asked, astounded. "We've been emailing him for months, we wanted him to take our engage—" She stopped herself and peered at Mal.

Henry only proposed recently, but they had been discussing the engagement for months. When Gwen realized the proposal was upcoming, she came to Mal to stop their liaison, but they ended up making love on his desk, and she didn't get the chance to tell him how serious things were with Henry. He was a drug more potent than heroin. Everything about him intoxicated her, and she just couldn't quit.

"Congratulations." Mal remarked coolly before inspecting the photo. "I guess it's time we pay Mr. Scott a visit."

#

"Are you alright?" Kasey placed a hand on her friend's leg, while steering with the other. Mal had been unusually quiet since they split up after the meeting.

"I've just been shot."

"You don't have to be glib about it. I know what's really bothering you."

He was in a mood. "If you know, then why are you still

asking?"

"Because if we had it our way, neither of us would ever talk about our feelings and we promised each other we'd stop doing that." Kasey knew he was brooding over Gwen's news, but she didn't understand why. He had to have known it would eventually happen. Or did he really think she would self-destruct and come running back to him?

"I thought she would." He spoke as if reading her thoughts. "I thought she would come back."

"Would you have taken her back?"

"I don't know. Somehow, her being engaged makes it real and final. I guess I'm processing."

"Nothing's final, Mal. Not even marriage," she whispered, comforting her friend with a small pat on the shoulder. He flinched as she grazed his freshly stitched wound. "Do you still love her?"

"Yes, and no." He responded as if he'd mulled over the question before. "I love what we had, but it's nothing more than a photograph. A capture in time. It was perfect, but it would never last. She deserves better. She deserves Henry."

Kasey winced. It was the first time he had ever used Henry's name.

"Do you love Selena?"

"It's complicated with her, too."

"That's your forte though, isn't it? Complicated relationships with complicated women." Kasey grinned, glancing at Mal as a small smile spread across his lips.

"My lot in life, I guess."

"Let Gwen go, Mal. You guys are toxic to each other. If you keep doing this, you'll never be able to form meaningful relationships with anyone."

"I've already got my meaningful relationship. I've got you." His smile widened as he clasped her hand.

"That's a sweet thought buddy, but I won't be your go-to forever." They laced their fingers.

"Yes, you will."

"I kissed Baker," she confessed.

"About damn time." Mal exclaimed, raising his hands in the air as if to praise an invisible deity. "I thought that guy would never close the deal."

"It was a kiss! There will be no deal closing anytime soon."

"Sweetheart, I love you and I love Bruce, but if we're going to talk about letting go, it's time you let my best friend go. Let the man rest in peace. He can't if he's constantly having to worry about you being a slobbery mess all the time."

"I'm not a slobbery mess," she protested. "Maybe a bit of a mess. You know how I feel about the whole situation."

"There's nothing to feel guilty about. We all want you to be happy." He squeezed her hand. "Do you like Terrence?"

"He has a lot of baggage, but I guess so do I. His divorce isn't finalized yet, though. I don't want to step into that mess."

"Quit making excuses. If you like him, promise me you'll give him a fair chance."

She caved. "I promise."

He playfully poked her. "That's my girl."

33

Abigail's apartment was light and delicate, just like her. Books were neatly tucked into place by cute, crafty bookends. Beach décor was placed strategically over the shelves, a bottle of periwinkle sand saddled next to a faded tan basket of seashells on the coffee table. For someone so wealthy, Abigail lived frugally. Her furniture was tidy, but well-used, and her entire apartment spanned the length of Gwen's dining room and living area.

"This reminds me of my apartment in college," Gwen commented, leafing through the mail on the kitchen counter.

"How old was she?"

"Old enough to make fatal mistakes, apparently."

"That's fresh coming from you, doc." Selena looked up from thumbing through a book. It was a Danielle Steele mimic, a place for young girls in their twenties to fantasize and to hide objects of their fantasies between the pages. "She fell in love. You can't fault her for that."

"I never would've pegged you for a romantic, Parish."

"And I thought you were a simpering sentimentalist. Yet here we are." The doctor's face fell and Selena sighed. "That was harsh. I'm sorry."

"It's alright. I know what you must think of me." Gwen picked up another book and flapped it gently. A receipt fell out from between the pages.

"I don't think anything of you. You fell in love. I can't fault you for that."

Surprised, Gwen shot Selena a curious gaze.

"So, you understand?" Her piercing green eyes grew wide, turning her into a desperate school girl.

"No, I don't understand your actions." Selena chuckled. "But I understand your emotions. Malcolm is easy to love. There's something forlornly broken about him. I get it."

"Why do we let ourselves fall for people who can't fully love us back?" Gwen thought of Abigail lying on a cold slab in the morgue, her once youthful, rosy skin now the color of ash. Alone, discarded, all because she loved the wrong man, a narcissist who had no love to return.

"We accept the love we think we deserve." Selena quoted absentmindedly.

They were now in the girl's bedroom, digging through her drawers and combing through her closet. In some ways, she was still a child. Stuffed animals in the shapes of starfish and whales lined the window alcove. Her comforter, a soft lilac print, was neatly tucked between the bed frame and mattress. Abigail was careful to the point of compulsion. Her closet was color-coded and arranged by length. She had notes and letters tacked to a corkboard by her desk, and numerous photos of friends and family lined the top of her dresser. There was no way a woman like this would hide her relationship, unless it was a forbidden one.

"What do you make of this?" Gwen laid a leather-bound notebook on the desk and ran her finger down the lined page. "It's written in some kind of gibberish or code."

"It's shorthand." Selena examined the small blocky markings. "But it's nothing I recognize. She might have developed her own style while in school."

"Why would she need to write in shorthand if it's a private journal?"

"Why indeed?" Selena mused. *Smart girl*. She deduced they had stumbled upon something important. Maybe this sweet child wasn't as naïve as they thought. If she had been careful enough to code her notes, the information contained within must be crucial, or even damning. Selena took photos of the pages.

"What are you doing?"

"Sending samples to my contact. He's a cryptographer. If he can't crack this, then he doesn't deserve his reputation." She foraged through the open desk drawer and found several more notebooks with the same blocked code, and stuffed them in her bag. "We need to take these."

"Selena, that's evidence. We should call Terrence. We can't mess with the chain of custody."

"Why? We don't even know what it is yet. Besides, don't tell me we weren't thinking the same thing. Someone is lining their pockets with Sandoff payoffs. Why would we trust them with this evidence?" Gwen pursed her lips, but silently agreed. If the information within these pages was damaging, handing it off would be a huge mistake. Once the evidence was logged into the property room, even Baker wouldn't be able to monitor it. The wary investigator pulled herself up and looked around a last time.

"Doc, there's really no sign of a boyfriend. Are you sure the semen samples weren't just one-night stands? Something casual? A girl has needs, you know."

"Possibly, but there's something else." Gwen hesitated. She wasn't going to reveal this tidbit until she issued her official report, but she had reason to ask Kasey to run the semen samples. She'd made another discovery during autopsy.

Abigail was pregnant.

34

Marc traced the naked folds of the figure in his arms, drawing invisible circles on her back with a freshly manicured finger. Her warm breasts were pressed against his torso as she laid on him, her breathing in sync with the heaving motion of his chest. He hadn't gone home for three days, choosing instead to camp out in his "smut condo", as Bethany liked to call it, with Giselle, a waitress-turned-"model"-turned-mistress to the millionaire attorney. She was beautiful, uncomplicated, and she stroked his ego as much as she stroked his cock, which was all he ever wanted.

Things had gotten so tricky with Abigail. She kept wanting more, never satisfied with the gifts and jewels he proffered. When she asked him to leave Lenore, he thought putting some space between them would put things in perspective for her. Instead, she forced his hand. The little minx had the audacity to get pregnant. He didn't know how; he was always careful, wearing condoms and providing all his mistresses with birth control pills prescribed by his private physician. He wasn't going to be tied to another Lenore if he could help it.

At first, he suspected Abigail had stepped out on him, that it was some sort of power play—leave your wife or we'll become the biggest political scandal since Bill and Monica. But when he arrived at her apartment the night before she died, there was a sense of puerile desperation in her voice, in her eyes, in the way she clung to his back as he fucked her on the breakfast table. It told him she genuinely believed the child was his and they would be a family, live out some white picket fence delusion she manufactured in her head. The naivete that once attracted him became vexing and trite.

After their tryst, he told her in no uncertain terms that he wasn't going to set his world on fire just to settle her tantrums. If she wanted to remain in his world at all, she would be a mistress, no more. He left a sobbing Abigail curled up on her bed, clutching a doll like a little girl. A sense of relief washed over him when he heard she was dead. One less thing to cross off his list.

#

"How may I help you?" a sultry voice blared through the speaker.

"Please tell Mr. Scott that Chiara Lisbon is here to see him."

"Certainly. Please come on through." A short buzz pierced the air and the metallic gates ground open.

"This is ridiculous." Kasey pulled down the borrowed white romper hugging her thighs. She didn't know whether to continue tugging them down or to cover the inconvenient cut-out in her midsection. Then there was the abnormally large bow, planted right on her chest, which kept catching strands of her hair.

How does Selena maneuver in shit like this every day?

"Stop fidgeting. You look great," Mal smirked.

"I hate you." Kasey stumbled from the height of her Valentino peep-toe heels. "Why do I have to dress like this, and why do you get to wear pants?"

"You *are* wearing pants!" Mal hissed.

After they left the Hanover, Selena called Mal to say that Gia grabbed a bit of gossip from Greg Scott's personal assistant. The agency was sending over an up-and-coming model for head shots, and since Scott had never met her before, it was the perfect cover for a bit of subterfuge. Of course, Selena wouldn't allow Kasey to show up in scrubs, so they made a detour to the hotel room. Kase showered and changed readily enough, but it took an hour of wrestling before Selena coaxed the pigheaded analyst to allowing her to fix Kase's hair and make-up. It was more exhausting than dressing a small child on sugar.

The plan was simple: gain access, get Scott into an office or studio alone, and then beat the crap out of him for the information they needed, all before the real Chiara Lisbon showed up and someone called the police.

"Brilliant plan, Mal. He's totally going to fall for this because I look like an actual model," Kasey continued. "Need I remind you, I'm only five feet tall? Just missing a dozen inches there."

"Kase, apparently this guy is a creep. He has a list of harassment lawsuits as long as my leg. Flirt with him long enough that I can punch his pervy ass in the face. He won't even notice how short you are if he thinks he's going to get in your pants."

"You know, until two days ago, I hadn't flirted with a guy in ages, and now suddenly I'm swinging my hips at everything with a penis. Selena should do this."

"Except he knows Selena, and he doesn't trust her. Just calm down. I'm going to be right next to you. If anything goes wrong, just kick him in the balls and run. He deserves it anyway."

Greg Scott was a world-renowned photographer who started out schlepping for the famous Gianni Bautista in Milan. After a whirlwind affair with Gianni's daughter, his black-and-white nude photos of her leaked, and they became media sensations. Rumor had it, Alessa Bautista leaked them herself, to spite a father who cheated with models, and therefore hindered her chances of becoming one.

As Alessa's career skyrocketed, so did Scott's. Supermodels from all over Europe wanted a session with him, and lesser models would go to any lengths, including taking off their clothes, to be in the same room as him. He was known as the "career launcher". Despite his lewd behavior, he understood aesthetics, angles, and lighting. He could deftly hide a scar on your face while highlighting your cheekbones. Scott went from carrying bags and testing camera flashes, to owning a villa in Tuscany, a condo in New York, and a sprawling mansion in Beverly Hills.

Just as his stardom reached new heights, the philandering photographer went on a drug binge with the barely legal daughter of a top casting director in Hollywood. The young socialite choked on her own vomit in the bathroom while he slept off a cocktail of prescription drugs and whiskey on the couch. After a week in an induced coma, her parents opted to pull the plug.

And just like that, Hollywood blackballed Greg Scott. The jobs dried up. Past associates stopped taking his calls, and soon, he found himself photographing weddings to make ends meet. It wasn't the worst vocation, capturing couples at the happiest moment of their lives, but it was a steep fall from grace. He soon sold all his properties and retreated to a mansion in the Memorial area of Houston, where he built a large studio attachment for boudoir shoots. Nowadays, his clients were either happy couples or lonely housewives looking to revive their marriages. If the pay was good, he would take on corporate sessions for company websites. Now and again, one of his old agency contacts would throw him a bone.

Which is how he heard of Chiara Lisbon. Or, rather, how she heard of him. The infamous illegitimate daughter of Carl Lisbon, premier oil mogul and philanthropist, wanted to make her modeling debut and had requested him personally. He knew this was his chance at redemption. No one had seen the heiress, but there were rumors she was captivating. He cleared his schedule to meet with her, hoping to charm his way back to luxury.

And now here he was, coughing nervously, smoothing his dark hair and combing over the blond streaks, cursing himself for not getting a touch up sooner. Sasha's voice boomed over the intercom, informing him that Chiara was in the foyer. Scott marched across the office, taking one last look in the mirror to smooth out the crisp Italian button-down he wore over loose black slacks. He made sure the sleeves were rolled up past the elbow and tightly held in place, hoping to convey a sense of professional but casual artistry.

Nice legs, he noted as he trotted down the stairs. She was a bit underwhelming for someone who created such a stir over the years. Born to a Korean mother and an Italian father, she was rumored to have a slender figure, smooth olive skin that looked practically sun-kissed, a strong jawline, exotic features, and raven-colored hair. The girl in front of him was pretty, but her posture was forced and awkward. She was paler and shorter than he imagined, and what she wore was loose and ill-fitting. Either way, her father was worth billions, so he turned on his charm.

"Chiara, darling!" Scott smiled, holding his arms wide open.

"Ciao, Greg." Kasey forced a smile, leaning in for a hug, stunned when he kissed both cheeks. She was supposed to be European, but had already forgotten how to act. This was definitely more Selena's territory.

"Let me look at you." He twirled her. "Stunning!"

Kasey rolled her eyes internally. *Liar.*

"I'm so glad you agreed to my request," she lied, trying her best to sound coy yet seductive. "Shall we go somewhere private to discuss business?"

"Of course, dear." He wrapped his arm around her shoulder, trying to ignore the tall, muscular guy with the permanent frown standing behind her. As they took a few steps towards his consultation room, he followed them. "Just a minute. Who is this?"

"Oh, this is my bodyguard, Jeff." She dismissed his presence with a wave.

"I'm sorry, Chiara, but I'm very shy about my art. I'm afraid it won't do to have a third person in the room with us."

Mal rolled his eyes. *What a blatant creep.*

Kasey broke into a cold sweat; she did not want to be in a room alone with this pervert. "Can't you make an exception? Father makes him go everywhere with me."

"My art is very sensitive. I *insist.*" Scott's voice deepened. "He can wait here."

Kasey eyed Mal and gulped. That put a damper in their plan. *Just kick him in the balls,* she reminded herself.

"Very well. Jeff, please stay here." She gritted her teeth.

"Sasha, no interruptions. None." The receptionist nodded, and Scott smirked. This was going to be easier than he thought. She was the one that asked to see him in private. Even Sasha heard it. He would open with his usual proposal, and this cute young thing would have no choice but to give him what he wanted, or he simply wouldn't take her photos. Of course, she had the money and the pull to get any top photographer in the world, but he'd seen her type. They fixated on a desire, and their spoiled little minds wouldn't rest until they get *exactly* what they want. Lucky for him, she was fixated on his work.

Mal tapped his foot impatiently, glancing around the makeshift reception area. Scott did a great job of converting his home into a professional office. The entire front area was encased in marble. Floor to ceiling windows bathed the room in natural light, giving the entire house a natural and airy flow.

The receptionist sat high on a leather barstool at a gun metal bar converted desk, typing away on a sleek black computer. She snuck a glance at the bodyguard. He was handsome despite his grimace.

"Would you like some water, or to sit down?" she asked timidly. "They might be in there awhile." Knowing Greg, he wouldn't let her leave until she gave him what he wanted, and Greg always got what he wanted.

"No, thank you."

She dropped into silence, and Mal counted the windows and

exits to his right. He noted the open kitchen area and the pool in the backyard. Force of habit. After several minutes, he'd seen all he needed, and he'd left Kase in there long enough. Time to play knight in shining armor and sneak into the "consultation" room. "May I use the bathroom?"

"Down the hall and to your left." She pointed as the phone rang. Without looking at him further, she returned to her other duties.

You OK? Which room are you in? He texted, hoping the hallway to the bathroom would lead him to Kasey. Just as he passed the gilded mirror, there was a loud yelp and then a crash coming from the double doors. He burst through, pulling his gun from its holster, in time to see Scott collapse from a left hook. The short, wiry girl then pummeled him to the ground.

"Kase, stop!" Mal closed the double doors, hoping the sounds hadn't traveled down the hall.

"Fucking pervert pulled out his dick!" she cried, clawing his face while sitting atop his chest. Mal wrangled her off his body.

"You stupid bitch!" Scott cried, getting up. "I think she broke my nose."

Mal held him on the ground, the heel of his right boot grinding into the photographer's chest. "Yeah? I'm going to break something else if you don't quiet down."

Mal aimed his pistol at Scott's face. "Answer our questions and we'll let you leave this room with your bones intact."

"What?" Scott tried to make sense of it, but nothing added up. The punch must have dazed him. Why was this model and her bodyguard attacking him?

"Information, asshole." Kasey spat out the words.

"Get up, creep." Mal pulled him up, ripping the soft Italian shirt.

Mal's hope had been in vain. "My shirt!" Sasha heard through the door. She thought there had been a crash earlier, but she didn't know if she should go in. Last time she walked into Scott's office without knocking first, she got an eyeful of some things she never wanted to see again. He had also been most definite about not being interrupted.

A grunt from within decided her.

"Greg? You okay in there?" She tapped the door softly.

Mal pressed his pistol on Scott's temple, cocking the hammer.

"Get rid of her," he hissed.

"I'm fine. Go away, Sasha!" They heard her heels retreat down the hall.

"Alright, Greg Scott, now that we're alone, here's the deal." Mal sat across from him on the metal coffee table, lightly tapping the barrel of the pistol on his knee. "We ask you some questions, you answer them. Then we walk out of here and leave you alone. If you call the cops on us, we'll report all the illegal shit you've been doing here. Deal?"

"I'm not doing anything illegal. I'm a photographer," he protested weakly. Kasey smacked him in the head.

"Let's try that again. Do we have a deal?" Mal's eyes narrowed and the barrel of the gun rose, making his grimace even more menacing.

"Deal," he whimpered.

35

R ight on time," Langstrom lauded. "I appreciate that."

"I tried calling him again, but he's not picking up." Baker responded as they walked through the courtyard of the modernistic townhouse complex. "Want to see my call log?"

Ian held up his hands, shaking his head.

"Place needs some work." Langstrom pulled open the rusty gate covering the small walkway and front door. He tapped the corrugated metal siding, murmuring under his breath.

"What's that?"

"Don't understand why they started making metal houses. What's wrong with wood and brick?" he complained.

"Galvanized metal is cheaper. Weather-resistant. Lasts longer." Baker smiled. "I would buy one of these if I could afford it."

"Then how does an out-of-work police sergeant afford this?"

"He bought this house more than a decade ago. Houses were cheaper when midtown was an abandoned lot." Baker rang the doorbell, all the while knowing it was a futile motion. "You sound ready to crucify him, Ian. You should give him a break."

"And why is that?" Langstrom's tone remained unchanged.

"He's had it rough."

"Not as rough as the kid he beat half to death. He's going to be eating his dinner from a straw for the rest of his life."

Baker leaned against the door, glaring at the veteran detective. "Listen Ian, I really appreciate that you came to me first instead of making a big hubbub about the shooting, but I don't appreciate you jumping to conclusions about my colleague."

Maybe I'm wrong, maybe Langstrom doesn't have what it takes to be a good detective. Seems he had his mind set and is gathering evidence to support his own conclusions.

"Then why don't you set me straight? I'm just going off what his file says."

Baker hesitated. As the next highest-ranking detective, he had approved the reports regarding Mal's conduct. He had to admit there was a hint of jealousy and definite bias when he signed them; he couldn't blame Langstrom for sensing that same bias now.

"I take it you read he was the lead investigator in that sex trafficking case?"

"Yup." They were walking back towards their cars; it was obvious no one was home. Baker motioned for Ian to jump into his vehicle so that they could continue the conversation while driving to Mal's office.

"Mal poured his heart and soul into that investigation. His marriage didn't survive."

"Marriages rarely do."

"His son didn't survive it either."

Langstrom grew quiet. The saddest part about the job was their collateral damage became a footnote in someone else's report. In the grand scheme of such an investigation, one officer's loss would occupy only two sentences in a thousand-page document. He obviously read the Cliff's Notes version of Malcolm Ly's career.

"So, the guy he beat up..."

"Low level foot soldier in the organization. He knew about the murder, but didn't really have any other information. Made the mistake of dangling the carrot in front of Mal, though, and then taunting him for it."

Ian whistled.

"Guy's lucky then. Can't say I would've done anything different." Though he lost nothing but time to the job, he lost a child once upon a time. A son who grew up wanting to be like daddy, who joined the Marines and then died overseas. Losing a child is all the same. The void remains with you until the day you die. At least he had closure, knowing how and why his son died. Mal would have to struggle with those questions forever. Truth of the matter was, even if he caught the killer, he would never find peace.

"I don't believe Mal murdered those guys." Baker stated; there was genuine concern in his voice.

"I don't either. But he is involved, so he needs to come clean. Eventually, everything will come to light. Better to have his version on record first." They sat in contemplation for the rest of the ride until Baker's phone broke the silence.

"Baker." A muffled voice spoke hurriedly from the other end. "Slow down. What is it now? Okay. I'm on my way." Baker turned the car around.

"Was that Malcolm?"

"No, assistant ME. They've got something for me on that murder from this morning. I'm going to drop you off at your car. It sounded urgent."

"Just take me along."

"You sure?"

"I've got time. Something tells me Malcolm isn't at his office, either." This time, Langstrom responded with a twinkle in his eye.

#

"You're sure about that?" Selena asked, astonished.

"Yes, I'm sure. I went to medical school, you know." Gwen responded.

"How far along?"

"Not far enough, if you're thinking paternity." Gwen shook her head. "The fetus was just a clump of tissue cloaked in maternal DNA." They were still standing in the colorful bedroom, the heat from the large alcove window beating down on both their faces. Selena didn't think the case could get any more depressing, but she was wrong. There was a reason she stuck to art theft. There was beauty in art, and every time a crime is committed, it's only because someone coveted that beauty and wanted to make it their own. Beauty in murder? It didn't exist, only defilement, destruction, and chaos.

Selena cleared her throat. "That's a downer, but it means we need to search harder. If you were a teenager, where would you hide your contraband?"

"I used to hide cigarettes in my shoes," Gwen offered. "And condoms."

"Well, well, doctor." Selena chuckled. "There is a wicked streak to you."

If you only knew, Gwen thought. In college, even without an au pair looking over her shoulders, she used to hide cocaine and weed in her closet, underwear drawer, places she deemed so intimate she would allow no one else to touch. Here they searched all of those, and more. They found nary a trace of a photo or love letter, no second cell phone or pager.

"Where would you hide your contraband?" Gwen couldn't imagine what her counterpart was like as a teenager. Did she come from a broken home? Or was she a rich girl with a sordid past who became good at lying and stealing as an adrenaline rush?

"Doc, if I told you about my hiding places, I would have to kill you." Selena stifled a laugh at the cliché while running through the photos lining the dresser. A young Abigail in an oversized hoodie sat laughing with her friends, her soft, full tresses glowing under subdued sunlight. A hint of a bed full of stuffed animals peeked from the corner. Another photo showed an impish child with the same-hued curls hugging a handsome couple. She was wrapped in their arms, while wrapping her own arms around a doll that looked identical to her.

"What is it?" Gwen sensed her partner's hesitation.

"These photos. What do you see?"

"A happy childhood, loving parents, lots of friends. Abigail was a wholesome girl."

"Do you notice what each of these has in common?"

Gwen's eyes flickered from one frame to the other, the realization slowly dawning. "The doll."

"It's like a safety blanket, right?"

"I had Mr. Muffins; he was a stuffed cat."

"Really?"

"I like cats!" Gwen defended. "And I was three."

"Do you still have Mr. Muffins?"

"Yes, in storage." Gwen eyed Selena sheepishly. "You don't think Abigail…"

They turned their heads towards the window ledge, where all of her stuffed animals were on display. Sure enough, lying prominently front and center, was the little blonde doll, with a head full of dirty curls and discolored blue eyes. Selena undressed the doll, looking for an opening, a battery latch, anything that could be taped to its plastic body.

"Selena, you really think she would put a photo of her lover into her childhood toy?"

"Why not? Next to her mother's photographs, it's the most emotionally comforting thing she has."

"That's kind of sick."

"I don't judge." Selena responded as she pulled at the doll's head. Finally, it gave out with an underwhelming *pluck*, revealing a round hole underneath the doll's chin.

"Got something." Using her index and middle fingers as pincers, she pulled out a thin parchment of paper. It was the color copy of a photo, faded and folded over many times.

"Contraband is right," Gwen commented, as they unrolled the scroll to reveal a half-naked Abigail, covered by a lace shawl, smiling at a sexy, shirtless man who seemed to be asleep, unaware a photo was being taken of him.

"Well, this explains everything." Selena clucked. The man in the photo was none other than millionaire attorney and mayoral candidate Marc Sandoff.

36

Kasey landed another smack against Scott's head, this time with a notebook she found on his desk. Her silk romper was stained with bits of spittle and blood. Despite being a tall, semi-muscular man, Scott was a wimp and a bully. He used his authority to sexually assault desperate women, but as soon as Mal put pressure on him, he cried like a baby.

"Will you stop it already?" Scott yelped, covering his head with his arms. "You're giving me a concussion."

"Good, maybe that'll teach you to stop whipping your nasty, unwanted penis out at women."

"Hey, I never gave it to anyone who didn't want it, okay?"

"You arrogant piece of...!" Kasey grabbed a book and raised it above her head.

"Kase!" Mal interjected. "We want him hurt, not dead."

He motioned for Scott to continue.

"Yes, I forge documents on the side. Can you blame me? Shooting weddings doesn't pay for this place," Scott explained. "Fake driver's licenses, social security cards, passports. Mainly for immigrants and college students looking to drink. That's my bread and butter. But once in a while..."

"Once in a while, you dip into some real dirty shit."

"Look, I don't ask questions. I do the job and get paid for it."

"Have you ever forged documents for criminals?" Mal

questioned, but he already knew the answer. Traffickers would pay top dollar for such superior work.

"Honestly, I don't ask questions." Scott rubbed his arm, remorseful and fully aware he did. He didn't have to ask. He would be handed passport photos in large manila envelopes. Most were of steely eyed, tattooed men he would never want to cross paths with in real life. He could guess they weren't "migrant workers".

Once Mal knew Scott was cooperative, he pulled out the envelope with the IDs used to rent the van and the storage unit. "Who did you make these for?"

The forger studied the photos and gulped. They were definitely his work.

"I don't know," he lied, but Mal caught the glint of recognition behind his eyes.

"Do you know what happens when a bullet shatters a knee cap?" Mal cocked his pistol, laying it squarely on Scott's knee. "You can scream, or run, but I promise you, a shattered kneecap hurts much less than a punctured kidney."

Kasey squirmed at that last threat. He was shrouded in a dark aura again.

Greg Scott was sweating profusely and weeping. "I really don't know. Please!"

"Let's change it up a little. How do your clients contact you for jobs?"

"Email."

"Seriously?"

"I take precautions. I use a VPN connection and an anonymous email service. My business is one hundred percent word-of-mouth. It's not like I'm handing out business cards or buying Facebook ads."

"Walk me through the next steps."

"They put in a food order and I respond with a time and location."

"Real cloak and dagger shit going on here," Kasey scoffed.

"Shut up." Scott glared.

"Focus," Mal snapped.

"When I'm done, I send an email. They send back another time and location. I make the drop, and that's it."

"How do they pay?"

"Half up front, half upon delivery."

"Who made this order?" Mal directed his pistol at the ID with Jamal's picture.

"I DON'T KNOW," Scott yelled, aggravated. "It's not like I ask for names and references."

He felt a sharp crack across his cheek. The analyst's stomach churned at the sound of metal to bone.

"Kasey, what time is it?" Mal gritted his teeth.

"Fifteen til."

He was getting impatient. With Selena's help, they'd called Scott's office to say that Chiara Lisbon's private jet had landed early, and she would be at the studio a few hours before her appointment. Sasha happily consented, saying Scott had cleared out his entire schedule for her. They already wasted forty-five minutes on this jagoff, and they were still no closer to getting what they needed. He sensed the photographer was holding back, that there was something he wasn't telling them.

"Do you want a matching bruise on the other cheek?"

"Mal…"

"Shut up, Kasey." Stunned, the analyst took a step back. She didn't know if it was the pain from his wounds, or the stress from being betrayed, but she could sense a steeping rage within him.

"I think you broke my jaw," Scott squealed. He prayed Sasha would hear his yelps and call for help, but knew it was in vain. The last time Sasha walked in on him, he berated and belittled her, screaming that the next time he told her to go away, she better make herself scarce.

"Take a long lunch and never come back," were his exact words. She was long gone by now.

"You're hiding something from me," Mal growled, his eyes narrow and exacting. He laid the barrel on the cushion between Scott's legs and pulled the trigger. The muffled bang sent a tremor through the chair. Greg Scott pissed his pants. Kasey felt the blood rush to her cheeks, and she cried. This was not her friend, but a rabid beast, untethered and unleashed, gnashing and foaming at the mouth.

"V-video," Scott uttered in between sobs. "I wear a pin camera as a safety precaution. I make the drops myself, so I record them."

Mal handed him a box of tissues, motioning for him to clean himself up. Shaking, he tore a bundle from the box and began dabbing his pants.

"May I?" he asks, pointing to his computer. With Mal's approval, he inched his way towards the solid oak desk. Tapping a few keys on the keyboard, he pulled up an email screen and searched for the order in question. "I have the emails auto delete every sixty days, but this order stuck out."

"Why?" Mal's tone was even, but icy.

"Because the pay was so good."

"How much?" Kasey asked, wiping her nose with the bow on her chest. Selena was going to have to burn this outfit anyway.

Mal looked up, suddenly contrite; she must have been horrified at what he did.

"Fifty thousand total."

"Fifty thousand? For three IDs? And you didn't find that suspicious at all?"

"Money is money."

"You really are a scumbag. Give me copies of the emails and your videos of the drops."

As soon as he handed the USB to Kasey, Mal nodded towards the door. "I'll meet you by the car."

Five minutes later, the side gate swung open and Kasey spied Mal limping towards her with a black backpack on his shoulder.

What the fuck? she mouthed. Mal signaled for her to get in and start the car. Before she could shift into drive, he pulled her into a hard embrace.

"I'm sorry," he whispered, "I lost it."

She wrapped both arms around him and buried her face in his shoulder. He smelled like gunpowder and exasperation. This was the man she knew and loved for more than a decade: gentle, kind, and compassionate. She'd heard of his episode on the sixth floor, but she never believed he was capable until today.

"Please don't do that again," she requested, her voice muffled by his shirt.

"I promise."

37

etective Baker." Louis Renfield looked up from his desk, a half-eaten sandwich in his hand. As assistant medical examiner in one of the most violent counties in the state, it was hard for him to get more than a few minutes for lunch every day. "That was fast."

"Lou, this is Detective Langstrom. We're working together." Langstrom nodded at the portly doctor. "So, what's going on? Why the urgency?"

"Ericka Thomas." He chewed and swallowed. "I'm calling it a suspicious death."

"Really? Something came back on the toxicology report?" Baker asked, stunned.

"No, that's just it." Renfield finished the last of his sandwich and dusted the crumbs off his hand. "Toxicology came back negative for heroin or anything else. Nothing out of the ordinary, so that's a no to the overdose theory." Renfield waved the two of them towards the morgue.

Baker shared a glance with Langstrom before following the examiner. "Could it be a suicide?"

"It's more. After the toxicology report came back, I put a rush on testing the syringe. Then I saw this, and I knew for sure I had to call you." He opened locker thirty-one from the multitude of metal drawers in the cold room, pulling it all the way out to

189

reveal a paper blanket covering Ericka's cold, gray corpse. Vitreous fluid was leaking from her eyes and the flesh smelled of rot and decay, despite being refrigerated.

"The syringe tested positive for heroine?" Baker surmised, connecting the dots of a well-laid plan.

"There's more." Renfield pulled the bottom of the sheet up and pointed at the soles of her ashen feet.

"Is that what I think it is?" Baker asked, appalled. Purple bruising appeared in large horizontal lashes across both feet.

"Caning." Ian stated.

"Ten points to Gryffindor!" Renfield responded. "I x-rayed her feet just to be sure. Microfractures scattered across both tarsals and metatarsals. This girl was tortured for information, then murdered to keep her quiet."

"Doc, is there any way you can test for insulin or GHB?" Ian requested, pulling his phone out.

"Unfortunately, no. Insulin is produced naturally in the body. I might test the levels, but even if there's an abnormally high level of insulin, it wouldn't do much to prove murder. GHB only lasts in your system for a few hours. By the time we found her, her body would have expelled most of it. Whoever did this was a professional."

"You know who did this, don't you?" Baker asked Ian, who was already on the phone with McGregor. He held out his finger and signaled for them to wait.

"McGregor, I need you to go to my house. In my study, there's a large blue folder, bottom of the filing cabinet. Bring it to Houston. I'll tell you where to meet when you start driving." He turned back to the duo, who were waiting for an explanation.

"I have a hunch. I can't be sure yet, but it sounds like his MO."

"Who?"

"A ghost from my past. I have to be sure before I let you know. Give me a ride back to my car? I need to meet with

McGregor first. You got somewhere I can work?"

"Yeah, my desk. I'll call ahead and let them know to expect you."

#

Selena laid back in bed, exhausted from the events of the day. It was almost eight in the evening and Houston was nowhere near dusk. The merciless Southern sun blazed through the windows, waking her from a short, dreamless nap. She checked her email. Still no messages from her crypto buddy.

After Gwen dropped her off this afternoon, she laid in bed, absentmindedly studying the photo of Marc and Abigail. In the back corner, she felt imprints, as though something were written and then erased. She shaded over the impression with a pencil to reveal the same blocked scrawling and a date. It wasn't hard to guess the message from a twenty-something completely infatuated with her love affair. She took a photo and emailed it to her guy: TRY "MARC AND ME" AS KEY.

That was two hours ago.

She let out an impatient huff and thought about the last ten days. The Marc Sandoff case should've been easy; he wasn't anything more than a tool, clumsily committing insurance fraud for some menial reason: an affair, a costly divorce, bankruptcy. She didn't expect to be swept into a whirlwind of indecent liaisons and murder.

It seemed every time she crossed paths with Mal, murder was thrown into the mix. The first time they met, he was still working burglary. He would sometimes find himself hot on the trail of a suspect and, unbeknownst to him, one step behind the insurance investigator. *He was always slower than me*, she mused as a nostalgic smile spread across her lips.

It wasn't until their last case, three years ago, that Mal, now working homicide, finally caught up to her. She followed the trail of a missing Manet straight to the dead body of one art dealer and cat burglar extraordinaire, LaRue. Bewildered by the violent bludgeoning, Selena did not hear Mal come in through the side door. As he let his gaze drift towards the body on the ground, she seized the moment to take a crack at his wrist with her baton. Mal dropped his gun, stunned, but refocused in time to block Selena's left leg as she dealt an impressive sidekick towards his head. She came at him, first with a right hook, followed by a quick jab of the baton. Mal deflected both, not wanting to throw a punch in return.

"What's the matter? Can't hit a woman?" she teased.

"I've never done it my life," he retorted, this time catching the baton and deftly grabbing her arm with the opposite hand, twisting it firmly behind her back. "Not trying to start now."

Her back was against him, his warm breath by her ear as he whispered that last part. The more she wriggled, the firmer his grip. She felt a pain in her left arm. In desperation, she used all her body weight to push back, slamming him against the wall.

"Goddamn it, woman. Just quit already."

"Not today," she grunted, slamming her head backwards.

"Fuck!" He thought he had a pretty hard head, but this feisty chick nearly cracked his skull. In a last effort to subdue her, he threw his arms around her slim body and took her to the ground, pinning her with his weight.

"Had enough?" he asked, as they breathily gazed at each other. Even with blood dripping from his nose, he was a sight for sore eyes.

That was their first dance.

Her phone vibrated, pulling her from her thoughts. It was a brief email.

VIDEO CHAT. 10 MINS. THE USUAL METHOD.

38

"Hello gorgeous," A heavily accented, cloaked figure spoke through the video conference.

"Hi Caduceus," Selena responded. "You're losing your touch."

"What do you mean?"

"Two-and-a-half hours?" She tapped her watch.

"Give me a break darling, it takes way longer to decrypt someone's made-up language than a text-based code." The voice scoffed. Selena didn't know why he always insisted on doing video chat with her when she never got to see what he looked like. Caduceus loved cosplay and wore them often. It was anonymity that he appreciated more than anything, and he cloaked it with humor.

"Raven, really?"

"Teen Titans is one of my favorite cartoons, alright?"

She long suspected that Caduceus might be quite young and also a woman, but who was she to question their anonymity? She encountered the hacker in another life, long before she became an insurance investigator. By her estimation, Caduceus couldn't have been over fifteen, but he was brilliant, and he adored her, prioritizing anything she sent him above anyone else's requests.

"I've been meaning to ask, why did you pick the name

Caduceus? Isn't that like a medical symbol?" Selena pulled one of Abigail's leather-bound notebooks from her bag.

"Contrary to popular belief, the staff of Caduceus belongs to Hermes, the messenger god. The rod of Asclepius is what should have been used as the medical symbol. US Military fucked up big time on that one."

"You are so wise," Selena quipped, but she was impressed. "Please tell me you solved the cipher."

"Unfortunately, no. Thanks to your hint, I got further than I would have without it."

"Oh." The investigator dropped her shoulders in disappointment. She was hoping for a key so she could spend the rest of the night translating the symbols in these notebooks.

"Don't be too disappointed. Thanks to you, we got the letter E, the most used letter in the English language. We also got A, R, C, N, D, and M. Worthy letters, all." Selena could hear typing on Caduceus's end. "So based on that context, and that our novice cryptographer did not bother to make up symbols for their numbers, a few things were repeated over and over on those pages you sent me."

Suddenly the video feed switched from Caduceus's ridiculous costume to a text screen.

ADAM _ _ AN_

"Great, I'll just look up all the Adams in Houston." Selena replied drily.

"O, ye of little faith. I'm not done yet." More heavy clacking on the keyboard.

1:10C_08532

"Using the process of elimination, I deduced that is a federal case number for a lawsuit filed in the Southern District, which makes the missing letter there a 'V'. Now I have the V, which isn't great because it's like the fifth to last letter frequently used." The hacker rambled on.

"Caduceus, focus."

"Right, sorry. I looked up that case number and it is a civil lawsuit against someone named Adam Hoang, which, bazinga, fits our missing letters!" Caduceus yelped triumphantly.

"Send me the lawsuit?" She was jotting down the name.

"Already did!" he replied as a file popped up in the chat box.

"Great work. You'll let me know when you solve the rest of the cipher?"

"I'll send you the key and any other bits of information I gather. You know, it would be faster if you could just scan the pages over to me or send me the originals."

"I can't. There are too many and I don't have enough time. Just send me the key and I'll have to work on it myself."

"As you wish, darling."

"Sending payment through the usual method."

"Received. Over and out." With that, the screen cut to black. She appreciated that Caduceus asked no more questions than necessary to complete his work, and he probably appreciated she never tried to haggle on his fees, which were exorbitant, if she were being kind.

She stared at the desktop clock. It was well past nine and the city skyline boasted impressive multicolored lights amidst the humidity. Downtown Houston bustled with the indignant, robust pace of a multitasking parent with too many screaming kids.

She opened the file Caduceus sent and sighed. It was time to order a late dinner; she was going to be up all night.

39

Carl looked up as the door made a soft *ding dong*. Mr. Lincoln Lawyer was back again, the third time this week, heading straight for the cell phone racks. As a gas station attendant making minimum wage, he never paid attention to anything going on as long as no one was stealing, pissing, or shooting up inside the store. However, this guy with his shaggy Stones haircut and his shabby Lincoln had been by the station a lot these last few months. Every time, he picked up pre-paid cell phones, sometimes four or five at a visit. That wasn't too unusual, but most of the customers waited for their change. Lincoln Lawyer didn't. He'd put enough cash to cover his bill on the counter and leave, which left a hefty tip for Carl. The only reason Carl knew he was a lawyer was because he overheard him talking on the phone about some oil spill case.

"Just the one for you today?" Carl asked, attempting to make small talk. He liked to make up stories for customers who bought strange items, and in his head, Lincoln Lawyer had one too many mistresses and needed the cell phones to keep them separated. It wasn't creative, but he never purported to be a writer, just someone trying to keep his wits about him during mundane twelve-hour shifts. The lawyer's mustache twitched slightly as if to say something, then he dropped a few bills on the counter without a word and walked out. To Carl's dismay, he didn't drop as many as usual, so there wasn't much extra for the underpaid cashier to pocket.

Outside the station, sweating through his Tommy Bahama linen shirt, Adam Hoang dialed the familiar number, willing his cohort to pick up the line. He cursed the heat, but he couldn't risk the chance of talking in his office, home, or car, knowing full well that the Feds were probably listening in all three.

"Carter, this is the fourth time I've called. You can't avoid me forever. I haven't received the last payment yet. Call me back if you know what's good for ya."

#

Carter LeBlanc leaned back on his chaise, a glass of Japanese whiskey in one hand, a freshly lit Cuban in the other. He placed the glass on the side table, took a big puff from his cigar and adjusted his plush white robe, pulling at the chest area and loosening it. Lifting his phone from the side table, he sighed, knowing he would eventually have to deal with those missed calls. When he saw the strange number on his caller ID this afternoon, he immediately sent it to voicemail, but there was no doubt about who was on the other line.

As a campaign consultant, it was his job to protect his employer, but it was getting difficult. He understood that the wealthy would always be immersed in one scandal or another; money makes people feel invincible, but Marc Sandoff was something else. Carter could cover sex scandals and drug addictions. He could pay off girls who became too clingy or call trusted dealers for anyone that needed a fix to prevent public arrests or accidental overdoses. However, this was the first time he had to fix a problem this big, a problem that had become a federal investigation, and Marc Sandoff would have been the center of it had he not caught it in time.

Adam Hoang was a disease. A plague to his own people. He used his influence within the Vietnamese community to gain their trust, getting them to sign contracts for mass torts that would benefit the attorney more than them. In the city of

Houston, a substantial population in excess of eighty thousand Vietnamese people lived and flourished. While most were immigrants, these immigrants produced first generation Americans, struggling to find their identity, trying to separate themselves from the disparate idea of the individual versus the good of the whole.

Hoang leeched off this disparity, siphoning from the older generation, their pride refusing to let them ask their children for help. He promised protection, representation, and, critically, a voice for a diasporic people when they had so tragically lost their own. He may have started out an idealistic student of law, ready to serve his people. Years of struggle and poverty had revealed him as an opportunistic survivor, ready to sell out his own grandmother for fame and fortune. Once upon a time, Hoang had political aspirations, but a failed local campaign left him humiliated. He turned to facilitating multimillion-dollar lawsuits by promising defendants plucked from his own community.

Sandoff bought into this propaganda. His team's research had led him to Hoang's cheesy commercials, broadcast on the Vietnamese satellite channels. It seemed people all over Houston's "Chinatown" agreed: they trusted Hoang. He further proved his dedication and pull when he signed almost ten thousand complainants to the Toyota lawsuit. Marc was satisfied this was the man to spearhead his Asian recruitment team for the oil spill case. After all, many of the fishermen, deckhands, shrimpers, restaurant owners, oyster shuckers and marshland owners along the gulf were of Asian descent. Plenty were Vietnamese or lived within the same communities, making it easy for Hoang to initiate his "call to arms".

When the first round of emergency funds was disbursed to those most immediately affected by the oil spill, Sandoff and Hoang gained traction amongst thousands of Vietnamese people. In a masterfully calculated move, Sandoff waived all attorneys' fees for emergency fund applicants. Millions of dollars were released and people flocked to Hoang and Sandoff, hailing them as the peoples' champions. More contracts were signed, more plaintiffs were added to the ever-growing lawsuit. By the third round of disbursements, they had over thirty thousand names stretching from Galveston through Louisiana and all the way to Florida.

Hoang knew the number of plaintiffs was growing thin. They had scooped up most fishermen, deckhands, and seafood restaurant owners, but the potential for a quick profit was too great. In his greed, he gave instructions to move further inland and sign anyone who might have come in contact with seafood, stretching logic to sign nail salon owners who might have been affected by the lack of clientele on the coast because of the disaster. Sandoff didn't care. The client list kept growing. They weren't planning on going to trial; they had already gotten word that the man in charge wanted to settle.

Marc flew them to meet Lieberman in his private jet. After the mediation, they flew back with champagne flowing and a sweet young thing in each of their arms. Then, just as quickly as methane gas rose into the marine riser and ignited, the lawsuit blew up in their faces. As each plaintiff packet was prepared for exhibit submission, a lowly intern noticed that many of them were missing copies of driver's licenses, social security cards, W2s, or even a paystub. As they dug deeper, some packets were missing complete addresses or were provided with false ones. An associate called Hoang, Hoang called his client recruiter, and suddenly it was impossible to go back to retrieve copies of documents and to verify information.

"They're nomadic people. If they're not working, they're spending their hard-earned paychecks in Vietnam. They'll probably be there for months," Van, their client recruiter, explained.

"Well, do they have family? Someone we can contact? Send word that we need copies of these documents? I don't care how you do it, this needs to be taken care of!" Adam yelled into the phone, puffing out his chest, sweating bullets in front of his co-counsel.

Carter could never confirm how much Hoang personally knew about the fake plaintiffs, though he suspected he was at the heart of the scandal, using Van as a scapegoat. On top of the hierarchy sat Marc, who feigned ignorance of the entire scheme. Just as well; Carter could do with a little plausible deniability.

He had to admit it was an elaborate and intelligent scam. Hoang would take the emergency funds released to these clients, including the fake ones, and deposit them into an Interest on Trust Accounts fund. From the IOTA account, he then dispersed funds. The actual victims received their money and went on their way, while the fake victims would then use *their* disbursements at various businesses that were owned by Hoang or someone he knew. These friends who rinsed the money through their businesses would then get a cut of the eventual payout.

His biggest sin was hubris. Not only was he pocketing money from the nonexistent victims, he also started embezzling from the genuine victims. Thinking that he was swindling uneducated farmers and illiterate village folk, he started ignoring their phone calls regarding disbursement. When he was finally tracked down, he'd be abrasive and disrespectful towards them.

His eventual downfall came when he cheated the wrong grandma, an old lady with a small seafood market in Baton Rouge. Since her livelihood depended on fresh catch from the Gulf, the oil spill devastated her business, resulting in a hefty payout. When she called about disbursement and was brushed off, she lamented to her grandson that she would never see her money. The compassionate young man, who carried a soft spot for the woman who raised him, was an FBI agent.

When the indictments started coming down, Carter began by completely distancing Marc from the criminal investigation. Of course, the civil suits couldn't be avoided, but if the press got a whiff of his name near the criminal investigation? God, he could see the headlines now: *Mayoral Candidate Under Investigation in Major Scam*. It was his idea to pay off Hoang to take the fall, a message he passed to Hoang over a discreet dinner.

"Just take the money, Adam. Your life is over, anyway." Carter spoke in a low, cool tone over veal and red wine.

Hoang remained silent, stone-faced.

"Marc promises his firm will represent you at trial, if you even go to trial. The Feds have nothing on you. Technically, it's all on Van and her group of *volunteers*. There's no way she didn't know all those names were fake," he continued, in between chews. "You'll get a slap on the wrist."

"Easy for you to say," Hoang whispered. "It's not your reputation that's going down the toilet."

"I hate to break it to you, but your reputation is already in the toilet."

"I could still salvage…"

"Do you think your people will trust you? I don't speak Vietnamese, but even I know what's going on in those news reports." He ran his tongue over his teeth. "All that's left is an image of you in handcuffs running across the screen and you're toast. You'll lose your license no matter what. If you leave Marc's name out of this, at least you'll have a nest egg for when it's over. Start fresh somewhere new."

"And what would I do if I'm not an attorney?" There was a tinge of sadness in his voice. "It has always been my dream."

"Find a new dream." Carter shrugged. He was losing patience. "Run a new scam somewhere else. I don't care. This offer lasts until I get up from this table."

"How much?"

From that moment on, they were beholden to the sniveling little weasel. The money was paid to Hoang's only child, a daughter who grew up without a mother. She adored her father but, despite Hoang's best efforts to put her through the right schools and make the right connections, she became a gambling addict. She wasted her college fund and every paycheck she ever made. Her biggest aspiration was to become a professional poker player. Unfortunately, she had little patience or strategy and absolutely no poker face. She would play until dawn in a local game room in Chinatown, and now owed the Laotian loan shark more money than her life was worth. Hoang would have no nest egg when he got out of prison. He would be broke and his daughter would most likely be dead.

Carter wouldn't have cared about any of this except Sandoff's money ran dry. The idea of running a campaign free of constituent contributions was a great one at first, but he had overestimated the attorney's net worth and his nasty habits. Between his numerous affairs and Lenore's coke habit, they were bleeding the firm dry. Then there was that little tart, Abigail.

God, that was a headache. He took another sip of whiskey and rubbed his temple. The worst part of that affair was that she wasn't after Marc's money. She actually *loved* him. Genuine affection was an enormous problem in his line of work; it couldn't be bought. They all heaved a collective sigh of relief when she died, horrible as it was to say.

He threw his cell phone back on the table after listening to the voice mail. He'll deal with Hoang later. If the insurance payout would come through, all their problems would be solved. Maybe he'd have a chat with the insurance investigator. He heard she was a fireball, but he liked them feisty. Pulling his robe further apart, he grabbed his laptop and opened his favorite website. The sensual sounds of heavy breathing and moaning permeated his spacious apartment as he pulled out his cock and tugged.

40

"Get out." Kasey nudged as she pulled up to Mal's townhouse complex.

"You don't want to come in for a bit? We could order a pizza."

"As much as I would love to, I'm about to pass out where I'm sitting and I hate your mattress. I want my own bed tonight."

"Are you going to work tomorrow?"

"Nah, I took the rest of the week off. It's questionable whether I still have a job." Kasey chuckled.

"I'm sorry, Kase. I didn't mean to get you involved in all of this."

"As if you could do any of this without me," she joked. "You're practically useless. Now get out. I have to meet Baker tomorrow. I promised him I would help look for your mystery renter."

"Alright, I'll talk to you tomorrow. Drive home safe and text me when you get home." He slipped out of the car, closing the door with a light shove.

"Hey," she shouted, cracking open the window. He turned around. "If you talk to Selena tonight, tell her I'm burning this outfit. It sucks."

"Tell her yourself, idiot," he laughed, deciding that he wasn't going to call anyone tonight. There was a lot of planning to do, and as much as he enjoyed her company, Selena always had a way of distracting him from the task at hand.

His house stood, dark and somber, sandwiched between two identical units. The front gate squeaked as he pulled it ajar. It wasn't completely latched, but Baker and Langstrom had stopped by earlier. The bulb in the hallway was out again; this was his fifth time making a mental note to change it, but truthfully, he liked the dark. There was something comforting about not having the ramparts of his life visible. It made it easier to visualize what once was. The street lamp shone through his windows, illuminating the scanty living room, furnished with nothing more than a plush, oversized sectional on one end and a large, overfilled bookshelf on the adjacent wall.

A worn copy of *The Road* laid flat on the couch, earmarked on his favorite page, his favorite quote:

You have my whole heart. You always did. You're the best guy. You always were. If I'm not here you can still talk to me. You can talk to me and I'll talk to you. You'll see.

Mal wondered if Georgie could hear his words. He spoke to him often, especially on those nights where sleeplessness hung lazily in the air and there was an unencumbered stillness all around.

Mal examined his bookshelf and smiled. Kasey came over to clean a few weeks ago, and as usual, had alphabetized his books. *Meditations* by Marcus Aurelius at the front of the pack, followed by a slew of Dumas paperbacks, with Sun Tzu, Seneca and T. H. White bringing up the rear. He used to get annoyed whenever Kasey rearranged his books, but now he found solace in her compulsion. Though both Lit majors in college, they were vastly different readers. Whereas Mal sought the advice of both Eastern and Western philosophers, relishing in anything from introspection to the dealings of politics and war, Kasey got lost in the dismal landscape of Dostoyevsky or the romantic musings of F. Scott Fitzgerald.

Home. Kasey texted as he moved towards the bathroom,

cranking on the shower. There were also several messages from Gwen, asking about his stitches and then finally asking him if he was alone tonight. He sighed and dropped his phone, ignoring her.

His mind raced as the scalding water hit his wounds. He had to call Baker in the morning. Even if there wasn't enough for a court of law, he had enough circumstantial evidence for a compelling narrative. Hopefully, Langstrom would understand enough to let them ride out the case. He would suffer the consequences later.

As he toweled off, the buzzing on the mattress caught his attention. Maybe Kasey was right, maybe his mattress was too hard. Hesitating at the name on the screen, he finally picked up.

"Hey Gwen."

"Finally. Why didn't you answer my texts?"

"I've been a little busy." His response was terse.

"How are you? How are your stitches?"

"They're fine. Just as you left them," he replied, crashing on the bed and switching to speaker phone. He was too exhausted to hold it up against his ear. "What do you want?"

"I-I just wanted to check up on you."

Silence.

"Are you mad at me?"

"Why would I be mad, Gwen?" He repeated her name, maybe a little too brusque. "Were you engaged when we had sex in my office?"

"No." She was nearing tears. "But I knew it was coming. That's why I came to your office that day."

"It's time to stop this charade, don't you think?"

"Malcolm, say the word and I'll leave him. I'll leave it all."

"No." Mal asserted, summoning his will. "This has to stop. We're toxic for each other."

Toxic. A word he would never use to describe a relationship.

"Toxic? Did Kasey say that?"

"No, I did," he sighed, exasperated. This was a battle he'd

fought many times before. "Gwen, why are you calling me? You're engaged, and you always knew you were going to say yes. You were contacting photographers and planning a wedding before he even popped the question. I'm unfinished business. Let's not do this anymore."

He heard quiet sobbing on the other line. "Henry might leave. He heard everything we said the other night. He knows I still love you."

"Well, I don't love you anymore." It was a half-truth, but still a truth.

"How could you say that?"

"Because it's true."

"Is it her? Is it Selena?"

"I forgot how much I enjoyed her company." Again, another half-truth.

"I hate you." More tears.

He hesitated. "That's fine. I'm sorry you feel that way."

Ruthless and cruel. This wasn't him.

"Who are you? I don't even know you anymore."

"Maybe you never knew me," he whispered. "I'm tired. Let's put this issue to rest. I wish you all the best in life, Gwen."

He hung up without waiting for a response. He supposed it was heartless, but it was the right thing to do. It was one thing for them to mess around when she had a boyfriend; it was a whole other thing for him to break up an engagement. He couldn't make that mistake again.

He pulled out another polaroid from his nightstand. It was a copy of the photo in his truck. There was a moment when he crashed into an abyss of existence, when his only reprieve was a single, subtle touch from the young doctor as she explained her report or when they saw each other in court. She was beautiful, vivacious, full of life. He remembered the way her lips parted as she spoke, their passionate first kiss, and the subsequent affair.

For a moment, there was a sliver of hope. Could he bathe in her warmth and affection, and somehow, could she heal his damaged soul? This lasted about six months before the repercussions of their actions destroyed them. She was just an addict looking for another fix, and he was too fucked up to fix himself, let alone her. He tore the photo and tossed it aside.

Throwing an arm across his forehead, Mal cursed himself for thinking about his own relationship when he hadn't even thought about Ericka. How would he tell Jamal that he had failed protecting his girlfriend and children? Did those poor kids witness their mother's murder? Joe reported that Jamal's injuries meant he would be in the hospital for at least another week. At least he would be safe, but that also meant Mal would have to deliver the bad news there.

When he worked in organized crime, it seemed the criminals were impoverished, disadvantaged children, who grew up to be impoverished, disadvantaged teenagers. They were neglected, discarded by society, and they joined gangs so they could finally feel a sense of belonging.

The irony of it was the real criminals wore thousand-dollar suits and brunched at Quattro on Sunday mornings, and sadly, those were the kinds of crooks that were virtually untouchable. Deep down, he knew even if they broke the case wide open, Marc Sandoff would probably get off scot-free. The rest of the punishment would trickle down to the underlings, with those at the bottom of the food chain getting the brunt of it. He needed to find the Stevensons' actual murderer and clear Jamal's name. It was the least he could do. The kid had suffered enough for his idiocy.

41

Baker marched into Homicide the next day and immediately dialed Townsend from Burglary. He was a man on a mission. Instead of opening an investigation into insurance fraud and risk alerting anyone on Sandoff's payroll, he was going to have Townsend keep the burglary investigation open. He deftly name-dropped Selena Parish, a highly skilled insurance investigator looking to recover the missing art for her firm.

"I think you guys could learn something from each other, Derek," Baker advised, knowing that he was young and ready to please any superior that could help further his career. Townsend earnestly agreed to call Selena to compare notes. Baker felt bad for the kid; Selena was going to play him like a fiddle. Worse, Baker was counting on it. It was time they took control of this investigation. They had been two steps behind Sandoff the entire time, and as much as he despised Mal, they were on the same team. He'd be damned if he'd allow the bad guys to win this one.

His phone rang, and he answered before seeing the incoming number.

"Hey Mal." Baker tried to sound nonchalant. He hoped it was Kasey on the other line. She was going to help him sift through the archives today.

"Terry, is Langstrom with you?"

"No, he said he had to check on a hunch and that he would be in later." Baker hesitated. "Mal, he has a hunch about Ericka's murder."

"What kind of hunch?" He sounded less growly than usual.

"I'm not sure. He said something about a ghost from his past and I haven't heard from him since."

"Does he know that Ericka's involved in our investigation?"

"No. I haven't told him anything, but maybe we should pull him in? It might be better if we all worked together. The way this case is going, we're going to need all the people we can trust on this."

"You trust him?"

"With my life."

"Give me his number. I think it's time I stop running."

"I'll text it to you." Baker hastily ended the call, spotting Kasey strolling towards him, a cup of coffee in each hand. Her wavy hair fell in a frenzy on sloping shoulders, thin body encased in a loose V-neck and ripped jeans. There was something insouciant about her strut, as if the kiss they shared was nothing more than a casual occurrence.

"Grande Americano." She held out the paper cup. "I'm sorry for being a bitch to you."

"You weren't a bitch to me." He cleared his throat, adjusting his collar while trying to ignore the stares from everyone else on six.

"Just accept the apology, Baker. I'm not saying it twice."

She's pushy even when she's apologizing.

He changed the subject. "Do you want to go through the dirty old files first? Or do you want to watch the footage from that USB?"

"Ugh, archives first. It's probably going to take forever."

Baker smiled. With any luck, he would get to spend all day alone with her.

#

"Langstrom."

"I heard you were looking for me."

"Malcolm?"

"Before I agree to meet with you, hear me out."

"I don't think you're in any position to bargain with me, son." Langstrom's voice was stern, but not harsh.

"If I wanted to go off the grid, you would never find me."

"I believe you, but then I would have to arrest your friend Kasey. She's already admitted to being at the Port with you."

"Don't touch her." Langstrom knew he struck a nerve. He could hear Mal's jaw clench as he uttered each word. "We didn't kill those guys at the docks."

"I know." Langstrom's admission surprised Mal. "But you were there. Wouldn't be doing my job if I didn't check on *every* lead. If you were still on this side, you would do the same."

"I *am* still on this side. I just… don't wear a badge anymore."

"Then let's meet. I'll listen. You have my word."

"Bring everything you have on Ericka Thomas's killer."

"What does that have to do with Galveston?"

"I'll tell you everything, but then you're in it as deep as we are. You okay with that?"

"Hell, why not? I've only got six months 'til retirement anyway." Langstrom clucked without hesitation. "When and where?"

42

True to his word, Ian Langstrom sat with his arms folded and listened intently in the dingy, mildewed office with the wilting fern and dirty laundry. At the conclusion of Mal's narrative, he sat up straight, cleared his throat, and intertwined his fingers.

"That's a hell of a story, son."

"It's more than just a story." Mal peered at the yellowed ceiling tile concealing the proof they gathered over the past few days. "We have evidence."

"Even if I believe you, what does this have to do with the mess you made in my city? You knowingly took part in illegal activity by the Port. Now I have four dead bodies, a crap ton of shell casings, a shot-up truck, and no way to explain this incident. All so, what? So you can procure some information from a source?" Langstrom raised his voice, incredulous at the gall of the figure sitting across from him. "And you won't even tell me who this source is."

"My source is shy."

"Someone has to go down for what happened in Galveston, and right now, the only name I have is yours."

"I'm not asking you to make this all go away."

Mal thought fast. How could he convince Langstrom that solving the Sandoff case would help him close those homicides?

He wasn't willing to give up Moua directly, but if he could tie Moua to Sandoff, it would give Langstrom another name, another venue for investigation. "I'm asking for your patience and help."

He saw Langstrom's deep-set eyes flicker as the wheels turned in his head. His brows furrowed, causing the creases on his dark forehead to deepen. Ericka Thomas was Mal's client, and now she was dead, murdered in a way that dredged up distant memories, flashbacks Langstrom no sooner buried when he returned stateside. If this ghost had indeed returned, then Malcolm and his friends were going to need all the help they can get.

"I'll make you a deal. We finish this investigation together, and if there isn't an alternative answer that will satisfy you, you charge me and I'll go back to Galveston with you." Mal pulled a revolver from his drawer, still sticky with dark-red stains from that night, and slid it across his desk to Langstrom, cylinder open, butt first.

"What's that?" Ian studied the weapon but didn't touch it.

"Insurance." Mal explained. "Bag it and keep it somewhere safe. If you're not satisfied by the end of this investigation, you have my blood. Ballistics can match bullets from the crime scene to this weapon." He left out the fact that he had wrapped his hand around the gun, smudging any remnants of Selena's fingerprint. After years of listening to Kasey, he also knew to clasp the grip tightly, making Selena's contact DNA nothing more than a mixture with his own. Ian grabbed a clean napkin from Mal's desk and nudged the revolver aside before unfolding the napkin and blanketing it.

"The man you're looking for is Corporal Anthony Scachi of Independence, Louisiana, and he's a sick son of a bitch."

#

"Stop squirming like a little bitch," the squat, brutal figure warned, clamping his arm around the boy's neck, nearly choking him. With his free hand, he loosened his buckle before yanking the belt free from the denim loops. The pudgy boy struggled, his face turning crimson with terror. At twelve years old, he had learned early on it was best to stay as quiet as possible or the abuse would increase twofold. The woman in the corner glanced at him, unapologetic, through vacant eyes. She was no mother, only a creature of greed and self-preservation. As the first crack of leather whipped across his skin, he closed his eyes.

Don't cry, he reminded himself. *Don't let him see you cry.*

A second and third whip broke across his bare legs and bottom. He could feel his skin rupture and the trickling of blood drops through the breach.

The son of a bitch was sadistic. He liked the feel of his belt across the boy's skin. What was it today? What triggered his ire against the boy? Was it the missing beer from the newly purchased six-pack in the fridge, or the twenty-dollar bill allegedly stolen from his wallet? Allegedly. Truth was, Tony drank that beer and he stole that money. He was going to get whipped anyway, so why not give the abusive prick a genuine reason to get angry?

"Close your eyes, Tony," his school counselor gently instructed. "Imagine you're in a different place, a different time, and nothing they say or do can hurt you. Think of the one thing you want to do that would make you the happiest and imagine yourself doing it."

When Tony Scachi opened his eyes again, he was stout, muscular, and seventeen. The yelling no longer fazed him and the beatings were like swats on his thick, leathery skin. One particularly turbulent night, the teenager came home from his neighbor's apartment covered in the fetid smell of pot and malt liquor. The man, drunk and tempestuous, felt especially disrespected by his existence and came at him with a kitchen knife. Tony expertly dodged the thrust and disarmed him, kicking the knife to the side. Inebriated and aged, the man's movements were now slow and feeble.

As a storm rolled through their hometown, the first thunderous crash synced with a hard slap across Tony's face, and something snapped. Tonight was going to be the last night this dog would ever touch him. He dodged the second blow and mustered all his training for a quick one-two punch to the ribs. His happy place was one in which this bastard was dead. The beating was savage, made even more merciless when his mom jumped in to defend her boyfriend. All these years, she blamed him for the beatings, saying his unacceptable behavior led to the abuse, and now she was protecting this piece of shit. She jumped into his left hook, and he could see her jaw disengage as her face met his fist.

"Get out, you son of a bitch." The jumbled words were barely audible. "I can't believe I gave birth to you, you bastard. I never want to see you again." That was the last image he had of his mother, bloodied, bruised, jaw hanging loose, barely able to utter those hateful words. She'd probably get another beating once the boyfriend woke up, but he didn't care. He was out, gone, and, crucially, he had tasted first blood.

And he liked it.

#

"The rest of Anthony Scachi's story was as tragic. A kid from small town Louisiana didn't have many choices. Join a gang or join the military."

"He chose the military?" Mal questioned. "Seems he made the right choice."

"Maybe for him, but not for society." Langstrom shook his head. "All the military did was hone his skills, sharpen his instincts, teach him to be a better killer. There was always something off about him, something dark."

"We all have darkness in us."

"Not like him. There were days when I would look into those eyes and see pure evil. He enjoyed the violence, the blood, the death. Hell, he thrived in it."

"What happened to him?"

"His dream was to become Special Ops." Langstrom leaned back, his face relaxed. "He failed the psych eval three times. He was discharged soon after, and I lost track of him for a while."

"Until?" Mal leaned forward.

"You mind if I smoke in here?"

"Didn't know you smoked, but go for it."

"Not so much since my wife died, but occasionally, especially when I'm talking about this guy." Ian reached into his pocket and pawed a pack of cigarettes, lit one, and inhaled deeply. He let out a strained cough as the smoke filled his lungs. "Got an ashtray?"

Mal pointed to the floor.

"When I got out of the military, there wasn't much I could do with a high school education. The world was changing, and I had been stuck fighting somebody else's war for too long. My choices were janitor, maintenance man, or the academy. Imagine my surprise when, four years later, this fresh-faced detective walked into a mob bar and came face to face with my past."

"So, you became a policeman, and he became a gangster."

"An enforcer for the Gambino family. With his skills? Of course, that's where they placed him. He was the best damn hitman they had. We crossed paths a few more times, and then Anthony Scachi disappeared without a trace."

"He change his name too?"

"Yup. I've tried looking up Anthony Scachi, Tony Scachi, even tried looking him up by his middle name. I know he's still alive because I can't find a death certificate either."

"You think Anthony Scachi is back, and he's here in Houston?"

"Remember when I said he was an enforcer for the mob?"

Mal nodded.

"Well, his favorite pastime was caning. Lots of nerves on the soles of your feet. Doesn't take long before you start talking."

"And he liked the needle for his kills?"

"Scachi is a diabetic. He once tried to kill himself, as a kid, with an overdose of insulin. I guess somewhere along the line, he figured, why commit suicide when he could just kill other people? A slow march to unconsciousness, where you're incapacitated, but aware you're going to die. Like I said, a real sick fuck." Langstrom took a last drag of his cigarette, threw the butt onto the ground and stomped on it.

"How do we find this guy if we don't even know what name he's using?"

"Oh, he'll still be using Anthony. That was his daddy's name, and he has some real daddy issues. That's the only thing he ever knew about old man."

"Any chance you can just walk into a bar and bump into him again?" Mal joked, stretching. His shoulder ached again.

"I really hoped I would never run into him again," Langstrom replied, his voice tinged with dread. "You got a racetrack around here, don't you?"

"Yes, up north. Why?"

"Because Anthony loves to gamble. I would start there."

Mal had a better idea. If this character really liked to gamble, there was one place that every high roller would have passed through at least once. It was time to pay his old friend another visit.

43

Tanya looked up from her magazine, indifferent to the two figures standing in front of her. Few people actually came down to Records anymore. There was infrastructure in place for requests. An email was sent to their inbox, which was then placed in a queue. The ladies would take turns pulling files and organizing them before having their delivery guys bring the files to whichever floor made the request.

"Send in a request." Tanya instructed blankly, flipping through her Cosmo article.

"This can't wait, Tanya," Baker pleaded. "We might need to look at some microfiche."

"Send in a cold case request."

"Can we bypass all the red tape this time?"

"Terrence Baker, you think I don't know who you are?" Tanya glared. "You think you're so cute with your boyish charms? I know what you did to my girl, Hannah."

"Hannah in accounting?" Kasey whispered.

"That's right, sweetie," the clerk continued. An intense glare pierced through horn-rimmed glasses held in place by purple straps. Kasey shrank back. "I'd stay away from this one. He's no good."

"Word travels fast around here," Baker murmured, as Kasey giggled.

"Tanya, I'm sure this guy is a jackass, but I'm just trying to do my job. We need to look at files from fifteen years ago and some of them are archived on film, so we'll need the machine. Can we please just go down there and look for ourselves? I promise we won't make a mess and we'll file everything back properly."

"And who are you?"

"I'm an intern. I'm on grunt duty, research." Word travels fast when there's only twenty-six floors. She didn't need it getting back to the director that she was traipsing around the building when she was supposedly taking personal days.

"Alright intern, this guy," the clerk nodded at Baker, "is not to leave your side. And you, I'm watching you." She slid two passes over the counter and pressed the access button, releasing the magnetized door and allowing them entry.

"Do you even know how to use the machine?" Baker muttered as they walked down the hall.

"I'll have you know. I've had to write research papers using old newspaper articles on film."

"In college?"

"No, in middle school."

"Nerd."

"What did you do in middle school?"

"Played football, hit on girls."

"Ew, you were twelve."

"What can I say? I hit puberty early." The duo stopped chattering as the doors to the records room swung open. A tall brunette in a navy pantsuit glanced at them as she walked past, a stack of folders in tow.

"Whoa, I've never seen this room before." Kasey sucked in her breath.

"I haven't seen it since they renovated," Baker replied, equally wide-eyed. Floor to ceiling white metal shelves lined the room. Rows of blue folders pressed against each other on each shelf, resembling flattened Smurfs. Labeled tabs stuck out from each folder, revealing a case number. The metal shelves were on wheels and could be electronically moved with the touch of a button. To conserve space, each shelf could be compressed tightly against its neighbor, leaving walking space only between the rows that needed to be perused.

"I imagined this room would be dusty and gross, like a basement. This looks like something out of the future."

The bright fluorescent overhead lights reflected off metallic surfaces, causing a celestial halo around the room. A row of computers, copiers, and other electronic equipment lined the back wall. Small cubicles were nestled on the side walls, each with its own desk lamp. The room resembled a university library more than the records room of a police station.

"Well, it used to look like a basement dungeon." Baker chuckled. "This is where the budget cuts for Homicide went."

"Where do we even start?" Kasey blew a puff of air and tied her hair up into a ponytail.

"Fifteen years ago, I guess."

#

"I should talk to my source alone," Mal appealed to Langstrom. "She's shy."

"This is the same source that almost led you to your death?"

"The same."

"And you still trust her?"

"Trust? No. But she never lied about it being dangerous."

"It's your funeral. I'm going to head back to the station and catch up with Baker. Maybe he'll need some help." They both knew Langstrom was lying and as soon as Mal started driving, he was going to trail him to Moua's place. The veteran detective understood the game. If he had spent years cultivating a valuable informant, he would be hard-pressed to give them up, especially if he weren't law enforcement anymore. However, if this person were the true cause of the ruckus in Galveston, he couldn't look the other way either.

Mal's borrowed Camry turned into the parking lot of a rundown shopping center with a small smoke shop and a larger tinted space. A faded yellow "Grand Opening" sign hung loosely to the top of the awning. There was no indication of what business lay inside those darkened windows. Langstrom drove around the block a few times, surveilling the area, before parking in an opening on the far side of the lot.

Where is that damn Chrome button? Langstrom fidgeted with his phone, trying to remember McGregor's instructions on how to search on "the Google". He hated everyone had smartphones now, and that the department required they used Androids was especially frustrating. There was nothing user-friendly about the interface, and he couldn't find applications or read anything without his glasses. He missed the good old days of flip phones, when there was nothing to do but make phone calls and send simple one-word texts. He sighed, giving up. He dialed a number.

"McGregor. Run this address for me. Let me know what business is registered here. I'm out front, trying to get a feel of what I'm walking into."

He waited while McGregor tapped away on his computer.

"Looks like it's a gaming establishment. They're licensed to hold poker tournaments, et cetera. Open since the eighties, been raided a few times, but nothing stuck. Owner is a Noy Moua, Laotian immigrant, no record."

Gaming establishment, my ass, Langstrom thought. Noy Moua was probably running an illegal gambling room on top of a long list of other illicit activities, which would explain the raids. Just because she was never caught didn't mean she wasn't guilty; it just meant she was smart. He needed to know what else Moua was into and how that resulted in four dead bodies in his city.

As Langstrom parked outside, pondering his next move, Mal sauntered straight into the back room without waiting for an invitation.

"Malcolm, I'm glad you're okay," Moua feigned relief but didn't stop counting cash in her stale, dim office.

"I'm touched by your concern," Mal replied sarcastically.

"We'll talk about that later. I need information."

"You know my rates."

"No, you're giving me this for free." Moua looked up, unprepared for the sharp tone in his voice. "You *owe* me."

"It's like I told your friend Selena." Moua spoke slowly, with a hint of enmity in her voice. "Business is business. You wanted information, and it was worth more than what you could pay. Don't take it personal, Malcolm."

"Did you get what you needed?"

She paused before answering.

"Yes."

"Did you find your mole?"

Another pause.

"Yes."

"Did you have to take out all four of them?"

Silence.

"Galveston PD likes me for the murders. I haven't said shit to them, but they'll find out soon enough. The detective on the case is no idiot."

"Then I'll pay him off."

"You can't. He doesn't have a price."

"Everyone has a price." She looked up and through him with her cloudy, damaged eye. He could see a faint twitch as her mouth curled into a small smile on the acid-wrecked side of her face.

"I think what I did was worth more to you than the information you gave us. You found your mole, you got your merchandise, and you didn't spend a dime. You'll give me this, Moua."

"Or what?"

"Or next time someone burns down your building, I'll bar the doors." He fixed a hard gaze on her; she met it with the same viciousness. All these peons were growing balls; she needed to nip this in the bud before word got out that she was turning soft.

"Is that a threat, Malcolm? Do you think I'm afraid of a weak imbecile like you? Someone who couldn't even protect his own family? I can slit your throat tonight in your own bed before you can whisper Georgie's name."

"Don't *ever* mention his name. You don't get to say his name." Mal reached for the SIG Sauer holstered securely in the appendix position. His trigger finger tingled with the rage pulsing through his body. "Come for me anytime. I'm ready for you."

"Yes, but is Kasey ready for me?" Moua spied the butt of the pistol jutting from his waistband. She inched her finger towards the panic button placed covertly underneath the wooden desk.

"You'll be dead by the time you press that button," he growled.

"Yes, and you'll be dead soon after. This button isn't for the police, Malcolm."

"Nobody is shooting anybody," a voice rang out. Mal turned towards the doorway to see Langstrom walking in with Tiny by his side. The seasoned detective had charmed the hulking bear into letting him in without a fight.

"Joy. More uninvited guests." Moua stood up from her desk and sauntered past Mal. "Detective Ian Langstrom of Galveston PD, I've been expecting you."

"You told her about me?" Langstrom asked in disbelief.

"No, I didn't say anything."

"He didn't need to say anything. I knew who you were the minute you drove into Houston. You both would do well to remember this city belongs to me."

"Look, I'm not here to cause trouble. We need information." Ian held his arms up in surrender. "I would appreciate any help you could provide."

"This one has respect," Moua muttered, before saying, more loudly, "Are you willing to pay?"

"I was hoping to owe you a favor," Langstrom bargained.

Moua groaned. *Another cheap detective.*

"What favor could I possibly get from a semi-retired detective?" No wonder Mal had been keeping her to himself, Langstrom realized. She was a wealth of information.

"Galveston, the docks." The detective squared his jaw as he started his dance with the devil.

"I don't know what you're talking about." Moua's seared skin and damaged eye made it hard to discern any emotions.

"I know you're tough. You're a survivor. I can see it all over your face."

Literally.

"I'm also prepared to send the slugs pulled from the four dead bodies in my morgue to the FBI. You're better than us local guys, sure, I can admit it, but I wouldn't have to do much more than drop your name in a report. Someone will make a connection. Once you're on their radar, how long before they bring you down on a RICO charge or tax evasion?"

Mal had to admit, it was flimsy, but it was a nice bluff. Moua survived all these years because she had local politicians and law enforcement in her pocket. Either they were taking bribes from her or she knew a secret that could destroy their careers. He didn't know how she would fare if the FBI or, God forbid, the IRS came down on her.

"What do you want?" The madame caved after a long pause.

"A name," Mal answered.

44

Carter LeBlanc received the call on a melancholy afternoon as large drops of rain cascaded down the wide, panoramic windows of his office. The dizzying view made him nauseous, but he wasn't going to complain about being on the top floor with the boss. The higher you are, the closer you are to God, or to becoming one. Next to Marc Sandoff, Carter had become the second most powerful person in this campaign.

His client's "tragedy" had moved him up several points in the polls, especially as he stood, dignified, next to his attractive wife and passionately vowed to reduce crime through stricter zoning laws and increased patrols. Marc and Lenore played their parts beautifully. Behind closed doors, Lenore was a frigid bitch with an expensive cocaine addiction. On camera? She was a blond Jackie-freakin'-O, sophisticated and stately in a pleated gray Chanel dress, adorned with a simple string of pearls and a sapphire broach that matched her husband's tie. A simple gesture of solidarity between husband and wife, as Carter explained when he picked their outfits.

"Mm-hmm," he grunted. "Call her. Log everything. I'll handle the rest."

He hung up the phone and straightened his tie, still staring out the window. The sky had become a blotchy pillow of gray and white clouds. The streets below were empty and subdued, save for a few cars circling the block for parking. Anyone unfamiliar with the city would be shocked at the unoccupied streets of downtown during the business day. Little did they know that twenty-feet below laid a network of subterranean, climate-controlled tunnels spanning six miles. This system contained over ninety-five different restaurants and shops, and connected to multiple office buildings. While the unknowing tourist trotted through the streets in searing Texas heat, thousands occupied the labyrinthian tunnels below. He paged his assistant.

"Courtney, did you get the number I asked for?"

"Yes," she replied, bursting through the doors, passing him a pink note that was stuck to her index finger. Her round face was set in a bright smile, revealing dimples on both leathery cheeks and crow's feet around her eyes. She reminded him of that sweet aunt who always showed up at your house with your favorite cookies. "Did you need anything else? A macchiato?"

"That would be great." That sweet aunt also always knew what you wanted before you knew it yourself. He took out a notepad and doodled absentmindedly. He needed to devise a plan to approach Selena Parish.

#

Kasey flicked a paper crane across the desk in boredom, her head snuggled in her arm. The yellow-lined origami joined a graveyard of other cranes of varying sizes. Baker paused the microfiche long enough to scratch her head and stroke her hair. He promised they would go to lunch an hour ago; she was probably hungry and annoyed.

The morning had started slowly. After they entered the records room, they had to devise a plan on how to organize and read through thousands of cases efficiently. Luckily, though the case files were archived physically by film, the case number and descriptions had been logged electronically with a handy search bar for entering relevant keywords.

Kasey initially typed in Mal's name, but the search returned thousands of entries. Seems Mal had his hands in multiple pots.

"Makes sense. He'd been on the force for over ten years," Baker reasoned. "Try narrowing it by adding Marc Sandoff's name?"

MALCOLM LY + MARC SANDOFF

No results.

"Try Sandoff. He might not have represented any of these guys personally, but his firm would have."

MALCOLM LY + SANDOFF

200 results.

MALCOLM LY + SANDOFF + WILSON

No results.

"Okay, two hundred cases aren't as bad as thousands." Terrence tried to sound optimistic as Kasey groaned and laid her head on the desk. She had hoped Jamal and his brother shared the same last name, and it would narrow the search even further.

"We're going to need a lot of coffee."

By ten o'clock, they had sorted the case numbers by date and relevance. Any cases where Mal was the lead or arresting officer were ranked last. By lunch time, Baker had painstakingly read over fifty cases, made easier by mug shots, courtroom sketches, crime scene photos, and any other relevant illustrations. Kasey had gone through two cups of coffee, made ten origami hearts, five cranes, and two dollar-bill t-shirts.

"I'm almost to a good stopping point," The machine whirred as he patted her. "Where do you want to e—"

"Go back." Kase's head bounced up from the desk, flipping her riotous black curls into her face. He turned to the machine and rewound the film a few images.

"Shit Kase. I think you found him." They studied the keen, soulful eyes of Kendrick Johnson, comparing it to the driver's license. In the black-and-white mugshot, the scrawny, beardless teenager didn't look like he could lift a Glock-19, let alone gun down another kid on the street. The photo from the forgery, however, showed an older, more seasoned criminal. The eyes were still soulful, but the gaze had grown calloused and depraved.

45

M s. Parish."

Carter nuzzled Selena's hand. He was ten minutes late, and his feeble attempt at a handshake annoyed her further. She studied his pointy chin and hawkish features. He was dressed in a charcoal Versace suit, no tie, his sandy hair perfectly styled. His smile was balanced, eliciting warmth and trust; he was made for politics.

Except for that handshake, she thought.

"Mr. LeBlanc, to what do I owe the pleasure?" Selena pulled back her hand, trying to hide her disdain. "You were quite vague over the phone."

"I apologize for my tardiness. It was raining something terrible earlier," he explained, dabbing the sweat off his upper lip with a monogrammed handkerchief. "I just wanted to meet the most renowned investigator at Mutual Financial Protection. It's been a few weeks since you've arrived in Houston."

He met her suspicious gaze with gunmetal blues, trying his best to inspire confidence. Malcolm Ly was a lucky man. She was a little old for his taste, but much more sophisticated than anything he could get. When he called her to rendezvous, she suggested meeting at a small, hole-in-the-wall café in thirty minutes. To his dismay, it was nestled in the heart of Montrose, an area with no valet, small parking lots and plenty of hipsters

228

on bicycles.

The shop was tiny, with a small wrap-around porch, metal tables and chairs, and bar seating along the awning. The interior was cramped with a cacophony of two-seater tables, mismatched couches, and a steep set of stairs that led to a wrap-around second floor, open to the first floor, set again with a mish-mash of furniture. The coffee bar sagged to the side on the left end of the first floor, and a small refrigerator with craft beers sat dead center.

He stuck out like a sore thumb in a place like this, and so did Selena. Her lustrous hair was elaborately coifed. She sipped black coffee in a silk wrap-top and white cut-off pants; a hint of strawberry gloss stained her lips. There had been an unfinished chess game left on the table when she sat down and she absentmindedly reset the board while waiting for Carter to arrive. Now she gingerly touched the pieces in anticipation of his negotiations.

"Thank you for meeting me." He cleared his throat. She made him nervous. "It's unusual. Wouldn't an insurance agent want to talk to the victim first?"

"Yes? My methods are a little unorthodox." Selena smiled. "I prefer to trace the crime first before the trail runs cold."

"Understandable. And what did you find?"

"Mr. LeBlanc—"

"Carter, please." He fingered the tanned pawn and moved it forward.

"Carter, you know I can't share the details of my investigation with you." Selena batted her eyes. The pawns have made their moves.

"I'm sure you've shared it with others." *Like your ex-cop lover*, Carter insinuated.

"Only with my boss. He insists on a report every week." Selena retorted. Her first knight was in play.

"You know, Mr. Sandoff is *very* friendly with the mayor, even though they're running against each other. He's absolutely livid that this crime could happen to his opponent." Another knight, bold move. Carter was an avid chess-player, but he underestimated Selena's prowess.

"Carter, what is it you need?" Their knights were now in play. She was almost done with her coffee and this conversation.

"The mayor wants nothing more than a fair campaign. As you know, Marc Sandoff promised early on he was going to do this with no financial help. Now that this heinous crime has happened, he, his family, has been seriously violated. He was wondering if your company could be *sympathetic* towards his predicament."

"And how sympathetic does he want us to be?" Selena asked, eyes narrowed, inching her second knight forward.

"*Very* sympathetic." He slid a photo across the board, ending the game. She could never have predicted Sandoff's gambit would be *this*. She peered down at the snapshot of "Maree basse aux Petites-Dalles". The Monet sold for almost nine million dollars a few years back to an anonymous buyer. She didn't realize the anonymous buyer was Sandoff, or that he had the audacity to send his minion to buy her off with such a *recherche* piece.

The temptation was there. Brilliant strokes of purple, green, white, and mustard hurtled across the canvass, forming an inconsolable cliff and the infinite, placid expanse below. Unfortunately, if she accepted this piece, it could never see the light of day.

"I will need some time to *conclude* my investigation properly," Selena responded, sliding the photograph back towards the consultant.

"How much time will you need?" Carter smiled. This was easier than he thought. The exceptional Selena Parish was nothing more than a greedy, corrupt insurance agent. She only differed in her preferred currency.

"A week." Her eyes fluttered as she spoke the next sentence. "I will also need an appointment with Mr. Sandoff. It's time I meet the victim, don't you think?"

"Of course." Carter pressed his lips in a forced smile. "Please keep the photograph. Think of it as *motivation*."

46

"Why in the hell would you meet with her?" Marc raised his voice. "Didn't we agree that I would have to approve everything you do as my consultant?"

"As your *political* consultant," Carter corrected. "Otherwise, I have carte blanche to clean up your messes, and let me tell you something Marc, you stepped in some deep shit."

"*We* stepped in some deep shit," the attorney corrected, pointedly.

The half-baked plan they concocted to have someone rob him for the insurance money seemed like a great idea at the beginning. He made millions a few years back when he shorted the oil and gas options, right before stocks took a dip and thousands were laid off. Since then, he had been resting on his laurels, making passive income from his property investments. He was rarely at his law firm except for publicity, leaving the day to day to a handful of trusted managing attorneys.

Then, something happened. The older Tremel decided to retire. Bethany stepped up as director and restructured the company her father built, adding new technology and younger analysts. She called in the million-dollar debt that old man Tremel loaned Sandoff, immediately after he announced he was running independently without constituent donations. Marc suspected this was no coincidence.

"*You* asked *me* to plan it, and we agreed it was best if you didn't know the details. I'm only bringing you in on any part that directly involves you, and Ms. Parish asked to meet with you," Carter reminded Marc. For such a renowned lawyer, he could be dense. "Do you want your money or not?"

"Fine, but I want you to schedule the meeting for here, in my office."

Marc had gone head-to-head with some of the toughest criminals and corporate honchos throughout his career. He was going to treat Selena the same way he treated any witness during deposition. First, he'll let her sweat a little in his gilded conference room, let them see the power, money, and influence he possessed, throw around some paperwork through another room, yell at a few interns, and then walk into the conference room fifteen minutes late and lay it on thick with his Southern charm. It was always the eyes that got them; the infinitely glacial stare even while his voice oozed charisma. It gave rise to a level of discomfort that disarmed his opponents.

"Fine. What about Adam?"

"What about him?" Marc shrugged, uncaring.

"You owe him, going on two months now. He's going to talk." Taking on Marc Sandoff as a client was the biggest headache Carter ever voluntarily gave himself. He did it because the money was good, but if this insurance payout didn't happen, it was unlikely he was going to get paid. Perhaps it was time to jump ship.

"Then pay him."

"With what? Charm?"

"Figure it out." Marc glared. "Isn't that what I'm paying you for?"

Carter gulped. It was one thing to bribe Selena with a nine-million-dollar painting. She was a connoisseur. Adam Hoang wouldn't be able to tell a Picasso from chalk art, which made those pieces useless to Carter as payola.

How was he going to liquidate enough assets to pay this

leech?

It was time to make a phone call.

#

"You son of a bitch! You promised!"

The pathetic wail wrenched the on-duty nurse from her station. She rounded the corner to trauma room 310, where their heavily guarded patient laid writhing in pain. The police officer was still guarding the door, but two men stood by the foot of his bed, heads down. The Asian male seemed especially contrite. He held his hand out to calm the patient, only for the heavily bandaged figure to slap it away, screaming curses at him instead.

"What is going on in here?" she demanded, fearing some sort of sadistic interrogation technique.

"Just police business, ma'am." The older gentleman held out his badge.

"What sort? Did y'all hurt that boy?" Her voice softened as she continued probing; there was a kindness in the weather-worn eyes looking back at her.

"No, but we've given him some bad news."

"What about my girls? Where are my girls?" The wailing intensified as the patient shook his head from side to side, beating his clenched fists against the sheets.

"They're with Ericka's parents. They weren't harmed." The Asian male spoke again, trying his best not to exacerbate the situation.

"Do I — Should I get the doctor? Should we sedate him?"

"No." Both men objected simultaneously.

"It'll only be worse for him when he wakes up," the Asian male whispered. "Trust me."

"You two need to leave." The nurse pointed at the door, her scrubs bunching at the waist as she turned. "He needs to rest."

"I'm really sorry, Jamal. She didn't deserve this." Mal grasped his hand tight.

Jamal's cries finally died to a whimper, but tears still flowed freely from his eyes. "Don't be sorry, motherfucker. Find the bastards who did this to her."

With that, he dropped his hand and turned away.

47

ethany? I mean, Ms. Tremel?" Clara croaked, knocking timidly on the mahogany door of her employer's study. The heiress looked ghostly in a pale silk kimono. The computer monitors cast a bluish hue, outlining her gaunt face and the jagged, sunken scar. That scar had always given Clara nightmares; it added a sinister air to Bethany's already chilling demeanor.

Clara's mother, Eleanor, had been Jeanette Tremel's housekeeper and Bethany's nursemaid. A hardworking widower, Eleanor was an indispensable figure in the Tremel household. She raised Bethany and Clara as sisters. Often, the girls played together, ate their meals together, and had sleepovers with each other. No matter how close they appeared to the adults, Clara was always uneasy around her brooding companion, despite her mother's rebuff that her "accidents" were innocuous, merely child's play.

Thanks to the generosity of the Tremels, the girls went to the same private school. Though she chucked it up to paranoia, Clara never felt like any of the incidents she had in school were actually accidents. At first, they were minor acts of sabotage, like her assignments would go missing even though she was sure she turned them in. Then, her test scans would be half erased and she would have to re-take her exams. The first time Clara kissed a boy at the Sadie Hawkins, Eric's tires were slashed and a large gash keyed across the passenger door.

Before things could get worse for Clara, tragedy struck the Tremel family. Jeanette Tremel died in a horrific car accident. They pulled her daughter Bethany out, barely alive, a large metal shaft jutting from her scapula. The rod had scraped down her face and ended in her shoulder, leaving the heiress looking akin to Carrie after prom night.

There were no more incidents during Bethany's recovery and Clara left for college shortly after. Years later, the ruddy-cheeked child was now a strong, athletic young nurse, who reluctantly took a job as caretaker for the elder Tremel in order to be close to her ailing mother. While most of his cohorts believed he had retired and was golfing in exotic lands, only Clara and a few members of the household knew the truth, that Aldrich Tremel had been on a steady decline after his dementia diagnosis. To keep the company stocks from plummeting because of the disheartening news, he had quietly stepped down, allowing his daughter full reign of his company.

Even fewer people knew the loathsome state in which Bethany kept her father. Constantly berated and abused, Aldrich would peddle around the house, half-naked, with expressionless eyes. When Eleanor got sick and before Clara arrived, he would stink of sweat and human feces, picking scraps from the trash cans, and getting feverish for days. Now, his caretaker tried her best to keep him out of Bethany's presence, so as not to incur her wrath.

"Ms. Tremel?" Clara cleared her throat, her voice barely above a whisper.

"What is it?"

"Aldr—I mean, Mr. Tremel has a slight fever tonight. He's asking for you."

"*Handle it.*" Bethany shot her a corrosive glare.

"I would, Miss, but he's relentless tonight. Please, won't you go see him for a bit?" The nurse swallowed, adjusting the chestnut ponytail hanging low on her neck.

"Please, Bethany." She pleaded with her friend. "He's lonely."

Bethany pulled the silk robe tighter across her thin frame and stood with an impatient huff. She traversed the room without breaking her gaze on her employee. Clara followed behind as her employer glided down the hall towards her father's sickroom. Since his diagnosis, he was removed from the master bedroom, languishing in the drafty converted library. Bethany didn't take over the master, either. She left it cold and abandoned, forbidding anyone to dust or clean in there.

"Give us a minute." She stopped short of the doorway. Clara nodded at her shadowy profile and walked off, only turning back and hovering by the unlatched door when she was sure the heiress was inside.

"Hello, Father." Bethany's voice was muffled. Aldrich whined in between gasps of air. Her voice died down to a whisper, and Clara could hear nothing more than the hum of the oxygen machine.

"I heard you have a fever tonight." Bethany lifted the damp cloth from his bedside, wet it in the water bowl, and dabbed the old man's forehead. "Well, we can't have that now, can we?"

Aldrich Tremel's eyes softened, his chapped lips moving as if to speak.

"What's that?" She inched her blanched face towards his mouth.

"Waaa-ter." His tongue thrust drily against tobacco-stained teeth. Her piercing eyes followed the sallow hand towards a plastic cup containing ice chips.

"Aw, are you thirsty?" Bethany jiggled the cup in front of his face, grasping a few ice chips and sucking them between her lips.

"Like what you see?" she whispered, eyeing the small, rigid pillow by his side. She leaned even closer to him; aware Clara was hovering outside. "You know, I could end it all right now. Smother you with this pillow and relieve you of all your pain."

Tremel gargled. His eyes widened in panic. His fingers wiggled slowly against the satin sheets.

"Looking for this?" Bethany taunted, holding up the call button. "No one's going to help you now." Her father's breaths deepened; the gasps grew louder as he hyperventilated.

She waited a few sadistic minutes before releasing a mirthless laugh. "Relax, old man. If I wanted you dead, you would be." She chuckled, dropping her voice back to a whisper, blowing hot air into his bristled ear. "But for your many sins, you will lay here, writhing in pain and filth like the dung beetle you are. And when I'm done watching your world burn, I'll come for you. I promise."

Her voice turned small and child-like. "Good night, Daddy." She laid a gentle kiss on his forehead and adjusted his pillow.

I will destroy you in the most beautiful way possible. And when I leave, you will finally understand why storms are named after people. She didn't look back as she glided toward the door.

48

It was nearing dusk before Baker walked into the conference room with bags of takeout in tow. Kasey munched on a bag of chips, clipping stills from the video Greg Scott provided. The entire video was pixilated, save a few close-up images that might be salvageable. After a paltry lunch of day-old sandwiches and juice, compliments of Homicide's budget meeting yesterday, Kase told Baker she wanted actual food for dinner. While he was out, she traded favors with Donna from Digital Media to clear up the video images after hours.

"Name your price, Donna. Anything you want," Kase offered, in between munches.

"Anything?" The technician played coy; her Southern drawl even more pronounced than before.

"Anything," Kase confirmed. Donna named her price, and, with a wicked grin and bit of negotiation, Kasey agreed.

"Send them." The line disconnected, and Kase had sent the last of the files as Baker returned.

"Sorry that took so long, babe. It's boiling outside."

"Um, Terry, maybe cool it with the *babe* stuff."

"Sorry, is it weird?"

"A little." *Especially when you hear this next part.* "I've finished snipping these stills from the video and sent them to Donna in digital. She's going to work on it while we eat."

"That's great." He exclaimed, unwrapping the rectangular containers containing shrimp scampi, steaks, and a slew of different sides.

"Are we feeding an army?"

"Selena called while I was out. She's on her way here with Mal and Ian. I figured I would buy a few extra dishes in case anyone was hungry."

"That's really thoughtful." The analyst shot Baker an endearing smile while he unfolded a napkin for her. "So…"

"What?"

"I had to trade favors with Donna so that she would get these images to us tonight."

"Okay. What does she want?"

"You." Kasey smirked.

"Come again?" Baker flushed.

"She wants to go on a date with you."

"Absolutely not!"

"Oh, come on Terry! It's one date!" Kasey pleaded. "Do it for the cause, man."

"You can't just pimp me out. I'm not a piece of meat!"

"It's hardly pimping," she snorted, trying to hold in her laughter. Baker's handsome face had turned a dark shade of red. "I'm sorry, Terry. I had to tease you for a bit."

"I'm not going on a date with her?"

"Well, that's what she wanted," the analyst chortled. "I told her I couldn't promise anything. I *did* promise I would set up a happy hour and whatever happens, happens." She shrugged, inching her eyebrows up and down while grinning deviously.

"I hate you right now," he exclaimed, relieved.

"No, you don't."

"No, I don't." He brushed a strand of hair from her eyes and leaned in for a kiss. Her lips were soft and tasted of grape juice.

She pulled away with his hand still caressing her face. "Stop. Not here."

"Ahem." They turned to see a stern-faced Langstrom by the

door, with Mal and Selena giggling like little girls behind him. Kasey blushed, feeling like she got caught by the principal.

"Just friends, huh?" The veteran detective grimaced.

"Hey guys," Baker greeted, a lopsided grin pasted across his face.

"If you guys are done canoodling?" Selena's face grew solemn. "I hate to be the bearer of bad news, but you have a plumbing problem, detective."

Baker's smile faded, and he motioned for the trio to come in from the doorway. He scanned the hall quickly and closed the conference room door, satisfied that everyone had cleared out of six for the night.

"Are we waiting for the good doctor?" Selena searched the room, while Mal and Kase shot each other a knowing glance.

"No. Let's leave her out of this if we can. She has her own problems to deal with right now," he replied, despondent.

Baker turned from the door to face the trio and directed his attention to Selena. "Are you sure about this problem?"

"What time did you drop my name this morning in the burglary case?" Selena crossed her legs, pulling at her leather belt pouch.

"Probably eight or nine."

"I hope you all don't mind, but I skipped lunch today." Langstrom stared intently at the steak. Kasey absentmindedly handed him a paper plate.

Selena pulled out a polaroid and everyone regarded the photo with a perplexed look.

"This afternoon, a man named Carter LeBlanc set up a meeting with me. He asked about the investigation and then slid this photograph across the table."

"It's a painting." Baker stared at the splashes of color, nothing more than chicken scratch against a canvas to his eyes.

"This, detective, is a nine-million-dollar bribe," Selena replied pointedly.

"Shut the fuck up." Kasey thought the surreal strokes

resembled something from the Impressionist period, but her knowledge of art stopped there. She had taken one art history class in college and slept through most of it while Mal took notes for her.

"Don't you find it strange I've been here for a little over two weeks and Carter LeBlanc calls me the day you officially invite me to join the investigation?"

Baker groaned, disappointed. He thought the kid had a bright future; he seemed hard-working and quick-witted enough. Terrance even had designs to pluck him from Burglary to join Homicide once Carmichael retired.

"There's no way it could be a coincidence?" Kasey prodded, reading his mind.

"It's possible, but not probable," Baker replied, his heart sinking.

"Who is it?" Mal asked.

"Townsend."

"Jesus, Terrance. You sure? He's a good kid." Mal protested.

"Yeah. It makes sense. His mom's in hospice. Breast cancer." He cracked his knuckles nervously. "They even had donation cans going around every floor trying to help him with some of the medical bills."

An easy target. Corrupt bastards look for the chinks in the armor, the weakest link in the chain, nasty divorces, a gambling problem, or, like Townsend, guys who had sick family. They start out slow, offering them a free meal, some sweet talk, maybe insinuate leaving their crappy government positions to go into something more lucrative. Maybe private security or private investigation for large equity firms. They plant a seed and watch the desperation grow as the relative gets sicker, or the divorce gets nastier. Then, they offer a cash reprieve, and these guys are drawn like moths to a flame.

"Just a small favor. Just this once." It was all familiar to the three detectives. They'd each encountered these words in their careers. Though they prevailed over temptation, it wasn't hard to see why some wouldn't.

"Guys, this sucks. I also really like Townsend." Kasey popped their collective thought bubble. "But can we back up a little? Who the fuck is Carter LeBlanc?"

"He introduced himself as Sandoff's political consultant," Selena explained, picking at the roasted enoki mushrooms sulking in their oily container. "I get the sense he's more of a fixer, though. Especially after he made this offer."

Baker pulled the unwieldy, outdated laptop away from Kasey and started typing furiously.

"Got a birth date from him?"

"Yeah, because we traded all kinds of niceties when we met up," Selena snarked.

"Well, let's see what we can find." Baker pulled up a search, which revealed more Carter LeBlancs than he cared to read about.

"God, you're so slow. Give it here," Kasey grumbled, yanking the laptop back. Mal smiled as he watched his friend work backwards. Give Kasey enough time and she'd pull up every one of Carter's ex-girlfriends since elementary school and probably every meal he had for the past month.

"Here." She pushed the screen back towards Baker.

"That's creepy." Langstrom pulled out his phone.

"What are you doing?" Mal asked, peering over his shoulder.

"Deleting what little online presence I have. I don't want people like cyber stalker over there to find my information."

"No one wants to stalk you anyway, Langstrom," Kasey retorted, rolling her eyes while her friends snorted.

"Carter LeBlanc, born Carter Jenkins," Baker read aloud.

"What a dorky name. No wonder he changed it."

"Well, that's disgusting," Baker proclaimed. "Charged with two counts of soliciting sex from a minor; acquitted on both."

"Recently?" Selena's face twisted in disgust.

"Once when he was twenty-three and the girl was fifteen, and then again when he was twenty-eight and the girl, another fifteen-year-old. Looks like our guy is a pedophile."

"And they let him go?" Langstrom inquired, though his face signaled he wasn't surprised. "Must be loaded."

"Father, Carl Jenkins, hedge fund manager. Mother, Lisa Jenkins, trust fund baby. Both deceased, but yeah, looks like they were alive through both indictments. They must have funneled a ton of money into his defense."

"If I were a betting man, I'd say Carter's the one pulling the trigger for Sandoff. Shall we bring him in, detective?" Mal asked, a twinkle in his eyes.

"How much you wanna bet he's still hunting?" Baker shot back.

"Honey trap?"

"Honey trap."

"On that note, our girl Donna's come through." Kasey chimed in. The antique printer, the one piece of out-of-date technology, whirred to life, wheezing erratically as it churned out large grayscale images of a mousy girl with dark hair. The image Donna enhanced the most showed her mid-sentence, lips slightly parted, with a tiny gap in between her two front teeth.

"Yeah, there's a real killer." Selena looked into the taut, round face of a young girl, only twenty-two. Her cheeks retained the baby fat of youth and her round eyes sloped with worry. "Email me this image, Kase. I have a meeting with Sandoff tomorrow at his office." She added the last with glee.

"When were you going to tell us that?" Baker queried.

"I just did." Selena replied.

"Okay, anything else we want to share with the class?" Langstrom interrupted, playing the principal again. Just then, a shrill beep cut through the tension in the room.

"Yeah, patrol brought in our mystery man from the storage unit ID a few minutes ago. Ian, care to join me in interrogation?" Langstrom nodded. "The rest of you can watch behind the glass."

49

Carter swallowed hard, taking in the sugary floral scent of her perfume. After an ungodly long day arguing with Sandoff, he stopped at his usual haunt, ready to squander a month's worth of rent on expensive booze, cocaine, and possibly a high-end hooker, when a pair of legs and dark tresses caught his eye. Two martinis and a full-bodied Monte Cristo later, Carter learned Roxie was a sixteen-year-old debutante who learned the art of fake IDs from an older classmate, Chelsea. Both hailed from wealthy and negligent families. The girls would routinely frequent high-end bars, scoring free drinks from equally wealthy strangers for sexual favors.

Gotta love a girl with some serious daddy issues, he thought, his erection growing. In her short, red bodycon minidress, she reminded him of a much younger Selena Parish and he felt his cock throb underneath his custom-tailored suit.

"I just texted Chelsea," the girl said in an almost infantile whine, "and she said she's DTF."

"DTF?" It was hard keeping up with kids and their lingo.

"Down to fuck," Roxie whispered, her tongue stroking his earlobe. "Or down to *whatever...*" she giggled, batting her guileless brown eyes at him.

"That's good news." He bit his lip. They were now practically on top of each other at the bar. "How old is Chelsea?"

"She just turned eighteen." A little too old for him, but he was getting a two-for-one deal. Fortune was shining her luminous smile on him, a little recompense for the week he'd endured. They barely made it out of the bar before the little minx was on him again, one arm pulling his face towards her o-shaped mouth, the other hand cupping his crotch, oscillating between fast and slow motions. Her dress was around her waist by the time they made it to his door. She straddled his leg, gyrating slowly while leaving a warm, wet spot on his sharkskin pants.

"Naughty girl. Where are your panties?"

"Oops. Guess I forgot to wear them tonight." They stumbled into his apartment, slamming against the walls like a broken pachinko machine, knocking over a vase from the console table and landing atop each other on the faux-fur throw laid casually across the couch. Carter pushed the girl's head down towards his groin. The mop of dark hair felt rough and ersatz around his fingers. Just then, there was a knock at the door.

"That must be Chelsea," she moaned breathlessly, planting feathery kisses on his bare chest and stomach. "Why don't you get comfortable and I'll get the door."

Carter let out a loud sigh as she stood up and undressed. The outline of her small breasts and taut waist excited him even more. He hurriedly took off his belt as the door unlatched and Roxie's sultry voice greeted the person on the other side. Then there was silence. Curious, he got up from the couch, pants around his ankles.

"Roxie? Everything alright, babe?" Kicking off his pants, he inched towards the foyer before lurching to a stop. A knot formed in his stomach as the sound of heavy combat boots and metal scraping across concrete filled the apartment.

"Ca-a-a-r-t-e-r," a male voice sang out while Roxie giggled maniacally. As the footsteps grew nearer, Carter grabbed his boxers, staggering sideways to slip them back on. He glanced feverishly around the minimalist room, searching for a weapon.

They turned the corner and his heart sank. Two males edged towards him, swinging metal bats from gloved hands like pendulums.

Swish, screech, swish, screech.

They were covered from neck to ankle in black trash bags. Their unmasked faces revealed ghoulish smiles. He opened his mouth to scream as the first swing caught him across the face. His ear exploded as a sickening crunch echoed through the exposed beams and reclaimed wood. Carter's nose twisted unnaturally to the left. Fresh, irony liquid commingled with chunks of flesh and teeth in his mouth. He gagged before the second blow twisted his neck the other way and then he faded into a swirl of Roxie's laughter and darkness.

50

Selena waltzed into the plaza, unfazed by the marble paneling and sleek interior of the lobby. The guard at the front desk regarded her with a mixture of intimidation and awe as she confidently scribbled her name across the log-in sheet. He was used to seeing political figures, oil barons, even athletes and minor celebrities come through Sandoff's office. He hadn't seen anyone who gave off the air of owning the building and the very marble that encased the law firm like Selena did.

"Right this way, Ms. Parish." He led her around the desk towards the bank of elevators for floors fifty to seventy-six.

"I believe Mr. Sandoff's office is on the seventy-eighth floor," she corrected, searching for that elevator.

"Yes, but you'll have to check in again at their front desk. The entrance is on the seventy-sixth floor," the guard replied in a matter-of-fact tone. He slid a key fob across the scanner, motioned for her to enter the elevator, slid the fob against the magnet inside the carriage, and pushed the top button.

"Sorry for all the security, ma'am, but you can never be too careful with a law firm this size." He tipped his hat and bid her goodbye as the elevator doors closed on his genteel smile.

Selena felt her ears pop as the car ascended, marking each floor she passed with a light *ding*. Sensual jazz surrounded her as characters danced on a digital screen, flickering between news reports, the weather, and relevant announcements regarding building clean-up and closures.

A slender blond girl greeted her as the doors opened. She studied Selena's two-toned, herringbone Alexander McQueen suit, the lacey deep-necked blouse, and expensive pumps with approval, her face finally cracking into a wide, fake smile.

"Good morning. Ms. Parish? May I see some ID, please?" It was more a demand than a question. After scrutinizing her driver's license, she led Selena through the foyer towards the back of the office. "Mr. Sandoff is running late, but he's asked that you wait for him in the conference room."

"I thought I would meet him in his office?"

"Ah yes, his office is being renovated right now, and he isn't ready to receive guests there." The girl lied without batting an eye. The entire law firm was what Selena expected: expensive, ostentatious, and gaudy.

Guess money really can't buy class, she thought, judging the mish mash of contemporary art with classics. As they passed the cubicles of interns, secretaries, and paralegals, Selena scanned through a sea of blondes and brunettes, trying to spot the mousy, dark-haired girl from the camera still. There were simply too many. She would have to figure out an excuse to get her hands on their employee records.

"Right in here, Ms. Parish." The girl opened the glass door to a gilded conference room. An oversized walnut table sat in the center, almost too large for the room. It was surrounded by leather chairs, with a television on the far end, and floor to ceiling, glass windows, which could electronically be shaded for graded levels of darkness. "Would you like anything to drink?"

"Coffee, black."

"Costa Rican, Sumatran, or Ethiopian?"

"Sumatran." Selena responded without missing a beat, trying to hide the fact she was impressed Sandoff had any taste at all.

"Mr. Sandoff likes variety," the girl explained, as if reading her mind, before vanishing.

By Selena's calculations, Carter LeBlanc should have been here by now to greet her. Then they would let her sit in this room and sweat for at least thirty minutes before Sandoff would show his slimy face. She looked at her watch impatiently as ten minutes went by and Carter had yet to appear. A different girl brought in her coffee and did not seem to know whether the political consultant was even in today. Something was off.

Much like this entire case.

Last night's interrogation had generated more questions than answers for the group. Selena watched from behind the glass as Kendrick Johnson played tough guy for about two seconds before Baker invited Mal into the room and threatened to turn off the cameras. He studied the three: the weathered veteran, with his bear claws folded, locked him in a placid gaze. The bulldog, with shoulders like a linebacker, giving him his options in a surly voice. Then, there was the leader, inimical, calm, skillfully twirling a Shivworks push dagger along the length of his hand.

"We don't give a shit what your dumbass has been up to, Kendrick," Baker pressed. "We want to know who hired you to rent the storage space."

"Man, I dunno what y'all talkin' about," Johnson quavered.

"Really, you little shit?" Baker pulled out a copy of the fake ID and contract. "You want to try again?"

"We already know about the theft. One kid is dead, and the other is in intensive care. We have a warrant on its way here for the space. How long do you think you'll last in jail when we arrest you for conspiracy to commit burglary?" Langstrom bluffed. The warehouse remained untouchable, but the kid didn't need to know that.

"I want immunity," he shot back, beads of sweat forming along his hairline.

"Fat chance." Baker continued the bluff. He was internally relieved the kid didn't call them on it, but he was what they called a "three strikes" kind of criminal. One more fuck-up and he was going to spend the rest of his life counting dust particles behind bars. He didn't have much leverage.

"Well then, what you offerin'?"

"How about you be a decent human being for once and we put in a good word? You can spend the rest of your life with white-collar criminals instead of the rapists and murderers in supermax?"

Johnson audibly gulped, then dropped his shoulders and nodded.

"Which one of these guys hired you?" Baker placed two head shots on the table.

"I never saw the guy." The kid stared at the photos. "But it's not this dude. I seent him on TV. He doesn't sound like the guy on the phone." Disappointment shrouded the room as he pointed to the picture of Marc Sandoff. Of course, he wouldn't have dipped his dainty hands in any of these pots.

"Well, what did he sound like?"

"Like a cowboy."

"What?" Baker looked confused.

Langstrom snapped his head and stared hard at Mal. "You mean with a Southern drawl?" The older detective demonstrated. "Like this?"

"Yeah, yeah," Johnson agreed. "Look, I don't know how this dude found me, but he asked if I wanted to make some quick money. He paid me ten thousand dollars to rent this storage space and…"

The kid realized his error.

So did Mal. "And what?"

"Nothin'. Ten grand for the rental, that's it."

"Don't fuck with us, kid. What else was the money for?"

Johnson clamped his mouth. From the other side of interrogation, Kasey grabbed a piece of paper and folded it.

"Kase, where are you going?" Kasey didn't answer Selena. She watched as the analyst walked to the other side, briskly opened the door, and announced, "Your warrant's here. Ready to roll?"

"Deal's off kid. Better luck next time." Mal shrugged without missing a beat. Baker staggered, but quickly gained composure.

"Wait, dude! Shit, hold up!" He glanced from Kasey to the three cops in the room. "Ten grand to rent the storage space and to off that dude and his daughter."

"Who?" Baker squeezed.

"I don't know their names, fool. In midtown. The one been on the news. But I didn't do it! I just set it up." He let out a weak protest.

"Malcolm, we should go." Langstrom stood and signaled for his colleagues to follow, leaving a bewildered Kendrick sitting in interrogation. The district attorney's office could sort out the details of what charges to lay against him; they had more pressing matters.

"We need to find him, fast," Mal whispered. It seemed all roads lead to Scachi.

#

As Selena mulled over last night's events, Sandoff was in his office swearing incessantly as he placed his twentieth call to Carter's cell phone. They were supposed to regroup this morning and figure out a game plan to shut Selena's investigation down. Instead, this pain-in-the-ass was a no-show, and Marc didn't even know what he promised the insurance investigator. His strategy was to have her sweating in his conference room, but now he was the one fretting over the situation.

"Somebody goddamn better get me LeBlanc on the phone!" he bellowed. "Where the fuck is he?"

This scene was supposed to be played out for Selena's sake on seventy-six, but there were no theatrics behind his anxiety.

They had a vicious fight yesterday evening over payment. Carter had moved some assets around to pay Adam Hoang, but he wanted reassurance that Marc had enough cash to continue paying him. They almost came to blows as the little weasel threatened to walk out on the campaign, whereas Marc promised litigation or worse, if he followed through.

"Listen, you snot-nosed, entitled little shit," Marc screamed over the phone to voicemail. "I don't know what kind of point you're trying to make playing hooky today, but if you don't show up in the next five minutes, I WILL KILL YOU!"

51

Kasey laid opposite from Mal on the bed, her feet resting near his chest, tossing a ball towards the ceiling. She listened intently as he rehashed their suspicions on Anthony Scachi, now that Moua had confirmed he was known as Anthony Rizzo. After the interrogation, he left Langstrom to catch Baker up to speed while he made a phone call to Moua. Rizzo had not shown up to gamble in a while, but she would call them if he did, for the price of another favor. Mal had no intention of keeping that promise, but complied for the time being. Baker was using his resources to dig up information on Rizzo. It seemed he didn't have much of an existence besides a social security number and some tax forms. He held a part-time job at a small bookstore in a rundown part of town. When Mal left the detective last night to take the girls home, he was running down current addresses for the guy.

"Which leads us to the present," Mal finished. "How do you think it's going at the meeting?"

"Selena's probably eating Sandoff for breakfast," Kase replied, still tossing the rubber ball.

"You guys became friends pretty quick."

"She has her moments. She's good at what she does," the analyst admitted, her head now dangling upside down from the edge of the bed. "Doesn't mean I have to like her, but I'll give her a break."

Kasey paused for a moment, letting the blood rush to her head. She could feel Mal absentmindedly tickling her feet, his breathing deep and even as if he were lost in thought.

"You know what I still don't get?"

"What?" Mal was playing with her big toes now.

"If Sandoff is such a big-time genius defense attorney, why are these crimes so blatantly pointing at him? Shouldn't he cover them better?"

"I was thinking the same." He put his arm over his forehead. "It could be one of two things. Everything we have is circumstantial, nothing direct. It could be he's cocky enough to think nothing can be directly linked to him, so he'll get away with it."

"Or?"

"He's being set up."

"Do you think someone would kill Abigail and her father to set him up? Bit ruthless if you ask me."

"We've both seen worse. Besides, she's the best link to him."

"Yeah, but how could they ensure anyone would find that photo? Selena said she and Gwen found it by luck. It wasn't out in the open."

"That part, I haven't figured out yet." Kase did a backflip over the bed, tossing her curls out of her face and dove back into bed to face Mal. "Can't you lay still for a second? Psycho."

"I drank a triple macchiato this morning," Kase retorted. "Let's say we run with your set-up theory. Who do you think is behind all of this?"

"Carter LeBlanc is definitely suspect. He holds the key to Oz right now. He has access to Sandoff's home and office, all of his finances. As a political consultant, he has to know all the skeletons in that closet. How hard would it be for him to pull the strings and manipulate the situation?"

"Yeah, but to what end? What's he getting out of this?"

"That's why there's gotta be a second. The mastermind. He's

working for someone who doesn't want Sandoff winning the election. They could even be working to destroy his law firm and his reputation."

"My money's on the wife," Kase joked, using Mal's chest as a pillow while throwing the rubber ball towards the ceiling again.

"Where are you getting that? If Sandoff were destroyed, her life would be in shambles too."

"It's always the spouse on Forensic Files." His best friend shrugged, chuckling.

"You're an idiot." It wasn't the worst idea. Lenore Sandoff was the long-suffering wife of a habitual adulterer; a condescending egomaniac who probably treated her like shit behind closed doors. Was she so full of fury she would take him down despite the cost to herself?

Maybe.

"That yours or mine?" Kase asked, feeling around the bed for her phone.

"Yours. Mine's on the counter."

"Hey Terry," she chirped, smacking her buddy with a pillow as he made kissy faces at her. "When?"

Mal's ears perked as her voice turned grave.

"Does Selena know? Okay, we'll see you there." She hung up the phone and shot Mal a bewildered look.

"What?"

"Well, your theory just took a hit. Carter LeBlanc was found beaten to death in his apartment."

52

Gwen trod gingerly around the perimeter of the body, directing her assistant to get close-ups on Carter's bloody hands. Baker had specifically requested she examine this scene, insinuating this death was related to their case. His face and brains were splattered on the floor like mashed potatoes. There were no teeth left for dental comparisons, but according to Baker, the victim had priors, so she would have to settle for fingerprints to make a positive identification.

"Bag his hands once you're done with photos," she instructed. Her youthful assistant looked like he was going to blow chunks from the violence.

The fledgling medical student wrapped a plastic bag around the battered hand.

"Paper bags," Gwen barked.

"Right, sorry," the kid muttered.

"And why do we use paper bags?" she quizzed sternly. Terrance turned from his witness to stare at her. She seemed especially mercurial today.

"Paper bags allow for better airflow, reduces the risk of mold growth on wet objects," the student recited.

Gwen nodded begrudgingly before rolling her eyes at Baker. "Rote memory, but can they apply it? Nope."

"Give the kid a break, doc. It's a gruesome scene. Even I'm

disturbed." Terrance chuckled.

"Hmph." She turned back to the corpse, noting the defensive bruises on his hands and arms. He tried to shield his face; tremendous help that was against a baseball bat, which she suspected was the weapon of choice.

"Looks like he put up a fight."

"Baker."

The hairs on the nape of Gwen's neck bristled at the familiar voice.

"Hey Mal." He nodded at the officer guarding the entrance. "It's okay. They're with me." Mal and Kase ducked under the crime scene tape, treading around the bloody footprints scattered across the concrete floor.

"Is it Carter?" Kase asked.

"Right build, right hair color. We can't confirm yet."

"Why—" Mal stopped mid-question when he saw the corpse. His face was concave, nothing left but a shallow bowl of flesh and bone. He looked up from the mess on the floor to see a flash of auburn plaits disappearing into the kitchen. Was she really hiding from him?

We're not going to play this game. He followed her into the kitchen. "Hey, what are you doing in here?"

"Oh, hey. Just checking for blood evidence," she replied with little conviction.

"In the dark? Why don't you come out here and fill us in?"

She met his gaze, and he flashed her an awkward smile, trying his best to make her feel more comfortable. They walked to the foyer where Baker stood, tapping his pen on his notebook. The pallid young girl was being escorted out of the apartment; a blanket wrapped around her shoulders. The detective pointed towards her.

"That's Katy Moran. Intern at the Sandoff law firm. When Carter didn't show up for his meeting with Selena this morning, the office panicked. Apparently, she's been sleeping with him, so she knew where the spare key was. She volunteered to come over and look for him."

"How old is she?" Kase raised her eyebrow.

"Just turned eighteen. Her uncle works at the firm. Thought she could get a leg up on law school."

"Oh great… he moved up three years at least," she replied facetiously. "Where is Selena?"

"She wasn't interested in the gore. When word got round that Katy found LeBlanc, she called me and then went back to her hotel," Baker stated with no inflection. He lowered his voice. "She said we should reconvene in her suite later."

"Any luck finding mouse girl?" Mal asked. Baker shook his head. "Gwen? What do we have?" He needed her back, involved, not going through the motions.

"Death was most likely caused by blunt force trauma. From the looks of it, baseball bats." Gwen rattled on; her voice robotic.

"Bats?" Baker scribbled furiously.

"Two sets of shoe prints, a men's size nine and men's size eleven. A set of bare footprints, women's size seven, possibly? There were at least three people in here with him." The doctor kept going, emotionless.

"Looks like someone beat us to the honey trap," Mal said. "Where's Langstrom? Does this look like Rizzo's work?"

"He was here." Terrance scanned the room.

"I'm here," a gruff voice grunted from behind the entrance. Langstrom towered in the doorway in a coffee-stained button down, accompanied on both sides by two junior CSIs. Each held long objects covered in two large paper bags, sealed at the middle. The detective held up another sealed brown paper bag in his gloved hand. "Three guesses what I have here, but you'll only need one."

"Where?" Terry asked.

"Dumpster, two blocks from here."

Terry turned to Kasey. "Can we get epithelials?" The analyst grabbed the camera dangling from the CSI's neck and peered at the photos.

"No. Make a DNA request anyway, then send them to Latents. You'll have a better chance there," she instructed Baker. "We need to confirm the blood on the bat belongs to Carter, but you won't get any skins cells from them, even if they weren't wearing gloves. The bats are metal."

"And to answer your question, no, this is too messy to be Rizzo," Langstrom chimed in, staring at the bloodbath in front of him. "This looks like the work of psychopaths."

"He did like them young."

"You think teenagers killed him?" Gwen's face twisted in shock.

"I think our bad guy is unraveling. Every murder we've encountered has been clean and concise. There's nothing calculated about this murder. It's almost..." Mal searched for the right descriptor.

"Desperate?" Baker offered.

"Yeah."

"I have to get back to the station and log this evidence. Put in a request, all that jazz. How about I meet you guys at Selena's around dinnertime?"

"Doctor, you coming tonight?" the detective asked as Gwen stalked off.

"I don't know. I have an autopsy to do. Seems like I'm missing out on a lot, anyway. Brief me on any necessary information later." She returned to her work, dismissing them.

Baker shot Mal a "what-did-you-do-to-piss-her-off" look. Mal shrugged.

"We'll call you then." She raised her hand in acknowledgement and started barking orders at the med student, who was, by now, trying unsuccessfully to bag the corpse.

Kasey followed Baker towards the elevators, tugging at his sleeve. His gaunt face broke into a smile, highlighting the dark bags under his eyes.

"Did you get any sleep last night?" she asked. "You look

terrible."

"Thanks. It's what every guy wants to hear from his crush." She blushed as he squeezed her hand. "I got a few hours on the couch in the lounge. You?"

"Same. A few hours."

"Did you sleep at Mal's?" It wasn't so much a question as a hope that the answer was no.

"Does it matter? It wouldn't be the first time." She could see a twitch of disappointment in his eyes and gently cupped his face in her hand. "You and I need to have a talk when all of this is over."

"When this is over," he repeated, and disappeared behind the elevator doors.

53

Sandoff paced the length of his condo, digging holes into the hardwood floor. He sent Giselle another text message, demanding she leave work to come relieve him of his anxiety. Ever since his office received the distress call that Katy had found Carter's horribly broken body in his apartment, he had holed up here, trying to buy time before the police found him.

What the fuck did you get me into, Carter? he thought, leaning against the glass monstrosity Giselle insisted they buy to host dinner parties. His bright blue Tom Ford jacket was draped across the dining chair. The suit that was supposed to spell power and wealth to Selena Parish this morning served as nothing more than a sponge for the stink of sweat and cologne. He fell back onto the bed and stared up at the beige ceiling, beige walls, beige curtains.

Giselle had wanted everything beige, just like her personality, beige and insipid. She didn't have two thoughts to string together, and unlike Abigail, the only thing she could do for him would be to ride him hard. Abby was certainly different. Sure, she was young, naïve, and a hopeless romantic, but she was also intelligent, willful, and useful to his many business ventures. He would have kept her around as a permanent mistress had it not been for her doing her job too well. What a gullible dove to see the world in black and white. When she used her discovery of Adam Hoang to blackmail him into leaving his wife, he knew he had to end things with her.

"Carter!" he gasped, bolting upright

After he left her crying in bed that night, he phoned Carter, told him to take care of it. Did Carter *murder* the girl? Sandoff meant to pay her off, convince her to get an abortion, but *murder*? Had he been too self-involved, too relieved that Abigail was no longer an obstacle to connect the dots? This was getting out of hand; he didn't know who Carter hired, but it looked like they were tying up loose ends, and he was afraid he would be next. Sandoff poured a tall glass of whiskey from the crystal chalice by the bar, downed it in a single gulp, and poured another.

First, he was going to call his broker and liquidate his assets. Then he was going to go to the police and get protection. He'd hide out here for a few days until he could set things in motion. Very few people knew about this place, not even Lenore; besides, he had a.45 in his dresser and a shotgun in the closet. They weren't going to get to him so easily, not like Carter.

A loud knock shook him from his mental preparations.

"Giselle, that you?" he asked, cautiously wrapping his hand around the butt of the .45. He edged his way towards the door, peeping through the hole. He knew it wasn't Giselle. She had her own key.

"Mr. Sandoff, it's the police."

Impossible. He bought this condo through a shell company, a subsidiary of a subsidiary. There was no way they found it this quick; unless it was that woman, that bitch Selena. Carter warned him she had resources and she was working with the police.

"Let me see your badges. Hold them up to the peephole!" he demanded, his voice cracking. The one on the right with the short army cut held his gold-plated shield up to the door. He cracked the door open, satisfied that it was real.

"Mr. Sandoff? My name is Derek Townsend, and this is Detective Terrance Baker with homicide. We'd like to bring you down to the station, answer a few questions about your employee, Carter LeBlanc."

"IDs." Sandoff snapped, holding out his hand through a crack in the door. He studied both men, comparing their faces to the photos. The detective named Baker smiled at him confidently, showing off a set of pearly whites, offset by his dark skin. He was tall and lanky, his forehead wrinkled and wreathed with dark, bushy brows. He looked like a basketball player past his prime. The shorter one, Townsend, reached out to reclaim his ID, baring a large tattoo on his forearm. There was something off about the pair. Their button downs were baggy and stained, and their ill-fitted slacks covered expensive tennis shoes.

"The department sure is slacking on the dress code." He eyed them suspiciously. The only thing that seemed real about them were the two SIG Sauers holstered by their sides.

"Sir, a man in your employ is dead. Now is hardly the time to be judging our clothes," the short one replied curtly. "Now, are you going to come with us quietly, or are we going to make a big scene out of it?"

"Fine, give me a second. Let me grab my jacket." Marc unhooked the latch and invited them in. He shuddered at the thought of being carted out of his building in handcuffs. Anyone with a cell phone could record the whole thing and he would be on YouTube before night's end.

"Thank you for your cooperation." The tall one had an awkward lilt in his voice, as if he were speaking unfamiliar words. Marc didn't want to mess with that one. There was something iniquitous behind the smile. "Though you don't seem surprised Mr. LeBlanc is deceased."

"Well, I heard the news from my office. I trust this won't take long." He raised his eyebrow, hoping to achieve his usual authoritative demeanor. "I have arrangements to make for his family."

"Oh, not long, sir." The shorter one grinned as he shut the door. "Not long at all."

\#

"Of course it matters!" Mal exclaimed in between bites of his bun-less chicken sandwich. The chicken had been grilled to the consistency of burned rubber, but at least he would feel a little healthier eating this than the bacon cheeseburger Kase was scarfing down.

They were squatting on the grass mounds of Discovery Green, watching children doing cartwheels barefoot or learning to fly a kite. Further north, he spotted couples sharing soft kisses on park benches and friends renting canoes for a lazy afternoon row on the man-made lake. He wondered what it was like to see the world through their eyes, to never see the dark, dirty, and basest of human behavior lurking behind every corner.

"It doesn't matter," Kasey argued. "Why does he have to care if I slept over at your place or not?"

"Because he likes you."

"Bruce never cared."

"Bruce was a unique creature. How would you feel if Terry slept over at another girl's house?"

"That's different. He doesn't have a best friend, not anyone like you, at least."

"That's not the issue, though." Mal took another bite.

"What is it then?"

"The issue is you're an annoying little snot who never gives anyone a straight answer." He ruffled her hair.

"Mal, you've got greasy fingers! I just washed my hair," she complained.

"All kidding aside, you really are annoying when you do that. Why couldn't you tell Baker you came over in the morning? Why couldn't you ever tell Gwen we never slept together? Your evasion drives people insane."

"Because it annoys me when they question my actions or motives," she shot back. "It's always the same dumb questions and they can never accept the answers."

"You can't assume they know what goes on between us. We're dysfunctional and you know it. It's all about respect. You never respected Gwen when we were together, and now you're disrespecting Baker. And to add to my point earlier, you stopped sleeping over once you and Bruce got together. Why? Because you *respected* him."

Kase rolled her eyes. She knew Mal was right, but she didn't want to admit it.

She yielded. "I'll talk to him once this is over."

"You should apologize and set the record straight."

"Fine, you're right." Kase conceded as Mal patted her on the back. "Please wipe that shit-eating grin off your face."

"Come on, Sherlock." Mal stood up, brushing the grass off his jeans. He held out his hands and pulled her up. "Let's solve this case so we can go back to fixing your love life."

"You're one to talk. How about we fix yours first?" She looked at those dark, umber eyes shaded with worry. For the longest time now, he had been tending to a bird with a broken wing, and she wanted nothing more than to reassure her friend it was time he let her fly again.

54

The team filed into Selena's suite, their shoulders slack, faces haggard and somber with defeat. Every avenue of investigation seemed cut off, as if someone were eavesdropping on their conversation. After returning to the station, Baker had Townsend removed from the building, his work phone and emails suspended until the end of the investigation. He would receive flak from the lieutenant in burglary for this, but he would gladly take it if it prevented more bodies from dropping.

Selena had fared no better at Sandoff's office. Though she could sense the anxiety through his fancy cashmere suit, he wouldn't budge on employee records. There was no one in the mass of cubicles who fit the description of the girl from the videotape, and the few employees she stole an interview with did not recognize her.

"You're kidding, right? You know how many people are employed here and how many walk in and out of this office every day?" a skinny brunette sassed as she flicked her newly shellacked nails. Then all hell erupted as news of Carter's murder spread like wildfire through the floor. Marc Sandoff slipped out unnoticed during the commotion and had not been seen or heard from since.

The air was stiff with humidity and fluctuating temperatures, which caused Langstrom to develop a discernable cough. It was the first time Selena had looked closely at the semi-retired detective. He looked every bit his age, maybe even older. Flecks of gray were visible on his sideburns and on his bristling mustache. All the trauma of his occupation seemed to have etched its way into the crevices of his face.

"I heard you were the one who found the murder weapons," Selena stated, handing him a glass of water.

"Alleged," he grunted in response, taking a big gulp between coughs.

"How long before we get results?" She directed her question at Kasey.

"The request probably won't be processed until tomorrow morning. Even then…"

"What?"

"I didn't examine the bats themselves, but from the photos, I didn't see any visible fingerprints. Highly likely, they wore gloves. I don't think forensics will help us in this case, guys. Sorry."

"One thing's for sure, though," Mal spoke, fumbling with his phone. "Sandoff was set up."

His words hung over them like a damp quilt. Someone had carefully maneuvered the pieces to divert suspicion towards Marc, but killing LeBlanc was a mistake. A mistake made by the nervous nelly on the phone.

"We've been looking at this from Sandoff's perspective, seeking reasons we think would motivate him. What if we shifted view?" Langstrom offered. "Who has the most to gain from his absolute destruction?"

"We thought Carter." Mal shifted his gaze from Kasey to Langstrom. "But he turned up dead."

"Doesn't mean he wasn't involved," Selena countered. "When he bribed me, he seemed awfully certain of his ability to make that offer. Believe me, he turned some of those cogs."

"Then why kill him?"

"Maybe he got too big for his britches? He was such a cocky sonofabitch. He might have overstepped."

"Who else has a motive?" Baker pulled out his notebook and ripped a page from its spine. He drew Sandoff's name in the center and circled it, then drew web-like extensions out from the center.

"I'm telling you, the *wife*," Kasey offered.

"Can you run Lenore's finances? Would she survive if Marc's entire fortune was in the toilet?" Mal asked, as Baker wrote Lenore's name down on one branch.

"I'll have McGregor run them," Langstrom volunteered. "The kid's a whiz with computers, and things are too complicated at your station right now."

"Adam Hoang," Kasey suggested, brainstorming. "This could totally be a revenge ploy."

"Less likely because he's under federal surveillance," Baker replied, writing his name on another leg of the web. "But I'll give the feds a nod and ask them to check on it."

"He doesn't seem the type," Selena rebutted. "From what I've read of that lawsuit, he's chickenshit. White-collar criminal, into scamming grandmas, mainly his own people. He's still scum, but I don't peg him for the murdering kind."

"Who else?"

"Who hated this guy so much that they're willing to kill four people to topple his empire and watch him rot in jail?" Mal posited.

"He's a lawyer. Pick a card, any card," Kasey retorted.

"Something else to add to the mix," Baker interjected. "I ran Carter's credit cards. Seems he was at a high-end bar called *The Anchor* last night. We're working on getting camera footage. My guys interviewed the bartender, said he was with some dark-haired chick; said they were all over each other." *The bait, no doubt.* Baker surveyed the faces before continuing. "I have more good news. I got a judge to expedite a search warrant on Sandoff's office. We'll get those employee records and much more."

"We should look into Marc's top clients while we're at it. Criminal cases. Any defendants with enough power and reach to get back at him." Baker started scribbling furiously as Mal continued to list possible motives. "Civil cases. Corporate clients who lost a lot of money. Mass torts."

"I can list one right now," Selena added. "The oil spill case he worked with Hoang. Hoang may be a sniveling coward, but what about the actual victims?"

"Shit. Who's up for another all-nighter?" Baker stared down at their web diagram; it resembled a high school English project. He could tell from everyone's bleary, bloodshot eyes they were all running on caffeine and adrenaline at this point.

"Why don't you go home and get some rest, Baker?" Kasey suggested. "We can take turns going through the files."

"That won't be possible." Mal looked down at his phone. "Sorry, Terry, but we have to go. Guess who walked in to Moua's game room?"

#

Tiny tapped on the door to the familiar, dim office hidden behind the bar. They had only been open thirty minutes, and the poker room was in full swing. The sound of cash registers opening and chips clattering rang amidst the shouts for bets and liquor orders. The usual machismo-fueled chest-pounding and cursing echoed over nauseating techno music. Mimi, her highest earner, had disappeared again, no doubt to share another line of coke with a client.

Moua made a mental note to teach her another lesson tonight after closing.

"Rizzo," Tiny said.

Moua's lips curled in disgust. Anthony Rizzo was a parasite who showed up at her doorstep one day with a single piece of useful information to sell. After he gambled away his payment, he tried to come back with morsels he collected from the corrupt wealthy who employed him. Moua would buy a few useful tidbits here and there, but never enough for more than a few thousand in credit. Once his usefulness ran out, Moua made it clear she was not a pawnshop, and he better bring cold, hard cash the next time he came to gamble. The girls were on alert to never exchange chips for him without her express permission.

So here he was, putrid sludge from the bottom of the ice machine, grinning his yellowed Cheshire Cat grin, thumbing the green in his palm as if he had enough to buy anything more than the dirt beneath her nails.

"How much?" She deigned to acknowledge the provenance of his cash. It would be gone by the end of the night.

"Twenty," he replied, disappointed she didn't ask.

"A hefty sum. What about Side-Eye?"

"None of your business." His tone bordered on insolent, and she resisted a twitch.

"It's my business when you run your mouth, claiming I'm vouching for you." She glared at Rizzo; the damaged eye appeared milkier than usual. Tiny delivered a tight, balled fist into his gut. He doubled over, gasping for air.

Sucker punched by a half-wit, he thought, clamoring to regain his dignity. A second, steeled blow crushed the soft folds of his belly. He doubled over again, inhaling through his nostrils and mouth while letting out a loud, flatulent rip of air. His instincts were usually better than this, but he didn't come here today looking for a fight.

"*Yuut*," she commanded in Laotian, then chuckled. "Did you shit yourself?"

"He hits—like—a—bitch." Rizzo wheezed, trying to sound tough. Tiny raised his fist, getting ready to deliver a third punch. Rizzo squared his shoulders to block.

"That's enough." She bent over, her face level with his, and whispered through gritted teeth. "Next time you think about fucking with me. Don't. Or I will feed you to my dogs."

She stood up, straightened her simple cotton blouse and smacked him lightly in the face.

"Change for twenty!" she shouted. A petite girl came to the doorway to ensure Moua had pocketed the cash. She began expertly counting out chips as Tiny escorted Rizzo to the front.

Moua reached for the burner phone tucked in her desk drawer and typed.

55

B aker slid into a parking spot in front of the smoke shop, turned the car off, and pulled the slide on his Beretta.

"There's no need to do that," Langstrom stated calmly. "He's not the violent type."

"Really?" Mal replied sarcastically, pulling the slide back on his SIG p365.

"I mean, he is, but he won't put up a fight," the old cop muttered, coughing. "He'll leave quietly. Especially when he sees me."

Baker glanced at the rear-view mirror, catching Mal's eye.

"For fuck's sake, holster your weapons. What are you going to do, anyway? It's a full house in there. You gonna shoot through innocent civilians?" Langstrom exclaimed, exasperated. He exited the vehicle muttering profanity at his two younger companions.

"They're civilians, alright, but knowing Moua's crowd, I doubt any of them are innocent," Mal joked as they walked towards the poker hall. The metal door rattled to the beat of obscenely loud trance music. They stepped into a hazy fog of cigarettes, the smoke exacerbating Langstrom's cough. Baker held his breath as they weaved their way through fevered bodies and sticky puddles.

"Oh my God, Mal baby!" A shrill voice rang out as a five-foot-nothing waitress in a black tank and shorts tackled the lanky investigator. Mal stumbled backwards as the surprisingly strong girl landed a wet kiss on his lips, inserting her tongue into his throat. Baker and Langstrom stared, wide-eyed, as she continued a full-on make-out session with their companion in the middle of the room.

So much for a discreet entrance, Langstrom thought, rolling his eyes. *Come on Mal, get rid of her.*

"Heyyy, sweetie," Mal greeted her, feeling her breasts pressed against his chest. He felt beads of sweat form on his brow as he struggled to remember her name. The surrounding patrons were staring.

"Mimi, get back to work!" The hostess by the chip counter barked.

"You never called!" Mimi pouted, ignoring the order. The tattered hem of her shorts rode up her voluptuous rear as she stomped her feet.

"I'm sorry, I've been busy. I promise I'll call."

Shit.

He felt a lightbulb flicker inside his head. In a moment of temporary insanity, after an especially obnoxious fight with Gwen, and with Kasey on one of her usual benders, he found his way to Moua's game room on a slow night. After too many shots and a few rounds of *Tien Len* with the cute cocktail waitress, he ended up in a furious make-out session on a furry bed surrounded by pink decor. He woke up the next morning, tasting heavily of whiskey and shame, on top of a glitter throw pillow with the words *BOSS BITCH* embroidered in sparkly gold thread. She lay spread eagle next to him, immodest and unabashed, the way only a twenty-something could be after a one-night stand. He snuck out quietly and tried to forget it had ever happened. He told no one about it, not even Kase.

"Alright sweetheart, he'll call you later." Langstrom gently guided her off by the shoulders. Her pupils were heavily dilated, and he guessed she was a coke fiend who wouldn't remember this encounter in the morning.

"Didn't figure her for your type, dude," Baker snickered.

"Shut up. It was a dark time in my life," he stammered, embarrassed. He motioned for them to move towards the bar, hoping to seem less conspicuous, though in a game room filled with blinged-out Asians in ostentatious jeans and Supreme LV jackets, even Mal stood out like a sore thumb.

"Do you see him?" Mal asked. It was pointless for either he or Baker to search, since the only picture they had of Scachi was a service photo from two decades ago.

"Where are the high stakes table? Tony's game was Texas Hold 'Em," Ian explained, sipping from a glass of murky ice water the bartender planted in front of him.

"You boys better look less like cops. You're making my regulars nervous," she whispered, pulling back her platinum hair into a high ponytail, her black roots inundating the heavy eye makeup and long, voluminous lashes.

"Good to see you again, Mal. Diet cola for you, hon?" She winked at him. Baker and Langstrom turned to stare again.

"Jesus Mal, how many of these girls have you slept with?"

"Just the one! And she's right, stop looking like cops." He slid a twenty over the counter towards the girl, who was now mixing a drink with a metal shaker, the motion stressing her high collarbones and perfectly formed breasts. "Shayla, poker tables?"

Her eyes are up there, Mal, he chastised.

"It's okay to look, hon." She flirted as if reading his mind. "Just don't touch."

With a subtle nod, she gestured towards the back corner of the room, where serious-looking men with serious-looking frowns sat, brows heavily furrowed under expensive aviators and a plume of smoke.

"Tan bomber jacket." Ian cleared his throat, bringing the glass of water to his lips.

Baker imagined the sun-kissed Italian with tightly cropped

hair to be brawny and robust, an older version of the mustached soldier from the photo. Instead, they were face to face with a squat, nearly pot-bellied uncle with leathery skin. They slowly made their way toward his table. Langstrom signaled for them to flank him from behind while he approached from the front. It wasn't long before Rizzo looked up to the figure casting a shadow over his cards.

"Well, I'll be. Ian Langstrom." He slid the plastic rims of his sunglasses down the bridge of his nose, an enormous smile plastered over his pock-marked face.

"Scachi. Never thought I'd see you again. Kind of wish I didn't have to."

"Quite the contrary. A little birdie tells me you've been looking for me." He chuckled, tapping his chips. "All in."

He was fucked anyway. He had managed to do the impossible, squander twenty thousand dollars in less than an hour, and now he was staring at the unholy pairing of the three of spades with the eight of hearts, knowing this was the second shittiest hand anyone could get. As the other players followed suit, he tossed his cards face up on the table and grinned.

"Well boys, I'm out. Gotta go with Detective Langstrom now," he taunted loudly. "What can I do you for, Detective?"

The gray-bearded mafioso on his left twitched nervously, reaching under the table, his trigger finger itchy.

"I wouldn't do that if I were you." Mal spoke up from behind, placing his hand squarely on Gray Beard's shoulder. "We're only here for him."

"Let's take a walk, Scachi. Or is it Anthony Rizzo now?" Baker nudged.

"It's whatever you want it to be, officer," Rizzo mocked.

"It's Detective." Langstrom grabbed Rizzo by the collar and pulled him to his feet. He bent his arms and cuffed him. "We're long overdue for a chat, Scachi. Let's go."

56

Selena tapped the down arrow on her laptop. Fortunately, Sandoff's employee files had been organized electronically, complete with a professional headshot for the company website. The law firm employed almost two hundred people. More than half were women, but sadly few ranked higher than associate attorney. A third of the men were promoted in less than five years; in less than ten they had made managing partners. The Board of Directors comprised of all men, including Aldrich Tremel.

Selena remembered reading an article a few years back on how his company's breakthrough in geological technology set the precedent for oil drilling practices. He reshaped the landscape for the entire industry, making close to a billion dollars selling the rights, and was now retired on some exotic golf course while his daughter took the reins.

She stole a glance at her companion.

Kasey let out a huge sigh and continued tapping on her keyboard. They agreed to split the work, with Kasey viewing hundreds of hours of security camera footage. Selena worked the inside job angle while Kasey followed the trail of the unhappy client. Unlike crime procedurals on TV, police work wasn't one tech genius on the computer punching out algorithms that eliminated suspects by age and hair color. Police work was the two of them, staring at photos of what looked like the same girl, in different lipstick shades and hair color.

"What were you like in high school?" Kase asked, her face glued to the computer screen.

"That's a random question."

"I'm a random person." She shrugged.

"That's the third bag of chips you've had in like an hour. Your diet worries me." Selena tried to change the subject.

"I quit smoking a few months ago. Gotta keep my hands busy," she responded. "You haven't answered my question."

"Why do you want to know?"

"Just trying to get to know you, I guess."

"And you figured you would start in high school? Why not my childhood, Dr. Phil?"

"High school is a determining factor in your outlook on the world. If you were popular, you view the world differently, handle people differently than if you were not. For instance, both Mal and I were outcasts in high school. Mal was always teased about his weight and me about my looks. Then we grew up and became the dysfunctional adults we are now."

"That's a pretty generalized summary of what makes a person a person. But it explains his complex with food." Selena chuckled.

"You noticed that too? He eats like a rabbit."

"And what's the deal with alcohol? How come he doesn't drink?"

"There's no deal. He doesn't like the taste."

"Here I thought he had a terrible experience, went on a drunken binge or something."

"No, sadly, the dude is historically boring when he drinks. He's the same person, except maybe even more responsible."

"Yikes, sounds like a good time."

"It's alright." Kase giggled. "I drink enough for the both of us."

Selena laughed, then grew silent for a moment. She thought

about the girl sitting next to her, the only child of strict immigrant parents who succeeded academically in high school. Then she caved to the enormous pressures of achieving a medical degree she didn't want and a barely existent social life. When she met Mal and her husband, things were great until Bruce was ripped from her life as well. Selena had seen more tragic backstories, but she had to give it to Kase for holding it together. She couldn't do the same for a long time after…

"I was… moody in high school."

"That's every teenager who has hormones," Kase chortled.

"Well, that's all you're going to get." Selena closed the file with the employee records. "She doesn't work at the law firm."

"Damn it."

"I know. I even checked all the women who were out of that age range."

"Then you should help me with the security footage. There's too many here."

"How far back are you going?"

"I started from about two weeks ago, right before the robbery."

"I'll go back two weeks before that. If we're viewing footage from a month out and still don't get anything, then we might be shit out of luck."

"I hope the boys are faring better than we are." Kase pulled up the still of mouse girl.

Who the hell are you, mystery woman?

#

"Gentlemen, let's get this show started, shall we?" Rizzo clucked with apparent good humor. Mal hesitated; he was way too cocky for someone who was about to go down for homicide. "Introductions please. You obviously know a good deal about me. How about you tell me about you?"

"This isn't a dinner party, Scachi." Langstrom spit out. "This is a murder investigation."

"Ian, don't be such a stick-in-the-mud," Rizzo sneered. "I

guess I'll start. First, we have the illustrious Malcolm Ly. I have to say, your career was a great read. The rise and fall of a rising star, HPD's very own Achilles. They found your heel, didn't they?"

His eyes glimmered.

"And they broke ya good."

Mal lunged across the table, grabbed Rizzo by the throat and wrestled him to the ground. Rizzo howled, his hands still cuffed in front, not even putting up a fight. Baker rushed over and yanked on his irate companion's arm.

"He's not worth it, man!" the detective shouted, but it was too late. All Mal saw was red. "You're going to rip your stitches!"

Unable to break his grip on Rizzo's throat, Baker bear-hugged him from behind and slammed him to the side. Langstrom dragged Rizzo across the floor, away from a kicking and screaming Mal.

"Hey! Calm down or you're out of here," Langstrom shouted, pointing a stern finger at Mal and pulling Rizzo's chair upright. He brushed his shirt, straightening out the wrinkles and wiping Rizzo's blood and spit off with his handkerchief.

"Sit your ass down, sonofabitch." The veteran detective wrenched Rizzo back to the chair. He couldn't believe he still had to deal with this rookie bullshit six months from retirement.

"Let me go, Terry. I'm fine!"

"Mal, I can't let you stay if you have another outburst like that."

Baker didn't blame him, though. Rizzo was a sick bastard who went way below the belt. If he were in Mal's position, tonight would be the night he lost his badge. However, someone had to have provided Rizzo with Mal's file, and Townsend was too low on the totem pole to have access to it. Did he send the wrong cop home?

"I'm fine," Mal growled again, jerking himself free from his colleague, his shoulder aching from the wound, drops of red bleeding through his cotton shirt.

"You cops are all idiots." Rizzo cackled. "Just like good ol' Ian here. He could never bust me in New York and now here he is, decades later, a has-been in Galveston, busting bar brawls and underaged spring breakers."

Did this guy have a jacket on all of us?

"How about you, detective?" Rizzo's gaze shifted to Baker. "What's your story?"

That answers that.

Whoever was providing Rizzo with information either didn't know that Baker was investigating all the connected crimes or didn't think he was important enough to keep a dossier.

"That's enough, Rizzo. We've indulged you for far too long. It's time to answer our questions. We have evidence that connects you to at least one homicide and one conspiracy. I bet if we dig deep enough, we'll be able to connect you to the whole thing," Baker stated. Langstrom picked up when he stopped.

"But knowing you for *decades*, like you so aptly stated, I know you're no point man. You're just the trigger. We want the top dog, not you, and we're willing to work with you, get you a deal."

"I've got four words for you, Ian." Rizzo replied with a glint in his eyes. Something wasn't right; he seemed more amused than worried.

"US Marshal Clint Lovell."

57

Henry leaned against their apartment door, his forehead touching the cool wooden surface.

It had been days since he saw Gwen, leaving before she woke up in the morning and returning in the dead of night when he was sure she was fast asleep. He didn't mean to eavesdrop that miserable night, but the door was slightly ajar, and the arguing got loud. What he heard broke his heart. He always felt she was holding back. No matter how hard he tried, she was never fully his, but he didn't know why. To come face to face with the reason as he stood drenched in blood in your dining room was like being sucker punched on the playground.

For days, he wrestled with options. His first idea was to move out. Then he thought of calling off the wedding. Finally, he escalated all the way to requesting a transfer overseas. However, cooler heads prevailed, and he made his way home, determined to talk to her first. Now here he was, standing awkwardly at the front door of his own home, dreading the conversation to follow.

He heard the knob turn and straightened as the door jerked open. Gwen's surprised face greeted him, her auburn tresses styled in loose curls and tucked neatly behind her ears. Her jaw tensed and her mouth drew into a tight line. There were bags under her eyes as if she hadn't slept in days.

"Henry!"

"Hello, darling."

She flinched at his tender words. "What are you doing standing out here?"

"Thinking, I suppose."

"About?"

"We should talk." He clutched her wrist and pulled her past the doorway.

"I was going to take out the trash." She bit her lip. It was the wrong thing to say, but she dreaded the conversation they were about to have.

"It can wait." They walked into the living room with Henry a few steps in front of her. She eyed the nape of his neck, the hair line trimmed with precision, his well-tailored suit. Everything about him was impeccable, never a hair out of place. If only she could love perfection.

"I'm sorry I've been absent these last few days." He scanned her emerald eyes for emotion.

"I called you a dozen times."

"I know. I was upset."

"Are you going to leave me?" she asked.

"I honestly don't know yet." He looked down at his leather oxfords, wishing he had gotten them polished during lunch. He struggled to form the right words. "Will you tell me the truth?"

"About Mal?" It wasn't as much a question as a confirmation.

He nodded.

She hesitated.

He poured himself three fingers' worth of whiskey, more than his usual, but the occasion called for it, and knocked back half of it.

"I thought I knew everything about you. I thought you shared everything with me. Am I just a romantic fool?"

"We all have skeletons, Henry."

"I showed you all of mine." His jaw clenched. "Did you mean what you said? Do you still love him?"

"Yes." She knew this wasn't the time to sugarcoat things and answered truthfully. "But I love you too."

"Did you ever cheat on me?"

"Yes." Her emerald eyes were brimming with tears. He knocked back the rest of the whiskey and poured another.

"The night I came home early from San Francisco." She nodded. "You were going to meet him, weren't you?"

"Yes." Her voice faltered.

"If it came down to it, would you pick me or him?" She diverted her gaze, wringing her hands, turning her ivory palms a deep pink, unable to speak. Choking back tears, he headed towards the bedroom.

"Where are you going? We're not done yet."

"You gave me all the answer I needed." He pulled a gunmetal suitcase from the closet and started packing. She stood sobbing by the doorway.

"Please don't go."

"Give me a reason to stay." The moonlight illuminated her silhouette, casting a halo around the soft curves of her jawline. Even tears couldn't tarnish that lovely face; she was a living Madonna, his own angelic tormenter, and maybe that was the problem. He worshipped her and when your idol falls, you're left with a chasm too deep to fill, no matter how desperately you wanted it.

"I love you."

"That's not enough anymore." He latched the suitcase. "I'm going to stay with Jimmy. I need time to think."

"Can I call you?"

"I don't think it's a good idea. I'll call you when I'm ready." With that, the front door swung shut with a tender finality. He had always been this way, gentle, warm, compassionate. It was no surprise his farewell would be the same. Gwen felt like the air had been sucked out of the room.

Not knowing what else to do, she dialed, hung up the phone, and dialed again. Better this addiction than the other.

"It's Mal. You know what to do."

Gwen took a breath and hung up the phone. She couldn't be helpless anymore. It was too exhausting. Maybe it was time to consider another city, another life, away from these toxic relationships. She packed a suitcase, put her coat on, and left. She wasn't going to stay another night in this sad, empty home.

#

Shari yawned. It was the third consecutive night she'd worked the graveyard shift, and it was wearing her down. The usual night shift concierge called in sick with the flu a week ago, but she had it on good authority that he was actually in Miami, partying up with his fraternity brothers. She hated him and was waiting until he slipped up and posted something on Facebook to rat him out. As she scrolled through her phone, devising her revenge plan, two shabby-looking men walked through the front door. Judging from their ill-fitting slacks and dirty button-downs, they were not residents of the Hanover. She straightened her shoulders, cleared her throat, and stared them down.

"Can I help you, gentlemen?" She put a subtle emphasis on the last word to make it clear how far short of that measure they fell.

The tall one pulled a leather square out of his pocket. It glinted under the chandelier. "HPD. We're detectives. We need to speak to Dr. Gwen Bixby. She lives on the nineteenth floor."

Shari eyed them suspiciously. She had never met detectives before, but something about the way they avoided eye contact with her just felt off.

"What's this regarding?" Shari asked, trying not to sound condescending. She knew Dr. Bixby was some sort of corpse doctor, but she'd never had so many detectives visit her home before. Why anyone would pick that as an occupation was beyond her.

"We're not at liberty to discuss," the short one replied curtly.

"Fine. I'll call her." The tall one reached across the counter, planting his hand firmly on top of the headset.

"Don't," he said, but Shari knew her business.

"Excuse me. Dr. Bixby will have to give you express permission to go up there."

The short one lied. "We're in the middle of a homicide investigation and Dr. Bixby hasn't exactly been forthcoming. If you alert her, we'll arrest you for obstruction."

She slid her hand away from the phone, seemingly unwilling to get into a confrontation with law enforcement. With a suppressed snarl, Shari pulled a key fob from the drawer and over her wrist.

"This way." She scanned the fob, opening the elevator, then scanned it again and punched nineteen. The doors had barely closed on the two detectives before she was back at her counter, dialing Dr. Bixby's extension. There was no way in hell she was going to lose such a great paying job for some dumb threat by two asshole cops. She had seen enough television to know they would never arrest her.

There was no answer. Maybe she was asleep. She tried again and this time got sent straight to voicemail.

"Dr. Bixby, this is Shari from downstairs. Two gentlemen are coming up to your floor. They claimed to be detectives, but I don't know. I want you to have a heads-up. Call the front desk if you need anything."

Short and Tall got off on the nineteenth floor and headed straight for the double doors.

This doctor was rich and her boyfriend was even richer. Their instructions were simple: grab the bitch and kill the boyfriend, but they weren't told they couldn't grab some valuables while they were at it. She must have some fancy jewelry.

Their source said the service elevators in the back didn't have cameras, but to be sure, they had paid the usual night concierge to disable the front cameras and to let them up. What they didn't count on was the idiot calling in sick and using his unexpected bonus to go on an impromptu holiday, leaving them to deal with that hoity-toity tramp at the front. Good help was hard to find these days.

Tall knocked gruffly on the door, holding a taser in the other, while Short pulled the gun from his holster, twisting the silencer on before cocking the hammer. They had rehearsed all morning. If the boyfriend opened the door, Short would shoot him in the chest and Tall would catch his body before it made too much noise. If the bitch opened, Tall would tase her and Short would go take care of the boyfriend.

"Nobody's answering. You sure it's this one?" Tall glared at Short.

"Of course, I'm sure. I wrote it on my hand." He opened his hand, showing smears of blue ink on his palm. "They're probably drugged up and asleep. You know how these rich fuckers are, always on Prozac or some shit, like they have any actual problems. Just pick the lock."

"Cover me." Tall pulled a kit from his pocket, inserted the tension wrench in the keyhole, deftly pulled it to the side and inserted the rake. In seconds, he heard an almost inaudible click as the lock gave way. He grabbed the handle and nudged; the door eased open, and he sighed with relief. No interior locks, or if there were, they hadn't bothered to throw them.

Short went in first. They silently closed the door, scanning the foyer and living room area. There were no lights on in the apartment, but street lights streamed through the large floor to ceiling windows, providing enough for them to poke around.

"What the fuck?" Tall whispered. "No one's here."

"Did you check the guest bedroom?"

"I checked both. I thought your boy said she's here most nights."

"He did! He said they don't have much of a social life. Usually come straight home after work and stay in. Order delivery almost every night."

"Well, where the fuck are they, then?"

"Fuck if I know!" Short pointed to the photos lining the walls.

"That's her though."

"Should we wait? Maybe they went out to grab dinner?"

"Let's give it a few hours." Short walked into the master and emptied a pillow case.

"What are you doing?"

Short was already searching. "We're already here, right? Waste not, want not. Don't make a mess in the entry. We don't want to alert them we're here. We have time, so poke around, electronics and jewelry only."

58

Clint Lovell was a simple man. Like most men of his time, the Marshals recruited him right out of the military. He let the job take over his life, let go of the girl of his dreams, gave up the white picket fence, children, grandchildren, all in the service of his country. Now, a heart attack, two gunshot wounds, and an alcohol addiction later, The Man was forcing retirement on him and what did he have to show for it? A gold watch, a shitty pension, and an empty house.

When Deputy Director Richardson told him Anthony Scachi, infamous enforcer for the Gambino family, was turning state's evidence, Lovell jumped at the chance to become his handler. One last job to fill the void. If he were lucky, the Gambinos would send someone after Scachi and he could die in the line of duty. Anything was better than sitting around ruminating on his mistakes, counting the seconds to a natural, undignified death.

Scachi turned out to be an easier gig than he thought, much to his disappointment. He checked in on time, worked multiple jobs at a bookstore and as a delivery man, and though he seemed to move around the city a lot according to his GPS tracker, he kept to himself and never got into any trouble. He went to bed every night by nine and got up bright and early for his shift. After a while, Clint stopped checking in on him as often and gave up on the idea that anyone would ever find this guy. He was truly retired and in hiding. Now, they were mere months away from trial and it seemed he would inevitably leave the Marshals service a forgotten has-been.

Which was why Clint was in his underwear, drinking a beer, and pan frying a porkchop when he received a pair of calls that ruined his day. First was a call from WitSec's dispatch system notifying him that his witness was in police custody in Houston, and then an irate call from the Deputy Director himself asking what the hell was going on? He barely had time to put on pants before he was out the door.

The briefing in Richardson's office had not been a pleasant one. It seemed Scachi had been a busy boy, and not at all the docile recluse the Marshal thought. He was in police custody, and not for light, easily explained and buried charges. No, he was there under suspicion of murder and conspiracy, charges that weren't going to go away with a wave of his badge. Richardson's instructions were to sit in on the interrogation and to brief the AG directly.

"We need this guy, Lovell. If there's a deal to be made, call the AG's office and let him know," were Richardson's exact words.

He had to give it to Tom. Here he was, looking at the biggest fuck-up since Nico "The Accountant" "hung himself" in his jail cell, and he had a straight face and not a hair out of place. Clint drove to the office, expecting to get his ass handed to him. Instead, Richardson gave him instructions and sent him on his way. The ass reaming would come later, after they had done proper damage control.

Three and a half hours and a bumpy car ride in a cheap rental later, a portly HPD officer escorted him to the sixth floor and down a long corridor of faded laminate and staid wooden doors, all labeled INTERROGATION. He stopped in front of door number six and knocked. There was something final and ominous about that room, the room at the end of the hall.

"Detective?" the officer called out.

A muscular, boxer-looking cop opened the door.

"Marshal Clint Lovell?" he asked, holding out his hand while staring them both down.

"And you're Detective Terrance Baker?" He returned the handshake and tried his best to reciprocate the firm grip.

"You've been briefed." Baker folded his arms in front of his chest; after the past few days, his trustmeter was running on empty. It wasn't personal. Frankly, right now he didn't trust anyone he couldn't vouch for personally. He found it hard to believe that an agent would let his witness run amuck without an inkling of what was going on. He either had to be an incompetent idiot or in on the whole thing.

"Before we go in there, I wanted to let you know that I've been authorized to make any deals necessary to keep this guy out of jail. That's how much he's worth to the AG."

"Well, that's nice. Do you have any idea what this guy's done?"

"Allegedly did," Lovell pushed. "From what I've heard, everything you have is circumstantial."

"The United States Attorney General wouldn't be talking deals if you believed that to be true," Baker pressed. Mal had warned him that the Feds would play hardball, put pressure on HPD to get what they wanted. It would have been near impossible to have this conversation if he had to go up the usual chain of command to reach Lovell. Instead, Mal called in a favor with an FBI friend and a few hours later, Rizzo's handler was standing hat in hand at their doorstep.

"I'd like a few minutes alone with my witness, please." Baker led him into the room, where Scachi sat across from an older, tough-looking gentleman and his disheveled, angry partner.

"Ian Langstrom, Malcolm Ly, meet US Marshal Clint Lovell." They both nodded at him. Scachi's smile grew wider as he saw his get-out-of-jail free card walk through the door. Clint wanted to slap the smug grin off his face.

"Gentlemen, this man is a federal witness and needs to be released immed—"

"Cut the crap, Lovell." Mal interrupted. "This bastard is a gun-for-hire. We know it, you know it, the federal government knows it. We found DNA in the needle he used to kill Ericka Thomas. Couldn't resist using one of your diabetic syringes, could you, you sick son of a bitch?"

"Gentlemen, I need a privileged conversation with the witness, by authority of the United States Attorney General." The smirk on Rizzo's face faded as he caught Clint's glare.

"He's bluffing," Rizzo stammered. "He's not even a cop!"

"Shut it, Rizzo," Lovell growled through gritted teeth. "A few minutes, *please*."

The trio shuffled out of the room, shooting each other uncomfortable glances. Rizzo was forensically adept. They had dusted the plunger and body of the syringe for prints and swabbed the inside for foreign DNA, but everything came back to Ericka. They were hoping, however, that WitSec wouldn't take that chance on their star witness.

"Baker, it might be time to bring in the DA," Langstrom whispered, as they shut off the microphone on the other side of the interrogation room.

"Her husband plays golf with Sandoff every other Sunday. I don't know if we can trust her," Baker replied.

"Goddamn it, who can we trust?" Langstrom lamented.

"Look, I'm not saying everyone here is dirty. Far from it. But the Marshal is right. All we have is circumstantial evidence. We run around with what we have now and people are gonna laugh in our faces, or the ones involved will catch wind and shut us down. We need to break Rizzo. Get him to tell us who hired him. Get some hard evidence." Baker's voice left no room for argument.

"And let him get away with murder?" Ian did not like that plan one bit.

"Baker's right. We can't win them all. Let's just get what we need and let the DOJ deal with this piece of trash," Mal opined.

"Yeah, but how?"

"You won't like it."

Their eyes widened as Mal relayed his plan.

"You're right. I hate it. I'm going to have to arrest you if you do it. Worse, they'll send the FBI to arrest you," Baker argued.

"Eh, I'm already wanted by Galveston PD. You want to solve this case or not?"

The kid had balls, that's for sure, Langstrom thought. It was a Hail Mary, but they were too close to give up now. He didn't care about his badge. The worst GPD could do was take away his lousy pension and Anita's life insurance policy more than made up for it. He couldn't let Baker risk his badge for these sons of bitches.

"Baker, why don't you go grab a coffee?" Langstrom assumed his high school principal demeanor again. Baker shot a glance at Mal. "Don't worry. I'll make sure he doesn't beat Rizzo to a pulp."

"I guess I can go check on the girls, see if they need coffee or dinner. Lord knows, Kasey's probably on her third bag of chips." Baker walked out as Lovell tapped on the glass, signaling to the officers Rizzo was ready to talk. Langstrom and Mal entered, and Lovell jumped right in.

"Look guys, Scachi is an asshole of epic proportions, but before he entered WitSec, he confessed his deepest, darkest sins to the Holy Trinity of the DOJ already. You have nothing on him but an alleged syringe with his DNA on it. The AG wants to see this report, or else let him go."

Mal held up his hand; it was his turn to talk.

59

In 1935, an American publisher commissioned Matisse to illustrate a novel for one of his authors. That author was James Joyce, and the novel was none other than his epic tome, *Ulysses*. The etchings were hilariously incongruous, as Joyce feared, Matisse never read his book, and incorrectly assumed it had something to do with the Greek myth he named it after. A few years ago, a talented, albeit misguided con artist decided it was a good idea to forge the set of six etchings, selling it to a huge literature and art collector by the name of Vittoria G. He scored a tidy sum from Vittoria, as her broker La Rue cleared the provenance on the sketches."

Rizzo rapped his fingers impatiently on the table. He yawned and glanced at Lovell, whose brows were shifted almost to the top of his forehead, furrowed in confusion.

"Is there a point to this history lesson?" Lovell's face was cherub-like, encased by rosy, almost scarlet cheeks, brought on by either the city's humidity or the intense situation in which he found his witness.

"Vittoria was unaware the grifter and her trusted La Rue were in cahoots, ripping her off for nearly a quarter million dollars," Mal continued, unthwarted by their confusion. "Now, what the grifter and La Rue neglected to do was check *Vittoria's* provenance. BA from Columbia, MFA from Oxford, soft-spoken, intelligent, well-bred? She was an easy mark."

Rizzo shifted uncomfortably in the plastic chair, the metal arms pressing against his sides. His prominent thighs were feeling like wrapped pork. Malcolm leaned forward, his eyes narrowing as if he were about to reveal a state secret. His smile was almost rapturous as he intertwined his fingers.

"You see, gentlemen, the G in Vittoria G. did not stand for Gallo as she originally told them. She was a young girl from Brooklyn with a checkered past and a more checkered family, who did all she could to suppress anything which could taint her future. But when the *capo* of Brooklyn heard his niece had been taken for that much money? They found the grifter without his tongue and his hands."

Rizzo stirred uneasily.

"How is any of this relevant, you ask? La Rue ran to Houston, where he set up shop and survived a few more years before someone bashed in his head with an antique bust he was offloading. As fate would have it, yours truly was put on the case, and then I met the illustrious Selena Parish. Not only did she recover the money for Vittoria, she also threw in a first edition *Ulysses* with the etchings. So, while you have no reason to be afraid of us law enforcement officers, or the law, as it seems to be on your side, Anthony Scachi," Mal paused for effect. "You have every reason to be afraid of Ms. Parish."

"Just a minute! You can't—" Lovell popped from his seat, his eyes wide and his breathing thicker. It was the first time Langstrom saw genuine fear in Scachi's eyes.

"You son of a bitch, I could arrest you right now for making that threat."

"You could, but would you be faster than Selena? I believe she has the *capo* on speed dial. After all, he owes her a favor for helping his favorite niece." Mal stood and leaned towards Rizzo, his face inches away from the repugnant mustache, feeling the bastard's desperate breath on him. He addressed Lovell, his eyes never straying from Rizzo's frightened face.

"You can arrest me, Clint, but can you catch Selena?"

"What are you offering?" Lovell murmured, sighing. Rizzo turned to look at him, indignant. "What are you looking at, you useless piece of shit? I'm cleaning up your mess."

"Tell us what we want to know, and this conversation never happened. The AG can deal with your witness. No doubt he'll get in trouble again," Langstrom said coolly. He really wanted to wring Scachi's neck, give him a taste of what his victims suffered, but Mal was right, this wasn't their fight.

"I'm sorry, gentlemen, but neither of you are HPD. I'm going to have to hear this from Detective Baker."

"Christ. Fuck you, you by-the-book asshole," Mal spit out as Langstrom laid a hand on his arm. Before Langstrom could pull out his phone, Baker walked through the door.

"Tell us everything and you can take your witness and get the hell out, Marshal." Baker turned to his colleagues as if to say *I never left.*

Lovell nodded at Rizzo, whose puffed out chest had shrunk considerably in size. He cleared his throat. "I received a phone call a few months ago. Anonymous. I was supposed to set up a hit, a father and daughter."

"Levi and Abigail Stevenson," Mal prompted.

Rizzo nodded in confirmation.

"Normally, I wouldn't have accepted. I don't like working for people I don't know. Too many factors I can't control, but the money was too good." There was more left unsaid, and Mal grabbed at it.

"How much are you in for with Side-Eye?" Mal asked.

"About a hundred grand," Rizzo replied sheepishly, avoiding eye contact with Lovell.

"When are you spending all this money? You're in bed by nine every night," Clint squeaked.

"It's easy to get past you, Clint. You're too trusting," Rizzo responded, rubbing his sweaty hands together.

"He has two phones, Marshal. He leaves the one you're

tracking at home. My bet is, he has another truck you don't know about too," Mal explained to a clueless Lovell. The older agent was a man out of time, a Luddite who didn't quite understand how GPS worked, let alone how easy it was to bypass.

"Look, it was supposed to be a few simple jobs, but it just kept getting bigger and bigger." Rizzo tried to distract from the many sins Lovell was ignorant of. "Besides the Stevensons, I was supposed to hire some kids to rent a warehouse, but the asshole, Tory, he tried to shake them down for more money, so then they paid me to clean up that mess, too."

"Them?"

"There's two of them I've spoken to." Rizzo admitted. "They tried to mask themselves with that stupid Darth Vader voice, but you can tell from their speech patterns. The first one was definitely the alpha. After, I dealt with the skittish one. They had me get rid of that Ericka chick because they were afraid her boyfriend told her things, you know, pillow talk. Then that Carter idiot. I didn't do that one, was busy, but I outsourced it. All I know is these two keep digging themselves a bigger hole and then bodies started falling, and it's all because of you." Rizzo nodded at Mal.

"What are you talking about?" Baker asked. "How is it Mal's fault?"

"He got involved, kept sniffing around, even went to the storage facility. You don't even know how close you are to the truth, do you? You're a good detective. It's too bad about the job."

"I have a great team," Mal replied through gritted teeth; Rizzo's compliment made him want to vomit and punch through a wall at the same time.

"No doubt. That Selena. Sexy and smart. I'd like a taste of her." Rizzo's lips curled into a lewd grin. Mal balled up his fists, his knuckles cracking from the pressure. "And that Kasey chick's a looker, too. You hooking up with both of them?"

"Shut your damn mouth." This time it was Baker who stood up, heated.

"Terrance, he's baiting us. Let it go," Mal commanded, coolly, back in control. "Get on with it, Rizzo. A guy as careful as you, you didn't continue working for some gravelly voice behind a telephone. You know who hired you, don't you?"

"Well, I hate to disappoint you, but it wasn't Marc Sandoff," Rizzo continued, as if reading their minds. He was a real Chatty Cathy now that he had immunity.

"How do you know that?"

"Because Malcolm is correct. I would never work for someone without knowing everything about them. I keep track of the news. I knew when the burglary went down. I had my suspicions it was Sandoff cleaning house, so after I got the phone call to take care of the two jokers in jail, I ran Sandoff's financials."

"And?" Baker pushed impatiently. Rizzo was like a diva at curtain call, pausing dramatically while opening his chest and shoulders, spreading his arms wide.

"He's broke. He can't afford to pay me what they paid me."

"How much did you get paid?" Langstrom asked.

"I'd rather not share that piece of information. It's not relevant to the case."

"Like hell it's not," Mal retorted.

"Hey, do you want to know who hired me or not? If so, let's move on." There was no way he was going to share with the Marshal how much he had squirreled away.

"Fine, then let's fast forward to the finish. Who hired you?"

This time, it was Rizzo who leaned in close; it was Rizzo with the rapturous smile. His voice dropped to a dramatic whisper.

"Lenore Sandoff."

#

Kasey raced towards the elevator with Selena's heels clacking rapidly behind. Baker set them up in the records room because it had better equipment, but now they were standing impatiently in a creaky elevator meandering down to six.

Terry's phone had gone to voicemail again, which she hoped meant that they were getting somewhere with Rizzo. She also hoped whatever Rizzo was telling them would help make sense of their discovery. It seemed the deeper they dug, the more questions they found.

"Mal's not answering either," Selena muttered, dialing again.

"I'll just text them," Kase replied as she entered their names into a group text.

Found her.

60

All three phones chirped simultaneously as Rizzo whispered Lenore Sandoff's name, as if the universe were confirming they were on the right track. Mal's screen lit up with a notification; a text from Kasey. Two short, sweet words. They found the identity of the mousy girl, and they were one step closer to corroborating Rizzo's story. Pushing the chair back, he eyed the repugnant hitman one more time before slipping out the door to meet the girls.

"If Marc Sandoff is broke, how is Lenore funding your little killing spree?" Baker continued the interrogation.

"Don't you dumbass cops ever do your research?"

"We're running her financials, but it takes a little time. Laws and things like that. Humor me, Rizzo."

"Lenore Sandoff is independently wealthy. Probably the only reason Marc stayed married to her all these years. He's been siphoning off her trust fund to keep the law firm alive."

"What are you talking about? Sandoff's law firm wins cases. They won a multimillion-dollar mass tort against that car manufacturer. They're spearheading the oil spill litigation. How could they not have any money?" It was Clint's turn to be surprised. As part of Rizzo's move to Houston, Lovell kept up with the local news in case he needed to make use of the resources in town. Sandoff had been headlining the Chronicle for the past few years, even more so ever since he announced his bid for mayor.

"The oil spill litigation is a bust," Langstrom replied. "They're under federal investigation right now. Don't you suits talk to each other?"

"Right, I must have missed the weekly newsletter," Lovell replied drily.

"Look, all I know is, in between the poor investments, the condos, the girls, the jewelry, and the gifts, Sandoff isn't even worth the Italian suit he's wearing. Lenore's been keeping him afloat for years. Whether she knows it is another story."

"Oh, she knows," Baker snorted. He turned to Ian and whispered.

"Are we done here?" Lovell asked as the two detectives headed for the door.

"For now." Baker turned, handing him a pen and a yellow pad. "Start writing."

"Wait a minute, you said this conversation never happened."

"And it didn't. It's not recorded, but you're going to write a confession and sign it: Anthony Rizzo. A few weeks from now, Anthony Rizzo will disappear from Houston and no one will find him. He'll be in the wind, a ghost. This confession will be the only thing we have of him and we'll put out a BOLO on a guy who no longer exists. But these murders happened and there's a kid out there who won't survive prison if we put him back in. In case you're interested, it's the kid whose girlfriend you murdered. So, you're going to do the right thing for once in your useless, pathetic life. Make it a good one," Baker commanded before slamming the door shut.

#

"Terry, it's Bethany Tremel." Kasey handed him a black and white printout as he entered the conference room. Mal was already thumbing through the pages of a thick packet they brought downstairs. The grainy, cropped photo showed a petite, dark-haired girl smiling coyly while handing a clipboard back to the busty blonde behind the oak counter. The background was laden with grandiose furniture and expensive artwork. It didn't take color to tell him he was looking at gilded frames.

"She doesn't work there. That's why I couldn't find her." Selena slid another thick folder towards him. "Whoever ran your warrant was thorough as hell. We got copies of everything, including the sign-in sheets."

"Are we sure this is the same girl?" Langstrom asked. From the downward angle of the camera, the girl's face seemed narrow, almost pinched. She wore a dark padded blazer that obstructed the contours of her body.

"It was hard to be sure until she smiled." Kase pointed to the crevice where her two central incisors should meet. "The gap."

"We matched the timestamp to the sign-in. Stacey Braddock, executive assistant at Tremel Technologies & Co. Purpose for visit? Delivering documents. Just a menial task she does every few weeks. She's in the logbook about a dozen times. She was there all along."

"Then why did it take all day to find her?" Baker asked, wincing at the way the question came out.

"Because she stopped visiting the last few months. We would have missed her if Selena hadn't pushed to go further back." Kase jumped in to respond before Selena could throw in one of her sassy quips. She had been prickly all day, probably from exhaustion. They were all tired and on edge.

"What about a motive?" Langstrom looked over Baker's shoulder at the lined pages in the folder.

"We're not sure. We didn't have time to dig deeper."

"Let's go ask her." Mal looked up from the paperwork. "Whatever it is, I bet it's financial. How about you ladies dig through newspaper clippings, financial journals, bank statements? Find me some ammunition."

"That's a good idea." Baker supported Mal. "Ian, why don't you and Mal pay Ms. Tremel a visit in the morning? I'll work on a warrant and bring in both Marc and Lenore Sandoff."

"What are you thinking? Separate them, sweat 'em, let 'em think they rolled on each other?" Mal offered.

"Something like that." Baker shrugged. "We'll figure it out in the morning. Everyone go home and get some rest."

"What about you?"

"I've got to make sure Rizzo finishes his confession, type up the report, and release Jamal. There's a lot of work to be done still." He squeezed the bridge of his nose, wondering how many days it had been since he last slept.

"I'll stay and help you type up the warrant." Mal volunteered. "Ian, will you take the ladies home?"

"Are you sure, Mal?"

"Pretty sure I remember how to type those up." He grinned.

"I can take Selena home. Ian, you go rest," Kasey volunteered. "We've got a big day tomorrow, boys."

As they filed out of the conference room, she paused and raised her arms in victory. "Oh, and for the record? I knew it was the wife."

61

Malcolm rounded the corner onto the dimly lit street. Darkness shrouded his neighborhood, flanked on both sides by titanic oaks, permitting only thin streams of light through their massive branches. Parked cars lined both sides of the one-way street. Some were parked illegally and might be towed by morning if HPD needed extra revenue from fines.

When he and Trish moved in ten years ago, they were two bright-eyed, fresh graduates looking to start a life together. Midtown Houston was an urban jungle, a mixture of small, derelict shopping centers with run-down businesses and older, dilapidated homes, not yet gentrified for the young professionals. Their invasion was still a few years in the future. His townhouse complex was one of the newer ones, a development project that ran into opposition from a mayor and a city that wanted to keep pieces of history alive. Money won out in the end, as it always does.

He grimaced and turned the radio on, immediately regretting it. It was on one of those Top 40s stations Kasey always listened to, and he was going to slit his wrists if he had to listen to another Ariana Grande song. Mal flipped through the radio channels. Not finding anything palatable, he switched it off in irritation.

He was trying to find some music to drown out the constant buzzing of his phone. Gwen had called an inordinate number of times today and had also texted him the equivalent of a college essay. He could only glimpse the messages while running around, but what he read wasn't good. Henry left, and she was holed up in some hotel, probably drinking herself to death. Usually, he would run to her side, console her, make love with her, and then fall back into blissful unawares for a few months before the suspicion and jealousy ripped them apart again. Each time this happened, it seemed the bliss got shorter and the quarrels more volatile.

"Well Georgie, it's almost over."

It had been a while since he spoke that name into the universe. He looked at the garish green clock blinking on the dashboard. Almost three in the morning.

The witching hour, he thought as a knot formed in his stomach. He didn't know if Kase's superstitions were rubbing off on him, but he had a bad feeling. Kase both loathed and feared the hour. Born and raised Catholic, she would say it was the hour for ghosts and demons. In college, he would chuckle every time they stayed awake until three, knowing he now had an extra hour ahead of him so she would feel safe enough to fall asleep. For a scientist, she had some weird beliefs, but who was he to question the supernatural? He still spoke to his dead son.

He called her, knowing she was probably drunk and asleep, but her phone went straight to voicemail. Strange. That girl usually lived on her cell phone. It was never off.

With the car secured and the front door locked, he jumped in the shower and cranked on the cold water, hoping it would wash away his paranoia. Tomorrow, no, today. Today was going to be a long day. They would have to force a confession out of one of the culprits if Baker were to have a chance of making the case. Marc Sandoff may not have been involved in the murders, but Mal didn't believe he was innocent, either.

As he sank into his pillow, his cogs turned with different

interrogation techniques, trick questions, and traps he could use against the weakest link. His breathing evened out, and he was fast asleep soon after.

#

Selena's eyes fluttered open. She blinked rapidly to adjust to the darkness, squirming against the cold concrete floor, struggling to move. At last, she stopped; her hands and feet were bound. Her shoulders ached from arching backwards to free her hands. She shook her head, trying to focus through the pain. Her blouse was soaked and the iron scent of dried blood hit her nose as she gained full consciousness. She was unsure if it was her blood or…

Kasey, where was Kasey?

"Kase?" she croaked through cracked lips. Her throat felt like sandpaper. How long had she been out? More importantly, where was she?

"*Kasey,*" she hissed again, swallowing some spit to moisten her throat. The last thing she remembered was playfully throwing M&Ms at the analyst while heading towards the hotel. Her heart sank as she remembered seeing the outline of a large, dark SUV before it crashed into them. She flailed her arms, waving her limp hands around in circles, feeling for another body. Did Kasey make it out of the accident?

62

Ian Langstrom smoothed out the collar of his light blue button down and straightened his tie. He scrambled to catch up to his companion, who double-timed it up the brick steps of the manor. The Tremel's mansion was every bit what he imagined it to be: immense, stately, and over-the-top. Solid monastery doors greeted them. Mounted on the side was one of those electronic webcam doorbells, looking somehow anachronistic amongst the brick and wood. He let out a string of hacking coughs as the doorbell played a sing-song chime.

"You okay?" Mal eyed the veteran detective, who doubled over in a coughing fit.

"I'm fine," he replied between gasps. "Just getting old."

"I'll walk slower next time." Mal smirked.

"Shut up, smart ass."

The heavy doors creaked open and a pair of cappuccino eyes stared out at them, followed by a warm, oval face and thick, chestnut braids.

"Can I help you?"

"Sorry to bother you, ma'am. We're the police." Ian flashed his badge. "I'm Detective Ian Langstrom and this is my associate Malcolm Ly. May we speak to Ms. Bethany Tremel?"

"She's not home at the moment," the girl replied cautiously. "Can I see that badge again?" Her eyes darted up and down while she studied Langstrom's photo. "This says Galveston Police. What are you doing in Houston?"

"We're conducting a joint investigation with the Houston police. Is Mr. Tremel home? May we speak to him?"

"Well, where's his badge?" she asked, eyeing Mal suspiciously.

"He's a consultant Miss…"

"Clara," she answered, shying away from the door.

"Are any of the owners home? It's pretty urgent that we speak to them," Mal pressed.

"Well, Aldrich is home, but you can't speak to him."

"Why?"

"He's indisposed at the moment." She searched for the right words. She was under strict orders to keep his condition a secret, but this was the police, and whatever their purpose, it seemed serious.

"What do you mean, indisposed?"

"I mean, he's not available to speak to you at the moment."

"Ma'am—" Ian started, but Mal interrupted.

"Listen Clara, if Aldrich Tremel is in the house, I suggest you tell him to make himself available. This is a murder investigation and we don't have time to play games."

At the mention of murder, Clara's eyes widened, and she flung the door open, beckoning for them to follow her. The detectives trailed the nurse up the stairs and down a drafty corridor. The interior was grimy and morose, a far cry from the neatly trimmed hedges and opulent arches out front.

"Aren't the Tremels billionaires?" Mal muttered, eyeing the cracked crown molding and splintered wood accents.

"Yes," Clara replied, timidly.

"They choose to live like this?" The nurse ignored his question and cleared her throat, halting in front of a half-closed door. They heard a soft hissing sound, and the clinical smell of disinfectant wafted from the room. Clara nudged the door open, and the investigators peered inside. Aldrich laid limp and gaunt on the hospital bed, eyes closed, mouth agape with an oxygen cannula trailing from his nostrils to a shiny tank.

"He was diagnosed with dementia a few years ago and then he had a serious stroke in December. The doctor doesn't think he has much time left."

"That's why he stepped down from the company?" Langstrom asked.

"Yes, but Ms. Tremel didn't want anyone to know, which was why I was reluctant to say anything at the door."

"Is she really not home?"

Clara nodded, her natural confidence returning.

"Do you mind answering some questions?"

"Sure. Let's go into the kitchen. Bethany never sets foot in there." They followed her down another corridor into a set of stairs in the back of the house. "Would you like some tea?"

"Sure, thank you." Langstrom nodded as they sat on the stools by the marble island.

"What do you want to ask?" Clara filled the kettle and placed it on the stove.

"How long have you been working for the Tremels?" Mal started.

"Six months."

"Oh," he exclaimed, disappointed. "I guess you wouldn't know much about Bethany?"

"I know more than I care to about the Tremels. I grew up with Bethany." She placed three mugs on the breakfast counter, dropping tea bags in them. "My mother was their housekeeper. Once she fell ill, I moved back and took a job as Aldrich's caretaker so I can care for my mom as well."

"What's Bethany like?"

Suddenly the confidence was gone. Clara busied herself with the kettle, pouring steaming water into all three mugs. Mal and Ian waited, not wanting to rush her and lose this potential lead. Finally, Clara put down the kettle and wrapped her cardigan closer to her body. Her gentle brown eyes were overcast with fear. She traced the rim of her mug, following the trail of steam from the surface.

"She's terrifying."

"How so?"

"I'm pretty sure she's a psychopath."

"Is she dangerous?"

"I can't prove it, but there's something sinister about her. I've never actually witnessed anything, though."

"Well, why don't you just tell us your suspicions? This isn't going into any official reports." Langstrom put his hand over hers, attempting to quell her anxiety. He and Mal shared a glance as the girl's hands trembled.

"Before I tell you anything, I want you to understand I'm grateful for everything Aldrich and Jeanette have ever done for me. It was the only reason I agreed to take this position and return to this house. They allowed my mother to bring me to work, treated me like one of their own, and even paid my private school and college tuition. Without them, I think my life would have been much harder."

She let out a breath as Mal and Ian nodded. "We understand."

"But Bethany, even as a child, was cold. Distant. Almost menacing. She would get into these fits of rage and break my toys or destroy my clothes. She would manipulate me into hurting myself. As a child, she almost killed me a few times."

"How?" Mal asked.

"One time, when we were, oh, seven or eight? She told me the pond behind their house was heated and we should go swimming. We snuck out on these floats and once we got far enough out, she ripped my float from me and swam back ashore. I couldn't swim all the way back before the hypothermia kicked in and I almost drowned. I don't know why she changed her mind last minute and saved me. I think she was testing the limits, to see how far she could go, or maybe to see how good it felt to have the power and control over someone else's life. I'm also sure she was the one who set my boyfriend's car on fire, but we could never prove it."

"But the worst thing…" Clara hesitated.

"Worse than all the times she tried to kill you?" Mal interjected.

Clara gulped. "I'm pretty sure she was responsible for her mother's death."

The kitchen grew silent, and Mal could hear the thumping in her chest as it synced with the ticking of his watch.

"I thought her mother died in a car accident? Wasn't Bethany in the car as well?" Langstrom asked, recalling the reports he read through last night as they researched Bethany and the Tremel empire.

"Like I said, it's only a suspicion, a rumor. She hated Jeanette, and I never understood why. Mrs. Tremel was a generous and loving woman, but she repelled Bethany. I think she had one of her fits and caused her mom to run the car off the road. At first, I thought the rumor was ridiculous because what normal person would put themselves in danger to hurt someone else? Then I remembered the pond and how she jumped in and risked hypothermia to kill me. Something is off about her."

"Well, my next question was to ask if she was capable of murder, but that answers that," Mal muttered, almost to himself.

"I think she's capable of anything, detective. Before I came along, Aldrich was eating out of trash cans. She starved and abused him. How can someone be so cruel to their parent?" Clara's eyes glistened.

"I hate to ask this, but did they abuse her as a child?" Mal questioned.

"I honestly couldn't tell you. Like I said, to me, the Tremels were extremely kind, but these walls hold many dark secrets."

"Does Bethany often have guests over? Dinner parties? Friends or a boyfriend?" Mal and Langstrom were going down the same road. If Lenore and Bethany were both jilted lovers, it would give them motive.

"Bethany…" Clara cocked her head to the side, deep in thought. "I didn't think she was capable of loving anybody, but I overheard some things. She was having an affair."

Mal's eyes glinted as things seemed to click into place. He nodded knowingly. "With Marc Sandoff?"

Clara shook her head.

"With Lenore."

63

Stacey Braddock examined the black and white photos the bulldog-looking detective slid across the table towards her. They were clearly stills cropped from a video, showing her walking from a distance and then getting closer to an unknown destination. She was wearing a pair of ripped jeans and one of her favorite t-shirts, so it was hard to place when this was taken. It could've been any normal weekend.

"Stacey, do you know why you're here?" Baker broke the silence. The officers who picked her up this morning were under strict orders not to answer questions or talk to her after their initial request to come down to the station. They then placed her in an interrogation room with the temperature turned down to a nippy sixty degrees. By the time Baker walked in, she was freezing, terrified, and going out of her mind with speculation and fear. It wouldn't be hard to get her to talk.

"No sir, I don't. The officers said I was a person of i-interest in a murder investigation?"

"Do you know what that means?"

She shook her head, hugging her body with both arms to stop shaking.

"Do you know who Carter LeBlanc is?"

She nodded. "He's a political consultant. He works for Mr. Sandoff."

"He was found dead in his apartment. We're trying to interview everyone who may have come in contact with him."

"D-dead?" Her eyes widened, teeth chattering. "I didn't, I don't, I mean…" She gathered her thoughts. "I've only met him a few times. I haven't even been to their office in months."

"Okay, tell me about it then." Baker knew she wasn't involved with LeBlanc's death, but it was a good pretense. He brought her in, and now he could work her for meaningful information.

"About what?"

"We know you work for Tremel Technologies, but the log shows you sign-in to the law firm a lot. Why are you there so much?" Baker feigned ignorance.

"Tremel Technologies has the firm on retainer. I'm only there delivering documents. I'm an executive assistant, a glorified secretary. Ms. Tremel is a private person. She doesn't even like it when I'm in her office. I prepare her coffee, answer the phones and emails. Most of the time, I don't even know what documents I'm delivering." Stacey rattled off her duties, pleased to have a question she could answer.

"The log shows you stopped going to the law firm about two months ago. Can you tell me why?" Baker asked, disappointed. Either this girl was a superb actress, or she wasn't any more than a mule.

"No," she responded, rubbing her clammy hands together. "Ms. Tremel had envelopes prepared and placed on my desk, and I would know to deliver it to the law firm. I don't mind those drops, really. Some of the girls and I are friendly, and it's a great waste of at least an hour. Sometimes, the girls have an envelope for me to give back to Ms. Tremel, sometimes they don't. They're always sealed."

Her eyes widened again as if coming to a realization.

"Was it drugs? Are they dealing drugs? If so, I was *not* a part of it!"

Baker raised his hand to interrupt. "No, it has nothing to do with drugs. Does Ms. Tremel ever ask you to deliver envelopes anywhere else?"

"No, that's the weird part. We always mail everything else. I only ever hand deliver to Mr. Sandoff's office. Except—"

Baker prompted her. "Yes?"

"There was one time." She touched the photos. It occurred to her where the video came from. "I met a man, handed him a small envelope, and he handed me a larger one. It didn't take a genius to know I was handing him cash. His envelope felt like documents, so I felt secure knowing I wasn't doing a drug deal or anything."

"Did Bethany have any instructions? What did she tell you to do about the envelope?"

"I'm sorry, I'm really confused. I thought I was here to answer questions about a murder?"

"You let me worry about relevance, Stacey. I just need you to answer my question." Baker was secretly holding his breath. Any savvy or guilty person would have asked for an attorney as soon as they heard the words "murder investigation", but she was young and naïve. He felt bad for scaring the crap out of her, but it wasn't play time.

"She did."

"What did she tell you? No, what did you do?"

"She laid it all out, and I did it. I met another man on a bench at Hermann Park. He sat next to me eating a burger, said a few words to me and I handed him the envelope. It was all really sketchy, but I didn't want to be involved or ask too many questions. I need this job."

"Can you describe this man?"

"Stout. He looked like he had been muscular once but was letting himself go?" She tried to recall any other details. He honestly looked like any other chubby, white male with too dark a tan. "He was wearing like a bomber jacket. It was weird because it was such a hot day. Oh, and he had a Southern accent. It was really distinct. He was definitely not from Texas."

Scachi. Baker now had a link between Bethany Tremel, Greg

Scott, and Scachi. Stacey Braddock was no longer a person of interest but a witness and had to be protected at all costs. Bethany was cleaning house when she took out LeBlanc, and an insignificant twenty-something girl from the Midwest would be a trifle in her murderous rampage.

"Stacey, listen to me." Baker's voice softened. "Everything you've told me was really important. I know you didn't want to be involved in illegal activities, but you were. You say you didn't know, and it's inadvertent, and you know what?" The scared young woman shook her head. "I believe you."

The look of relief in her eyes was immense, and Baker hated that he'd have to smash it. "You have a choice. You can help us testify and we can offer protection, or you can end up like Carter LeBlanc." He needed her to agree to protection voluntarily.

"I don't even know what I'm involved in! How can it be that important? I delivered envelopes. I was basically a mailman!" She burst into the frightened tears of a teenager, shrinking into the chair and trembling.

"Trust me. It's important and it will all be explained to you. Will you help us?"

It took a few moments, but she agreed, right as Baker's phone went off. He felt a sense of foreboding as he saw it was CSU's office line. He excused himself and walked outside to take the phone call.

"Baker."

"Baker, thank goodness. It took me forever to convince someone to give me your cell phone number."

"What's going on? Who is this?"

"It's Cherise, from CSU. We processed a really nasty car accident last night."

"Okay? Did someone die?" He was confused, he was homicide, he didn't deal with motor vehicle crimes unless someone shot up that vehicle.

"Baker, there was only one vehicle there, t-boned. The driver was gone, but the first responders on the scene saw blood, lots of blood. That's why they called us."

The detective stayed silent. He still didn't know where she was going with this.

"We ran the vehicle, and they went to the owner's house. A lady answered the door and said she lent the car to her daughter. Baker, it was Kasey's mom."

64

Mal and Ian bid Clara goodbye as she closed the large wooden door behind them. They asked her to leave the residence and go somewhere safe until this was all over, but she declined.

"I can't leave Aldrich, and he can't be moved right now. I also can't leave my mother. There's nowhere I can go safely with two sick elderly patients. I'll take my chances with Bethany." Clara smiled softly before assuring them she would call if she heard from her employer.

"Let me get this straight. You started out investigating a burglary and ended up on the heels of a psychopathic killer?" Langstrom addressed Mal, coughing violently and wiping his mouth with a handkerchief.

"What can I say? My life's never boring." Mal shrugged as they walked down the brick steps.

"Sure isn't." Langstrom sighed. "All the money in the world, and these fuckers can't even act right. What is wrong with humanity?"

"Some people want to watch the world burn."

"Did you quote Batman to me? I may be old, but I've seen the movie."

"Well, I quoted Alfred, but I'm impressed." Mal laughed, feeling a vibration in his pocket.

"I was wondering how long it would take for that bitch to rat me out." A silky voice purred through the line. Mal's smile instantly disappeared as he signaled Langstrom. He put the phone on speaker, noting the number was blocked.

No way to do a trace.

"Bethany?"

"Who else?"

"How did you know we were here?" Mal asked as Ian leaned closer to listen.

"Take a guess."

"The doorbell."

"You're as quick as they say." Her tone remained flat. He bit his lip. He couldn't believe she actually checked her own cameras.

"Well, you obviously know we're looking for you, so why don't you come in, save us some work, and we can have a chat?"

"Nice try. There's only one problem."

"What?"

"I'm not that stupid, but all of you are." She paused for so long Mal almost thought she'd hung up. "Let me tell you what's going to happen. You will give me all the evidence against Marc that you've hidden. You'll tell your pal Baker to close this case and let that bastard take the fall for this shit. Then, you'll slither back to the holes you crawled from and maybe, just maybe, I'll let you live."

Mal knew that would never happen. She was going to kill them all once she got what she wanted. "I can't do that, Bethany. I've got a duty to protect these people. Even if you let me live, what about Clara? What about your father?"

"They're none of your concern. That traitorous bitch will get what's coming to her. You're no longer a cop. I don't even know why you had to stick your nose where it didn't belong."

"Guess I'm just nosy," Mal sassed.

"You have an hour to get me what I want. I'll call back to give you an address."

"And if I don't comply?"

Another baleful pause.

"When was the last time you spoke to Kasey and Selena?"

Mal froze and his heart sank. Langstrom immediately pulled out his phone and dialed Baker.

"Is your cop buddy calling Baker to verify? Don't worry, Mal, I'm a woman of action, and a woman of my word. I don't bluff." Mal's eyes darted towards Ian, who was now whispering urgently into the phone.

Silence.

"Please don't try that strong, silent bullshit with me. I know these women mean something to you."

"Fine. Where?"

"You'll find out in one hour. Come alone and don't try anything stupid. Just remember, I'm smarter than all of you."

"If you fucking touch a hair on their heads…"

"Save your threats. Oh, and Mal?" He could practically hear the menacing smile coming through her voice. "Don't be late; Kasey is bleeding out."

The line cut and his phone vibrated with a text message.

A present for you.

Underneath the green text was a photo of Kasey and Selena, hands and feet duct taped, sitting with their backs against each other. Selena was blood-soaked, but her eyes were alert and angry. Kasey slumped onto her companion's back for support. Her head hung limply, chin touching her chest. A newspaper with today's date was positioned in the photo's corner, held up by an unknown hand. Ian walked towards Mal, still on the line with Baker.

"Mal, is it true?"

He struggled to find his voice.

"Yeah, she sent me a picture. It's not good," he croaked.

"Are they alive?"

"They might not be for much longer."

"Kasey's hurt bad, isn't she?" Baker asked, choking back

panic.

"How do you know?"

"They found her mom's car last night. Bastards t-boned them on the driver's side on Louisiana, as they were about to get on I-10. I got word it was her car. I tried calling both of them multiple times, but it went straight to voicemail. Then Ian called."

They must have been followed. Why didn't Kase just drop Selena off at her hotel? Mal's attention was pulled back by Baker, continuing.

"It gets worse. Sandoff's in the wind. We went to pick him up this morning, and both he and Lenore were gone."

"He's not in the wind. He might be in danger too," Mal surmised. "It's Lenore, Terrence. She's having an affair with Bethany."

"Boys, we can walk and talk at the same time. We need to figure out a plan." Langstrom nodded towards their car.

"What should we do?" Baker asked.

"We give her what she wants," Mal responded definitively.

65

Selena searched her damp surroundings for a sharp edge or object, twisting her hands as much as she could to introduce friction to the tape. She hazily remembered two large guys with ski masks pulling her from the wreckage and a few more voices in the car as they were thrown in the back. She slipped in and out of consciousness as they drove for what seemed like hours, trying to focus on the conversation in the car over the pounding in her head. She remembered blinking through the blood dripping from her forehead and spying a sign labeled Fulshear.

Where the fuck is Fulshear? she thought, before blacking out completely.

As sunlight beamed through strips in the boarded windows, she realized they were stashed in some sort of partially converted barn. Some of the walls had been stripped down to the studs, exposing wires and pipes. It looked like someone had started the work before giving up. She spotted the frame for a bar area to one side, and another with plumbing designated for a restroom. The muffled voices in the other room crescendo-ed to a full-blown argument.

"We agreed to kill him. You promised me!" A slender, thin woman with elven features and a blond ponytail screamed. Her cream-colored slacks ruffled as she stomped her feet mid-

323

tantrum.

"I said *maybe*." The shorter, pale woman replied adamantly. Her voice was calm, her features glacial. A long, ugly scar ran down the side of her face and onto her jutting collarbone.

Bethany, the alpha.

"I want him to pay! FOR EVERYTHING!" Lenore Sandoff screamed. As they waltzed around each other, Selena glimpsed a heavier figure, duct taped to a chair. His head flopped to the side, but his chest heaved up and down steadily.

Sandoff. He's still alive.

"And I told you, this is the best way! Let him live with all the shame." Bethany raised her voice for the first time in the argument. "Why won't you listen?"

"Because I want him dead and you said you would!"

"Quit being a child, please!" Bethany tenderly caressed Lenore's face, calming her instantly.

"Isn't it obvious?" Selena chuckled. She was playing a hunch.

Both heads snapped at the sound of her voice.

"What are you talking about?" Lenore demanded.

"Bethany, she wants him dead because she's still in love with him."

"You don't know what you're talking about." Lenore glowered and Bethany's eyes narrowed.

"She was only using you to get back at him," Selena pressed as Bethany inched closer to her.

"I thought you were smarter? I thought you wouldn't be used like that," Selena continued, taunting her. The frail figure reached behind the waistband of her silk slacks and thrashed Selena with the butt of her pistol. Sensing she was about to be hit, Selena snapped her face and neck in the opposite direction, leaning away from the slap, lessening the intensity of the blow. It didn't stop the butt from cutting her lip.

"Shut up, bitch."

"You hit like how I imagine Marc would." She laughed maniacally, her teeth and gums stained with blood. "Face it,

Bethany. No one will ever love you. Your parents didn't."

Bethany slapped her again, then held the muzzle of the gun towards her forehead, furious past reason at the mention of her parents.

"She's right, you know," a weak voice concurred. Kasey lifted her head. "You're a sad, pathetic loser who's doing all of this for daddy's attention."

Bethany turned the pistol towards the analyst, who was sitting in a puddle of her own blood, her skin almost translucent.

"Don't! We need them alive. We can't trade damaged goods!" It was Lenore's turn to be rational.

"Fine." Bethany hesitated before lowering the gun. She lit a cigarette and blew the smoke in Selena's face. "They won't be alive for long, anyway." The lovers turned and walked towards the entry of the barn. Marc screamed as Bethany put out the cigarette on his palm, then planted a deep, passionate kiss on Lenore's lips.

"Jesus, Kasey, I thought you were dead," Selena whispered to her companion.

"Damn nearly, and the polls aren't closed yet," she wheezed. "And what were you trying to do, join me? Why did you taunt her like that?"

"I was trying to play them against each other. See if I could talk Lenore into letting us go, but Bethany's hold on her is too strong."

"I feel like I've been hit by a truck." Kase groaned in agony.

"Well, we kind of were. Are you hurt bad?"

"Pretty sure my leg's broken."

"So, no chance of running if I can cut our tape?"

"Selena, if you can get out of this duct tape, you get your ass out and go find Mal."

"Nuh-uh. I'm not leaving you."

"I'll only slow us down. I'll be fine. You heard them. They can't trade damaged goods. They gotta keep me alive, at least until they have what they want."

"No offense, Kase, but you're pretty damned damaged right now. Besides, Mal would kill me if I left you here."

"He'll understand, trust me. He cares about you just as much."

I sincerely doubt that, Selena thought.

"I can get out of the duct tape, but it would be too obvious. Those thugs would pounce on me before I can break both bonds." She counted five guys, at least, all armed.

"Then you need a distraction."

"Fine, but I don't even know where Fulshear is. I think it's better if we go together."

"Fulshear is far as fuck. You won't be able to run anywhere for help." Kasey felt her eyes getting droopy again. "Can you see a vehicle outside? Would you be able to hot wire it?"

"Are you kidding me? Who do you think you're talking to?" Selena chortled.

"Dude, you're more fucking criminal than these wannabe thuglets here." Kase laughed, then groaned as she felt the throbbing in her chest.

"Somehow I doubt that, seeing as how they *all* have guns."

"Don't make me laugh," she chuckled weakly. "Let's sit tight and think about this, Selena. Too many variables right now. I'm sure Mal's already looking for us."

He'll find us. I know it. Kasey's head slumped onto her chest and Selena felt her friend's full weight as she fainted and fell to the side.

66

Malcolm?" A voice sniffled over the phone.

"Gwen, are you okay?"

"No, I called and texted you all yesterday—" She started to chide him, but Mal was having none of it.

"Fuck that. Gwen, are you physically alright? Are you safe?" She sensed the urgency in his voice.

"Yes. Mal, what's going on? What's happened?"

"Where are you right now?"

"At the Four Seasons. Malcolm Ly, you tell me what's going on right now!"

"Kasey and Selena's been kidnapped. Baker sent men to your place and it was ransacked. They couldn't find you or Henry. I thought something happened to you."

"What?" She dropped onto the lounge chair in her suite, realizing how lucky it was she left last night. Then it dawned on her Henry might be in danger if he came back to talk to her, unlikely though it seemed.

"Gwen, stay in your hotel room. Call in sick. Do not leave and *do not* open the door for anybody. You understand me?"

"Yes, I understand. Mal, I have to call Henry. What if he came back last night?"

"Then call him and stay put. Send me a text to let me know if you get a hold of him." He was racing back to the office, while shouting instructions over the phone to Gwen. The tires screeched as he banked a hard left; Ian gripped the grab handle as his body swerved with the car.

"I will. Malcolm, please be safe."

"I'll call you later."

He left Langstrom in the car while he sprinted up the stairs to his office. He didn't want the old-timer huffing and puffing, trying to catch up. Shoving the door open, he yanked the chair from the corner of his desk, its legs bouncing and thumping against the carpet. Thrusting the rotting tile aside, he sighed in relief. The envelope containing the tape and documents still perched on the crossbar.

As he made his way back to the car, the phone rang. He jumped in and signaled to Ian before turning it on speaker.

"Did you get it?"

"Yes."

"Good boy."

"What's the address?"

"Drive to Fulshear, turn left on a road called Dixon. Drive until you can't drive anymore. You'll find your precious princesses there."

"It would be easier if you just gave me an address."

"You'll figure it out. You're a smart guy. Oh, and lose the luggage." Mal glanced at Langstrom before his phone rang again. Baker was on the other line.

"Did you get that?" Mal answered. He had to remember to change his number after this. Circumstances forced him to allow Baker to wiretap his cell phone.

"Yeah, we have the map open right now." Mal could hear computer keys clacking away on the other end. "There are three properties on Dixon in the area she described. Best guess is a secluded barn. 550 Dixon Road. Mal, be careful. There's nothing but untended land surrounding the barn. You could walk into an ambush."

"Could? Almost certainly. It wouldn't be the first time. I'm driving Ian to you and then hauling ass. You get the arrest warrant?"

Langstrom shot him a *look*.

"Not yet, but we will. Judge Holden is allowing Stacey Braddock to recount her story verbally in chambers. Exigent circumstances. They're bringing in a court reporter now."

"Fine. Hurry, dude."

"Mal, I'm sending SWAT ahead with you. We won't be able to get to you in time, otherwise."

"Okay, but tell them to hang back. No telling what Bethany will do if she hears all of you. Crazy, not stupid, Terrance."

"Like hell you're taking me back," Ian exclaimed as soon as Mal hung up.

"Ian, I appreciate everything you've done, but Terrance is right. This is probably an ambush. You have no dog in this fight. I can't let you risk your life."

"I'll be damned if I let you go on a suicide mission by yourself," Ian proclaimed. "Son, you have a knack for shouldering the burdens of the world, but you are not alone. You have friends and family who care for you, and right now I'm one of those. We're making one stop, and it's for damn sure not the police station."

Mal stayed silent, acknowledging that he would have died last time if the girls hadn't showed up. It would be useful to have someone watch his six.

"Where are we going?"

"Old Marine buddy," Ian grunted, satisfied. "We need supplies."

67

Mal parked the car a distance from the end of the dirt road. Staying low in his seat, he studied all the visible sides of the barricaded barn.

It was no fortress. The front doors were left open and unguarded. This was no sophisticated military outfit, so he didn't expect snipers. Still, he opened the car slowly, slithering out from his seat, using the door as a shield. He gave Ian a few minutes to crawl through the tall grass and flank the side.

Staying low, he cut across the open land in front of the barn, then pressed his body flat against the wall next to the open doors.

"Bethany?"

"You came! I was wondering if you were going to let your girlfriends rot and die in this godforsaken place," a voice rang out from inside.

"Why are you playing hide and seek? Come on in," another voice chimed in.

"I would love to, but I'm not stupid," he mocked. "I need to know you don't have men inside waiting to shoot me where I stand."

"I don't," Lenore growled.

"Not how this works. I need to hear it from the girls."

"Malcolm, there are five guys—" He heard the familiar sound

of metal against bone. Selena stayed quiet. *Bad move, bitch.* He needed to figure out how to free Selena first. If he were ever in a fight, he wanted her fighting alongside him.

"Selena, you okay?"

"Yes."

"Kasey?"

"Not so much," Selena responded.

"I'm alive. Good thing I didn't hold my breath waiting for you, though. Grandma-ass driver," a breathless, low voice rasped.

Same old sense of humor. Thank God.

"Hey, I drove *your* piece-of-shit car."

"Great, let's fuck up both our cars. Cause we're *rolling* in cash to buy another one."

"Bethany will buy you another once this is all over," he joked.

"Enough with the chatter," Lenore cried, impatient. "Tell him no one is aiming a gun at him."

"These fuckers wouldn't know their guns from their dicks, Mal." Both girls giggled at Kasey's comment. Another slap.

"*OWWW* bitch!" Kasey was not the strong, silent type, but he was glad it sounded like an open-handed slap.

"Stop! I'm coming in." Mal trudged in with both hands raised. He assessed the situation and cursed silently. It looked like Bethany had hired Sandoff's entire lineup of criminal defendants. They weren't professionals, but Mal knew a gun in an amateur's hands was much more dangerous.

"You can stop right there," Bethany demanded, before signaling one thug to search him. The tallest one dropped his MAC 10 and let it hang loosely to the side. He was tall and lean, sported a buzz cut, and displayed hardened features and eyes.

Probably the oldest of this bunch, Mal concluded.

He thoroughly ran his rough, dark hands over Mal's torso and up and down each leg, patting down the pockets firmly.

"Thanks. I feel thoroughly violated now." The thug met his remark with silence and a death stare. "Real wordsmith,

Bethany."

"They're paid to kill, not to talk. Where's the evidence?"

Mal examined the petite heiress in her silk pants and cashmere blouse. She was beautiful, despite the scar which gave her a rakish air, but who would suspect a stone-hearted killer lurked beneath her gilded veneer? He pointed to the envelope secured in front of his shirt by his waistband. Time to start the dance. "Let the girls go."

"Not gonna happen," she chuckled.

"Well, then sorry."

"You know, I've been dealing with men like you all my life. Men who see me as frail, damaged, even pathetic. My father was one. He used to come into my bed at night and then buy my silence with gifts. He would tell me the twisted things we did under those covers were all signs of his love. I believed him for years. Then, one day, he said we couldn't do it anymore." Bethany paced back and forth while recounting her tragedy.

"At first, I thought it was me. I thought I had lost his love because of something I'd done." Her eyes became wild and chaotic. "Then I saw them in bed together and I realized men will stick their pricks wherever they want, but they never leave their wives."

"Just like this one here." She buried her hand into the thicket of matted hair and yanked until Sandoff's contused face was inches from her own. He whimpered, opening his mouth to cry.

"Poor, naïve Abigail fell for his charms. She thought he would leave his wife for her; that they were in *love*." Bethany let out a mirthless laugh. "She never for a second suspected that it was all by design. That *I* had planted her within his inner circle, so I could have access to his books. It worked out better than I planned; the stupid child told me all about Marc's idiotic plot to bleed Lenore dry, and I knew it was perfect. Lenore over here had a secret camera in his office, hoping to catch him in another affair. What did she stumble upon instead? This idiot and Carter clumsily trying to plan insurance fraud. It wasn't hard to intercept their plan. All we had to do was pay Carter more."

"The most brilliant attorney in history," she mocked. "In reality, just another corrupt, debauched man. So, what do I do with men like that?"

With one deft movement, she reached behind her waistband. A loud crack echoed through the barn. Selena jumped on a barely conscious Kasey as the hired thugs flinched or ducked for cover. Mal stood motionless as he realized what she had done. Lenore's eyes grew wide, a large maroon stain oozing through her chest, growing in diameter before she finally crumpled to the ground.

"I take away their wives, and then I ruin their lives." She cackled as Sandoff trembled and wailed.

"Are you crazy? She's your lover!" Mal exclaimed, clamoring towards the heiress, hoping to disarm her before she shot anyone else.

"That's close enough!" she ordered. "Please. She was no more than a means to an end. They will charge Marc Sandoff for the murder of his wife, Lenore. When he's convicted, he'll live in a cage for the rest of his life while his entire world crumbles."

"So, Mr. Ly, if I can do this to my *friends*, people I love, imagine what I can do to the people *you* love."

"Break her good leg," she commanded. One of the younger thugs dragged Selena off Kasey, while another aimed his foot at Kasey's bended knee.

"No!" Selena screamed, twisting her hands even harder. She felt the tape fatigue.

"Here, take it. You win. Leave her alone." Mal slid the envelope across the concrete floor towards Bethany's foot, never taking his gaze off Kasey.

"Thank you for your cooperation." She picked up the envelope. "Now, I'm afraid I must leave. Planning such an elaborate setup has been exhausting. It really was foolish of you to come here unarmed and without backup. Love makes you weak."

"Good bye, Malcolm Ly." With that, she pulled the trigger a second time. Another crack echoed, blending with the women's screams into a funereal dirge. Mal's knees buckled.

68

T sk. Tsk. Tsk. I'm sorry, ladies. Did you think things were going to end any differently?"

Bethany wiped the gun with Sandoff's torn shirt. She pressed his clammy right hand over the slide and grip, rubbing it around before dropping it on the ground by his feet.

"Kill them all, call the cops, and then release Sandoff," she instructed the older, tall henchman. He nodded wordlessly. Envelope in arm, she sashayed towards the door, satisfied how well her plan had come to fruition.

For a streetwise detective, Malcolm Ly really did not live up to his reputation. Soon, Marc would be found with four dead bodies, including his wife. They would eventually have cause to open the storage facility where he stored his art since the burglary. Evidence will be mailed to the police of his involvement, and even if Baker knew differently, he wouldn't be able to prove anything. They would go through Sandoff's books and discover Abigail had laundered political funds for him, albeit inadvertently, and he would go down for two more murders.

Lost in thought, she stepped over Malcolm's body and felt calloused hands close around her ankles, jerking her to the ground. She crashed face first onto the floor and felt a painful pressure on her back as Mal pulled her arms behind her.

"I'm not that stupid. I wore a vest," he remarked, keeping his knee firmly on her back as she squirmed and railed. As the thugs paused in confusion, Selena balled her fists and pushed them away from the small of her back. Scrambling to her knees, she puffed out her chest and exhaled as she violently pulled her arms past her hips to the front. The already-weakened tape snapped.

As she made her escape, the delinquent assigned to finish her turned around, poised to fire. Kasey swiveled, tripping him with her legs, using her body to entangle his feet. Her hands free, Selena threw a hard right onto the kid's jaw, landing an elbow on his nose with a satisfying crunch. A shot rang out as Selena and Kasey glanced up to see the forehead of a second hoodlum rupture.

In the chaos, the discombobulated thug freed himself from Kasey, kicking her hard in the stomach. The analyst doubled over, coughing blood onto the floor. Enraged, her raven-haired companion wrapped an arm around his neck, mustering all her anger, pain, and strength. She locked both arms until she felt his pulse fade and his eyes roll backwards.

With another swift movement, she hopped to the floor, driving her hands between her thighs and dove on the duct tape around her ankles. The adhesive frayed and she ripped it off easily. She began to help Kasey, but glanced up to see Mal in a melee with the other two henchmen. Bethany was curled in a ball on the ground as the fight took place above her. Langstrom appeared at the door, rifle on his back.

"I couldn't get a clean shot," he yelled, pointing towards the two thugs exchanging punches with Mal.

"Help Kasey!" Selena pointed to the figure on the ground as she sprinted towards Mal, springing onto the back of the shorter one, clawing at his eyes and face. Distressed, he backed up from the mosh pit, desperately trying to flip her off of him.

Free of the second attacker, Mal concentrated on the taller one, who had his throat in a tight grip. Driving down hard on the crevice of the muscular arm, the elbow joint popped and his opponent writhed in pain, loosening his grip. Using the momentum, Mal thrust the palm of his hand upwards towards the square jawline, causing the thug's eyes to tear. The assailant folded in pain as Mal delivered a one-two to the kidneys. With a finishing move, he brought his elbow down hard on the top of his skull.

"Hey Kasey, come on." Langstrom knelt by Kasey's limp body, feeling for a pulse. "Kasey, honey, talk to me."

She was motionless and clammy, her skin a pallid, ashen color.

"Stay with me now, dammit." Pulling a utility knife from his belt, he effortlessly sliced through the binding.

"I'm still here, but please stop shaking me." Kasey rasped, pulling a faint smile from Langstrom.

"Jesus, girl. Thought we lost you."

"Nah, I'm not that easy to get rid of."

Suddenly, her breath quickened as she tried to raise her arm.

"Ian, watch out!" Langstrom turned to see a bewildered but furious Bethany grasping the gun beside Sandoff's tortured body. She aimed at Kasey and screamed, "This is for you, Malcolm!"

Kasey closed her eyes as the sound of firecrackers popped off in rapid succession. She felt Langstrom's bear hug as he slammed her to the ground, then a warm, viscous spray spattered her face. She felt no pain.

"Ian?" She heard a gurgling sound. *Oh God, oh God, don't let it be him.* She pressed against his neck, trying to plug the warm liquid with her hand. "Help, Mal? Selena?!"

Ian's body had gone slack; she couldn't flip him over or administer proper first aid. The sound of sirens scattered across the quiet fields of Fulshear as another figure appeared at the door. Mal raced to Langstrom's side as a familiar voice screamed out commands. The cavalry was here.

"Bethany Tremel, this is the police. Lower your weapon."

Baker raised his Beretta. "We have a warrant for your arrest. Lower your weapon!"

Baker studied the figure standing before him. Dirt and blood covered her ruffled blond hair; she was no longer a picture of dignity and composure. In its place was the aftermath of abuse, the semblance of lunacy, a lust for revenge, and an eerie determination.

Don't do it, don't do it, he prayed as the SWAT team filed through, surrounding her. They gawked at the bloodbath before them, and in the center, the mastermind.

In the debriefing later, nobody could pinpoint what made them react, whether it was a twitch of a finger or a tremor or a move to one side. But they opened fire as one in reaction.

The first few bullets hit her chest and stomach before Baker could give the order to desist. She had nothing left, so she chose death.

69

Mal leaned against the couch, his thighs numb from the weight of Kasey's head. Her heavily plastered leg was propped on the chair's arm. He twirled an envelope in his hand, studying its thickness and pondering its contents.

It had been a week since the "Fulshear Massacre," as the headlines were calling it. Peter MacGregor, Langstrom's partner, gave a poignant eulogy at his funeral to a cemetery full of teary-eyed friends. Langstrom had few relatives left, but he touched many lives. The entire boys' basketball team from the Galveston Recreation Center came out to mourn their coach. Half of the people in attendance were old military or law enforcement buddies. Of course, the motley crew that pulled him out of semi-retirement were among the faces in the crowd. After they lowered his casket into its final resting place, MacGregor approached Mal and handed him an envelope.

"Ian emailed this to me with some instructions. It's for you."

"I'm really sorry for your loss," Mal offered, guilt-ridden.

"Don't worry about it, Malcolm. He spoke highly of you. Knowing my partner, this is how he would've wanted to go out. Beats the alternative."

"The alternative?" Mal cast a quizzical look, but MacGregor only managed a small smile, shook his hand, and walked away.

It rained all the way home from Galveston, the first storm

"

since they caught the case. Kasey was inconsolable, blaming herself for Ian's death. He couldn't bring himself to leave her, so two hours later, he nestled on her couch, stroking her hair as she sobbed herself to sleep.

Fuck it. No time like the present. He tore the envelope.

"Malcolm,

If you're reading this, then I didn't make it. It's alright son, don't blame yourself. Either way, I knew this case would be my last. Ever since my Anita died, I didn't have much to come home to. Nothing but the ghosts of dead loved ones and fallen comrades to soothe these weary bones. Then, last month, my doc gave me 'the news', the kind you don't come back from. Ain't it something? The war didn't kill me, the force didn't kill me... and here I'm supposed to rot in my bed from lung cancer. Fuck that.

Don't worry about the mess in Galveston. I told MacGregor to close it, blame it on a ghost we both know. Wonder where they're moving him next? You'll be short a revolver, though. I dumped it. Sorry. I'm sure you can find another.

You're a good man, Mal. You remind me a lot of my son. If he were alive, he would've been about your age. I've never been chatty, so the only other advice I have for you is to let your son go. Don't let this obsession drown you. Look at all you have, and I don't mean the three beautiful women you have in your life. (What they see in you, fuck if I know).

By the way, choose one and move on.

Thanks for one helluva ride,
Langstrom"

Kasey stirred as he wiped away tears. Then, without warning, the dam shattered, and he cried exhausted tears, tears of contrition and remorse, of boundless sadness. She peeked from between strands of damp hair, wordlessly caressing his face. He passed her the letter, and she offered him her sleeve.

"Don't blame yourself, sweetheart," he muttered between

sniffles. "The man had a death wish."

"Still doesn't make me feel any better." She levered herself upright and hobbled to the kitchen.

"Want me to stay tonight?"

"No. Unless you need company?"

"Nah. I want to be alone."

"Thought so. Go home." He could hear ice clinking against glass as he departed.

#

The headlines ran for weeks. Every newspaper from the Houston Chronicle to the Daily Court Review delved through Lenore and Marc Sandoff's lives, printing one scandalous affair after another. Opportunistic vultures circled the dead carcass of Sandoff's reputation, offering paid interviews for any dirty tidbit, any scorned mistress willing to tell their story. The Houston Press wrote an in-depth narrative of Bethany Tremel's troubled life while trashy tabloids linked other mysterious deaths to the heiress, hoping to create a stir for the novel conspiracy theorist.

Lenore Sandoff miraculously survived the shot to her chest, the bullet narrowly missing her aorta. ADA Haddock personally walked into her recovery room to take her statement, where she tearfully admitted to the conspiracy to frame her husband for insurance fraud and murder. Thanks to a pen recorder Mal stuffed in the back pocket of his jeans, there was no pushback when Baker demanded a warrant to search the Tremels' office, manor, and Bethany's highrise, where they found evidence corroborating Lenore's statement.

Officers found email correspondence between the two friends in which Abigail recounted her growing suspicion of what her lover was having her do. She'd found discrepancies in old accounts between Sandoff and the elder Tremel. Sandoff mishandled funds, recording them as bad investments, and cheated the old man out of millions, causing the first of many strokes. Mal had a theory that Bethany did all of this out of some perverse devotion to her father, a sort of Stockholm Syndrome.

This was never proven, though motive was hardly necessary once Bethany went postal in front of multiple credible witnesses. Armed with a team of lawyers from the next largest law firm in Houston, Lenore was going to do some jail time, but less than she deserved. However, after her deposition, the team agreed that she had suffered enough, having been thrown over by both of the people she thought she loved.

The written confession of an "Anthony Rizzo" was enough to get Jamal Wilson released from custody, though the man had escaped custody and left no trail. When they arrived at his shoddy apartment with a warrant, they discovered it mysteriously cleared out and cleaned. Mal suspected it had never been more than modestly furnished to begin with. Mal gave Jamal a ride to the bus stop and bought him a one-way ticket to West Virginia, where his children and Ericka's parents were waiting for him.

"Don't waste your second chance, Jamal. Be good to your children. Change their fates."

"No worries, man." He peered out from his one good eye, the other one still bruised. He held out his hand. "Thanks officer. You're good peoples."

"I'm not an officer anymore. Take care. I'll be checking in on you." Mal gave his hand a firm shake and then handed him a black backpack. "I have one last thing for you, but don't open it until you get to West Virginia."

"What is it?"

"Let's just call it a scholarship fund for the kids, from the Greg Scott Foundation." Mal winked.

"Whatever, five-o. You take care." With a broken grin, he mounted the steps onto the bus and disappeared down the aisle.

"Say!" Jamal shouted out the window. "Whatever happened to that hot insurance lady that was with you? Don't let that go, man!"

"Mind your business, Jamal." He smirked and waved as the

bus rolled off.

70

Mal was supposed to meet Kasey and Selena for coffee, but he had a stop to make. The wind chime sang as he walked through the bent metal door. Seems they had another fight last night. Tiny was sweeping glass in the corner and nodded absently when he walked through.

"She in?" Without waiting for an answer, he ambled behind the bar towards the office door.

"What is it you want now?" Moua's slow, even voice rang out, eyes never straying from the bundles of cash on her desk. The wrinkled hands deftly counted the bills before stapling them together.

"Heard you got your wish." He leaned against the doorframe.

"What wish is that?" She glanced up slowly, her lips still moving to the count of the bills.

"Galveston. Got pinned on Rizzo."

"That is not a wish. It was a trade. Your Detective Langstrom is an honorable man."

"Was. He died. But you knew, didn't you?"

"I may have heard. I'm sorry for your loss," she said coldly.

"You're not sorry. It's all business to you."

"Whatever makes you feel better," she replied, as an impatient mother would address her insolent child. "Did you come to insult me, or has business picked up for you? You've made quite a name for yourself."

She referred to the one newspaper article which gave him credit for the case and the subsequent arrests.

"I'm not looking for information. You did me dirty, but you're right, we're not friends, so I'm not here to argue that point anymore. I wanted to tell you our professional relationship is over. I'm no longer a cop, so I can't arrest you for anything, but don't expect any help from me in the future."

"Malcolm, you walk in here with some impertinent notion I ever needed your help because you pulled me out of a fire once? Every day, I walk from my home to this game room, and every day, I know it can be my last. Some enemy may come from the bushes to slit my throat, that a bullet has my name on it, that Death has finally drawn my card from her deck. I can live without you, Malcolm, but you can never live without me."

"And why is that?"

"Because every day, desperate junkies and gambling addicts come to me to sell information. And one day, the information will be about your son. On that day, Malcolm Ly, you will learn it's better to stand in the fire with me than to burn down my house."

#

Mal walked up to Selena and Kasey in the coffee shop across from the HPD building. After hearing how she almost lost her life cracking one of the biggest multiple homicide cases to rock the city, Kase's supervisor let her go with a slap on the wrist. She was supposed to meet all three supervisors and the lab manager for a huge ass reaming. She'd do all the expected things, apologize profusely and grovel for her job back. In return, after much faux indignation, they would relent. Mal walked through the door as she hobbled towards her coffee order.

"Oh, for God's sake, please sit down. I'll get it," Selena chided, but Kasey ignored her. She grabbed the cup and returned to the table, but didn't sit.

"Nah, one of you drink it. They took so long I'm going to be late for my meeting if I don't head out right now," she responded, with a dismissive wave of her hand.

"You need help to get over there?" Mal asked.

"No, you two catch up. I'll see your ass later. It's Friday, bring the pizza." She grinned as Baker walked through the door. He pecked her on the lips before slinging her work bag over his shoulders. The detective then nodded at the pair before walking out behind Kasey.

An awkward silence brewed as he sat opposite Selena for the first time in a week. He had ignored her phone calls for a few days after the funeral, feeling it was unfair to see her while he was still brimming with unresolved emotions.

"Did you do this?" He pointed to the TV hanging from the corner. Since six this morning, multiple media outlets reported they had mysteriously received audio files linking Carter LeBlanc, and indirectly Marc Sandoff, to Adam Hoang, a local attorney who was under federal indictment for collusion, embezzlement, creating false plaintiffs, and a whole slew of other charges regarding the oil spill case.

The District Attorney, who had been reluctant to charge a mayoral candidate for anything more than insurance fraud, was asked to step aside once the recordings were released to the public. A federal investigation was opened. Facing a civil suit from Mutual Financial Protection on top of upcoming federal indictments, Marc Sandoff had no choice but to withdraw from the race so that his law firm could mount a full-time defense. Many board members and investors hightailed it out of there. The Sandoff Law Firm was a sinking ship, and they were scurrying off like rats.

"I don't know what you're talking about. It was an encrypted email. Untraceable, I heard." Selena shrugged, straight-faced. "If you ask me, he deserved it. He caused all this misery, and he almost got away with it."

"We can't win every battle, Selena," Mal cautioned.

"But we can try," she retorted. Awkward silence again. "Did you want to drink Kasey's coffee?"

"Hell no. I might as well dump a cup of sugar in my mouth." Selena threw her head back in laughter, her cheerful gaze meeting his.

"So, why didn't you answer my phone calls?" She traced the mouth of her coffee mug. In the fresh light of day, without the constant strain of work and danger, Mal's feelings swelled with renewed vigor. She was not some damsel that needed saving. Hell, she'd saved him more times now than he can count. Maybe they were all right. Maybe he needed to move on.

"I'm sorry. I needed time to think."

"About?"

"Gwen called. She and Henry broke up. She wanted me to come back to her. I needed time to think about me and her. Me and you. Everything I was feeling, what I was dealing with, it was unfair to put you in the middle of it."

"You didn't—" she protested.

"I care about you deeply, Selena. I know we feign some sort of casual relationship, but it was never casual for me." He held her hand. "I don't know what we are now."

"My flight leaves in an hour. Come to New York with me," she suddenly pleaded. Her vulnerability was palpable; she felt it, Mal felt it, but she didn't care.

"I can't up and leave—"

"Why not? What's holding you back?"

Mal started to say, "I have unfinished business here." It was the same answer he gave when people asked him why he stayed at the run-down office, the decaying townhouse.

Then he thought of Langstrom's letter. What had the old-timer said? To let his son go. But how? Maybe it wasn't about letting Georgie go completely, but to start fresh, come at the case from a different angle, develop new contacts. If he stayed here, he'd be depending on Moua. She'd have her hooks in him, whether he wanted it or not, and he'd be obligated to her for a piece of information he might never get.

Finally, he thought back to their conversation in the shower. Hadn't he told Selena all she needed to do was ask and he would move for her?

"Okay. I'll do it."

"What?" Selena's eyes, which had faded almost to despair, brightened.

"I'll come with you to New York." He looked to the analyst hobbling towards the blue windows with large white letters, to the detective gently guiding her over the curb. She didn't need him anymore.

"Well? Let's go." He held Selena's hand, interlacing their fingers as they walked to the waiting rideshare. She kissed him passionately as they settled in the backseat. The sky rumbled, turning dismal under heavy clouds. A gust of humid wind gathered dirt and leaves around the car. Houston's scorching pavement soon flooded with another bout of torrential rainfall.

Mal smiled. For once, he wasn't standing alone in the rain.

Author's Note

Malcolm Ly and the characters within these pages are a figment of my imagination, though I modeled them heavily off the personalities and daily goings-on of my friends. There was a crime lab on the twenty-sixth floor of the Houston Police Department, though that lab has since moved. The inner workings of the lab, medical examiner's office, and police department in the book are modeled after my own experiences, but the processes and interactions are highly hyperbolic and does not represent the actual work performed by the highly-skilled men and women of forensics and law enforcement in real life.

When I started this story, I never realized it would become such a huge part of my life. There are many drafts of this manuscript in the recycle bin. And yet, I have many people to thank for its rescue from the bin, its development, and the spit and polish that's made *Maelstrom* what it is today.

First and foremost, to my editor Adam Gaffen. Fate. There's no other way to explain the fact when I needed an editor, you appeared. Thank you for tightening my writing, polishing my plot, and for your sage advice at every twist and turn. Working with you has made me realize I still have much to learn, but I'm excited for all the opportunities to hone my craft.

To my lab friends Brittany Beyer, Becky Gonzales, and Jessica Powers for your undying support and your willingness to buy this book no matter the format, even if it were written on tree bark and bound with twine. My deepest gratitude for allowing me to use your personalities and experiences to shape my characters and bring them to life. To my supervisor and friend, Tran Nguyen, for always believing Malcolm Ly was a special character, despite never reading a word of this manuscript, (and she probably never will).

To all my friends and family far and wide, for never forgetting to check in, and for always asking, "how's the book coming along". Your words of encouragement did not fall on deaf ears.

To my brother Kevin, with whom I've probably planned more than twenty fictional murders, each gorier and more detailed than the last. Don't worry, I'll eventually use them all. Thank you for always hooking me up with the latest high-tech gadgets or else I'd still be writing this with pen and paper.

To my parents, Thai and Natalie, or simply *bố mẹ*. I know it wasn't easy coming to a foreign country, learning a whole new language, and breaking your backs to earn a few dollars, only to turn around and spend it on books for me to read. It was one of the best gifts you have given me.

To my friend Victor Hung, who has worn many hats and played many roles during this entire process. Thank you for being my sounding board, my technical advisor, and my ever-optimistic cheerleader. I am now a highly skilled locksmith, duct-tape escape artist, and mixed martial artist thanks to you. (Just kidding… only on paper, maybe). Many thanks for allowing me to take creative liberties with your life so that Malcolm Ly can be the funny, vibrant character that he is.

Finally, to my beloved husband Andrew. Thank you for always nurturing my passions, and for keeping my feet firmly planted on the ground while my head is in the clouds. You are the only reason anything gets done around here. Thank you for always picking up the slack and for making up for my shortcomings, of which there are plenty. I may have written *Maelstrom*, but you breathed life into it. I am eternally grateful for your love and support.

To all my readers, thank you from the bottom of my heart. A book is only the beginning for a writer. A reader completes it, and you are an example of this. Thank you for taking the time to read my work. If you so feel inclined, please leave a review in Goodreads or on Amazon!

Malcolm Ly will return in
Animal Sanctuary